STRANDS OF SORROW
D0092253
BAEN
New York Times Best-Selling Author
JOHN RINGO
R
go is] sure to satisfy the most demanding action junkie."
—Publishers Weekly

$7.99 U.S.
$9.99 CAN.

SAFE AND SOUND?

"It is secure," the sergeant major said. "We've established a vaccination program and obviously the infected cannot access the ship. The reason that arms must be secured is, in fact, to ensure it *is* a secure area, sir. Point of order: *Sergeant?* Unofficial title or official?"

"I'm a National Guard staff sergeant, Sergeant Major," the man said. "Light cav."

"In that case, Staff Sergeant, let me be the first to welcome you to the United States Bloody *Navy*," Sergeant Major Barney said, smiling coldly. "I was *retired* bloody light cav and now I am forced to stand here explaining *plain sense* to you bloody Yanks! As soon as that information is verified, you are transferred at pay rate to the Navy. And as a member of U.S. Navy combat arms, you are *automatically* detailed to the rate of master-at-arms. Therefore, Sergeant whatever your name is, *you* are my new next senior NCO and *I* am your *boss*. Which means that *you* can stand here, after you get a bloody *haircut* and shave that *unmilitary* beard, and explain to your bloody Yank gun-huggers that, no, they are *not* carrying bloody arms onto *my* bloody ship! Is that *clear*, Petty Officer?"

"Clear, Sergeant Major!"

"So you lot go turn in your weapons," Barney said, in a softer tone. "You're at the barracks, for God's sake. You don't keep a bloody shotgun in your room at the barracks. You keep it where, Sergeant?"

"In the arms room, Sergeant Major."

"Get some bloody food, take a breath. You're safe. No bloody tricks, no bloody zombies. This is not a movie. This is not a video game. We are not going to stick a wire in your head or something. You are *safe*. It is *my* job to keep you safe when you're on this ship and I take that job *seriously*. Which means not allowing persons who are untrained in shipboard firearms use running around with bloody arms. So if one of you keeps a holdout and I find out about it, I *shall* feed you to the bloody gators."

BAEN BOOKS by JOHN RINGO

BLACK TIDE RISING: *Under a Graveyard Sky* • *To Sail a Darkling Sea* • *Islands of Rage and Hope* • *Strands of Sorrow*

TROY RISING: *Live Free or Die* • *Citadel* • *The Hot Gate*

LEGACY OF THE ALDENATA: *A Hymn Before Battle* • *Gust Front* • *When the Devil Dances* • *Hell's Faire* • *The Hero* (with Michael Z. Williamson) • *Cally's War* (with Julie Cochrane) • *Watch on the Rhine* (with Tom Kratman) • *Sister Time* (with Julie Cochrane) • *Yellow Eyes* (with Tom Kratman) • *Honor of the Clan* (with Julie Cochrane) • *Eye of the Storm*

COUNCIL WARS: *There Will Be Dragons* • *Emerald Sea* • *Against the Tide* • *East of the Sun, West of the Moon*

INTO THE LOOKING GLASS: *Into the Looking Glass* • *Vorpal Blade* (with Travis S. Taylor) • *Manxome Foe* (with Travis S. Taylor) • *Claws that Catch* (with Travis S. Taylor)

EMPIRE OF MAN (with David Weber): *March Upcountry* and *March to the Sea* (collected in *Empire of Man*) • *March to the Stars* and *We Few* (collected in *Throne of Stars*)

SPECIAL CIRCUMSTANCES: *Princess of Wands* • *Queen of Wands*

PALADIN OF SHADOWS: *Ghost* • *Kildar* • *Choosers of the Slain* • *Unto the Breach* • *A Deeper Blue* • *Tiger by the Tail* (with Ryan Sear)

STANDALONE TITLES: *The Last Centurion* • *Citizens* (ed. with Brian M. Thomsen)

STRANDS OF SORROW

JOHN RINGO

STRANDS OF SORROW

This is a work of fiction. All the characters and events portrayed in this book are fictional, and any resemblance to real people or incidents is purely coincidental.

A Baen Books Original

Baen Publishing Enterprises
P.O. Box 1403
Riverdale, NY 10471
www.baen.com

ISBN: 978-1-4767-8102-0

Cover art by Kurt Miller

First paperback printing, January 2016

Library of Congress Catalog Number: 2014038690

Distributed by Simon & Schuster
1230 Avenue of the Americas
New York, NY 10020

Pages by Joy Freeman (www.pagesbyjoy.com)
Printed in the United States of America

As always
For Captain Tamara Long, USAF
Born: May 12, 1979
Died: March 23, 2003, Afghanistan
You fly with the angels now.

ACKNOWLEDGEMENTS

The first major acknowledgement is that I didn't mean to write this book. But like the rest it just said "write me." I'd really hoped I was finished with the main story of the Black Tide universe with book three: *Islands of Rage and Hope*. As the book said at the end, "The Beginning." I really did not and do not see it as the ending of *Alas Babylon*: "And they turned away to face the thousand year night." Better words were from the chorus of "Last Ride of the Day": "This moment the dawn of humanity."

However, after finishing book three I couldn't stop pacing. Finally my wife Miriam more or less forced me to sit down and write this one. It's all her fault.

The second acknowledgement is to a group of "friends" on Facebook. When I started thinking about how to proceed on the east coast, I asked on FB about coastal facilities. I've never been in the Navy or Marines, just Army, which is why I occasionally "glitch" on Navy and Marine stuff. The Black Tide first-readers, many Navy, Coast Guard or Marine, have been invaluable in finding those glitches and correcting them. But Captain Steven "Wolf" Smith would have his people as well as the Hole to draw upon to figure out where to go now that there is some hope for the future. So I, as well, had to draw upon support from friends to figure out where to go. Blount Island had been nowhere on my radar screen until the *invaluable* Jon De Pinet (former USMC embarkation specialist) pointed out that just about *anything* you could want was there, and it was entirely clearable.

The next goes to Byron Audler, resident of Mayport, for directing me to info on HELMARSTRIKERON 40 with the very appropriate name "Air Wolves." That is probably what kicked this over the edge. Sigh.

Last but oh so certainly not least, Captain Kacey Ezell, USAF. (Who has no resemblance whatsoever to Captain Kacey Bathlick USMC, AKA Dragon, in the Keldara books. None. Really.) Kacey has been my regular technical consultant on helo ops over the years. My writing in this novel on the subject simply proved that an occasional ride in the cargo compartment of a Huey or Blackhawk many year—err . . . decades ago does not an expert make. When it became apparent that I couldn't write helo scenes in detail to save my butt, Kacey graciously (and rapidly) stepped forward and thoroughly rewrote them. For which I am eternally grateful.

Kacey has also already submitted her short story for the upcoming Black Tide anthology. Yes, that was a plug.

PROLOGUE

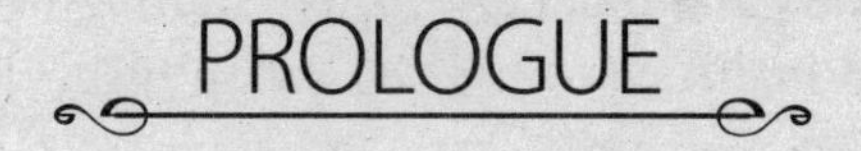

"This is so wrong," Lieutenant Lyons said. "I'm trying to count the ways this is wrong."

Commodore Carmen J. Montana, AKA Lieutenant General Montana, AKA "Mr. Walker" AKA so many other AKAs even his redoubtable memory couldn't remember them all, Commander in Chief, Pacific Forces, had decades before come to the philosophical conclusion that anyone who said "I have never failed a mission" rarely got the sort of missions that were his forte.

The first mission of his career in special operations was called Operation Eagle Claw and was a *spectacular* and very public failure. He wasn't in charge or anything, but it was still a failed mission. It was also where he had earned his first award for heroism while pulling air-crew out of a burning chopper. Operation Urgent Fury, a cake-walk for most, had been for his team another high-body-count failure that resulted in his first Distinguished Service Cross. Mogadishu: another spectacular, and public, failure had earned him his *second* DSC. He had, personally, failed to stop Osama Bin Laden from escaping from Tora Bora. But let anyone guess which of two thousand, mined, trails the bastard was going to use. Trying to get that

Soviet physicist out of the middle of Siberia, those two days in Shanghai, that thing in Berlin . . . and, oh God, if he never saw Beirut again it would be too soon . . .

But Navy Base San Diego was starting to get *right up there* in his personal best of utterly fucked up missions.

There were various military bases scattered all over the San Diego valley. Miramar, playground of the Airedales. Pendleton up the road, playground of the Hollywood Marines. NAVSEA based deep in the heart of Dago. Then there were the three main attractions: Point Loma, North Island and Navy Base San Diego.

NBSD was out of the question. It was on the city side of San Diego Bay. You might as well try to clear New York City. Given enough time, Subedey bots and helos . . . Well, they'd do it eventually. Heck, some working Abrams could do it. But it was never on the original game plan.

Point Loma, home to most of the submarines, was equally out of the question. It was a peninsula that was backed by a sprawl of suburbs and really didn't have much of interest.

North Island, on the other hand . . . had looked doable. Bad points. It was attached to the mainland by both a bridge and a narrow causeway. It had a vast sprawl of housing. Good points. It was *only* attached to the mainland by the bridge and a narrow causeway. And the causeway was both long and went to a, relatively, uninhabited area. Relatively because this was, after all, southern California and nowhere was exactly "uninhabited." There was limited water. By all that was holy, they should have only had to deal with the infected that were the survivors of the base personnel. Those that hadn't already died of thirst. Couple, few, thousand. Close the bridges and the causeway, get some of the survivors oriented, get some of the landing craft up and going, go clear Pendleton and he'd be CINCPAC in more than name.

Should have. Probably. If only.

They'd been informed there was "a light." Satellites had detected "heavy infected density." He'd noted the same thing before he'd left from the Atlantic. But . . . Sigh.

It was worse than Mog. Every freaking street was packed. It looked like naked Mardi Gras. Half the population of San Diego and Tijuana seemed to have moved to North Island. Because, well, there was "a light."

Specifically, the Seawolf-class submarine, USS *Jimmy Carter*, SSN-23, was alongside North Island. And under power. And shining a very powerful spotlight almost straight to the heavens.

Which light had drawn every freaking infected in the San Diego region.

"As I recall, all the Seawolfs are supposed to be based in Bangor," Montana said, looking over at Lieutenant Commander Halvorson.

"Yes, sir," the commander of the *Michigan* said. "That is where it should be."

In the Nineties, with the nation facing "multiaccess threats" that often required more finesse than destroying cities with nuclear weapons and new strategic arms agreements limiting the number of nukes subs could carry, four of the older Ohio-class ballistic missile submarines, notably and hilariously, the *Ohio*, *Michigan*, *Florida* and *Georgia*, were reclassed and repurposed for "littoral insertion" of special operations and "cruise missile" support by converting some of their missile space into housing for SEAL teams, with special lock-out arrangements, and modifying the rest to hold an absolute slew of Tomahawk cruise missiles on rotating launchers.

The admiral in charge of the program, rather clueless on modern acronyms, initially dubbed this the "O-M-F-G Program" for "Ohio-Michigan-Florida-Georgia" until it was pointed out that the initials were probably not the best choice and the program name was changed. Nobody, however, could remember the new program name: The acronym stuck. Given they could fire up to 154 Tomahawk cruise missiles in less than five minutes, it was entirely appropriate. The absolute barrage of cruise missiles that broke the back of the Libyan Army's response to the "pro-democracy" uprising came from *one* OMFG.

"So that's one thing," Montana said. "And isn't the sub base at Point Loma?"

"Yes, sir," Lieutenant Lyons said. "So I would suppose the next question is why is it snuggled up to the *Ronald Reagan*?"

"Those two *never* got along, I'll tell you that," Montana said with a snort. "In fact, if there was any rationale to the universe either the *Gipper* would have crushed the *Jimmy* by now or they'd be forced apart by mutual loathing."

The conversation was taking place on the sail of the guided missile-class submarine. So the commodore had to look up, then look up again, to see the open hangar deck of the *Ronald Reagan* and the flight deck above. Both of which were packed tight with infected.

Occasionally one would slip over the side from the crowding. Looking down, it was apparent that the sharks were enjoying a regular bounty. Not only sharks.

"Lieutenant Lyons," the commodore said. "I have a very extensive, most people would describe it as exhaustive, knowledge of just about, well, *anything*."

"I've played you at Trivial Pursuit, sir," Lyons said.

"But you are from this area and used to occasionally play in these waters."

"Yes, sir."

"So what the *fuck* are *those*?" Montana said, pointing at the boiling water's surface where large, hooked, tentacles occasionally flailed.

"That is something you don't usually see in San Diego harbor, General," Lyons said. "Those are Humboldt squid. I didn't think they could or would come in here. Generally they're only found in deep pelagic areas. Deep. They normally only come up to the last couple of hundred feet at night. About ten feet long including tentacles and nasty as they come. Frankly, I'd rather fight a shark."

"If you used to swim within a thousand miles of those things you are a braver man than I," Montana said. "And that's saying something. Commander Halvorson. Refresh my memory again. If that light has been burning for better than nine months, the boat has got to be under power. Correct?"

"Yes, sir," Halvorson said.

"And the *Topeka* already went active trying to wake up the reactor watch."

"Yes, sir."

"Which means no reactor watch."

"Yes, sir."

"Is there any reliable data on how long a reactor can continue to run, safely, without someone at the controls?" Montana asked.

"I think the answer is 'somewhere around nine or less months or possibly more depending on when the reactor watch died and when this reactor finally goes critical,' sir," Halvorson said. "In other words . . ."

"This *is* the test case," Montana said. "This is probably as long as any reactor has ever gone without someone manning it."

"Yes, sir. And the generators, sir. Rather . . . amazing, sir. I'd have said impossible for more than a few hours. And terrifying. 'Active reactor' and 'no reactor watch' are two phrases no one in their right mind wants to hear."

"Duly noted," Montana said. "Go Navy. A real credit to your nuclear reactor designs and SOPs. But unfortunately it has made North Island a bit of a pickle. Right. Let's find a good spot to open fire and have Leuschen rig The Beast. We certainly have enough targets."

"Aye, aye, Commodore."

"Frankly, I'd say just hammer it with your payload but even with this swarm there might be survivors," Montana said. "And we need the personnel, gear and materials. Not to mention a full reload on one of these boats is a major Congressional line item. Eventually we *shall* have a Congress again and I do *not* want to explain firing off four hundred *million* dollars worth of cruise missiles. So . . . Rig The Beast!"

"COB," the skipper said over the 1MC. "Tell Leuschen to rig The Beast."

The Beast was the sort of weapon you'd only get in a zombie apocalypse.

It looked a bit like a large machine gun. A bit. Or possibly a large paintball gun, which was closer to its actual form and function. There was a long, fairly flimsy looking barrel that had obviously been hand-machined from some sort of tube. There was a breech. There was a butterfly trigger. There was even a bit of a sight. So far so good. Pintle mount that hooked into a lock on the deck. Even the most modern submarines in the U.S. fleet retained provisions for a deck gun, which in this case was to the good.

Then there were the odd bits. Instead of a belt feed, there was a large vaguely conical hopper on top. There was an air hose running from a fitting on the deck to a similar fitting on the breech.

There was the seaman first class pouring two-inch steel ball bearings into the hopper.

"Loaded, sir!" Petty Officer Second Class Leuschen said, beaming for all he was worth. As inventor, designer and creator of The Beast, it was universally judged that he should have first crack. There were others onboard crazy enough to try it out but they mostly spent their time these days trying to chew through the straps. "Permission to open fire?"

"Commodore?" Commander Halvorson asked.

"Oh, why not?" Montana said. "Fire at will, Commander."

"Open fire!"

The chosen target area was the northeast corner of Quay Drive on North Island. Maneuvering the *Michigan* in close quarters, without tugs, was no picnic but the XO had managed to get it right in position.

And The Beast had plenty of customers. The infected were as dense there as they were everywhere on the God-forsaken island. And shore side. And Point Loma. Normal humans would have mostly succumbed to dehydration and starvation at this point. But not the infected. Oh, no, not the infected.

At least some were about to succumb to The Beast.

The sound was surprisingly muted. Accustomed as he was to gunfire, Commodore Montana was unsure at first if it was even firing. The sound was an odd *whip, whip, whip*...

But then the ball bearings reached their targets.

The concept of The Beast was simple. It was, at heart, nothing but an oversized, insanely overpowered paintball gun. As Leuschen had pointed out, the one thing a nuclear submarine has in near infinite supply is compressed air. Replace paintballs with steel ball bearings and what you got was a brutal and extremely efficient slaughter-machine.

The infected were moving more or less randomly on Quay Drive. Generally the densities they were looking at would only have occurred with a true alpha swarm. They weren't shoulder to shoulder but they were often bumping each other. Which occasionally erupted into fights and even small riots; infected did not get along with each other much better than with the rest of the world.

There was no clear view down Quay Drive from their position, which meant "aiming" was sort of moot. And the ball bearings could hardly miss.

Infected started to drop and Leuschen didn't even bother to walk his aim from side to side. There was always another target straight ahead. And infected were going down. Nine times out of ten, an infected hit by a two-inch ball of steel going not much under the speed of sound is going to die. Though far less spectacular than the water-cooled fifty-cals used by Wolf Squadron, The Beast was at least as effective.

"Now if we just had a hundred of them," Commander Halvorson said. "I can get to work on more, sir."

"The choke point isn't weapons, Commander," Montana said. "The choke point is bullets. We have only ten thousand ball bearings. And while I suspect that Leuschen's concept of using small cylinders made from machine steel is sound, at a certain point we'll have to either cannibalize your submarine or run out of steel. Nonetheless, with a successful test, do start making more. But quit when The Beast has used up seventy percent of its ammo. We're sure to need it somewhere else."

"I'd suggest we need to find more ball bearings, sir," Halvorson said.

"I'll put it on the agenda," Montana told him. "We first need to get that damned light turned off. Preferably with extreme prejudice. Lieutenant Lyons."

"Take a boarding team and get the light turned off, aye, sir," Lyons said.

"Anyone onboard familiar with the Seawolf class, Commander?"

"The COB served on them, sir," Halvorson said. "And Petty Officer Gomez."

"Take them and a security team," Montana said. "And put that light out. Take a hammer. Break it if you have to."

"That would be tricky, sir," Halvorson said. "It's recessed and extremely robust to withstand pressure.

I would suggest the lieutenant take a small explosives charge, instead."

"Already on my list, sir," Lyons said.

"Betraying my lack of knowledge of all things subnautical," Montana said. "What in the hell do you use something like that light for?"

"Hull shots," Halvorson and Lyons said simultaneously.

"And helping lost SEALs find their way back to a submerged boat, sir," Halvorson added.

"Quite quite helpful in that regard," Lyons said. "If somewhat untactical."

"Technically it's a standard navigation light," Halvorson added. "That's how it's listed in the white papers, anyway."

"Love to have seen that line item," Montana said. "'And we need a navigation light that can light up the moon!'"

A RHIB was duly deployed; the boarding team boarded, carefully, given the reception committee in the water, and headed over to the *Jimmy Carter*.

However, before they even began to board, they came to the furious attention of the infected crowding the hangar deck hatches and the flight deck.

"This might not be good," Commodore Montana muttered as the first few infected dropped from the flight deck.

In the case of the increasing shower of infected from the flight deck, it was, as it were, hit or miss. The flight deck loomed out and over the smaller submarine. Thus the infected who were not so much jumping off as being pushed trying to get to the RHIB were aiming at water. It was sixty-six feet, as any Naval aviator knows, from the flight deck to the water line on a Nimitz-class carrier. Sixty-six feet is survivable under some conditions. It is approximately the same height as a twenty meter diving board in the Olympics. However, surviving the impact is one thing. Surviving it conscious is another. Absent careful entry, water at that speed tends to feel somewhat like landing on concrete. Thus the "miss." The waters of San Diego Bay were home to not just the Humboldt squid but the great white as was *immediately* apparent. Conscious or not, there were not going to be many infected surviving the fall.

Some, however, were aimed more or less at the RHIB. Thus the "hit."

"Back up!" Lyons said as the first infected landed on Petty Officer Gomez. The infected didn't survive, not to mention it wasn't all that great for Gomez. And the impact very nearly tore the bottom out of the RHIB. Which would have made it, very briefly, an "IB."

The COB threw the outboard into reverse and backed up as fast as the boat could manage as the water around it started to churn with impacting infected.

"Zombilanche!" the *Michigan*'s chief of boat shouted, then cackled madly. There was essentially a *wall* of infected falling off the flight deck.

"Just get us out of here, COB!" Lyons shouted, then, "Incoming!"

The remaining crew dove to the side as an infected impacted square in the center of the RHIB.

"I don't know how many more of those we can take," Lyons said. "Jefferson, Garcia, toss those over the side."

"Aye, aye, sir," Seaman Jefferson said, grabbing the legs of the infected. Who, as it turned out, was sufficiently cushioned by Gomez and the previously impacted infected to survive. Albeit with two broken legs. "Sir!"

"Got it," Lyons said, drawing and giving the infected a "Mozambique tap" to the chest and head. "Now toss it."

"Aye, sir," Jefferson said, gulping. He and Garcia tipped the dead body over the side, then reared back. "JESUS!"

A particularly greedy great white had not even waited for the body to fully hit the water. Its teeth sunk into the body and ripped it out of Jefferson's hands.

"Think we need a bigger boat, sir!" Garcia shouted nervously.

"It's like feeding the dolphins at Sea World," Jefferson's voice quavered. "But way, way, way grosser."

"Which is probably how the fish feel," Garcia said.

"Just *toss* the next one," Lyons said. "Carefully."

Fortunately, the COB had backed the RHIB out of the "zombilanche" and slowed it as the shower continued.

"Oh, that's just wrong," the chief of boat said, shaking his head. "Look at the *Jimmy*."

The hangar deck openings were lower and more in line with the *Jimmy Carter*. Most of the infected being shoved out as the mass tried to reach the RHIB were landing on the deck of the submarine. Or the sail. Or the fairwater planes. All of which were very hard steel. Most of them were surviving but only with severe orthopedic trauma. Which was exacerbated when another infected would land on top of them.

The top deck of the *Jimmy* was also curved, somewhat slippery and seemed to be the primary territory of the Humboldts. As the writhing mass of screaming, broken infected would discharge a member, the giant squids would reach up *out* of the water and pull them in with claw-covered tentacles.

"That is a behavior never before witnessed," Lyons said. "And it just put paid to swimming off the Southern California coast for *my* lifetime at the very least. These things have been proven to be smart, adaptable and to have very good memories. There are some indications they even learn socially. Which means this behavior might just be passed down generations. Okay." He keyed his handheld. "Commodore?"

"Just come back to the boat," Montana replied. *"Back to the drawing board . . ."*

"Are we there yet?" Gomez asked, groaning.

"The positive aspect to this latest debacle is that Lieutenant Lyons found an easy way to kill zombies in job lots," Montana said.

"Pull a boat up and let them avalanche?" Lyons said.

"Got it in one," Montana replied. "The tricky part is making sure the boat crew survives."

"I'd prefer not to bring this boat in any closer, sir," Commander Halvorson said.

"They wouldn't recognize it as a target, anyway," Montana said. "But using the RHIB again is out of the question. We need a better boat."

"This is San Diego Harbor, sir," Lyons said. "Even with people punching out due to the plague there are plenty of boats available."

"However, this is an untenable objective at the moment," Montana said. "We're going to drop back and punt. We need a base and to start building personnel.

Let's fall back to the NALF for now. See about clearing that first."

"Aye, aye, sir," Halvorson said.

"More infected than I'd expected," Lyons said, looking at the shores of the barren island.

San Clemente Island was a twenty-one-mile-long brown, barren bit of rock sticking out of the Pacific Ocean about ten miles from the California coast. Part of it was an impact range but on the north end was a support facility and the Naval Air Landing Field. And there were infected. Not as many as North Island. *New York* didn't have as many as North Island. But quite a few. Most were clustered near a few of the large buildings on which, yes, there were clear survivors. Quite a few of those as well.

"If you start rhyming every statement I *shall* have to find a new aide, Lieutenant," Montana said.

"Noted, sir," Lyons said, looking through a stabilized scope on the sail. "And the relatively high number of survivors as well as infected is now explained."

"Oh?" Montana said. "Don't keep me hanging."

"I recognize people on the buildings, sir," Lyons said. "Looks as if NavSpecWar moved..."

"Damned right we moved."

Captain Owen Carter was the former commander of Navy Special Warfare, Basic Underwater Demolitions/SCUBA School, universally referred to as BUD/S. It was the West Coast's SEAL school normally based at Coronado on North Island.

The good part about the introductions was that Carter recognized him. There were no questions raised as to why a former Army lieutenant general was now a commodore and CINCPAC. Nobody in Special Operations questioned his competence. Now if he could just figure out a way to take *anything* on the land side . . .

"Holding Coronado was untenable, sir," Carter said. "Freaking infected were coming over the fences. Most of the teams were out trying to control the infected. I obtained orders to move the dependents, instructors and students to San Clemente. Various others joined as they had transport. Pretty much the entire Special Operations boat contingent moved over when it all came apart, along with some civilians and Team survivors. We moved sufficient supplies for a long siege, especially given the loss rate due to infection. What we did *not* bring is enough ammunition to deal with all the infected. I'm not sure there's enough in the world."

"And we, too, are about out," Montana said, trying not to sigh. The Beast had shot through the last of its ball bearings and all the subs in the area were about shot out on machine-gun rounds. But they had a land base and an infusion of fighters. "Commander Halvorson."

"Sir."

"Have the *Hampton* and *Topeka* do a run back to Gitmo or Blount, whichever Captain Smith prefers. Pick up more ammo. See about ball bearings. They might have found some on Blount. Vaccine. Medical supplies if they have spare. General supply run." For better or worse, most of the pregnant female dependents seemed to have already given birth so he wouldn't have to repeat the nightmare that had been Gitmo when the baby wave hit.

"Aye, aye, sir."

"Captain Carter," Montana said, looking at the small beach by the NALF. Drawn up on the sand or anchored in the tiny cove was an amazing cluster of just about every type of small boat imaginable. There were Special Operations Boats, yachts, off-shore inflatables and "hard" hulls; there was even one ten-foot inflatable dinghy that must have been a real joy to maneuver across the strait.

"Sir?"

"Any of those SOCs still operational?"

The eighty-one-foot "Special Operations Craft Mark V.1" were just the ticket to handle a zombilanche. They should even be robust enough to handle the impact.

"Unsure, sir. They've been parked for the better part of a year."

"Well, time to *get* them operational," Montana said, humming "Roland the Headless Thompson Gunner." "The FAST boat guys have a new mission . . ."

"Ball bearings?" Isham said, looking at the video transmission.

Commander Halvorson gave a brief précis of The Beast.

"That makes so much sense I don't know why Steve didn't think of it first," Isham said. "Okay, I'll put the word in to Survey and Salvage to keep an eye out. There might be a container or so at Blount Island. There might be a container of the Holy Grail for that matter. But I'll add ball bearings to the list of critical items . . ."

There was more to do. Zombie bodies had to be dealt with since they needed the facilities. There were some backhoes. More boats were gotten operational and spread out to see about at-sea rescue. They'd used up most of their machine-gun ammo but husbanded their small-arms rounds. Clearance happened. The nice thing about finding a bunch of BUD/S instructors and students was the instructors were specialists at clearing boats and ships. All they needed was a bit of touch-up on the "Wolf-Way." On the other hand, it wasn't much different from normal SEAL clearance techniques. Although they occasionally trained to sneak aboard boats, once they were onboard they rarely bothered to keep quiet. It was all about fast and hard. The only thing they had to be retrained on was "bring the zombies into your killzone, don't go into theirs." And Lyons had spent enough time around the Wolf Marines to be able to hum the tune.

But the land. Oh, the land...

CHAPTER 1

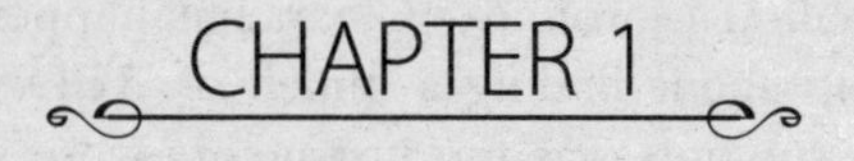

"Once again, let me congratulate everyone on the mission to London," Steve said. "You did an exceptional job. So you get the usual thanks for a job well done. Another one."

Captain Steven John "Wolf" Smith, Commander Atlantic Fleet, had been a high school history teacher prior to the Plague. At this point there were any number of professional submariner officers who had far more experience and could easily take over as Commander Atlantic Fleet. The reason that no one had so much as broached the subject was that the only reason they could now take over was due to the efforts of one Steven John Smith, his redoubtable family and the massive and almost entirely volunteer rescue effort called "Wolf Squadron" that had allowed them to finally climb out of their steel cans.

"As I remarked to Stacey, now we can really get started. The question, of course, is start what?" Steve continued. "And the answer is: Triage."

"I don't really think we're up to repair, sir," Lieutenant Colonel Hamilton said.

Craig Hamilton was another rescuee of Wolf Squadron. The Marine lieutenant colonel had been the senior surviving officer at Guantanamo Bay when a ragtag fleet of yachts, liners and trawlers converted to gunboats had sailed into the harbor. Since then the Infantry branch former interrogator had been running the Wolf Marines doing various clearance operations. Including commanding, up to a point, the near debacle in London.

"No, we're not, Colonel," Steve said. "But we have to figure out where to start working the problem of clearing the mainland. My initial plan was to start with Key West and simply work north. There are arguments for it. It keeps us on one vector. It is, how to put this, fair? Start at one place and work towards another and that's it. People can't complain that we overlooked them. That plan may still have some validity. However, there are problems . . ."

He paused and considered the ceiling for a moment.

"The continued clearance of London is going slowly," Steve said carefully. "The reason being that Prince Harry cannot decide between saving people and training more helo pilots. Captain Wilkes," he said, nodding to the Marine captain, "and the prince, of course, recovered some helos from Wattisham. All good. Parts? Crews? He's having to make his own."

"As we have, sir," Hamilton said. "And trained them as we went. Sophia is coming along well as a helo pilot."

"Thank you, sir," Sophia said, rubbing her new wings.

Sophia Smith, Steve's oldest daughter, had made ensign at fifteen. She had just turned sixteen when she made her first "pilot in command" flight on a helicopter. It helped that her father was LantFleet. Not to mention that they were in a zombie apocalypse. But mostly she had done both those things because she was a founding member of Wolf Squadron and just that damned good. The main argument for "just that damned good" was commanding a rescue yacht for nearly a year and making that first "pilot in command" flight on an MH-53 Sea Dragon, arguably one of the hardest helicopters in the world to fly.

"Which is why she wore her stupid flight suit," Faith said.

Lieutenant Faith Marie Smith, USMC, was two years younger than her sister and already had more combat hours than most grizzled gunnery sergeants. She had come to the conclusion her dad made her a Marine officer not so much because she was an over-the-top crazed zombie-killer or because her Devil Dogs worshipped her for it but because he knew she'd go for the Marines as boyfriends and he was putting as many as possible off-limits.

"Lieutenant," Colonel Hamilton said.

"Aye, aye, sir," Faith said, smiling faintly.

"Frankly, I'd love to have some of my original Marines back, sir," Captain Wilkes said. "The new crews are . . ."

"Spotty," Steve said. "We'll work on that, Captain. Some of the sub crews are going to be transitioning to helo mechanics. And they're about as good as you're going to find in any world, much less this fallen one. But don't expect Januscheitis back any time soon. The point is . . . There are no specific personnel or material targets going up the peninsula that way. Boca Chica has virtually nothing that we need. Notably, we need helos, helo crews and helo parts."

"With due respect, sir," Hamilton said, frowning. "You can't kill all the infected on the continent with helos, sir. Nor save everyone."

"On the first point, you'd be surprised," Steve said. "I'm still keeping some cards on my chest. On the second point, you're correct. But we can save many. Especially those in land-based materials points. Not to mention accessing them. However, all of that is moot."

He brought up a satellite image and dialed in.

"Before I zoom much more," Steve said. "Lieutenant Smith?"

"Sir?" Faith said.

"You are specifically ordered not to squeal," Steve said. Then zoomed in more.

The image was of a large island. That it was on a river near a city was all that was clear. As the image zoomed in more, it revealed a huge mass of military material, including M1 tanks.

"Squeeeeeee!" Faith squealed, then clapped her hand over her mouth.

"And, no, Faith, you don't get a tank," Steve said, grinning. "Probably."

"You didn't get me a present for Christmas, Da," Faith said, grinning back.

"Enough," Steve said. "But that is your next objective."

"That is Blount Island," Colonel Hamilton said. "Correct, sir?"

"Yes," Steve said. "This is one aspect of not being, admittedly, a professional. I was entirely unaware of Blount Island until it was brought to my attention."

Faith nodded sagely for a moment, then threw up her hands.

"Okay, I give up," Faith said. "Do the other newbies get to find out? Sirs?"

"Blount Island is an MPF support and conditioning

facility, Lieutenant," Colonel Hamilton said. "Are those MPFs alongside, sir?"

"Yes, they are," Steve said. "They were drawn into port at the beginning of the plague to change out their equipment and, well, never managed to leave. The same was done with all the other MPFs."

"MPF, sir?" Sophia said, raising her hand.

"Maritime Prepositioning Force, Ensign," Captain Wilkes said. "Three ships carrying all the material to support a Marine Expeditionary Unit for thirty days. Roll-on/roll-off capable. Also capable of loading or unloading on unsupported ports."

"So . . . geared freighters and ferries with lots of military equipment and supplies," Sophia said. "Thank you, sir."

"Their usual mission was to float around somewhere off-shore for months at a time, waiting for an emergency," Steve said. "If they had done that, they'd probably be uninfected. Instead, they were brought in to switch out some of their combat gear for disaster support materials. Bad call on someone's part. As it is, they are all alongside. Somewhere. Notably Blount, Diego and Guam. The problem being, as usual, mass. As in too much of it. However, that is better than not having what you need. And it should be quite clearable. Blount Island only has two access points. Half of it is military, the Marine pre-po base, the other half is civilian, a container and car port."

He slewed the image around to the civilian side.

"No problem finding wheels," Faith said sarcastically. There were about a hundred thousand cars parked in the port. "Threat, sir?"

"Some infected were spotted on the one pass that's

been caught," Steve said, zooming in again. He hit the play button and it was apparent there were infected roaming both the military and the civilian side of the port. They seemed to be clustered around certain buildings. And on at least one of those there were some clothed, thus noninfected, people.

"Survivors," Colonel Hamilton said. "Which would be useful. Just finding your way around in Blount Island is a chore."

"There is one other issue. Minor. There is a POL point," Steve said, referring to a supply point for petroleum, oil, and lubricants. "But it is accessible to the infected and, frankly, way too large to clear and get into operation. So we'll be depending on Statia for the time being. The *Alexandria* poked its head into the St. Johns River channel and it's clear enough to get the *Grace* in with care. Not as bad as the Thames, that's for sure. So, mission of Kodiak Force: Clear Blount Island and prepare to get it back into operation as a forward logistics and support base. You'll be augmented with Navy submariners as well as some nugget sailors from here who have been halfway trained. Usual odds and sods. You'll also be augmented with your usual divisions of gunboats for this mission since you're not going to have to cross the Atlantic this time. Your mission after that will be Mayport, which we'll get to later. Questions, comments, concerns?"

"Fuel," Captain Gilbert said. The civilian captain of the *Grace Tan* was merchant marine but it was hard to tell the difference these days between civilian and military. "And parts. We've got some issues cropping up."

"We've replenished POL stores here from Statia in your absence," Steve said. "And there are still all the other stores here. You're scheduled to replenish this evening. You'll want to take on extra aviation fuel since you are, hopefully, going to need it. And we'll send the *Ho Yun* up with more when you're getting low. Anything else?"

"No, sir," Colonel Hamilton said, looking around the group.

"Again, good job on London," Steve said. "Enjoy Jacksonville."

CHAPTER 2

This is Devil Dawwwg Radio, coming to you live from sunny Guantanamo Bay! An here's yer hourly sitrep, Devil Dogs!

Those of you Devil Dogs in the Great White North may not like to hear about our sunny weather and tropical days, but that cold's biting the hell out of the zombies! We're starting to get reports from across the northern tier of the U.S. and into Canada of breakouts by survivors! Oorah! Keep 'em coming!

U.S. Navy forces under the command of Lieutenant Arnold Trim recently made a port call in Rockland, Maine, delivering critical medical supplies and ammunition for the locals. Some requested to be evacuated but a small cadre stayed behind.

With Portland still reporting scattered infected, Rockland is the designated secure point for Maine and Upper New England. The flotilla will continue support and clearance operations in support of Operation Mayflower...

Master Sergeant John Doehler, NCOIC, Imagery and Overhead Analysis, Strategic Armaments Command, started at the sound of a phone ringing.

He was the Duty NCO in the Hole and, it was the middle of the night, there were no major crises and he was thus trying not to nap. Until the phone rang.

Phones just didn't ring. Every communication they were getting these days was on computer terminals. There might be a polite *ping, ping, ping* but not the harsh sound of a bell. Now there was a phone ringing.

He looked at it. It had a light coating of dust. The label on it said: "Topside Security Station."

He picked it up.

"Master Sergeant Doehler, Duty NCO, Strategic Armaments Command, how may I help you, sir or ma'am?"

"Master Sergeant, Sergeant Williamson, Base Security. Infected numbers have dropped enough we've staged a breakout. We are in the process of ensuring topside security. What is your status if I may ask, Master Sergeant?"

"Nominal," Doehler said. "Uninfected so until we can get some vaccine we're locked down."

"Roger," Williamson said. "Orders?"

"Survive and clear," Doehler said. "Look, don't try to maintain that position all night. Have someone there tomorrow at zero nine hundred hours if security situation warrants. I'll get someone to brief you then. And congratulations on your breakout, Sergeant. Really good news."

"Can I get a quick status update, Master Sergeant?"

"Broadly, the whole world was shut down by the infected," Doehler said. "There are groups getting organized. Main force, currently, is LantFleet and primarily Wolf Squadron. Long story. There are also civilian groups ground-side organizing, mostly in northern zones, but there has been no broad movement. Most are waiting for the spring to start moving beyond local areas. Do you have sufficient supplies for the time being?"

"Now that we've gotten out of the warehouse," Williamson said. "We've accessed another. We were getting short."

"Just hang in there, Sergeant," Doehler said. "And get someone back to the phone at zero nine. Call us. I'll have someone more senior available to brief you and give you any orders."

"Roger," Williamson said.

"Hole, out," Doehler said, then hung up the phone.

"Huh," Doehler said, making a note in his log. "That's a hell of a thing... Must be cold as a witch's tit topside..."

"Not as pretty as the Caribbean," Faith said, looking at the low, scrubby shoreline of the river entrance. "Better than fucking London, though."

February in Jacksonville was significantly colder than in Guantanamo. While not a patch on London, there was a biting north wind under an iron gray sky. It reminded Faith a lot of when they'd left Virginia so many months before.

They'd taken up a position on the side of the bridge of the *Grace Tan* to observe their newest objective. Neither was particularly impressed.

"Not much," Sophia said, gesturing.

The Naval Station was just inside the harbor mouth. They could see the masts of a few Navy ships, probably frigates, tied alongside. What was immediately apparent, though, was that the fuel storage bunkers had burned to the ground. The fire had also consumed what looked like a trailer park right at shoreline.

"Survivors," Faith said, looking through binoculars.

"Where?" Sophia asked.

"Big warehouse in by the docking areas. Think that's the same building. See them up top?"

"Got it," Sophia said. "Well, that's a target, then. That's a stores warehouse for the squadron that was based here."

"And more fuel tanks," Faith said, pointing west. "Amazingly not burned."

"That's the aviation fuel," Sophia said. "It'll need to be re-refined, but good to see. The airfield is over there."

"I can figure out where stuff is on a map at this point, Sis," Faith said. "So seems like you're good for av-fuel. As long as we can clear this sucker and hold it."

"Ensign Smith to ready room," the tannoy blared. *"Ensign Smith to ready room."*

"And so much for sightseeing," Sophia said. "See you later."

"Try to keep it in the air, Sis," Faith said, still looking through the binos.

"Lookouts detected some survivors on a building in the base area," Captain Wilkes said, putting on Nomex gloves. "Time to rig up."

"Yes, sir," Sophia said. She'd started training in helo operations in England since Dr. Shelley had the vaccine production well in hand. Actually, she'd started on the trip over when she borrowed one of the captain's flight manuals as something to read on the voyage. Then in England she'd taken some very quickie tests and acted as a copilot, switching between the three "trained" pilots. In two weeks of clearance over burned-out London she'd gotten eighty hours of "copilot" time, then soloed. They left the Seahawk in London and brought back only the Super Stallion. On the trip back, she'd continued to fly, including dropping in some SAR and salvage crews on ships in the Atlantic. She was still a little unsure in winds like today, but she could manage to keep the bird in the air most of the time. "Has anyone told the rest of the crew, sir?"

They had one Marine, Sergeant Christopher L. "Smitty" Smith, who was a qualified Air Crewman. Oddly enough, he was considered more useful for his proven clearance skills than flying around in the back of a helicopter. Especially given some of the missions after the London Research Institute battle. Many of them hadn't been just "search and rescue," but "combat search and rescue." Then there were the two liner clearances the Marines and Gurkhas had performed. And, of course, Faith had gotten her titties in a wad about losing "her" Marines. Smitty was a grunt for the foreseeable future.

Shortly after returning from London, they'd picked up a medically retired Air Force flight engineer, what the rest of the services called a "crew chief." His name was Eric "EZ" Ezell, and he was a veteran of the storied 20th Special Operations Squadron, which had flown the MH-53J/M. General consensus was that he was a godsend. The Super Stallion needed a flight engineer to do the kinds of missions they were doing, and EZ was fully trained, albeit on the Air Force version.

"EZ's got them at the bird already," Captain Wilkes said, putting on his bail-out harness. Almost as soon as he'd arrived, EZ had taken on the task of training up their inexperienced back-end crew. As a flight engineer, he'd explained, he had one of two jobs. He'd either sit in "the seat" behind the pilots and monitor the aircraft's systems and run the crew, or he'd be in the right door, running the hoist and generally, manning a minigun. Therefore, he was in the best position to teach their baby gunners their jobs. Though he was diplomatic about it, it was clear that in his world, the flight engineer ran the show, second only to the aircraft commander. It wasn't quite the way that the Navy and Marine Corps had operated, but no one could deny that EZ was getting results with the gunners, and so Wilkes let him do his thing.

Sophia reached for her own survival harness, letting out a mental sigh. She was of two minds about the survival gear. If they survived at all, it would be useful. It included, among other things, a lifting harness so they could be airlifted out.

But they were flying over zombie-infested territory. Their survival if they went down was measured in how fast how many of the infected humans could close on them. Then they'd be eaten.

And since they were the *only* qualified helo pilots around, being airlifted out was currently a moot point.

She'd never even mentioned those thoughts to Captain Wilkes, though.

She was putting *her* faith in her 1911 if they went down. She squirted CLP into the action and worked it several times before holstering it on her chest.

"I'd say you carry an insane number of magazines for that," Captain Wilkes said. "But probably not."

"If we ever go down, there's going to be no such thing as 'too much ammo,' sir," Sophia said. "I'm still figuring out where to rack two Saigas in the bird."

"Ask EZ," Wilkes said. "I'm sure his pilots at the 20th did something similar with their M-4s. And anyway, we won't be feet dry for long this time. Just a quick hop."

"I saw the survivors when I was up on deck, sir,"

Sophia said, grabbing her helmet. "Agreed it's a short hop."

"I'll still be checking your pre-flight," Wilkes said. "You can die on a take-off, especially off of this monstrosity."

The helo platform on the *Grace Tan* was just about the highest point on the ship, stuck incongruously above and forward of the bridge. The only higher points were the radio and radar masts. Just walking out onto it required a fundamental lack of fear of heights, and since you could only approach from the bow, taking off and landing were interesting, especially when the ship was moving.

While the task force had been on the London mission, the M/V *Boadicea* had been modified to support helicopter operations. A portion of the aft sun deck and Marquee deck had been cut away. The pool had been removed and a large helo platform had been mounted at the bridge deck level. It would have made a better spot as a primary platform for the helo, as it was way less nerve-wracking to climb out on, but the *Grace Tan* was where all the mechanical support was located.

Sophia couldn't deny, however, that the view from the *Grace Tan*'s helo deck was spectacular. She could clearly see the skyscrapers of Jacksonville in the distance as well as their objective, Blount Island. And their companion craft. The *Grace* was preceded by three divisions of small craft, fishing trawlers converted into gunboats and yachts that had once seemed large to her, as well as the USS *Alexandria*, a nuclear attack submarine, which had, carefully, checked the channel using both state-of-the-art sonar and small boats using old-fashioned hand-lines. It was immediately in front of the large oil platform supply ship, guiding it into its anchorage. The ship was followed by two tugboats to make sure it could get into the right spots. Behind the tugs was the cruise liner M/V *Boadicea*, brought along in the hopes that they would find enough survivors to make it worthwhile. In all it was about half the "throw-weight" of the entire "Atlantic Fleet." At least if you didn't count the subs, which she was still getting used to.

She did the preflight slowly, and with great care, conscious of the watchful eyes of both Captain Wilkes and EZ. The flight engineer had already checked everything she looked at, of course. His own training demanded it. But she needed to know the aircraft systems for herself, and neither she nor Wilkes was willing to dispense with the ritual of "seeing for themselves." The survivors would be fine for the time being. They'd survived this long, they could wait another ten minutes, she thought.

She glanced over at the flag they used as a primary wind indicator. It whipped from right to left, indicating gusty and variable winds. That was another thing. She was not looking forward to trying to take off in this wind while the ship was moving. In fact, she'd "protest" if it was suggested. The aircraft was longer than any of the boats she'd captained and damn near heavier. A nice stable platform for take-off and landing that wasn't stuck out in a constant stream of dirty, turbulent air was high on her list of birthday wishes.

"Some day, I might actually be able to fly one of these things off of a ship that's designed for it," Sophia said as she completed the pre-flight in the cockpit.

"Well, think of this as good training," Captain Wilkes said. "Although, I'm taking this take-off and landing."

"Please," Sophia said. "I'm worried about the winds, sir."

"Did worse in England," Wilkes said, shrugging. "Finished?"

"Yes, sir," Sophia said, keying the intercom. "Crew, you up? Port?"

Following tradition, and because it made sense to minimize intercom chatter, the aircrews used the shortest, clearest, callsigns internally. Sophia's normal handle of "Seawolf" had been cropped to "Wolf." Captain Wilkes's callsign was "Tang" for no reasons he was willing to admit. As for the rest of the crew, they answered with either their position or their personal callsign, though EZ tended to insist on the former.

"Port ready to roll, Wolf," Olga said from the rear. "But I'm sort of disappointed we're not arming up. There are zombies to shoot."

"Not on this mission, Legs," Captain Wilkes replied. "Just hoisting ops."

"Starboard, you up?" Sophia said.

"Ready to go, Wolf," Gunner Apprentice Leo Yu replied. He generally handled the hoist while Olga rode the cable down. A trained person was required on the ground to hook the survivors to the hoist or handle a "basket" if they needed that support. Generally, that would also be a specialist, since there were also "issues" with hovering close to the ground. But they just were still that short on personnel.

"Tail?"

"Tail's up, Wolf," Anna "Wands" Holmes said. The British once-child-star of the Wizard Wars movies had been picked up on St. Barts where she'd been participating in the reality show *Celebrity Survivor:*

St. Barts. She'd decided immediately that she was firing her agent as soon as she got done with the truly inane show. It wasn't like she'd needed the coverage, unlike the rest of the celebutantes and "famous for being famous" women on the show.

Then it had turned to *Celebrity Survivor: Zombie Apocalypse Shit Just Got Real* and dear, sweet, thoughtful Anna had turned out to be the only one in the storage compartment with the guts to strangle the members who'd "turned."

After which, she found it much easier to hang out with people who understood what it meant to take a human life: notably Sophia and her even more violent sister, Faith.

"Engineer," Sophia said.

"FE is Set and Checked," EZ replied, mild disapproval in his tone. He sat in his seat and had his plastic sleeved checklist open in his hands. A quick look around the cabin to the three crewmembers reminded them that checklists had proper responses, and they were to be used appropriately. "Starting Engines Checklist when you're ready, Pilot."

They'd briefly considered changing EZ's callsign to "Moshe" after the one-eyed Israeli general Moshe Dayan. EZ had been medically retired after a "green on blue" incident in Afghanistan where the Afghan interpreter on his aircraft had "accidentally" shot him in the back of the head, blowing out his right eye.

While having a flight engineer with two working eyeballs would have been great, in a zombie apocalypse, having a *trained* flight engineer was something to cry happy tears over. However many eyes he might have. And sitting in the seat didn't require the same binocular vision that manning a weapon did. He mostly had to keep an eye on the instruments and run checklists, which he did just fine with one.

"We appear to be up," Sophia said, holding up two hands with crossed fingers.

It was only after she'd started training on one of the most complex, largest, and most difficult to fly helicopters in the world that anyone had mentioned it also had the record for most accidents per hour of flight.

"God spare us this day from wayward mechanics," Captain Wilkes said, bowing his head and clasping his hands. "As well as the vagaries of airflow dynamics. Amen."

"Amen," Sophia said as the captain hit the start button.

"Go with checklist," Wilkes said. EZ stepped him through the start sequence, and as Wilkes hit the ignition button, the three massive turbines whined to life. "So far so good," the captain said. "Thank you, God."

"Gunner First Class Olga Zelenova, sir," Olga shouted over the beat of the rotor wash. She threw a half salute to the tip of her smoked helmet visor as her feet touched down. "U.S. Navy at your service!"

"We thought you were just going to pass us by, there, Gunner," the Navy lieutenant commander waiting for her said. He stood back and made no move to grab the cable as she unclipped from her harness. As soon as she was unclipped, Yu began to retract the cable in order to clear the line.

"We were headed up to anchorage, sir," Olga shouted. The group on the roof looked to be about half Navy and half civilian. A couple of the women were carrying newborns, and most of the rest were pregnant. "We'll send up the people in the basket, first. Then those who can use the harness."

"Roger," the lieutenant commander said.

When the basket was down, he helped get one of the pregnant women into it and strap her down.

"You seem familiar with this, sir," Olga said, giving the three tugs on the cable that signaled Yu to begin hoisting the basket up.

"I've been in the Navy a few years, Gunner," the commander said. "Lieutenant Commander Lloyd Wiebe, by the way."

"My training consisted of 'Here's how you hook up a harness. Here's how you run the hoist. Here's how you hook up a basket. Good luck, hope you survive,'" Olga said, chuckling. She stepped out of the way of the swinging basket and let it touch the ground and ground out before pulling it over and waving the next woman in. "I was a model before the Plague. Long story. Sorry, long story, *sir*. Still not totally up on that."

"I'd wondered about the civilian ship," the commander said, frowning. "*Is* this U.S. Navy?"

"Sort of," Olga said. "And yes, sir. Controlling legal authority and all that. But it's about half civilian and it's been pick-up ball the whole time. You'll get the full story later, sir. Right now, next customer . . ."

"Kind of bouncing around, there," Wiebe said, looking at the slack cable dancing on the ground as they hooked up the first harness lift.

"You can tell when Sophia's on the controls," Olga replied, tugging on the cable above the slack. The slack came out and the survivor's feet came off the ground relatively smoothly. "Sorry, sir, that would be Ensign Smith. She's still learning. And Captain Wilkes was a Sea Cobra pilot from the *Iwo*. We use whoever and whatever we find, sir. Best anyone can do these days."

"Well, as long as we're getting the job done," Wiebe said.

"Just a matter of finding the people to get it done," Olga said, shrugging. "Only a few thousand of us, still. And we just sent a bunch to the Pacific."

"What is the mission?" Wiebe asked. "Besides general rescue? Or is that it?"

"Right now, get Blount Island up and going," Olga said. "As a support base on the mainland. Then do clearance and rescue ops on this base. We're really hurting for helo personnel so we're hoping to find some here. We're hoping to be able to get *this* base cleared and under control. We'll see if that's possible. After that, up to LantFleet. And you'll get the story of who LantFleet is and why when you get to the boat, sir. This isn't the pre-Plague Navy . . ."

The gigantic helicopter was capable of lifting all the survivors on the rooftop. It just took awhile. Finally, the last survivor, Commander Wiebe, was loaded and Olga followed.

"All the chicks are in the nest," Yu said over the intercom.

"Roger," Captain Wilkes said. "Copilot's controls. Return to the *Boadicea*."

"Roger," Sophia said as she wrapped her hands around the cyclic and collective. At a pointed nudge on her shoulder from the direction of the engineer's seat, she repeated the call. "Copilot's controls."

"Co's controls," Wilkes reconfirmed, amusement in his tone.

Sophia eased forward on the cyclic, bringing the aircraft's nose down, and simultaneously added collective, which resulted in a powered forward climb. You could, technically, go straight up if you had to do so. But with this amount of weight on board, there was a real possibility of asking more from the aircraft than it was able to give. When power demand exceeded power available, the bird *would* descend, and that could be catastrophic. That was just one of the reasons why taking off from the *Grace Tan* could be so nerve-wracking.

"More survivors, Tang," Olga commed. "I can see some people up on houses in the base housing area and a few over by the airfield on a building."

"Roger, Legs," Captain Wilkes said. "We'll get to them later. We're gonna be here a while."

The hop to the liner was short and Sophia slowed as she approached from astern. The *Boadicea* was swung more or less into the wind. But only more or less. Sophia looked at the flag as a telltale, and decided to approach from port and attempt to align with the pad once she was in a hover.

She managed to put it down on the platform, but the helo was at an angle.

"Given the hours of training and the conditions, that's a fair landing, Ensign," Captain Wilkes said while the gunners directed the rotors-turning offload of their passengers. EZ remained in the cockpit, but kept his one good eye on the goings on in the back. "But only fair."

"Yes, sir," Sophia said.

"Force Ops, Dragon Three," Wilkes radioed.

"Dragon Three, Ops."

"Spotted more survivors in base housing," Wilkes said. "Continue mission, query, over?"

"Stand by."

"Fuel state?" Wilkes asked.

"Eighty-six hundred," EZ said instantly, glancing over his shoulder to check the fuel panel readout.

"Dragon Three, Ops. Negative. Reconnaissance of Blount Island. Check status of fencing, determine infected levels. Pick up survivors, Marine and civilian side. Repeat back."

"Ops, Dragon Three," Wilkes replied. "Reconnaissance mission Blount Island, aye. Check status fencing, infected levels, aye. Pick up survivors, Marine and civilian side, aye."

"Roger. Discuss rescue ops, Mayport, on RTB."

"Roger," Wilkes said. "Continuing mission." He turned to Sophia. "Think you can back this off the pad?"

"Yes, sir," Sophia said. The wind had steadied out a bit, and would only help her power situation.

Wands came on the radio. *"Tail's in and secure, sir,"* she said. *"Clear back and up fifty."*

"Starboard," Yu said.

"Port," Olga replied.

EZ slewed back around in his seat, a satisfied look on his face. "Before Takeoff Checklist Complete," he said. "Watch the dirty air from the tail rotor, Co. You got this."

"And we are away..." Wilkes said as Sophia added collective and lifted off.

"Pilot, Port. Permission to engage infected targets of opportunity," Olga commed.

The Marine side of the island wasn't exactly crawling

with infected, but there were fair numbers. Many of them had been down by the water's edge where there was a line of dead infected. Most of the kills appeared to be old; they were mostly skeletal. But apparently the infected had gotten used to feeding there.

What there did not appear to be were any survivors.

"Negative, Port," Wilkes replied. "We need this stuff and rounds do bounce everywhere. Continue to the civilian side, Ensign. But make a swing by each gate."

"Aye, aye, sir," Sophia said.

"And do note the great big power lines," Wilkes added. "Wires like that are the bane of any helicopter pilot's existence."

"Note the wires, aye," Sophia said. "I've been keeping an eye on them. They scare the hell out of me."

"As they should," EZ said. "Call them out for your scanners, Co. That's what they're there for."

"Roger," Sophia said. She approached the fence line cautiously, slowing her forward airspeed so that her scanners could get a good look. She continued to decelerate until they reached a normal hover speed, though their hover was well out of ground effect, being well over the approximate eighty feet of their rotor diameter. The massive primary power lines were just on the far side of the fence.

"Fences are intact in this area," Wilkes said. "Cruise the line. Starboard, you got those wires?"

"Contact wires," Seaman Apprentice Leo Yu replied.

"Roger, keep us clear. Can you spot the gates?"

"River side gate is closed," Yu said. "Fence appears to be in good shape."

"Pilot, Tail: We've got a bunch of infected just following along," Anna said. "I can take them with the fifty."

"Port: no shot this side," Olga said, regret in her tone.

"Hold off on engaging right now," Wilkes said. "Keep your speed down, Wolf, and let's see how many follow us. Starboard, how are those wires doing?"

"Wires at fifty feet," Yu replied. "Doing good, Co. No drift this side,"

"Thanks," Sophia said, although her teeth were clenched slightly with the effort of keeping everything under control. Thankfully, the wind was tending to push her away from the lines rather than towards.

They followed the fence line looking for breaks, slowly gathering a larger and larger group of infected. But even then, it certainly wasn't the masses they'd seen in London.

"If one *small* group had survived in this place, they'd have been able to take out the whole lot of these," Captain Wilkes said. "Hold your hover here."

Sophia eased back on the cyclic, arresting the forward motion of the aircraft. "Here" was a large, elevated, scrubby but otherwise open area on the northeast corner of the main base area bordered by a vehicle parking area on the south, a container storage area on the east and two drainage ponds to the north and west.

"Starboard, can you engage oriented away from the base and materials?" Wilkes asked.

"Negative. They're gathering under us or on the base side," Yu replied.

"Tail's got targets," Anna put in.

"Roger, clear to engage."

"Roger," Anna replied, followed shortly by the deep *thunk thunk* of the tail mounted .50 cal. "Get Some," she called into the intercom, which made everyone, even EZ, smile. That phrase had a long history, particularly among helicopter gunners. The flight engineer swiveled back in his seat to see Wands standing with legs spread in a highly aggressive stance, the .50 pointed almost straight down as she waylaid the crowd that continued to gather below.

Wilkes looked out his window, and then turned back to the front. "Are we clear forward and down? Into ground effect?" he asked. "And turn the tail port, toward the fence? I want to slide south with the nose pointing east, so we can open up with the starboard gun as well."

"Clear forward and down port," Olga said.

"Starboard," Yu replied.

"Tail," Anna said, still firing. "Tail's clear port your discretion."

Sophia pushed down gently with the flat of her hand on the collective and nosed it forward just a little more. They returned to the hovering speed they'd had a moment before, and the digital numbers on their altimeter began to decrease.

"Altitude one hundred," EZ said, calling off of that instrument.

"Clear down port," Olga said.

"Starboard."

"Tail."

"Good," Wilkes said. "Keep coming down to about a twenty-foot hover, then turn your tail."

Sophia complied, slowly pulling the collective back in to arrest her descent as her scanners called for her to "slow her down." "Tail to port," she called.

"Tail clear port," Anna replied, her calls punctuated by the sounds of the .50.

Sophia started to feed left pedal in, slowly at first,

then with more assurance as the Super Stallion's massive tail began to pivot toward the fence.

"Go easy on it, Co," EZ murmured into the intercom. "Treat her like a lady."

Sophia eased up on the pedal pressure, and the helicopter slowed in its pivoting motion.

"I've got targets, Tang," Yu said.

"Engage targets of opportunity oriented away from the base," Wilkes ordered. "Legs, how're we looking?"

"Plenty of room, Tang," Olga replied.

"Does that mean clear to slide port?" EZ asked sarcastically.

"Roger, clear to slide port," Olga said, apparently unaffected by the engineer's remark. "Lots of room till we hit the trucks. We could use this as an LZ, though we're kicking up some FOD."

"See that," Wilkes said. The blast from the powerful rotors was throwing up masses of sand and debris.

"Sliding to port," Sophia said, pushing the cyclic slightly to the left, tilting the rotor ever so slightly to begin moving the helicopter toward the base.

"Lots of targets," Yu said, his voice nearly as gleeful as Anna's had been. "We are having a good killing."

"And *you* get all the luck," Olga said.

"Starboard's winchester," Yu said, using the brevity code for out of ammo.

"Can we rotate?" Olga asked eagerly.

"Pick it up and let's get a look at what we've got," Wilkes said.

"Clear forward and up," Olga replied.

Sophia gratefully nosed down and forward, feeding in collective to bring the aircraft up into forward flight. She circled around half of the base to bring it back to the killing field. The mass of infected hadn't tried to follow the helo. There was too much protein on the ground available for feeding.

"Shoot an approach to a hundred-foot hover," Wilkes said. "Nose oriented west. Winds are calm here, so you should be fine. Legs, your turn. Clear to engage as soon as you have range and azimuth."

Sophia slowed and descended on her normal angle to take up the hundred-foot hover. About midway down the approach, Olga opened fire, though she continued making her approach calls. Anna, too, joined in, swiveling the .50 on the tail as far as it would go to the port side, calling the tail clearance as they stabilized in the hover.

"This is fish in a barrel, Tang," Olga said, the frame of the helicopter shuddering slightly from her fire. "But what we really need are miniguns."

"They go through their whole ammo load in thirty seconds, Legs," Wilkes replied, even as EZ nodded emphatically.

"But what a thirty seconds!" Olga replied. "And . . . I'm not seeing any moving infected, Tang."

"Nor am I," Wilkes said. There had been, at most, a couple of hundred infected on the Marine side of the island. They were now scattered on the scrub field.

"Got one," Yu said. "Late to the party. Permission to engage?"

"If you can hit it without hitting any of the equipment," Wilkes said. "Which means including bouncers."

"Can do that," Yu said.

"Engage."

"Clear. No movement."

"Weapons cold," Wilkes said. "Circle the fence line slowly. Keep an eye out for breaks."

"There are openings," Yu said. "But I'm not seeing any breaks. Most of the water areas are open. No original fences."

"Got that," Wilkes said. "Okay, pick it up higher than the power lines and let's go check out the civilian side. Kodiak Ops, Dragon Three."

"Go Dragon Three."

"Limited infected presence on Marine side of island. Approximately two hundred. Infected concentrated away from river and cleared. Fences solid. Looks clear enough for landing. Doing recon, possible engagement, civilian side."

"Roger. Continue mission. Will discuss landing with ground force."

"Like they're going to be able to hold Faith back," Sophia said.

"Lieutenant?" Colonel Hamilton said. "What do you think?"

"I think if there were just two hundred we could have done it ourselves, sir," Faith replied. "And now it's just a matter of walking around the motor pool, sir."

"Remember London," Hamilton said. "Don't let yourself get trapped. With that caveat: Frago is ground clearance and security for survey and salvage teams."

"Aye, aye, sir," Faith said. "Time to take a stroll. At least till I can get a *tank*!"

CHAPTER 3

This is the Voice of America.

In the News: Forces of the U.S. Naval Services have begun clearance operations in the Jacksonville, Florida, region. The primary focus of initial clearance is the Blount Island Marine pre-position site, containing critical military equipment and supplies, as well as the Mayport Naval Station. Persons in the Jacksonville area are advised that in most cases direct rescue will not be possible. At a later date, clearance of the area to permit self-extraction is possible. Persons unable to self-extract should place signs on their roofs indicating such. . . .

"Jesus, that's a lot of cars," Sophia said. Dragon Three was doing a high circle to get a look at the civilian side of the island.

The civilian side, just one part of "the Port of Jacksonville," was the same square area as the Marine side. However, the Marine side had both an inset "port" area where the three MPF ships were tied up and several large drainage ponds.

The civilian side, by contrast, had all their piers either on the main St. Johns River or the deep channel to the west of the base and there were fewer and smaller internal ponds. Thus the land area was about three times the size of the Marine base. And it was packed, from side to side, with . . . stuff. Dozens of buildings, hundreds of acres of containers, even more acres of vehicles. There were cars, pickup trucks, mini-vans, SUVs, medium commercial trucks, construction equipment, dump trucks, semi-trailers. There were even more military vehicles. Every sort of vehicle in the world seemed to be parked in the port.

It also seemed to have an ungodly number of infected given the area. At least twice as many as the Marine side, if not more.

What there didn't appear to be was a good area to fire them up. There was just no room without hitting something with either direct fire or ricochets.

"Starboard's got an open area by the west river," Yu said. "Big open area in the west car park. Looks like it might be large enough to use."

"In the car park?" Wilkes said, gesturing for Sophia to bring the bird around. "Any power lines or other obstructions?"

"Lots of big light poles, Tang," Olga replied.

"Contact," Sophia said, indicating that she saw them.

"On the west edge, Tang," Yu said. "Right by the water. But there's a ship docked there, too. Need to be careful not to get bouncers off it."

"Roger, got that," Wilkes said, pointing to the open area.

"Port has survivors," Olga announced. "Building in the container area. Long, gray building. Metal roof. By the north road that parallels the river and continues to the Marine base. Near the Marine side."

"Call her to it," EZ prompted Olga.

"Port turn, Co," Olga said. "You're clear."

"Turning to port," Sophia said. She'd brought the

helo around, following Olga's calls until her eyes landed on the building in question.

"We'll extract, then see what we're going to do with the civilian side," Wilkes said. "Guns cold, get the hoist ready."

"A dangling we will go, a dangling we will go . . ." Olga caroled.

"How many?" Olga asked as she unclipped from the line. There were only three men on the rooftop. "Is this all?"

"No!" The man replying was short and burly with sandy blond hair and wearing an unfamiliar uniform and a pistol on his hip. "We've got more below. Some of the women are pregnant or just had babies! Can you get them up in a basket?"

"If we can get them to the roof," Olga said, holding up a finger. "Stand by. Dragon Three, Ground. More people down below. We'll need to get them up to the roof. This roof is pretty open. What do you think about doing a ramp load? You," she said, pointing to the man. "Start getting *everybody* up here. It's not like we can pick you up from ground level."

"Okay," the man said, waving at his buddies.

"We can do that," Wilkes replied.

"Let me get them all assembled up here," Olga radioed. "Then we'll call you in."

"Roger."

"Well, this is interesting," Olga said as she climbed, carefully, through the hole in the roof, avoiding the sharp metal edges.

The roof had not, originally, had a roof hatch.

The survivors had cobbled together one by a ladder up to the top of one of the containers parked inside the shed, then another ladder up to the roof. Then they'd simply cut through the metal roof to get access.

"Gunner First Class Olga Zelenova," she said to the man when she got to the top of the container. "U.S. Navy."

"Senior Agent Brad Johnson," the man said, shaking her hand. "DHS customs and border patrol. God *damn* are we glad to see you guys! We thought *nobody* was ever going to come! And I am flat out of rounds."

"When you get the whole story, you'll realize why it took so long," Olga said.

"We've got shortwave," Brad replied. "We know the deal. Are you with Wolf Squadron?"

"Yep," Olga said.

"Love Devil Dog radio," one of the other men said, grinning. "Wait... *You're* Olga? Like, *the* Olga? Seawolf's sidekick?"

"I am *not* a sidekick," Olga said. "And... yeah. Seawolf's one of the pilots."

"When did Seawolf start being a pilot?" another asked.

"Can we just get on with this?" Olga said. "There's plenty of time later for questions. What is this place?"

The large shed was filled with containers still on trucks. Many of them were opened. There were, in places, large pieces of equipment with radiation symbols and warnings liberally scrawled on them.

"Customs inspection point," Johnson said. "Bunch of workers brought their families to the port when things got bad thinking that it was secure and there were plenty of resources."

"Then people started turning and . . ." Olga said, nodding. "I've heard this story a million times. How do we get everyone up to the roof."

"Carefully," Johnson said. "We'll get it done."

"First things first," Olga said. "Hope you've got some blankets or something 'cause we *are* going to cover the edges of the hole . . ."

They got it done. Getting the pregnant women and the two surviving elderly up to the roof was a pain but they got it done. Two of the women had babes in arms. Olga just tucked the babies into her flight suit and carried them up one by one. She was afraid one of the pregnant women was going to have a baby right there on the ladder.

When they were all up on the roof, Olga had them line up on the peak with Johnson anchoring the rear. The other surviving customs inspector, Agent Simon Miller, took point.

"Dragon Three: We're ready for extract," Olga said.

"Took you long enough," Sophia replied.

Olga could tell by the steadiness that Captain Wilkes had taken over the controls of the aircraft. This type of extraction was tricky, especially with high winds.

The ramp was at about waist height and was moving around slightly. Anna stood at the top, legs spread wide as the "duckbill" style grip of the .50 cal. rested against her thighs. This allowed the barrel to be pointed straight down, and therefore not at any of the loading survivors. She kept one hand on the grip, so that she could use the intercom switch, but she held out her other hand to help those who might need it. The ramp wasn't hard to mount for someone in decent condition. Miller got up on the ramp and started assisting Anna with getting everyone aboard. Yu came to the back and started helping as well. The ladies with babes in arms handed them up to Yu or Miller, then clambered up easily enough. For the pregnant ones it was a touch harder, but with Olga and Johnson boosting and Yu and Miller pulling them up, they finally all were boarded.

"Tang, Port," Olga said, plugging into the intercom as Anna raised the ramp. "All in. Advise Force that one of the women appears to have gone into labor."

"Roger," Wilkes replied. "Heading to *Boadicea* at this time."

Nicola Simpson settled into a chair in the Piano Lounge of the cruise ship and looked at the lady next to her.

"In all future catastrophes," Nicola said, grinning. "Remind me to bring along maternity clothes."

Nicola was wearing a "maternity dress" made of stitched together bits of NavCam. The other woman, girl really, was in a size 6X T-shirt for much the same reason.

"I know, right?" the woman said. "When are you due?"

"Your guess is as good as mine," Nicola said. "Any day now, I hope."

"Same here," the girl said. "Kiera Murphy."

"Nicola Simpson," Nicola said, shaking her hand. "I was in Mayport. Where are you from?"

"Blount Island," Kiera said with a strong Southern accent. "My boyfriend worked at the port and said 'Hey, there's plenty of stuff there for an apocalypse.' Then he turned," she added with a frown. "I got the flu but I got better. What did you do at Mayport? Secretary?"

"Aviation engineering," Nicola said drily.

"Oh," Kiera said, her eyes wide. "Sorry."

"No problem," Nicola said. "I get that all the time. Not many girls in my field."

"Can I get your name, please?"

The speaker was a very pretty young woman with a distinct Slavic accent who was about as pregnant as the two refugees.

"Nicola Simpson," Nicola said.

"As soon as terminals get freed up we'll get you checked in," the woman said. "There are snacks if you'd like, as well as soup and drinks. After you're checked in, you'll get scheduled for a maternity check-up. The 'doctors' are Navy medics but at least we finally have more than two. One of them told me that, unbelievably enough, they're starting to get tired of looking at vaginas."

"I can imagine," Nicola said, laughing. "I'm just so glad to get out of that warehouse."

"Try starving to death on a yacht while being forced to have sex all the time," the woman said. "But those thugs are not with this group."

"Can I ask . . . What *is* this group?" Nicola asked.

"Here," Kiera said, handing her a brochure. "I'm finished with it. Besides, we had a radio. Since Devil Dog Radio came on, we've been getting the story."

"What story?" Nicola said, looking at the brochure.

Welcome to Wolf Squadron . . .

"Shewolf, Seawolf, over."

"'Sup, Sis?" Faith replied.

"Be advised, we're apparently celebrities to anyone with a shortwave. Last group of survivors was asking about you. Over."

"Sweet," Faith said. "And, by the way, you could have left some for us."

"Heading over to the civvie side again. Going to do our best to make your day boring. But that one you'll probably have to fine-tooth. Big place. Really complicated."

"Got it."

"Where you at?"

"Upside down in the hatch of an M1 trying to figure out if we can get it to start," Faith replied. "Figure if you get a helicopter, I should get a tank, right?"

"Like you can drive so much as a car."

"Everybody says these drive like one," Faith said, grinning at Januscheitis. "Maybe I'll take my first lessons in a tank."

"You would. Gotta go. Seawolf, out."

"You probably should try something smaller for your first lessons, ma'am," Staff Sergeant Januscheitis said. There was a distant sound of firing from the helo and the usual squawk of seagulls arguing over who got the zombie carrion.

"Do you know, honestly, my favorite teething toy was a little rubber 1911?" Faith said, pulling her head out of the tank. The interior was surprisingly clean due to the sealed hatches. That didn't mean it was ready to run.

"Ask my da or mum some time, they'll tell you. It wasn't even a teething toy, it was some SWAG Da picked up at a gun show. Just a little rubber gun. I'd go past other stuff to chew on it. At least according to them. So, what do you think they'll say in some future time about General Faith Smith, when you're the Master Guns of the Marines and I'm the Commandant, Staff Sergeant? 'She teethed on a 1911 and her first car was a tank.' Sound about right?"

"Sounds about right, ma'am," Januscheitis said, laughing.

"We only need *one* of these running, Staff Sergeant," Faith said. "We're not going to be using it that much. I know they're a bitch to run and maintain. But I do think we need *one*. So . . ."

"Make it so, ma'am?" the staff sergeant said. "You're talking to the wrong staff sergeant, Lieutenant. Decker's the armor guy. I'm helos."

"Crap," Faith said, dusting off her hands. She keyed her radio. "Force Ops, Ground Force, over."

"Ground Force, Force Ops."

"Base clear for Sierra and Sierra. Require Decker and Condrey for armored ground survey. Send over with Sierra and Sierra."

"Roger. Will dispatch with Sierra and Sierra."

"Now to get him to understand that all we need is it *running*," Faith said.

"Good luck, ma'am," Januscheitis said. "Getting one of these up to Decker's standards will take—"

"Forever, since there is no such thing as absolutely perfect," Faith said. "I'll try to explain it to him."

"I understand the vehicle does not have to meet full ORS inspection requirements, ma'am," Decker said, standing at attention. "However, this vehicle will require a minimum of two hundred man-hours of depot-level repair, ma'am."

"I'm not getting that, Staff Sergeant," Faith said. "I'm not disagreeing with you. You're the expert. But can you explain in terms simple enough for a second lieutenant to understand?"

"When armored vehicles are left unused, various materials break down, ma'am," Decker said, breaking into lecture mode. "Rubber seals are almost the first to go. The air filter for the engine is paper based and often becomes a nest for pests both invertebrate and vertebrate. At the minimum, this vehicle needs: new batteries, complete seal replacement, adjust fuel injection system, full lube, replace hydraulic fluid, hydraulic seals, oil. . . . That is before even inspecting the vehicle, ma'am. Depot level maintenance, two hundred man-hours, ma'am. And despite the hatches being closed, watch out for brown recluse and black widows in the ammo storage area. That was a recurrent issue with material from this depot, ma'am."

"Sounds about right," Januscheitis said.

"Really?" Faith said.

"That's what we were doing for *weeks* at Gitmo, ma'am," the staff sergeant said. "Just with helos. Which had all the same problems. Think you're going to have to settle for a LAV, ma'am."

"What's a LAV?" Faith asked.

Decker was far too dialed in and wired to wince. Januscheitis, not so much.

"It's times like this that I recall your age and relative inexperience, ma'am," the staff sergeant said. "If you would care to walk this way . . . ?"

"That's a tank, too," Faith said. "All I said was, I want a tank!"

"With due respect, ma'am! *That* is *not* a *tank*!" Staff Sergeant Decker, the Marine Armor Staff NCO, barked.

"S'got armor," Faith said, gesturing at the LAV. "S'got a gun. S'atank!"

"With due respect, ma'am," Januscheitis said, trying not to grin. "I have to agree with the staff sergeant on this one. It is a light assault vehicle. So . . . Not a tank."

"'Cause it's got wheels?" Faith asked.

"'Cause it's got wheels, light armor and a light gun, ma'am," Januscheitis said. "The LAV-25 is an eight-wheeled, four-wheel primary drive, amphibious reconnaissance vehicle built by General Dynamics and based upon the well-proven Swiss MOWAG series of eight by eight vehicles. The LAV-25 has a crew of three and can carry up to six deployable Marines. Armaments: One twenty-five-millimeter Colt Bushmaster auto-cannon, two M240 machine guns. Light assault vehicle. Not a tank."

"'Cause an *Abrams* could roll over one of these toys and crush it like a tin can, ma'am!" Decker said tightly. The staff sergeant was starting to twitch. Never a good sign.

"Very well, Staff NCOs," Faith said. "I concur to your experience. Not a tank. But can we get it running?"

"I am less familiar with the operation and maintenance of the light assault vehicle, ma'am," Decker said, calming down. "However, many of the same issues apply to a lesser degree, ma'am."

"LAVs are way less maintenance intensive than Abrams, ma'am," Januscheitis said. "Or helos. We can probably get one of these running in a day or two if the colonel okays it."

"We need these for more than just to give your lieutenant a driving lesson," Faith said. "I haven't discussed it with the colonel, but there's an argument for having some amphibians. I know the tank doesn't count for that. But we need some amphibious vehicles. And also not just because we're Marines and Marines without amphibious vehicles are, well, Army."

"Ma'am?" Januscheitis said.

"I'll discuss it with the colonel," Faith said. "This is amphibious, right?"

"Yes, ma'am," Januscheitis said. "Barely. Not rated for ocean."

"Can it swim the river?" Faith asked.

"It will operate downstream, ma'am," Januscheitis said. "Upstream? Possibly. The last SLEP eliminated most amphib capability."

"SLEP?" Faith asked.

"Service Life Extension Program, ma'am," Januscheitis replied.

"Why would a program eliminate amphibious ability from one of its vehicles?" Faith asked.

"That is one of those questions that falls into 'God and the Pentagon work in mysterious ways,' ma'am," Januscheitis said. "We *all* asked that."

"So what do we need if we need an amphib?" Faith asked. "Some of those hovercraft?"

"No, ma'am," Januscheitis said. "If you'll follow me, ma'am?"

"And this is or is not a tank?" Faith asked, looking up at the tall slab-side of the AAV. "'Cause, again, sorry, it *looks* like a tank. Sort of. Cross between a tank and a Winnebago maybe."

"This is not a tank, ma'am," Januscheitis said. "This is an amphibious assault vehicle, ma'am. Specifically an AAV-7A1. Crew of three, can carry up to twenty-five Marines in adequate discomfort. It is fully ocean capable and can easily negotiate the river, ma'am. This, ma'am, is what most Marine infantry use to get from ships to shore. And if you want to swim the river, probably a better choice than the LAV."

"How long to get one of these running?" Faith asked.

"Not as long as an M1, ma'am," Januscheitis said. "Less to break. Few days with some manuals, parts and tools."

"Which should be somewhere on this base," Faith said, hands on hips. "We'll spend more time looking for the stuff than getting these things running, I suspect. And first S and S has to get some of the base operating."

"Getting a class on Marine vehicles, Lieutenant?" Gunny Sands asked, walking up.

"Yes, Gunnery Sergeant," Faith replied. "I have been respectfully informed that just because something has armor and a gun it is not a tank, that for some reason the Pentagon decided that Marine vehicles didn't have to be amphibious, that any military vehicle that has been sitting out for months requires more than new batteries to run, unlike half the civilian cars we've gotten into operation, and that I lack patience. But we all knew that last one."

"For that matter, I knew the other ones, ma'am," Gunny Sands said. "The LAV was never very good at amphibious ops and keeping the drive train for the propeller operating was always one of those things that failed on inspection. So they just removed all the parts. It will still move in water using the wheels for propulsion but not very well. And they have a hell of a tendency to sink at the worst possible moment. If you're thinking of using something to cross the river and clear the base using this as your safe point, I'd suggest the AAV. For clearance on the civilian side, which we're going to be assigned pretty quick, I'd go with the MAT-V."

Faith paused, then opened her mouth.

"Before you even go there, ma'am," Januscheitis said. "With due respect, it's a type of fighting vehicle based on the MTVR. Five tons, ma'am. But I didn't see any."

"Should have looked closer at the satellite image, Staff Sergeant," Gunny Sands said. "If you would care to follow me, ma'am?"

The walk was long. To a completely different parking area near the river. The walk had taken them past lines and lines and lines of Humvees, MTVRs, wreckers, what looked like weird forklifts, LVSs and every other kind of support wheeled vehicle. They all showed signs of having been sitting out in the weather for a while. It might as well have been Patton's used car lot. Finally the gunny pointed at something that looked like what you'd get if a five-ton mated with a tank.

"That is a M . . . whatchamacallit?" Faith asked, looking up at what was basically a massive armored truck.

"Mine-resistant, ambush-protected, all-terrain vehicle, ma'am," Gunny Sands said. "M-ATV. Armored. Pintle mount accepts M2, M240 or Mark 19. TOW for that matter, not that we're going to need those. Also has a very nice climate control system. Stereo was an option the Corps in its infinite wisdom did not choose to purchase. Last but not least, change the oil and fuel, change the battery and I'd bet my life it just cranks up and goes."

"Tires are sort of flat," Faith said, kicking same.

"They have a central inflation system, ma'am," Januscheitis said.

"But not amphibious," Faith said.

"No, ma'am," the gunny replied. "But you can use this to clear the civilian side while Staff Sergeant Decker, Lance Corporal Condrey and Sergeant Hocieniec's team get five AAVs functioning."

"Five," Faith said.

"Enough for one per team and plenty of room for survivors if we have to pick them up that way, ma'am," Gunny Sands said.

"Do I even have a job here?" Faith said. "I was sure it was thinking ahead to the future of operations so as to be prepared to give orders about them. I know I read that in one of them manual thingies. But it seems my gunny has that well in hand."

"Somebody has to sign for them, ma'am," Gunny Sands said. "They're very expensive. Above my paygrade, ma'am."

"I knew there would be paperwork," Faith said, shaking her head. "Gunnery Sergeant!"

"Ma'am!"

"We're going to need some sort of vehicle for ground clearance on the civilian side," Faith barked. "I have selected the Mat . . . the . . . the Matathingy as the optimum vehicle. You'll have three up and running by zero eight hundred tomorrow!"

"Aye, aye, ma'am!" the gunnery sergeant replied.

"In addition, it may be necessary to do an amphibious assault on Mayport," Faith said. "The optimum vehicle for that I have determined to be the amphibious assault vehicle. We will need five of those when the time comes. You are to detail such personnel as necessary to get five of them up and running. We'll determine the schedule on that at a later date."

"Aye, aye, ma'am," Gunny Sands said.

"I'm going to go see the colonel about the paperwork necessary to draw these from stocks," Faith said.

"Aye, aye, ma'am," the gunny said, saluting. "We'll get started on that right away, ma'am."

"Carry on," Faith said, returning the salute, then walking away.

"Staff Sergeant Decker," Gunny Sands said as soon as Faith was out of sight and earshot.

"Yes, Gunnery Sergeant!" Decker barked.

"Building Fourteen is the tank repair depot. There are four M1A1 main battle tanks in Building Fourteen in covered 'hurricane prep' condition and in apparent good order. In addition to your other duties, you, Lance Corporal Condrey, Sergeant Hocieniec and Staff Sergeant Januscheitis *shall* get *one* M1A1 into operation suitable for mobility *only* prior to the nineteenth of this month."

"Aye, aye, Gunnery Sergeant!" Decker said.

"I will get with Sierra and Sierra on location of additional parts, tools and supplies," Gunny Sands said, referring to Survey and Salvage. "That is in addition to getting five AAVs up and running as well as three M-ATVs. *That* will be an all-hands evolution. However, only you, Lance Corporal Condrey, Staff Sergeant Januscheitis and Sergeant Hocieniec will work on the tank. Nor do I think that mission needs to be discussed with, by or around higher including specifically the lieutenant. Is that understood?"

"Aye, aye, Gunnery Sergeant," Decker replied.

"Permission to speak, Gunnery Sergeant," Januscheitis said.

"The nineteenth is the lieutenant's birthday, Staff Sergeant," Gunny Sands said.

"Aye, aye, Gunnery Sergeant," Januscheitis said, trying not to grin.

"NCO only word, pass the word that the lieutenant is *not* to be given driving lessons until then," Gunny Sands said. "Skipper wants her first car to be a tank, we are by God going to get her a tank. Semper Fucking Period."

CHAPTER 4

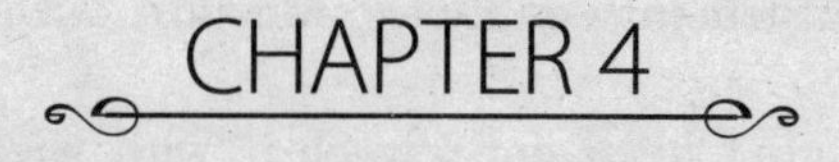

Anchors Aweigh, Shipmates!

Naval forces under the command of Lieutenant Colonel Craig Hamilton continue their clearance of the Mayport Naval Station and Blount Island Marine pre-position base. Blount Island has been entirely cleared with the help of local gator Navy forces. In this case, though, we're talking actual alligators . . .

Nicola sat down at the console and examined the first screen. Besides the general "This is to sort out the sheep from the goats" stuff there were several preference links. Civilian including LEO, Current Active Duty Military, Reserve/National Guard, Veteran.

She chose "Reserve."

She was asked for her social security number which she typed in and hit "Enter."

She was asked to enter and reenter a password which would be used to "Access the Wolf Squadron Network."

She entered and reentered the password, then hit "Enter."

The screen filled with her military, veteran and even employment information and asked if there was anything incorrect.

Reserve Captain, U.S. Army, check. Military and civilian helicopter qualifications, with list of qualified airframes. Check. Blackhawk, Chinook and Bell Jet-Ranger qualified instructor pilot, check. Masters degree in aviation engineering, check. Aviation technical support instructor contractor, Mayport Naval Station. Check.

She hadn't been entirely clear with Kiera. Pretty much every job she'd ever *had*, she was one of the few women.

She hit the "All Correct" link.

"Thank you for your information. You are automatically reactivated as of this date at the Rank of LIEUTENANT, United States Navy Reserve, Aviation Branch. After being medically cleared, see the Military Reactivation Sponsor for processing. Again, thank you for your contribution to saving the world and welcome to Wolf Squadron, LIEUTENANT."

"You're welcome," Nicola said, breathing out tiredly. "Like I'm going to be medically cleared in my current condition."

"Okay," the corpsman said, shaking his head. "I've seen a lot of weird maternity clothes since getting out of the sub. But that's a new one."

"I was in a Navy warehouse," Nicola said, getting up on the table without asking. "It was what we could make."

"There's a sewing shop downstairs," the corpsman said. "They're putting out all sorts of maternity clothes since it's not the sort of thing you just run across. You should show them that. They'll want to put it up on a bulkhead. Any notable health problems? High blood pressure, aching headache?"

"Just morning sickness," Nicola said.

"Heard your baby's heartbeat, yet?" the corpsman asked.

"No," Nicola said.

"Well, pull off the maternity gown, put on the paper one and I'll get a fetal heartbeat monitor hooked up..."

Nicola put her hand over her mouth and tried not to cry as she heard her baby's heartbeat for the first time.

"That's a strong one," the corpsman said, looking at the monitor. "We'll schedule you for an ultrasound but this one looks pretty solid and you're not exhibiting any of the symptoms associated with major side effects, thank God. Is this your first child?"

"Yes," Nicola said.

"Don't slap me for this next question," the corpsman said, making a note. "Any idea who the father is?"

"Yes," Nicola said. "I take it that's been an issue?"

"Five guys, one woman in a compartment?" the corpsman said. "You think? Any idea when you conceived?"

"It's one of two cycles so, no," Nicola said. "I could be due this month or next."

"This one, most likely," the corpsman said. "We'll be able to figure out better with the ultrasound. Assuming you don't pop before then. Okay, clothes back on. We only brought ten expectant mothers with us and two corpsmen. We rescue many more like you, Terry and I are going to be busy as hell."

"I'm surprised *any* corpsmen survived," Nicola said.

"Guess you didn't have a shortwave, huh?" the corpsman said. "We were in subs. Uninfected. We got uncanned, thank God, when the Squadron started making vaccine. And most of us have been landed pending the arrival of the baby wave. Which is shaping up to be a doozy. Twenty corpsmen, six physician's assistants off the boomers, one SF medic, two if you count a guy who turned out to be a general and is on his way to Pac, one, count 'em, *one*, female nurse. Nearly two thousand pregnant women most of whom appear to be scheduled within a month of each other. So far we've had fourteen viable births from the Wave. A few from earlier who were pregnant when the Plague hit and survived everything. But fourteen, so far, from the Wave. And, unfortunately, a bunch of stillbirths and a few ladies we've lost due to complications. When it hits in earnest... it's going to be interesting. Don't figure on seeing any of us unless you've got serious complications. You're probably going to be handling most of it on your own or with a friend."

"Okay," Nicola said.

"There are umas," the corpsman said. "Midwives that is. Some of them have experience, some of them just went through the class. You'll probably have an uma. Who might be a guy, by the way. Main thing is sanitize the area, both the bedding and your pubic region. *Clean* and fresh newspapers, if you can find them, work well for that. They're disposable and the ink is antiseptic. Shave the pubic region for sanitary purposes. Wet it down with Betadine of which, fortunately, we have a shit load. Then grit your teeth and dig in for the ride. Nine times out of ten, even first mothers just manage to push the baby out eventually without a lot of problems. Pain, yes. Seriously life-threatening complications? No. There's classes going on on how to breathe and what not. You'll find the schedule posted on the bulletin boards or on the Squadron net. Questions?"

"Anesthetics?" Nicola asked.

"The only good one, for values of good from what I hear, is an epidural," the corpsman said. "The only person barely qualified to administer one is our single MD, who is in Gitmo. And he'll be busy doing C-sections when there are complications. We've got some soma which is supposed to help, some. Other than that, it's the really old-fashioned way. Big thing is keep the area as clean as possible. More questions?"

"No," Nicola said.

"You're going to be fine," the corpsman said breezily. "You've got a good strong baby there from the heartbeat, and you're in good physical condition. Right now, our PA and our SF medic are performing assembly line C-sections of women from the civilian side of Blount's Island who are at death's door and still carrying a fetus. You seriously want to *complain*?"

"No," Nicola said after a moment's thought. "One issue. I'm reactivated."

"What are you?" the corpsman asked. "Or were or whatever?"

"Captain, U.S. Army Reserve," Nicola said. "I got activated as a U.S. Navy lieutenant for some reason."

"Oh, sorry, ma'am," the corpsman said. "And, yeah, if you're reserve, you're reactivated, ma'am. At rank but into the Navy or Marines since we don't have an Army right now. Wasn't on your paperwork, ma'am. I'll clear you for light duty, ma'am."

"I'll need a flight physical as well," Nicola said. "I'm a pilot."

"Great," the corpsman said. "Just great. Sorry,

ma'am, but that's not going to happen any time soon. I'm not even sure what all a flight physical entails. I'm clearing you for light duty right now. When Captain Wilkes gets back, you can see him about the flight physical issue. I wouldn't suggest putting you in a bird until you're cleared on the baby thing. After that... somebody else will have to decide how to handle it. Fortunately, our one MD may be learning the baby thing, but his actual PhD is in astrophysiology. Should know the requirements. Any other questions, ma'am?"

"No," Nicola said.

"Here's your profile," the corpsman said, pulling off a receipt and handing her a pill bottle. "And some neonatal vitamins for what they're good for at this point. For what it's worth, again, you look like one of the ones who has done okay. Baby seems healthy as hell. You're healthy. It all looks good. Which is much better than some of the stuff I've seen, ma'am."

"Thanks," Nicola said.

"Now I've got a slew more of these, ma'am," the corpsman said. "If you'll excuse me?"

"Lieutenant," the woman behind the desk said, pointing at her screen. "This service record is a sight for sore eyes. Squadron has been screaming for qualified pilots and aviation maintenance people and you're both. The only problem will be deciding which is more important."

"Glad you think so," Nicola said. "I'm not too sure about a cross-service transfer to the Navy."

"We're getting more Army personnel now that we're clearing land areas," the woman said. "But for right now, we're consolidating to Navy and Marine until there's a skeleton of Army personnel to set it back up."

"I suppose that makes some sense," Nicola said. "But I personally don't think I should be flying at the moment, though. I have to pee every ten minutes."

"Tell me about it," the civilian said. "I've left a note for Captain Wilkes to look you up. Right now you have three days to get comfortable with being back in civilization, such as it is. After that we'll find a slot for you. Company grade cabin space is at a premium. You've got a choice of interior solo, for now, or exterior shared. If you're sharing, it will probably be with an O-1 or O-2."

"Exterior, shared," Nicola said.

"Either of the Bobbsey Twins it is," the woman said. "Would you prefer your roommate to be a fellow, if extremely junior, pilot, Navy ensign, or a vicious, psychotic, zombie-killing Marine second lieutenant?"

"You make the choice so difficult," Nicola said, laughing. "I'll take the Navy pilot."

"Shewolf isn't that bad," the woman said. "Once you get to know her. Which you will. You eventually get to know everybody in this gypsy band, and Shewolf and Seawolf are two of the main stars. Okay, you're bunking with Seawolf. Room One-Seventeen, Marquee deck. It's right by the helo pad ready room."

"Okay," Nicola said, taking the room key.

"The key acts as temporary ID as well as rations and materials draw," the woman said. "I don't know if you want to hit your room, first, or the clothing store. Despite your being an officer, due to exigencies of conditions all uniforms and rations are issue rather than pay. Because that basically *is* the pay. There are some Navy maternity uniforms. Another reason to have people Navy or Marines is those are the uniforms we've got. You also get to draw civilian clothing. You don't have to be in uniform until the third day of your three days off. Day three, report to the S1 at oh-nine-hundred hours in uniform."

"Roger," Nicola said.

"Welcome back, Lieutenant," the woman said.

"You seem to be pretty experienced at this," Nicola said.

"I was a Navy dependent for thirty-two years," the woman said. "And a civilian DOD employee for a good bit of that. I know the dance. When you get some downtime in your room, I'd suggest you sit down and watch three videos. The usual series is the Welcome to Wolf Squadron video first, but I'd save that for last. Watch the Cruise Liner Boarding video, then the London Research Institute. I didn't mention it, but your new roommate is a fairly badass zombie-killer in her own right and she used to be a boat skipper and division commander. Then watch the Welcome to Wolf Squadron video. It's better on a big screen, but you've got a fair-sized plasma. At that point you'll be more or less caught up on the major players in the Squadron and you'll get my description of Shewolf. She considers 'psychotic zombie-killer' to be a compliment."

"Okay," Nicola said, puzzled.

"But you probably want to get some more comfortable clothes, first," the lady said, standing up and holding out her hand. "You're going to fit in just fine, Lieutenant. And by the time your baby grows up, he or she won't have to fear the zombies."

"That's a cause worth fighting for," Nicola said, shaking her hand.

"Oh, hi," Sophia said as she entered her room. There was a very pregnant lady in civilian maternity clothes she'd never met occupying the other bunk. Five eight or nine, black hair with a faintly Asian look, slim for being pregnant but not starved. She looked as if she'd recently been crying. "Um, are you sure you're in the right place?"

"Hi," Nicola said, clambering to her feet. "They're running out of company grade officer's quarters. So we have to share. Sorry."

"Not a problem," Sophia said, setting her flight bag down. "I'm Ensign Sophia Smith. And you are . . . ?"

"Lieutenant Nicola Simpson," Nicola said, sticking out her hand. "I *was* 'Captain' Nicola Simpson, U.S. Army Reserve. Aviation. Now I'm Navy. Gotta love it."

"A pilot?" Sophia said, her eyes going wide and shaking her hand. "Hooray! Wait, fixed or rotary?"

"Rotary," Nicola said, sitting back down. "But I'm not going to be flying any time soon," Nicola said, patting her stomach. "I could, but it wouldn't be prudent."

"Only one airframe at the moment, ma'am," Sophia said. "But God knows, we can use instructors."

"You don't need to use rank in quarters," Nicola said. "You're not used to dealing with many other officers, are you?"

"No, ma'am," Sophia said. "Or, not new ones. We get a trickle of them, of course. Almost the first time I've shared a compartment, though."

"Call me Nicola," Nicola said. "Is Sophia okay?"

"Yes, ma . . ." Sophia said. "That's fine . . . Nicola. What are you qualed on?"

"Blackhawk, Chinook, Kiowa, IP," Nicola said. "Seahawk, Little Bird, Super Stallion and some others you've probably never heard of. If it's Sikorsky, I'm qualified. Quite a few others as well."

"That's great to hear," Sophia said. "We're bleeding for qualified pilots."

"So I heard," Nicola said. "I thought the in-process lady was going to ask to have my baby. I'm also an aviation engineer. I was one of the civilian technical instructors at Mayport. I'd guess you were the pilot of the Sea Dragon that pulled us out."

"Ah, that explains it," Sophia said, nodding. "Well, really glad to have you aboard. And please feel free to fine-tooth the bird we're using. It's the only one we've got and our people are sort of green at the maintenance. Our maintenance boss is a Navy nuke that got cross-trained in about a day. Good guy, don't get me wrong. He's sharp as hell. But not experienced. If it's not in the manuals, he won't know about it. Our experienced people are all Marines who got cross-loaded to infantry. They still help out as needed but they're not turning wrenches every day. It makes both the captain and me nervous. Do you know the parts situation at the base, ma'am?"

"Intimately," Nicola said, grinning. "I even know where they're at. Most of the parts are for MH-60s but there's a fair suite for MH-53s. There are twenty-three 60s on the pad and nine in hangar. Three MH-53s on the pad, two in hangar. The ones in the hangar were prepped for long-term storage. I think some of the tools disappeared right at the end, but there are sets of those stored as well. That assumes you can clear the base. Can you?"

"That's the general plan," Sophia said. "After Blount Island, which is mostly cleared at this point. Zombies follow the sound of helos and don't seem to mind my crew machine-gunning them."

"Some of them were my friends," Nicola said. "I had a fair degree of interaction with Blount since there was a UTC officer over there. And you can feel free. I think they'd appreciate it."

"I'll keep that in mind," Sophia said.

"I don't suppose you've had dinner?" Nicola said.

"No, ma'am," Sophia said. "That was next on my list."

"I'm starved," Nicola said. "And I assume it's something other than MREs or humanitarian rations?"

"There's no fresh fruits or vegetables," Sophia said, shrugging and standing up. "But it's pretty good. We got a lot of cooks from the liners. They knew where the food was stored. So the food's as good as you're going to get with prepared. Ready for dinner?"

"Very," Nicola said. "One last question," she added as they were walking out of the compartment. "Any clue how to find other people on this ship?"

"You can use the Squadron Net, ma'am," Sophia said. "That has a list of all the survivors and their general locations and you can send them a message. Anyone in particular?"

"The guy who *should* have spent the afternoon looking up the captain of the ship," Nicola said, patting her stomach. "But he was last seen leaving in your helo for some reason. As soon as I track him down I'm going to ask him if he's going to make me a respectable woman before or *after* our baby arrives . . ."

"Ah, here you are, *Commander*," Nicola said, walking up to the commander's table in the dining room. He was talking with Colonel Hamilton and two civilians.

"Colonel, Captain Nicola Simpson, U.S. Army Reserve, Aviation and Aviation Maintenance Contractor at the base pre-Plague. Now, apparently a Navy lieutenant. Pleasure to make your acquaintance, but if you'd indulge a pregnant lady for just a second, sir," she said, turning back to Lieutenant Commander Wiebe and crossing her arms on her bulging stomach. "I don't suppose you've even *asked* if there is a captain on this ship and if he is qualified to perform marriage ceremonies?"

"That's the captain, honey," Commander Wiebe said, pointing at one of the civilians with both knife hands. "And I was just getting around to that, honest!"

"Lieutenant," the ship's captain said, gesturing to a chair. "Captain Tarn Fletcher. If you'd care to join us for dinner, it would be an honor and a privilege. And I'll be happy to perform the ceremony at some reasonable convenience. I've had four requests so far today and I'd suggest tomorrow afternoon for a group ceremony if that's soon enough?"

"Thank you, sir," Nicola said, sitting down. "You, at least, are a gentleman."

"Seawolf, you can join us as well if the colonel has no objection," Captain Fletcher said.

"No objections," Colonel Hamilton said. "I'm still waiting for the commander's response, however."

"I don't have a ring?" Commander Wiebe said desperately. "Of course, I want to marry you, Nicola. As soon as possible. But I don't have either the engagement ring *or* a wedding ring."

"What size do you wear?" Sophia asked.

"A six and a half," Nicola said. "Normally. My fingers may have swelled."

"I used to do a lot of small boat clearance," Sophia said. "I've got a stash in my room. Salvage. I'll let you look it over and find something you want to wear that fits. Or more or less. There's a guy who can fit it. So . . . ring's fixed," she said, looking at the commander and crossing her arms. "Ball's in your court, sir."

"Captain Simpson," Commander Wiebe said, getting on one knee. "*Lieutenant* Simpson. Would you be willing to marry me?"

"Well . . ." Nicola said, looking up at the overhead. "You're Navy, which is sort of a problem. Mixed marriages *never* work. But . . . wait, now I am too, so . . . Oh, okay! If you insist!"

"Congratulations, Lieutenant," Colonel Hamilton said when the happy couple were both seated again. "You were, in fact, a subject of discussion when you walked up. Although we hadn't touched on the personal aspects . . ."

"There should be no issues, sir," Commander Wiebe said, frowning. "Lieutenant Simpson was a civilian at the time and an officer of a different service . . ."

"No issues, Commander," Hamilton said, holding up his hand. "I'm just glad things worked out with so little drama. You have no clue, yet, how much drama there has been in such things. The point of the discussion, however, is professional. The commander was filling us in on your qualifications although he'd missed the Army captain part."

"I wasn't reactivated until I boarded, sir," Nicola said.

"The automatic 'Congratulations, you're back in the military' screen?" Colonel Hamilton said, smiling. "And welcome to the U.S. Navy. One of the most popular moments of joining Wolf Squadron from what I hear."

"Did come as a bit of a shock, sir," Nicola said. "The information was stored in the Hole?"

"Just the basics of the files," Hamilton said. "No evaluation reports, commendations or for that matter discommendations. It's sort of a new slate. The point to the discussion being that Captain Smith, LantFleet Commander, is insistent on having a large fleet of helos. The edict has been a limited number of airframe types, notably 60s, 53s and some type of small reconnaissance bird. That is going to consume a high number of personnel resources so I'll assume he has some plan other than flying around and rescuing people off of rooftops, however noble that may be. However, it will also require instructors and people with maintenance and engineering background..."

"So I fill all the billets, sir," Lieutenant Simpson said, nodding. "I understand, sir. I guess I'll be busy."

"Starting as soon as you can," Colonel Hamilton said. "Captain Wilkes has been actively engaged in flight operations with a very few exceptions since we got the birds. So someone has to design a training plan as well as recruitment and selection. Since I assume the corpsman put you on light duty...?"

"Yes, sir," Lieutenant Simpson said, trying not to wince.

"Take your three days, Lieutenant," Hamilton said. "Not interfering with that. Get your feet on the ground, get married, congratulations again, have as much of a honeymoon as you two can, given the circumstances. On that note, I believe the commander is not sharing a room..."

"No, sir," Commander Wiebe said. "And there's a queen-size bed."

"So I lose my roommate, too?" Sophia said. "Damn!"

"But when you report for duty, I'd like you to have some outline in your head," Colonel Hamilton said. "How we are going to turn refugees into crew and maintenance personnel."

"That's a tall order, sir," Nicola said.

"We crossed the Atlantic in boats crewed by people who had two or three days' training," Sophia said. "I was in charge of a division and I had no formal training at all. It was all OJT.

"Helicopters are, obviously, lots more complicated than yachts and I'd appreciate it if the people had some clue. But we're . . . driven. We have to be . . . Fatalistic? Shit is going to happen. Bad shit. But. There is an entire *world* out there filled with people who need to be rescued, towns and bases that have to be cleared.

"We had boats sink, crash, run aground, catch on fire. Most of it from people who were asked to do more than they had the knowledge and in some cases ability. But the *net* effect was more people saved. People like you. And I don't want to die in a crash because some maintenance guy, or girl, forgot to attach the wiring on a rotor. But before I do, I'll have saved ten, twenty, a thousand more people. And some of them, like you, will be *good* enough to take my place. So it's a win. World isn't perfect. We're just trying like hell to make it a *little* better."

"Welcome to Wolf Squadron," Colonel Hamilton said. "Where the better is always the enemy of the good. So your good, Lieutenant, had better be very good indeed."

"Yes, sir," Lieutenant Simpson said.

CHAPTER 5

"Plan looks good, Lieutenant," Colonel Hamilton said, looking over the written plan for getting the Marine equipment up and running. "Only question has to do with all the work being done outside. The island is littered with equipment bays."

"Yes, sir," Faith said. "However, the main tracked vehicle depot is Building Fourteen which, according to S and S and the gunny, is stuffed with M1s which are, currently, immobile. So we'll do the work on the AAVs exterior. Eventually, we'll get a tank mover operational and pull them out. Or get one to the point of rolling and clear the others. There's not a lot of use in this world for a main battle tank, sir. Except maybe as a wrecker."

"I thought you wanted one for your birthday, Lieutenant," Colonel Hamilton said.

"Personal isn't the same as professional, sir," Faith said. "What we need for clearance is the amtracks, especially in this area with the river and all, sir. The only reason to get the tanks running is to clear them out of the building and we can get around to that, sir. We'll need a tank mover anyway, sir, since one of the AAVs is bound to break down at some point. Which means we'll also need some way to move it from here to the objective. That's part of our Navy portion recommendation that they get a barge into operation that can load and unload over a beach. That is until we obtain a landing craft from somewhere. That was one thing the MPFs don't seem to stock."

"Marine equipment, not Navy, Lieutenant," Hamilton said. "And something big enough to carry a tank is defined as a ship by the Navy. M-ATVs are already up?"

"Worked on them yesterday and last night, sir," Faith said proudly. "Really have to commend Staff Sergeant Januscheitis and Staff Sergeant Decker on that, sir. They and their people were working until past midnight. Three are up and in good running order. So we can do ground level clearance of the objective. Also two container movers are operational and we've already identified some empty containers that can be used to block the bridges. Two of the Marines are qualified on using those, sir. We are ready to roll on that objective at your command, sir. Give us the word and we'll have the bridges blocked in an hour, sir, and the civilian side cleared to pretty solid green by the end of the day. Biggest hassle will be having to roll all over the zone. Lots of zone, sir."

"Captain Wilkes?" Hamilton said.

"Pick up additional survivors in Mayport, sir," Wilkes said. Sophia and the captain were already in flight suits. "General survey of Mayport and nearby areas looking at infected presence and density. As time remains, survey of the outer areas starting with Greater Arlington. Mark survivor or potential survivor points for later pick-up."

"How's your bird?" Hamilton asked.

"So far so good, sir," Wilkes said. "The Marines did

good work on it in Gitmo and the Navy maintenance crews are pretty well dialed in at this point. Petty Officer Simmons is damned detailed which is to be expected. He does good work and makes sure his people are doing good work. We're going to need some parts soon, but parts inventory is sufficient so far."

"Roger," Hamilton said. "Lieutenant Commander Kinsey. As soon as Survey and Salvage turn in their report, I'm handing over the base."

"Yes, sir," Lieutenant Commander Tommy J. Kinsey, Jr. said. The USS *Boise*, one of the older 688s, had suffered several irreparable mechanical failures post-Plague. The former commander was now the designated Blount Island commander. He'd brought part of his crew along to set up the base as well as refugees newly inducted into the Navy and civilian technical experts.

"Use the *Alexandria* for power initially," Hamilton said. "Tugs are bringing in your old boat. Be planning the power hand-off on that."

"Yes, sir," Kinsey said. "All under control. After it comes in, three days to restart the reactor from cold. Then we can hand-off and the *Alex* can resume operations."

"First priority after getting power restored and the computers cracked will be to set up a land-based helo operations center," Hamilton said. "I want to get the Sea Dragon off that crow's nest and in a hangar. Possibly before we get power restored. Second priority, to be handled in tandem, is getting Marine equipment up and running."

"Aye, aye," Kinsey said.

"Any questions?" Hamilton asked.

"May not be . . . uh . . . Girl's name, oorah? . . . germaine, sir," Faith said. "I understand that the long-term program is to clear multiple bases up the east coast, sir?"

"That would seem to be the plan, Lieutenant," Hamilton said. "Your father is still keeping some cards close to his vest. You may know better than I."

"He never really talked about it with us, sir," Faith said. "Da's always kept his cards close. The point, and it might be getting ahead of where we're at, is that this equipment will be useful doing that. And we don't have amphibs or landing craft, sir. Any ideas on getting it there, sir?"

"It is getting ahead of where we're at and outside this meeting," Hamilton said, making a note. "But it's something we'll have to fix when we get there. We'll set up a planning meeting next week to look at that. Off the top of my head, you can drive AAVs off the back of the *Grace Tan* and she should be able to carry at least four. I'm less sure about getting them back on other than alongside with a crane. But we'll cover that next week. Lieutenant Commander Chen."

"Yes, sir," the commander of the small boat flotilla replied.

"We so far don't appear to need your services," Hamilton said. "Once you get past the Jacksonville sprawl there are numerous small towns along the river. New mission. Run upriver and do light clearance of small towns along the river. You are not permitted to do landings. We will be way too far off to support your forces, and we're not going to get a repeat of London. Understood?"

"Aye, aye, sir."

"Northern limit of operations is the Florida 16 bridge," Hamilton continued. "Take one of the tugboats with a support barge along for fuel and supplies. No landings, but the rural areas... People have guns. With luck they'll be able to self-extract if we can get the infected numbers down."

"Understood, sir," Chen said.

"That's about it for commander's intent," Hamilton said. "And it gives your people something to do. Leave two of the yachts here for support, the rest head upriver."

"Aye, aye, sir."

"For now, clearance, salvage, survey and rescue. Oorah?"

"Oorah!" Faith said. "Ready to rock and roll, sir."

"We ready to roll, Gunny?" Faith said.

The Marines were gathered by a set of M-ATVs that had been moved closer to the *Grace Tan's* pier. The ship had been tied off at one of the RO-RO piers and was in the process of disgorging a mass of material to get the base up and going again.

"Please say 'Yes,'" Faith added. "I just told the colonel we were prepared to begin clearance."

"All ready, ma'am," Gunnery Sergeant Sands said. "Teams have been detailed."

"I suppose this is as good a time for a driving lesson as any," Faith said, looking up at the M-ATV with a frown. "It's not like I can wreck this thing and hitting a few things on the civilian side probably won't be a problem."

"With due respect, ma'am," the gunny said. "You'd be surprised how easy it is to wreck one. You might not kill the vehicle hitting something but you might kill *crew*. Also, there are several ponds on the far side. And these are not amphibious, ma'am. Last, officers don't drive themselves, ma'am. Private First Class Freeman has already been detailed as your driver, ma'am."

"Very well, Gunnery Sergeant," Faith said. "If you insist. But at some point, your lieutenant needs to learn how to drive."

"Possibly when you're *fourteen*, ma'am?" Januscheitis said.

"Not long on that, Staff Sergeant," Faith said. "But for now . . . let's go see if my sister left us anything to kill . . ."

"Do you have any idea how awesome it would be to have a professional facility to fly out of, sir?" Sophia asked. They were hovering over a building hoisting up refugees but she'd gotten experienced enough to be able to look around while in a hover. And at the moment she was looking at the hangar at the Mayport Airfield and the lines and lines of Seahawks and Dragons. "I mean, a real hangar and shops and everything?"

The airfield was small as such things go but it was well stocked with helicopters. The base had not only been the support base for a squadron of surface warfare ships, each of which had a helicopter, but the training base for Seahawk and Sea Dragon pilots for the east coast as well as pilots from foreign navies which had bought the well-tested aircraft.

"I'd be damned thrilled to have the *Iwo* back," Wilkes said. "Which would also resolve your sister's point about how to move the stuff around. But, yes, that would be a wonderful thing."

"Screw a tank," Sophia said. "I want a hangar and a decent shop for my birthday."

"I'll be sure to tell the colonel that, Ensign," Wilkes said. "We had that at Gitmo, you realize."

"Cuba is not the primary objective, sir," Sophia said. "And the *Iwo* was trashed, sir. I was inside it more than you were, sir. Totally trashed. Dockyard job."

"We're in and secure," Olga commed. *"One of them's having some labor signs. Again."*

"Roger," Wilkes said. "RTB, Wolf."

"RTB, aye," Sophia said, nosing down. "You'd think we could at least *refuel* from the *Bo*."

"Again, something to put on the list of birthday wishes," Wilkes said, grinning.

"Dear Santa . . ."

"Well, I know where to get a car, anyway," Faith said.

The masses of containers, which contained Ganesh only knew what, were probably more impressive in their own way. But they were just closed steel boxes and since they could be stacked they covered far less area than the vehicles. So what was noticeable on the civilian side was the cars and trucks. And vans. And everything else.

They were currently driving between lines of cars, SUVs and vans. Every kind imaginable.

"Since I can't get a tank for my birthday, I'll take a Mustang," Faith said. There were about a thousand of those. "Or maybe an Expedition." Two thousand. "Charger?" Five hundred. "Seriously, I can take a driving lesson in one of these. Any of these. Ooh! Mini Cooper!"

"Shewolf, J, over," Januscheitis radioed.

"Wolf," Faith radioed back.

"Recommend divert to west river area," Januscheitis said. *"Interesting activity this AO."*

"Infected, over?" Faith said.

"Negative. Just . . . interesting, over."

"Thataway, Freeman," Faith said, making a chopping knife-hand gesture to the west.

"Aye, aye, ma'am," Freeman said.

"Son of a *bitch*!" Faith said as they pulled up to the cluster of vehicles. The "interesting activity" was apparent.

The helo run the day before had dropped a mass of infected bodies at the edge of the car park. Part of the plan to get the base up and running involved eventually gathering them up, using front-end loaders, then probably burning them. There weren't any good areas for a mass grave.

However . . . body clearance was being taken care of for them. There were the usual flocks of seagulls and vultures but in this case, alligators were crawling out of the nearby river in a virtual tide. As she watched, a gator that seemed be the size of one of the parked Expeditions dragged an already partially dismembered corpse towards the water. Another, smaller, gator grabbed the corpse by the leg and the two engaged in a tug-of-war that resulted in a ripped-in-half corpse. The first gator dragged its partial prize into the water, leaving behind a trail of intestines.

A coyote, or a dog that looked a lot like one, darted in and grabbed the trailing intestines, then ran with them as a gator lunged at it. There were more coyotes, and even recognizable dogs, circling the pile of carrion and avoiding the snapping gators.

That sort of thing was going on everywhere, well up into the car park area.

The Marines were keeping a safe distance and generally staying up on or in their vehicles.

"Don't go near the water," Januscheitis radioed.

"We're Marines, J," Faith replied. "It's sort of what we do."

"Ground ops, Force ops, over."

"Ground ops," Faith replied.

"State nature of unusual activity, over."

"Reptilian, mammalian and avian local inhabitants doing body clearance, over."

"Reptilian inhabitants?" Petty Officer Third Class Sahms said.

"Snakes?" Seaman First Class Gardenier replied.

"Gators," Petty Officer First Class Querce said. "Probably. Ask for a clarification."

"Ground Ops, Force Ops. Clarify 'reptilian,' over."

"Gators are dragging the bodies and parts into the water," Faith replied. "The vultures, coyotes and seagulls are fighting over the scraps. Over."

"Dragon Three, Force Ops, your camera working, over?"

"Force Ops, Dragon Three," Wilkes replied. They were just taking off from the *Boadicea*, having dropped off the latest group of refugees.

Despite being the only known Sea Dragon in inventory, they used "three" as their number. The reason was a tiny bit of military trivia. Any military airframe that had the number "One" was carrying the President. Any that used "Two" was carrying the Vice President. So "Three" was the lowest number they could use.

"Do a pass over the kill zone from yesterday's civilian side clearance. Break. Get a shot. Over."

"Roger," Wilkes said, gesturing to the west. "Nature of shot, over?"

"You'll see it when you see it, Dragon. Multiple requests for video, over."

"Roger," Wilkes said. "Proceeding."

"Wonder what that's ab—" Sophia started to say over the intercom. "Holy *shit*!"

"What's up?" Olga said. *"Wolf, Tang, talk to us!"*

"It's a visual, Legs, Lee," Wilkes said. "Lean out and look."

"Son of a bitch!" Yu replied a moment later.

They'd seen the circle of vultures over both kill areas. That was expected. They'd seen that before and learned to avoid the spirals. But most of the bodies they'd left behind yesterday were already gone. And the waters of the river were *churning* with alligators. The coyotes were basically background to the mass of at least a hundred alligators.

"Tang, Legs. Two-thirty, ground level. In the river up by the bend."

"What?" Sophia said, skewing her head around. She was carefully circling the feeding frenzy as Wilkes handled the camera.

"Okay, that's . . . Look there," Wilkes said, pointing. He'd also directed the steerable camera on the bird's nose to the sight and zoomed in.

The majority of the gators were swarming halfway

down the section of river on the west side of the island. Right by the bridge something was swimming in the river. Sophia had an odd moment of not being able to get the scale. It looked like a house cat. No, it was too big to be a house cat. Either the bridge was *really* small or it was too big to be a bobcat. As it clambered out of the river and shook itself off, she realized what it was.

"That's a fucking TIGER!" she screamed.

"I know," Wilkes said.

"It's a fucking TIGER!" Sophia shouted again.

"Calm down, Ensign," Wilkes said.

She spun the bird around for a better look, shook her head, then keyed the radio.

"Ground force, Dragon, over."

"What's up, Sis? You diggin' this?"

"Be advised, you have a *Panthera Tigris Tigris* approaching your location," Sophia radioed. "Potentially hostile."

"Location, over?"

"Approaching from north on bank having swum the river," Sophia said.

"This I gotta see," Faith said. She wriggled into the back past the gunner, then out the rear hatch and onto the roof. "Freeman, hand up the mike!"

"Roger, ma'am," Freeman said. He handed the microphone to Lance Corporal Harvey, the gunner, who handed it to Faith.

"J, Shewolf," Faith said. "Check out what's approaching from the north."

"Roger, Shewolf. Care for a skin, over?"

"Possibly gator but not tiger," Faith said, looking through binoculars. "Look at the dugs. She's nursing."

The tigress walked through the surrounding packs of coyotes and dogs like, well, a tigress and settled down to feed at one of the corpses. When a smaller gator approached she growled at it and when it didn't back off, she spun around, landed on its back and bit down on the back of its head. The alligator was left shuddering in death throes. She went back to eating man.

"Did that tiger just kill a gator?" someone radioed.

"Calling station, Shewolf," Faith replied. "They do that. They've been observed to kill saltwater crocodiles in the wild. There's a reason mammals rule the earth. Ground force. Coffee break's over. This is not getting the mission done. Load up. Container Group. What's the status on containers to close the bridge?"

"We're ready when we get the call, Shewolf, over."

"Ground force, move to escort container force, break." She paused and looked at the feeding frenzy again. "Upon bridge closure, return this AO. Fire is authorized on canines and canines only. They can't swim off the island once the bridge is closed and clearly they're a potential threat. We'll let the reptilians clear the bodies. Move to link-up with container force, now. No readback. Just follow me."

"Okay, Freeman, head back to the base," Faith said as soon as she was back in her seat.

"Aye, aye, ma'am," Freeman said, starting up the M-ATV and turning it around.

"You know how they call amphibious forces the 'gator Navy'?" Faith said as they drove through the vehicle park.

"Yes, ma'am."

"Takes on a whole new meaning, don't it?"

"Civilian side is blocked, locked and the usual chartreuse cleared, sir," Faith said, saluting Colonel Hamilton. "Any more we'd have to do night sweeps, sir. Should I schedule those?"

"Not at this time, Lieutenant," Hamilton said, looking around at the mass of equipment. "We're probably not going to activate the civilian side until we have this side up and going fully. When the lights come on at night, any infected will be drawn to the fence line of this side. Where they'll be easy enough to eliminate."

"Aye, aye, sir," Faith said.

"Don't plan on getting any rest this evening, though," Colonel Hamilton said. "While the enlisted are hard at work on the AAVs, you and I will be going over plans for clearance of Mayport as well as looking at amphib assault concepts using other than designed ships."

"Aye, aye, sir," Faith said.

"No rest for the weary..."

All four of the Marines started at the pounding on the hatch of Building Fourteen. It had already been a sucky night and none of them needed to get heat from higher.

None of the M1s were in anything like useable condition. Everything rubber had succumbed to the heat, humidity and just sitting. Even Decker was scratching his head at getting the fuel system on their chosen tank working again. He was an experienced tanker which meant he knew more than just "Level One" repairs. But this was something he'd normally be talking to a master gunner tank vehicle repair specialist about. It didn't help that they were trying to do it all using hand lights and one generator. But they were, by God, going to get the lieutenant a tank. Might be a bit late for her birthday. This was a fucking depot level job.

Januscheitis got up from where he had been replacing another of the sixteen million fucking seals on the bitch and walked over to the hatch.

"Who's there?"

"Somebody who can knock politely, talk and who would like to get out of the zombie fucking haunted dark!" a voice said. "Open the fuck up!"

Januscheitis cracked the hatch and was surprised to see at least a dozen Navy pukes standing there clutching M4s, shotguns and tool bags.

"What?" he asked.

"Get out of the way, Jarhead," the short, burly machinist mate first class said, pushing past him. "No way four of you were going to get an M1 this worn-out up and going in four days. Faith was the only entertainment we had for *months* so now you have some *real* mechanics. Where's the manuals . . . ?"

CHAPTER 6

"Survivors, one-thirty, half a mile maybe," Olga said. "Livey. Up on the roof of a house. Clear to starboard."

"Roger," Sophia said, banking off of the search pattern.

They'd been crisscrossing East Arlington for an hour. Greater Arlington "town," more of a small city, was not so much a suburb as an extension of Jacksonville, which was across the river.

As with London, it had burned extensively. Whole neighborhoods were gone. But the road network tended to act as a fire-break and while one neighborhood would be nothing but ashes and debris with the occasional infected wandering through it, the next would be relatively untouched. They all were damaged, though. Overgrown, unkempt, yards and gardens run wild. In fact, one way to spot survivors was the occasional carefully tended backyard gardens, always with a fence. They probably snuck out during the day, quietly, to plant, weed and harvest. It was a living.

The other way to spot them was the roofs. There were survivors who had found some stash of food in an industrial building of one sort of another. Some were in grocery stores, others in warehouses. But some had survived in their homes or apartment buildings.

In most cases, at some point they had climbed up or chopped through to the roof and painted a distress sign. H-E-L-P and S-O-S being the most common.

Spotting those signs, with a single helicopter, was tough. Not only the satellite people in the Hole but sub crews and pretty much anyone with free time was combing the satellite overheads for them. But they were spotting quite a few that were missed from the chopper.

And, unfortunately, some of those locations were now deserted. They never were sure why and wouldn't be until someone checked them out on the ground. If that ever happened.

"Force Ops, Dragon, over," Wilkes said.

"Force Ops."

"Request permission to discontinue sweep and start doing active rescue, over."

"Stand by."

"Roger," Wilkes said as they passed over the house. There was a woman on the roof waving a sheet. "Mark this."

"Aye, aye," Sophia said, hitting the waypoint marker on the GPS.

"Dragon, Force Ops. Permission granted."

"Roger Force Ops. Dragon, out." He switched to intercom. "Crew. Get the hoist ready. We've got clearance to start rescue ops. We'll start with this one, then go back towards Mayport and work out from there."

"Roger," Olga replied. "'Bout time."

"You know, sir, this is almost a waste of time," Sophia said.

They were hovering, ramp down, over the roof

of an apartment building. Five survivors were being loaded, all who had survived in the complex off of Wonderwood Drive.

"Because we can do this all day, every day, and still barely make a dent in the world?" Wilkes said. "I agree."

"We need to get rid of the zombies," Sophia said, looking down at the parking lot of the complex. Every time they hovered for any time, infected from the surrounding area closed in. "We could just hover and machine gun them. That way the survivors can self-extract."

"There's a lot of bullets on Blount Island, Wolf," Wilkes said. "But not enough to clear an estimated one hundred million infected. Or weapons barrels or weapons for that matter."

"We're loaded and ramp up," Anna commed.

"Figure out the strategic later," Wilkes said, pointing southeast. "Next pick-up. Thataway."

"You never realize how many cars there were in the world till you see something like that," Wilkes said, looking down.

The I-295 bridge out north out of Greater Arlington was jam packed with vehicles. There were wrecks, places where people had desperately tried to ram their way out of the traffic jam, some evidence of fire, nothing huge. And now they were rusting ruins, roamed by a few infected.

"Same thing in London, sir," Sophia said. The Queen Elizabeth Bridge had been dropped but the M25 had looked much the same. Heck, most of London was just as packed with cars. "Not sure how we're going to move on the ground."

"By going around the bridge," Wilkes said. "Okay, do we see any obstructions?"

There was a group of survivors camped out on the mid-river island the bridge crossed at a sand quarry. Possibly they were from some of the people who had gotten stuck on the bridge. Or maybe they'd gotten there by boat but with the exception of one canoe, there didn't seem to be any boats. What there was was a *huge* S-O-S composed of dump trucks and construction equipment. It was easily visible from space.

"Negative here," Olga said.

"Nothing here," Yu added.

"Negative, Tail," Anna said, earning her a smile from EZ for her correct terminology.

The small camp had fifteen survivors and one of them apparently knew something about air-mobile operations. He'd set out a set of cloth panels anchored by metal parts that were in a Y indicating the wind direction and had the survivors lined up for boarding. He even had them to the side so they were out of the way of the rotor. The one sticky bit was that more than half of them were armed with bolt action or semi-automatic rifles.

As soon as the helo settled, the group moved forward, women and children first. A couple of the women were armed. Anna held up a hand, pointed to the weapons and motioned that they had to be cleared and pointed down.

The women who were armed showed that the chambers were open and she nodded and waved them in. Same with the men. One wanted to load with the magazine in an AR-15 and she shook her head and motioned for it to be dropped.

"Not only no," EZ said on the intercom, which the passengers couldn't hear. *"But* fuck *no. Keep an eye on that asshole, Port."* His own fingers twitched toward his .45 holstered on his vest, but he stayed in place. Sophia abruptly remembered that EZ'd been shot during an op, and the interpreter who'd done it had been on board his aircraft. The flight engineer was out of his seat, standing in front of the cockpit access, watching the onload with steel in his remaining blue eye.

Leo was forward, casually leaning on his machine gun which *could* be swung inboard.

"Keep the rounds *out* of the chamber," Olga shouted, moving down the line of refugees. "Rounds, magazines, *out*."

Some of them had pistols. She was just going to have to accept those. This group didn't look like the type to try to fully disarm.

"Tell the *Bo* that the incoming group is fairly heavily armed," Olga said. "Somebody is going to have to explain that they're turning in their rifles at least."

"Saw that and called ahead," Wilkes replied.

"And one of the women is going into labor," Olga added.

"We'll call medical."

"I do so love this job," Olga said. "Seriously. Like rescuing people. Tired of the question 'what took you so long?'"

"Would you rather be back on the *Money*?" Sophia asked.

"Before or after you jacked it?" Olga asked.

"I didn't jack it," Sophia said. "Officers of the United States Navy do not hijack nor pirate ships. We *requisition* them for the duration of the emergency."

"Pirate."

"Slut."

"Can it," Captain Wilkes said. But you could hear the grin in his voice. "Coming into the *Bo*. Get 'em ready to move."

"We're not giving up our guns," the man said calmly. He was nearly seven feet tall, dressed in jeans and an Ozzy Osbourne T-shirt with an old jungle cammie top with staff sergeant's rank on it thrown over the top, and as unshaven and burly as a biker. "We are citizens of the United States, not subjects of Great Britain."

Sergeant Major Raymond Barney, late of Her Majesty's Light Cavalry, British Army, was not a happy camper. He'd been left behind from the mission to secure Prince Harry and therefore was still stuck helping out the bloody Yanks, but at least now with some controlling legal authority. However, he also was still in their bloody Navy, even if he had retained his rank of sergeant major. It was confusing to Naval professionals and even more confusing to the raw, untrained, recruits that they were getting through the process of saying "Do you want to be in the Navy? Here's a uniform. If it's moving fast, don't salute, if it's moving slow, salute, if it's standing still, paint." Since he tended to move at what he considered a "measured" pace, he was so constantly being saluted he'd given up and just returned them.

He understood Yanks had a bloody love affair with their guns but he also understood Naval law and tradition and the reason for them.

"I respect that, sir," Sergeant Major Barney said. "And if you were on land, I would be the first to insist upon retaining your arms. You are not on land.

You are on a ship. A ship flagged by the U.S. Navy. Only officers of the U.S. Naval forces and designated persons, masters-at-arms such as myself, may retain arms on a ship, sir. I and my men shall be pleased to escort you and your people to the arms room. There you shall be given the opportunity to clean and service your weapons and turn in your ammunition. Or you may simply turn them in and clean them after you've gotten some food in you and a bit of rest, sir. But you are not boarding this ship further without turning in your firearms, sir. It is not going to happen."

"Just give us a second," the man said, his head down and the AR-15 clutched with white knuckles. Finally he looked up and breathed out. "Follow the sergeant major to the arms room."

"Sergeant..." one of the younger members of the group started to protest.

"It was not a *suggestion*, Terry," the man barked. "The sergeant major is absolutely correct in his reading of Naval Law. And this is, or *should* be, a secure area."

"It is secure," the sergeant major said. "We've established a vaccination program and obviously the infected cannot access the ship. The reason that arms must be secured is, in fact, to ensure it *is* a secure area, sir. Point of order: *Sergeant*? Unofficial title or official?"

"I'm a National Guard staff sergeant, Sergeant Major," the man said. "Light cav."

"In that case, Staff Sergeant, let me be the first to welcome you to the United States Bloody *Navy*," Sergeant Major Barney said, smiling coldly. "I was *retired* bloody light cav and now I am forced to stand here explaining *plain sense* to you bloody Yanks! As soon as that information is verified, you are transferred at pay rate to the Navy. And as a member of U.S. Navy combat arms, you are *automatically* detailed to the rate of master-at-arms. Therefore, Sergeant whatever your name is, *you* are my new next senior NCO and *I* am your *boss*. Which means that *you* can stand here, after you get a bloody *haircut* and shave that *unmilitary* beard, and explain to your bloody Yank gun-huggers that, no, they are *not* carrying bloody arms onto *my* bloody ship! Is that *clear*, Petty Officer?"

"Clear, Sergeant Major!"

"So you lot go turn in your weapons," Barney said, in a softer tone. "You're at the barracks, for God's sake. You don't keep a bloody shotgun in your room at the barracks. You keep it where, Sergeant?"

"In the arms room, Sergeant Major."

"Get some bloody food, take a breath. You're *safe*. No bloody tricks, no bloody zombies. This is not a movie. This is not a video game. We are not going to stick a wire in your head or something. You are *safe*. It is *my* job to keep you safe when you're on this ship and I take that job *seriously*. Which means not allowing persons who are untrained in shipboard firearms use running around with bloody arms. So if one of you keeps a holdout and I find out about it, I *shall* feed you to the bloody gators."

"Lieutenant, ma'am?" an unfamiliar petty officer wearing master-at-arms insignia said as Faith was tightening a torsion bar.

Faith had insisted on it. Officers do not normally crack track or do other maintenance. By the same token, they are "familiarized" with it in Officer Basic

Course and need to know the general outline so they can do planning. Faith's insistence was based on that. She needed to know, generally, what was involved in getting the tracks back into shape to "increase her general military knowledge."

The fact that it got her hands dirty and got her out of an office had nothing to do with it. Really.

So Staff Sergeant Decker was "instructing" her on the Preventative Maintenance and Service Schedule of an AAV-7A1. He was telling her what needed done, politely, and she was doing it.

"Stand by," Faith said. She braced and hauled back on the massive fucking wrench, letting out her breath in a controlled "saaah."

"Right there, ma'am," Staff Sergeant Decker said. "That's the right tension."

"Roger, Staff Sergeant," Faith said, letting up. She undogged the wrench and set it up on the track, carefully. Decker had already, politely, read her the riot act for just dropping it on the ground. You did everything perfectly by the book with Decker, which is why she liked him as an instructor.

"Yes, Petty Officer?" she barked.

"Lieutenant Commander Kinsey would like to see you at the Headquarters Building at your earliest convenience, ma'am," the PO said.

His uniform was straight out of the package and missing a nametag. His facial skin also had a reddened look and a very distinct beard tan-line. Together with the buzz-razor burns on his head, she could spot a "veteran" refugee who had been shanghaied.

"Roger," Faith said. "Staff Sergeant!"

"Ma'am!" Decker said.

"Receive tools!"

"Aye, aye, ma'am," Decker said, making a mental inventory of the present tools. "One seven-eighths wrench is not in inventory, ma'am!"

"My bad," Faith said a little sheepishly. She pulled the wrench out of a cargo pocket after a bit of patting, wiped it down with a cloth and set it in the toolbox. "One seven-eighths wrench, Staff Sergeant."

"Tool receipt complete, ma'am!" Decker said.

"Carry on with maintenance, Staff Sergeant!" Faith said.

"Aye, aye, ma'am!"

"Headquarters building is . . . Nine, right, PO?" Faith asked.

"Roger, ma'am," the petty officer said. "Do you know the way? I am to act as escort."

"Only at night, PO," Faith said, smiling thinly. She picked up her battle rattle, put it on and got it adjusted, then attached her M4, dropped the mag, racked it a couple of times to check the action, then did the same with her H&K. The H&K felt a little sticky so she squirted in some CLP.

"Ma'am, with due respect," the PO said. "If you are unaware, 'at your earliest convenience' actually means 'right away.'"

"I am aware, Petty Officer," Faith said, holstering the H&K now that it cycled to her satisfaction. *Then* she started walking. "And I will walk from here to there with only a master-at-arms whose combat capabilities I do not know when I am assured that my safety is as fully as possible in *my* hands and not his. Including duly functioning weapons.

"You will note that Lance Corporal Condrey is on

security, as I have been familiarizing with the maintenance procedures of an amtrack. For your information, zombies just pop the fuck up no matter *how* many times you've swept an area like this. So if you have just been *strolling* around this base, we may shortly be less one petty officer second class. And if a zombie gets you 'cause you're not being paranoid enough, it will be no great loss to Naval Landing Security Force. Is that clear, Petty Officer?"

"Clear, ma'am," the petty officer said in a certain "tone." The tone an experienced soldier uses on a second lieutenant who thinks she's salty.

"Heh," Faith said. "Where'd Sophia pick you up?"

"Ma'am?" the PO said.

"The helo pilot is my sister, Petty Officer," Faith said. "Where'd you get picked up?"

"On a nearby island, ma'am," the PO said. "Doesn't really have a name, ma'am."

"I am aware that you are prior service," Faith said. "Not Navy, right?"

"Army, ma'am," the petty officer said. "Florida National Guard light cav."

"I know all about 'butter bars,' oorah?" Faith said. "I get your assumptions. It's sort of like the assumptions about me being a teenager. And a girl. And cute. Although the scar on my cheek should be a dime for a clue, Petty Officer. I don't even care at this point, especially not about assumptions from some No-Go sergeant who just got off the chopper. So I'll just go on and let you assume. No reply is necessary."

"Lieutenant Smith reporting as ordered, sir!" Faith barked as soon as she found the commander. She added a salute since she was, in the vernacular, "Under arms."

"Shewolf," Lieutenant Commander Kinsey said, returning the salute. He was sitting at a desk that was part of a large "cube farm" and had turned around as she approached. The gunnery sergeant was at another desk, keying through an inventory. "We're in."

"Mr. Lawton, sir?" Faith asked, looking at the screen. All it was, from her perspective, was a mass of long numbers and strange acronyms.

"The man is a wizard," Kinsey said, spinning back around to the screen. "Dismissed to security post, Petty Officer."

"Aye, aye, sir," the PO said.

"Defense Logistics Management System," Kinsey said, pointing at the screen. "Version 9.6. Which is, amazingly, an improvement over versions one through nine point five. Fairly intuitive, easily sortable, pretty good search functions. You need to become familiar with it. From now on, all your requisitions will be by computer and we're actually going to have an inventory control system. If for no other reason than to anticipate when we're going to run out of stuff and get more. Logistics was never my chosen field but here I sit and I do intend to do a good job. So you can't just grab stuff anymore, Lieutenant. Got it?"

"Aye, aye, sir," Faith said.

"Sit down with the gunny," Commander Kinsey said. "He's going to fill you in on the system, then the two of you are going to figure out what you *already* grabbed and get it released properly..."

"The basin is double fenced and the airfield is double fenced," Faith said, pointing at the satellite images. "Priority should be elimination of infected inside those fenced areas . . ."

It had taken thirty some-odd Marines, with occasional help from Navy nuke machinists, four *days* to get the amtracks up and running. Getting the computers hacked so they knew where the parts and tools were had helped immensely. On the other hand, she was, personally, tired and frustrated from spending most of the four days in front of a computer or in meetings. In fact there seemed to be an organized conspiracy to keep her away from the actual *work*. She knew that officers were supposed to sit in the office and handle the paperwork while the NCOs got the "real" work done. That was the point to the old saw about "I work for a living." Officers sat in offices, note the similarity of name, and did important paperwork "stuff." NCOs did the "real" work. But the last few days had been *insane*. Any time she put on her battle rattle and tried to exit the building, something had come up that needed her attention "right now, Lieutenant."

And most of it just did not seem to be life and death. She hadn't gotten so much as a *ride* in an amtrack, yet. It looked like the first ride she was going to get was on the op. The only way she knew they were up and running, other than reports, was that they'd spent what sounded like half the day, yesterday, driving them around to find any remaining faults. And most of the time it was around the headquarters building. Around and around and around honestly sounding like they were circling it. And, *damn*, were those things loud. You could barely hear yourself think.

Worst of all . . . She knew that birthdays weren't a big deal in the military. She knew that. And she wasn't going to bitch about getting some time off or anything. But today was her birthday. And nobody had even *mentioned* it. Not a call from her mom and da, not so much as a "Happy Birthday, Sis" from Sophia who was sitting *right there* in the freaking meeting. Nothing. Four days of nothing but paperwork and working her butt off on "Operation Rattlesnake" and nobody had even said "Thanks, Lieutenant, and happy birthday." It sucked.

"Following airborne clearance, Marine personnel, using amphibious assault vehicles, will enter Mayport Naval Station at this boat launching ramp," Faith continued, pointing out the ramp on the screen. "The boat launch is outside the perimeter fences. Outer perimeter fence will be breached at this gate, which has to remain in useable condition, and again here. Method on that:

"Amtrack One will move to block the gate with the rest of the team spread out to cover. Entry team will exit Amtrack One. Perform breach doing as little damage as possible. If the key reader will accept standard ID, use that. Key reader is probably nonfunctional and may be set for specific keys. Try it anyway. If that doesn't work, then use the breacher charges. Once gate is breached and opened, Amtrack One will move inside the gate and to the side. Amtracks Two through Five will move through the gate maintaining overwatch until all personnel are inside the secure area. Close and secure gate.

"Amtracks and dismount personnel will then perform ground level sweep of the basin including sweeping all buildings for infected and survivors, then move to the airfield where they will repeat entry here and here, then sweep the airfield for ground level infected. Once the area is secure, Survey and Salvage personnel will be inserted via helicopter to the two facilities. Marine personnel will remain as security for Survey and Salvage. Amtracks One, Three and Five will remain at the airfield. Amtracks Two and Four will move back to the basin to support Sierra and Sierra on the basin.

"Assault commences at zero seven-thirty hours with departure of amtracks from Blount Island. Helo takes off at same time. Clearance of primary areas scheduled for zero eight hundred hours. amtracks should be to ramp basin by that time. Pick-up of Survey and Salvage personnel by helo currently scheduled for zero nine hundred hours depending upon security condition.

"Extract begins at sixteen-thirty hours. Extract from the airfield will be by helo with amtrack extract to the basin as a back-up for all personnel. Extract will be one flight for the Sierra and Sierra personnel, then one flight for the Marines in the airfield. Extract from the basin will be by boats and will not commence until all personnel have been successfully extracted from the airfield. Marines will leave their amtracks in place for the next day's operation. In the event of failure of one or more of the amtracks, they are to be towed to the basin for repair if possible and removal at a later date if not possible. In the event of failure during amphibious operations, small boats will be accompanying to support the landing, standard extract to the small boats. In the event of failure of the air unit while in operation, small boats will maneuver to assist personnel if in the water and amtracks will move to assist if on the ground. If the bird can be landed lightly on the ground and isn't sufficiently damaged to require evacuation, hunker down and we'll come get you. In the event of overwhelming infected force, extraction will be ordered by force commander and follow same model.

"Question remains whether to permanently base on Mayport or move all stocks and materials back to Blount Island. That is to be determined based upon ongoing security conditions. Other than that, any questions?"

"Are we going to be airlifting the helos tomorrow?" Captain Wilkes asked.

"Negative," Colonel Hamilton said. "Survey only. Security survey most importantly. Any other questions? Lieutenant."

"Rehearsal for all operations scheduled for this afternoon, starting at thirteen hundred hours," Faith said. "The amtracks have been briefly water tested but we'll be moving them around in the river more and making sure they don't sink, basically, as well as testing their ability to land on a similar ramp using one over on the civilian side. Rehearsal will involve moving upriver to the bridge island, performing amphibious landing then reenter water, move to civilian side Blount Island, perform entry using similar ramp, then we're done. Drive back on land. Whole operation should take less than two hours. Following which is the after actions review, PMCS on vehicles and final day-before prep. Any questions?"

"Sounds good, Lieutenant," Hamilton said. "We'll have a working lunch before the operation, officers only, to go over any last concerns. And we're done."

CHAPTER 7

"So, any concerns?" Colonel Hamilton asked as they were "enjoying" lunch. One reason to get some land cleared was so people could start growing food again. Canned rations were starting to get old.

"My main concern is I've been so snowed under with meetings and paperwork, sir," Faith said, picking at her food. "I'm supposed to command one of the amtracks and I've never even been in one that was moving, much less in the water, sir."

"You've got a driver, Lieutenant," Hamilton said. "All you have to do is point. It's not hard. I figured it out right away when I was a nugget."

"None of our drivers were amtrack drivers pre-Plague, sir," Faith pointed out.

"Which is why we're having the rehearsal, Lieutenant," Colonel Hamilton said. "You sound like you're taking council of your fears. That isn't like you."

"I'm just ready to get back into action, sir," Faith said. "I think I'm getting better at paperwork, but you know it's not my first love. At a certain point, it is time to shoot someone. Not getting any younger."

"Good thing for you the chances of running out of infected any time soon are slight, Sis," Sophia said. "No matter what we do, there'll always be somewhere else to clear. And based on General Wa— I mean Commodore Montana, you've got, what, sixty more years in you?"

"Something like that," Faith said, then looked up and around. "How old was he exactly?"

"Not too sure," Sophia said. "He was never really clear on that. Never even found out his birthday. He never mentioned it."

"I'm concerned that if the amtracks cannot negotiate the ramp, there are limited choices for entry," Colonel Hamilton said, frowning.

"We can always swim out to the beach, sir," Faith said after a moment. "There are some issues about the tides but even if the tide is against us we can probably make it in and out."

"Good thing we've got a nice, clear beach," Colonel Hamilton said. "You're not a real Marine till you've hit the beach. Maybe if we get it clear enough, we can get some time off and have a beach party again."

Faith tried not to sigh.

"I don't always get along with Faith," Sophia said, her face working. "But I really was starting to feel like I was pulling the wings off a fly at lunch."

"Which is why you kept bringing up age, right?" Captain Wilkes said, grinning. "I was just waiting for her to burst out 'Does anyone at all remember it's my birthday?'"

"Me too," Sophia said. "She's actually starting to exhibit self-control. Which is, like, *bizarre*."

"Thataway, Freeman!" Faith said, pointing at the river.

She'd finally gotten to ride in an amtrack. She still wasn't sure she was enjoying the experience. The fucker was loud as hell and made about a bazillion weird noises. Faster on land than she expected, too. Now she was going to get to find out if it floated.

The track nosed down the bank alongside one of the unused piers. It was actually in the docking port right by the river, on the easternmost point of the island. The *Alexandria* was tied up across the basin and a bunch of the crew were out on the deck of the sub to watch the amtracks sink.

The driver gunned the engine and drove down into the water. Faith was up in the TC hatch, confidently expecting she'd have to put the inflatable life vest to good use. She was putting a game face on things, but she really didn't think something made of steel and the size and general shape of an ocean-going Winnebago had any chance of floating.

It floated. Remarkably enough. Once the tracks were clear of the ground, Freeman opened up the water-jet drive, really just a couple of propellers, and cranked that puppy up to its blistering top speed of seven knots.

She looked over and back to check the bilge pump. It was pumping but not much. Good that it appeared to be working. "Not much" could mean it wasn't working well or, remarkably, they weren't taking on much water.

She ducked down in the TC hatch and looked at the Marines in the cargo, sorry, "troop," compartment.

"How's the leakage?" she yelled.

Sergeant Hocieniec made an "OK" sign. She could barely see him by the weird, green-brown light filtered through the water and let in by view-ports in the interior.

She shook her head and got back up in the TC hatch. So far, so good.

And it wasn't a bad day. Sky was clear. Temperatures were fairly balmy. And they were boating in a not-tank that was sticking all of ten inches, in places, out of the water. Amtracks were kind of like icebergs that way, with ninety percent below the water line.

The amtrack had cleared the small harbor and she used her left hand to knock her right upwards, then outwards to the west.

"TO ZEE LUMBER YARD!" she radioed, her arm jutting out as if mechanical. "TAKING ZEE BEACHES VE ARE! UND VE'LL HAFF SOME STREUDEL UND SOME SHERRY..."

"Looks like she's getting her mojo back, over," Januscheitis radioed on an encrypted frequency.

"We should have done it before *she got to ride in the amtracks,"* Gunny Sands replied. *"I'll get with the colonel on finding something to bring her down. Out..."*

"Ground Force Commander, Force Ops, over."

"Ground Force, over," Faith replied.

"Reminder from higher to maintain radio protocol, over."

Faith growled and glared balefully at the water for a moment.

"Roger, Force Ops."

"Force Ops, out."

"Son of a *bitch*. I need something to shoot." She switched to intercom. "Twitchman! Any zombies in sight?"

"Negative, ma'am," PFC Twitchell replied. "No targets."

"Give me a target," Faith said, clasping her hands and looking at the sky. "Please. It's my birthday..."

"Force Ops, Ground Force," Faith radioed. "Ready to try the ramp landing, over."

Good news. Still nice weather. Amtracks could make it up to the island, onto the island, around the island, off the island, back onto the island, across the island, back off the island... The things they were told to do got longer and longer and screwier and screwier while Sophia circled in her bird probably laughing her ass off and half the base seemed to have turned up in Zodiacs.

Bad news: Force ops had been on her *ass* all afternoon, at least half of it relayed from the colonel. And she hadn't seen any valid targets. She'd considered having Twitchman shoot up some of the gators that infested the area, but since they were basically part of the island's defenses that seemed counterproductive.

They'd, finally, "completed all certification tasks" and were now up for the last task of the day: pulling up on the relatively narrow boat launch ramp.

The boat launch, probably to support the many outboard boats a port like this needed, was nearly at the back side of the island by the older Blount Island Boulevard Bridge. And it was narrow compared to the amtrack.

"Freeman, if you miss the ramp I am going to turn the matter over to the gunny," Faith said. "Who will use nearly fifteen years of experience making you regret it."

"I will not miss the ramp, ma'am," Freeman said. He lined up on it and pulled forward, tracks churning.

As the tracks grabbed, the amtrack heaved itself out of the water for about the hundredth time that day and pulled easily up the concrete ramp.

The other four followed like baby ducks, one after another.

Faith could practically hear the sarcastic applause from the circling helo. Why they couldn't have sent it off to rescue people she had no idea. It was part of the "emergency assistance plan" the colonel had insisted on.

"Force Ops, Ground," Faith radioed. "All tasks complete. Ramp exit successful. RTB, over."

"Stand by, Ground Ops," Force replied. *"Hold position for further task . . ."*

"Aaaah!" Faith shouted, grinding her teeth. "What *now*?"

"Ground, Force Ops, over."

"Ground Force, over," Faith said sweetly.

"Admin task. Pick up critical inventory hardcopy, civilian side, Building Fourteen."

Colonel Hamilton was trying to maintain his composure watching the retrans from the helo above. Faith was banging her helmet on the upper deck of the amtrack. Then she threw her arms in the air wildly, banged on the top deck with both hands and finally keyed the microphone.

"Roger, Force Ops," the lieutenant said in a remarkably sweet voice. *"Which section, over?"*

"Stand by for steers, over," the petty officer said, then looked at the colonel.

"Take her and the group all over the civilian side," Colonel Hamilton said. "Make sure that you make it as confusing as possible and repeatedly have it seem to be, or at least convey that it is, her fault."

"Roger, sir," the petty officer said, shaking his head. "Remind me never to get on your cruel side, sir."

"I want her thoroughly pissed off when she gets to the building," Colonel Hamilton said. "I need to go. Make it good."

"Ground force, order was turn left, *over."*

"This is left!" Faith replied. Because of all the cars and other vehicles in the way, there were few direct routes to the building. It was like trying to negotiate a maze. Especially the way that Force Ops was taking them. "And the damned building is *that* way! I *know* you can see me from the helo! It's *that* way!"

"Left from the angle of the helicopter, over..."

"I *did* turn right!"

"You wanted steers from your *angle, Ground Force..."*

"God I wish I was there," Commodore Montana said, laughing. Getting started in the Pacific had him as busy as a one-armed paperhanger, but he was willing to take time for this. "If there wasn't something nice at the end of this, she *would* kill someone."

"I hope everybody is behind cover when she gets there is all," Lieutenant Lyons said, shaking his head. "She is armed."

"Lieutenant Smith is *always* armed, Lieutenant," the commodore said. "She sleeps with a gun *and* a knife under her pillow. Even *I* only sleep with a gun."

"I won't ask how you know that, sir."

"Ma'am?" Januscheitis radioed in a dubious voice. *"Are you sure you wouldn't prefer me to lead the convoy, ma'am? Some of the troops are getting a little concerned. We're heading completely away from Fourteen at the moment, ma'am."*

"This is *not* my fault, Staff Sergeant," Faith radioed as they had to turn around, again! "I'm getting my steers to Building Fourteen from *Ops*!"

"Yes, ma'am, but we can see *Building Fourteen from here . . ."*

"Oh, J," the gunny radioed. *"Nice salt in the wounds! 'I'm not saying you're lost, LT, but you're lost, LT.'"*

"Thanks," Januscheitis replied. "Just want it to be special . . ."

"Get the helo up a little higher," General Brice said, laughing so hard tears were coming out of her eyes. "I wanna see how close she is to the objective . . ."

"We are cruel, cruel, people," Undersecretary Galloway said.

"All in a good cause, sir," General Brice said. "All in a good cause. Lieutenants need a certain amount of frustration in their lives so they can handle being generals and dealing with politicians."

"Touché, General," Galloway said. "Touché."

"GAWWWWWWDAMNIT, OPS! I'M JUST GOING TO DRIVE *OVER* THESE FUCKING *CARS*! I CAN *SEE* BUILDING FOURTEEN!"

"Colonel," Steve said over the video link. "I believe we have tortured my daughter enough. She is armed and not particularly self-disciplined. Let her pick up the 'paperwork' before she drives back and opens fire on the *Tan*. And *everyone* higher wants me to reiterate that they had *better* see her face when she opens the door."

"Concur, sir," Colonel Hamilton said. "We've got the camera pointed *right* at it." He keyed the portable radio and assumed a stern voice. "Force Ops, Force Commander! The unit needs to turn *left*, there, not right! Ground Force, Force Commander!"

"Ground Force," Faith said in a defeated voice.

"Follow *own* direction to Building Fourteen," Hamilton said. "Critical paperwork in main hangar area. Door on the south side marked nine has been breached. Paperwork is Federal Inventories, Special Materials, Top Secret. Ground Force Commander and Ground Force Commander only to observe. Read back, over."

"Main hangar area, aye," Faith said dispiritedly. *"Door on south marked nine entry, aye. Ground Force Commander only, aye."*

"Just get it *done*," Hamilton radioed sternly. "A simple errand should *not* have taken this long, Ground Force. ForceCom, out."

"There is one, last, issue, sir," Gunny Sands said, from over his shoulder. The helo was carefully following the movement of the Marine convoy as it approached the building.

"How we're going to keep her from drawing and firing automatically?"

"Roger, sir."

"All personnel!" Hamilton said. "Gather on the *far* side of the objective from the door and *silent running*! Thirty seconds . . . twenty . . ." he could hear the amtrack pulling up by the door. "Ten . . . take cover! *She's almost here!*"

"Fuck," Faith said, sliding off the side of the amtrack. "I hope this building isn't clear. I *really* need to kill something."

She stomped over to the door as the Marines exited the amtracks and took up security. The door, as promised, had already been breached. Probably clear but she jacked a round into her M4 anyway. She might get lucky. She didn't remember clearance on this building but there had been some missions she couldn't get involved in 'cause of all the God-damned, motherfucking paperwork and fucking shit God-damned meetings and fuck this SHIT . . .

She opened the door, weapon on point, and stopped as lights came on all over the building. There was what looked like a brand new M1 Abrams, painted pink with flames along the side, sitting in the middle of the large maintenance building. On the side was written TRIXIE in big, bold, gold letters. A massive banner above the tank read HAPPY BIRTHDAY, SHEWOLF.

"SURPRISE!" about a hundred voices bellowed. Most of them were hiding behind the tank and poked their heads up warily at best.

"If you think this means I'm *not* going to kill somebody, you are OH SO VERY WRONG!" Faith screamed. "And I'm going to kill you by RUNNING YOU OVER WITH MY *TANK*!"

CHAPTER 8

“Oops,” Faith said as the M1 banged into the Ford Expedition. The tank didn’t even notice. It was a good thing they had plenty more trucks if they ever needed them. And they made nice traffic cones for a tank so Faith could have a proper driving lesson.

“Little more care in the steering, ma’am,” Staff Sergeant Decker said from the commander’s cupola. “Recommend you take it a bit slower.”

“Aye, aye, Staff Sergeant,” Faith said, grinning as she gunned it. “You said slower, right?”

“There’s no way we’re ever going to need two hundred Kia Sorentos,” Colonel Hamilton radioed. *“Go for it.”*

“HEE HEE!” Faith squealed, gunning the Abrams as she drove up on the first of the mid-sized SUVs. It crunched like a tin can under the foot of a giant AND THERE WERE A HUNDRED AND NINETY-NINE TO GO. “THIS IS THE GREATEST BIRTHDAY EVERRR . . .”

“Sir!” Faith said to the colonel. “I know I’m not maintaining professional demeanor but this is the greatest birthday EVER!” She threw her arms around him in a hug. "Thank you!" She grabbed the gunny and hugged him. "And thank *you*, Gunny, 'cause I know that a colonel couldn't have pulled this off on his own! Us officers aren't that smart!"

More than half the Force was gathered at the party in building Fourteen. The *Alexandria* turned out to have only left a small security and watch detachment onboard. Most of the Naval Landing Force was there, the helo team had landed and, of course, her Marines. Most of them were gathered around the cooling tank, admiring the detail work. Undersecretary Galloway, General Brice, Commodore Montana and Mum and Da had all chimed in via satellite. Turned out they were all in on the surprise party.

"Frankly, we were stumped, ma'am," Gunny Sands said. "It took the machinists mates from the *Alexandria* to get the fuel system working. And we couldn't have gotten it up without their help all around."

"That's just . . ." She looked at Commander Vancel and shook her head. "I am just having the best birthday ever, everybody. Just . . . the best. But . . ." She paused and shook her head again. "This is not the best use of our scarce available resources, you know?"

"Lieutenant," Vancel said, frowning. "I'm trying to figure out how to put this . . ."

"May I, sir?" the COB asked.

"Of course, Chief," Vancel said.

The Abrams had been parked back in the building after Faith's "driving lessons" so the COB climbed up on it and shouted: "AT EASE!"

"I got a few words to say," the chief of boat said, raising his glass of punch. Since everybody was armed, and in honor of the only teetotaler Marine lieutenant in history, the party was dry.

"We spin words around stuff," the COB said. "My daily report for the day the *Voyage Under Stars* was spotted had the notation that 'Crew Morale Could Use Improvement.' But what did that mean? We're a weird bunch, submariners. We're chosen from people who are functionally insane in the civilian world. Just being in a sub is being under pressure. And the ones that stay in the business just adapt to that. You know you're in a tin can that can sink any time and be crushed to smithereens. You gotta have a sort of definite sense of either fatalism or invincibility to handle being in the sub service.

"But we weren't looking at our own deaths. We were looking at... I'll just leave it at we left people behind on the strand. I'll just leave it at that. And higher had us looking anywhere and everywhere for signs of... well, recovery, hope, anything. And there wasn't a *fucking* thing. Not one fucking item. Every base was crawling with infected. Every ship. Every port. Hell, every God-damned beach. Six and a half billion people. Half of 'em were dead, the other half were vicious, insane carnivores. Infected carnivores. Three billion of 'em, maybe. Not a fucking thing you can do about that. We knew the truth. There was no home to return to. And as the days and weeks and months went by, there was no hope. It was that Fifties movie *On the Beach*. At some point, we were going to have to make the choice, do we go and let ourselves get infected or just... take the pill. And some of us already had. Guys had just hung themselves. Stuck their heads in bags...

"*That's* what 'Crew Morale Could Use Improvement' means.

"Now, we'd picked up the chatter from a group of civilian boats that were doing some rescue and clearing. But . . . that's all it was. Chatter. Just a bunch of boats. Not really under discipline, barely getting anything done. *Trying*, mind you, but not really what we'd call 'serious.' It wasn't really . . . hope. It was just . . . It wasn't really hope.

"Then the *Voyage* got spotted. We'd seen others. We knew what was happening. Crew Morale Could Use Improvement.

"And that group of boats just said; 'Screw this, we're going to save those people.' But what the fuck could they really do? Huh? *Voyage* was the second largest liner in the *world*, people! It was like clearing a fucking supercarrier. Thousands of infected left, probably. What the *fuck* could they do?

"And the first shooters to arrive, were these two young ladies," the COB said, pointing at Faith and Sophia. "We didn't have their ages, then. But we'd seen 'em. Okay, we'd watched 'em quite a bit. We knew they were young. Teenagers. And what the fuck could they do? Against that? But what they did . . ."

He shook his head and turned away for a moment.

"We were *all* watching. Everybody was, high, slow, radio up and linked in. The boats that were there. The boats that were away in the Atlantic, Pac, Indian. Then this young lady, she called her 'Da,'" the COB said, nodding at Faith. "And when she answered with her back-up plan . . ." Again he shook his head.

"There was a pause. Long one. Then you could *hear* the laughter start all over the boat. Not much at first. I hadn't heard one single laugh on the boat, not even in black humor, since . . . forever. It was slow at first, as if people had forgotten how. Then it was . . . hysterical. Out of control. It has been duly reported that more than one watch officer fell out of his chair he was laughing so hard. A submarine that shall not be mentioned nearly lost ballast control when the planesman was laughing so hard he took her into a banking dive.

"Then when she *did* board? When she just . . . fucked over more infected than God? By herself? Most of it hand-to-hand?

"You could *hear* the hope start. Like dawn coming up over a force ten sea. Like spring under the arctic ice. Groaning at first, unsure, then breaking. You could *hear the hope.* In every voice. And her sister," he said, pointing at Sophia. "She was just *right there*, Johnny on the Spot, every moment. *They* weren't giving in to the impossibility of the situation. They were just . . . driving the fuck on.

"Lieutenant, when we got word that the Marines were trying to get an M1 up and going for you, and trying to keep it secret which Marines *suck* at, *every machinist on the boat* wanted to help. Every *crew member* wanted to help. We had to tell guys they couldn't land 'cause they had watch, then listen to their bitching.

"Everybody in that first Wolf Squadron threw into the *Voyage*. But you, Lieutenant and you, Ensign, you were what gave us back *hope*. Not that things would be the same. Not that . . . those we left on the beach were going to be waiting. Just . . . hope. Hope that we could, some day, feel the land under our feet again and *do* something. Not just rot to death in a tin can until the choice was give up to the infected or take the pill. What you and your da and Sergeant, sorry, *Captain* Fontana and Sergeant Hocieniec and all the rest of your crews did—what you did in reality, the clearance and the rescue and all the rest—that should have been fucking impossible. But you did something more impossible than that.

"When the night was darkest. When hell was risen and heaven seemed to have left the building. When everything seemed impossible, when God had abandoned us, when there was no future but the zombie . . .

"You gave us hope.

"So if you want a fucking tank, Lieutenant, you get a fucking tank."

"Thank you," Faith said in a very small voice as the applause died down.

"And the plan was retroactively approved by your chain of command including Undersecretary Galloway and General Brice," Colonel Hamilton said. "All work was done on-own-time. Well, most. We had to test it initially during the day."

"So I *was* being deliberately kept in the headquarters building," Faith crowed.

"And you learned a lot," Commander Kinsey said. "Which isn't a bad thing."

"I learned not to trust my chain of command," Faith said, grinning. "Seriously. Thank you. Thank everybody who worked on it. But what are we going to get Sophia?"

"I've already said what I want," Sophia said. "A working helo repair and support facility."

"Then I will clear the fuck out of Mayport for you,

Sis," Faith said. "I'll sort of be sad I can't use Trixie, but getting it across the river would be a nightmare."

"Lieutenant," Colonel Hamilton said. "There's a *bridge*. The M1A1 has a three hundred mile range."

"I can drive it over?" Faith asked.

"There are about six hundred cars blocking the bridge, sir," Sophia pointed out.

"I get to run over *six hundred cars*!" Faith squealed.

"Not tomorrow," Colonel Hamilton said. "But the M1 may be somewhat useful in clearance operations. We'll see on an ongoing basis. There's also the issue that the bridge may not support the weight of both the cars and the Abrams."

"Yes, sir," Faith said. "I really love my tank, sir. But what is important is getting the clearance done. With our still-limited personnel, moving the facilities from Mayport to here would be a major logistical hurdle that, if it was due to the security situation would, obviously, be harder. Bottom line, there has to be a way to secure the base."

"Half a million infected within ten miles, Lieutenant," Hamilton said.

"Which just means half a million targets, sir," Faith said. "Just need to get the number down. And Lord knows, we're no longer limited in ammunition or equipment, sir."

"The mission is to get the local area up and running, then clear bases north, Lieutenant," Hamilton said.

"We've looked at the time it would take to get the major components of the support facility from Mayport to here, sir," Faith said. "Thirty days, minimum, with the personnel we have available. If we take less time getting the infected level down to the point the base is no longer in threat, it's a net win in terms of time, sir."

"That is a point," Hamilton said.

"Do it both ways, sir," Sophia interjected. "Mechanicals."

"Mechanicals?" Hamilton said.

"Mechanical infected... eliminators?" Commander Kinsey said. "Removers? I'm not sure what the nomenclature is. They used them in the Canaries as a test. Containers with some sort of cutting blades on the inside and light and sound attractors inside and out. Set exit end over the water, entrance end on land. Lots of lights on top. Zombies go in, they don't come out. Or, rather, they come out either in pieces or so damaged that they drown. Problem being, the ones in the Canaries only worked for a few days then failed."

"I've seen the redesign, sir," the COB said. "It uses the full tranny and cruise control from a light truck to gear down if necessary. I think it will work."

"I just wish that my tank was more useful for clearing infected," Faith said.

"Unfortunately, they're primarily designed for clearing other tanks, Lieutenant," Colonel Hamilton said. "Even using the machine guns would tend to be spitting in the wind. But as I said, we may cross that bridge when we come to it."

"Funny, sir," Faith said, shaking her head.

"Sir," Gunny Sands said.

"Yes, Gunny?" Hamilton asked.

"M1028, sir."

"Oh," Hamilton said. "I hadn't thought of... Lieutenant Smith's comment that we officers are not very smart was just proven, wasn't it, Gunny?"

"That is why you have gunnery sergeants around, sir," Gunny Sands said. "And Decker was the first one to bring it up. I checked the magazine inventory, sir."

"How many rounds?" Hamilton asked.

"Sorry," Faith said, raising her hand. "Clueless lieutenant? M whatsit?"

"Two *thousand*, sir," Gunny Sands said lovingly.

"Canister rounds," Januscheitis said to Faith.

"Canister, canister, canister . . ." Sophia said, frowning. "I know I know that . . . Oh! Really?"

"I know I've heard the name, too," Faith said, frowning. "Wait . . . Hornblower! Like grapeshot, right?" Her eyes lit up. "For my *tank*? Really?"

"Two thousand rounds in the magazine, ma'am," Gunny Sands said, grinning. "Eleven hundred and fifty rounds of ball bearings, per. Basically a one hundred and twenty millimeter *shotgun*, ma'am. Way better than a Saiga."

"Oooh," Faith said. "Sweet. We really could have used that in London . . ." She paused and frowned. "But getting a bunch of them in one place . . ."

"That's the way to do it," Sophia said. "Drive around the city. Slowly. We'll hover the helo in one spot, maybe near a park, draw them in. Needs to be noise."

"Should be psy-ops bullhorns in the inventory," the machinist mate said. "They're fielded with an ARG."

"You know," Colonel Hamilton said, looking at the overhead and rubbing his chin. "If we *start* from Mayport and they *follow* you . . ."

"Pied piper," Commander Kinsey said, nodding.

"We did this as a . . . well, because it was the right thing to do," Colonel Hamilton said. "But maybe refurbing a tank wasn't the worst use of resources ever. Two *thousand* rounds?"

"I'm going to get to shoot zombies with my tank, aren't I, sir?" Faith said, her eyes lighting.

"You just might, Lieutenant," Hamilton said. "You just might—"

"SQUEEEEE . . ."

CHAPTER 9

"Oh what a beautiful morning, oh what a beautiful day," Faith sang over the radio as the amtracks churned into the Mayport Naval Station boating basin. "Shooting zombies with my taaank, everything's going my way . . ." She unkeyed the radio since it was lousy radio discipline.

"We're not shooting zombies with your tank, yet, ma'am," Januscheitis replied. He was in the trail amtrack of the convoy. "And this ramp is narrower."

"Target," Twitchell said over the intercom.

The landing objective was outside the fence line of the basin and the airfield which is where the helo had concentrated and where it still continued to circle, looking for targets. But there were more infected outside the wire than inside. And some of them were up on the pier, attracted to the sound of the approaching amtracks.

"Oh what a beautiful morning," Faith sang again as they approached the ramp. "Oh what a beautiful day. Shooting zombies with my amtracks, everything's going my way. . . . Forty millimeter. Open Fire!"

The amtracks were armed with a dual system: 40mm Mk19 grenade launcher and .50 caliber M2 Browning machine guns. All the gunner had to do was choose or, in this case, have the choice made for him.

The basin where the ramp was located was small but not so small that five amtracks couldn't squeeze into it. And there was a fairly large welcoming party.

Mark 19 40mm was designed as an antivehicle round. They hadn't bothered to load the armor-piercing, discarding sabot, only the high-explosive incendiary. There wasn't, unfortunately, a canister round. That would have been spar.

The sealed turrets were controlled entirely internally and really did look like something from Star Wars. At Faith's words the turrets, which had been tracking the gathering infected, all opened fire. And immediately disproved the statement: there is no such thing as overkill.

Overkill can be defined as: Five amtracks whose turret operators had limited training more or less simultaneously opening fire with 40mm antimaterial rounds at a hundred rounds per minute at a scattered line of possibly, max, a hundred infected, using a weapon that has a 2200 meter range, with a minimum arming distance of 100 meters, in the confines of a 180 meter long, 88 meter wide basin, into which said amtracks were more or less packed and, in some cases, at functional arm's length to said infected.

"JESUS CHRIST!" Faith yelled as she ducked into the vehicle then keyed the radio. "CHECK FIRE, CHECK FIRE!"

The rounds shredded the infected, in many cases not even bothering to explode. Often, they simply hit and bounced off, the speed of the baseball-sized rounds being hard enough to kill the infected by impact alone. The ones that missed, and they were more common than the ones that hit, impacted the buildings around the basin. And the cars. And in some cases the walls of the basin. The entire area was pinging with fragments. When the rounds *had* detonated on contact with the infected, the zombies were not so much "blown up" as obliterated. Bits and pieces were still raining down when the last gun stopped firing.

"We seriously need more adult supervision," Faith said, picking a severed arm up off the deck of the amtrack and tossing it over the side with a slightly nervous flick. "They let *lieutenants* make these decisions?"

"Okay, Tex," Faith said over the radio. "I think we got 'em. Let's mount up that ramp and see what else is in store for us. And next time . . . Maybe just have the team fire them up from the crew hatch?"

"In retrospect, that might have been a superior choice," Januscheitis said. *"I'll remind higher that my background is air ops, not amphib. Holy cow. Over."*

"Ground Force, Force Ops."

"Ground Force," Faith replied.

"Reminder from higher. We need the base more or less intact, over."

"Roger that, Ops," Faith replied, then unkeyed the radio. "Jesus Christ. I think I wet myself. Oh, no, that's just spla . . . That ain't water . . . Crap. Just once, I'd like to *not* end up covered in blood. . . ."

Their path out of the basin led them right past the burned POL facility. The reason that the infected had been able to gain access to the small boats basin was obvious at that point: the fire had effectively melted the heavy steel fencing. It was breached in several places and the half melted posts were bent over at more.

Unfortunately, the breaches were more or less directly

away from their line of travel. The armored vehicles could just push the fence down, but it was a dicey proposition. They were just as likely to get stuck. So they had to go to the gate for the facility and breach it.

Moving there wasn't difficult and didn't take long. But by the time they got there, there was another reception committee. And their plans on breaching were for entry into clear zones, not exit. On the other hand, with this fence down at multiple points, they really didn't *need* the gate.

"Can we just ram this thing down and run into them, J?" Faith asked, looking at the infected on the other side of the gate. She'd seen them on the decks of ships plenty of times and, often, at very close ranges. But this was different. They were just . . . there. Right on the other side of reinforced link. Howling and keening and trying like hell to get through.

"Need to get with higher on that, ma'am," Januscheitis said. "Again, amtracks not my specialty."

"If we had my tank this would be easy," Faith muttered. "Force Ops, Ground, seeking counsel, over."

"ForceCom, over."

"Small boat fence compromised multiple points," Faith said. "Breaching plan for exit . . . nonfunctional. Exit gate swarmed. Exit gate also functionally useless due to compromised fence line. Getting slightly surrounded," she added, looking over her shoulder. There were more infected closing from the rear. "Easiest and most direct method, ram gate, ram infected, spread out and clear with light auto fire and, well, Patton quote. Query: probability of ramming gate causing . . . Are we gonna get stuck on the gate? Jan's not sure, over."

"You shouldn't," Colonel Hamilton said after a

moment. *"Fencing can jam treads in some conditions but if you get a running start you should slam right through."*

"Roger," Faith said. "We'll try that. This would be a lot easier with my tank, you know."

"Tungsten ball bearings going as fast as those go ricocheting off the concrete walls of the basin could have holed the amtracks, over."

"Will keep that in mind. Ground Force, out. Right," she said, switching back to intercom. "Freeman, back up to the edge of the basin. To the edge, not into. Hooch, get up and out and watch where we're going. And wave to get people out of the way." She switched back to the platoon frequency. "Everybody back up a bit. We're going to ram this gate. Following that, we are going to move into the parking lot and engage infected with direct fire. Break. Air ops, you up on this frequency?"

"Roger, Ground."

"Once we're in the car park, can you give some overhead fire, break. And to be clear, *away* from us so we're not getting hit by bouncers. Over?"

"We can do that," Captain Wilkes replied.

"Okay, hold it there, Freeman," Faith said as Hooch signaled for them to stop. "You've got the target?"

"Yes, ma'am," Freeman said, gunning the engine with his foot on the brake.

"Stand by," Faith said, ducking into the interior and going over to the team inside.

"I'm not sure how this is going to work!" she shouted. "We're going to ram the gate. We might go through like it's not there. We might get stopped cold. I don't know. So hang the fuck on!"

"Ma'am!" Hooch shouted.

"Yeah?"

"We're gonna go right through!" the sergeant said. "I looked at the gate. Not a chance in hell it's going to slow us down!"

"Roger," Faith said. "Hang on anyway! Following, I want to get the SAW gunner up and out. We'll spread out and use light fire to clear."

"Aye, aye!" Hooch said. "Permission to go topside on the run?"

"Roger," Faith said. Hooch, as one of their few actual infantrymen, had the most experience with amtracks. He really should have been one of the commanders. She'd kept him on the dismount group mostly to have his experience in her vehicle and close to hand. "Watch yourself when we hit!"

"Will do," Hooch said.

"Okay," Faith said, getting up in the commander's cupola and bracing herself on the hatch. She held one arm back like throwing a baseball, ready to point. "R—"

"FREEZE!" Hooch called.

The command was drilled into every Marine, even Faith. They all froze.

"Freeman," Hooch yelled. "Make sure the track is in *forward*. Not *reverse*!"

The newbie amtrack driver looked down at his controls and sheepishly put the vehicle in forward.

"You had it in *reverse*?" Faith said angrily. She looked behind her. They were backed to the edge of the basin and if they'd gone into reverse, between the three-foot drop, the angle and the fact that the BACK HATCH WAS OPEN . . .

Amtracks only floated because all the water was *outside* the track. The bilge pumps would not have helped. And there were, yes, sharks in the pool. They'd nearly done a full Anarchy. With a whole fire team and the crew.

"Sorry, ma'am," Freeman said. "I'm a truck driver, ma'am!"

"Got it," Faith said. "Hooch, thanks once again for saving my ass."

"Well, as usual, Miss Faith," Hooch said absently. "It was mine too. Ready to rumble, ma'am?"

"Okay," Faith said. "Are we *sure* we're going forward? I dunno. I'm just learning to drive."

"Yes, ma'am," Freeman said.

"Then roll it."

The amtrack didn't accelerate fast but by the time they hit the gate they were doing a solid ten miles an hour. And Hooch was right. The gate didn't stand a chance against thirty tons, with crew and ammo, of rolling steel and aluminum.

Nor, for that matter, did the infected. Most of them had been pressed up against the closed gate. Which collapsed over onto them.

The AAV bumped up on the gate, then back down.

Faith didn't look behind her to see what the effect of reinforced mesh with thirty tons of steel on top did to a human body. They'd be back around to check, later. What *was* noticeable was the decided lack of infected to engage.

"Ground Force, air, over."

"Air, ground, over."

"Do you enjoy making sausage, over?"

"Freeman, pull it along that edge of the car park," Faith said over the intercom, then switched frequencies. "Whatever gets the job done, Air, over."

"Roger."

"Ground Force. Form a circle, sides oriented out like wagons and let's just fire this AO up for a bit," Faith said. "Primary weapon, SAW gunner. Use the main guns for long-range targets only. Commanders designate targets and let's take a little more *care* this time. We need this facility intact. Read back. Track Two . . ."

"Okay, I think we've got the level fairly reduced," Faith said over the radio. The ground around the circled tracks was littered with dead.

A few infected had managed to make it through the concentrated fire and get up to the amtracks. Which were not particularly easy to mount from their angle. But they also couldn't be fired upon, given the height of the vehicle, once they got up close.

The simple answer was grenades. The shrapnel, equally, was not going to hit the people in the vehicles. So when the guys inside heard banging on the sides, the TC would toss a grenade over. It didn't, primarily, kill the infected. Grenades tended to wound, not kill. But it did ruin their day.

"Let's roll out of here," Faith said. "We're behind schedule to breach the basin gates. Freeman," Faith said over the intercom. "Roll out to the basin gates."

"Roger, ma'am," Freeman said, gunning it. They were in a sort of spiral called a "lager" and he had a clear shot.

"Don't run this one down," Faith added.

"No, ma'am," Freeman said.

When they reached the gate they backed up to it, close but far enough away to drop the ramp, then waited as the other amtracks got into position. The entrance was narrow, only admitting their one amtrack. The others were arrayed at the beginning of the lane, parked sideways, oriented at the car park filled with derelict and, at this point, pretty shot-up cars.

"Track commanders, engage with careful fire," Faith said. "Use forty. Carefully. And get the grunts up and firing."

Fortunately, the main buildings in their direct line of fire were just part of the sports and fitness complex. Not a big loss there.

Infected were still closing from all over the base, attracted by the sound of the amtracks. As she watched, the amtracks opened up on them with forty-millimeter grenades. Unfortunately, the gunners had had only a couple hours practice with the turrets and were still getting dialed in. So some of the infected were making it through the fire.

The troops, on the other hand, were also up. Instead of the usual twenty-five Marine passengers per amtrack they only had five apiece but that was enough. The unit had "up-armed" for the insertion so only the squad leaders were carrying M4s. The rest were either broken down into M240 medium machine gun teams or were armed with M203 grenade launchers or M249 squad automatic weapons. The Marines had started to substitute a redesigned H&K 416 taking Colt style magazines as the SAW. But fortunately there was a sufficiency of the high fire-rate Fabrique Nationale small machine guns in inventory. Because the difference in firepower was notable.

The infected were not making much headway against the combination. If the Mk19s didn't get them at range, they ran into a hail of 7.62 NATO from the M240s and if that didn't get them, there was the wall of 5.56 from the SAWs and more 40mm grenades from the M203s.

Faith's track dropped its hatch and Hooch's team dismounted. There were two gates at the entrance, a main vehicle gate and a personnel gate. There was also a small guard shack to control access. Hooch checked the guard shack, first, but the controls were powered and without power they couldn't automatically unlock the gate. That left the hard way.

The swing gate was constructed of military link reinforced with heavy wire. It had an electromagnetic positive lock holding the two gates together as well as a ram-opening system. Both systems had to be overridden to get the gate to move. First they breached the personnel gate with a small explosive charge. Then Lance Corporal Quade covered by Randolph entered the interior through the personnel gate and hammered free the pins holding the ram-opener. In the meantime, Hooch fitted another small explosives charge to the main gate. As soon as the two Marines were back on the AAV and the ramp was up, they triggered the charge to blow the gates.

"Main basin outer gate breached," Faith reported in. "No major problems from infected."

"Copy," ForceOps replied. *"Secure gate and move to airfield. We're behind schedule."*

"Be advised," Faith said. "Only outer perimeter gate breached, over."

"Copy. Move to airfield."

"Roger," Faith said. "Hooch. Secure the gates, we're moving to the airfield." She switched back to radio. "Jan, how's the weather?"

"Overcast with light showers," Staff Sergeant Januscheitis replied. *"No big deal. So far."*

"We're moving out to the airfield instead of doing clearance here," Faith said. "Make sure we're ready to roll. You take point this time."

"Roger."

Faith walked into the Sea Dragon as the Survey and Salvage crew was unloading on the airfield, proceeded forward to the cockpit, then hooked her vehicle crewman helmet into the intercom.

"You guys having fun?" Faith asked.

"A blast," Sophia said. "Not as much fun as you, though. We saw the firepower demonstration at the basin."

"Turns out there's such a thing as overkill," Faith said. "Who knew? One thing missing from the plan. You guys sticking around?"

"We're going to do more SAR," Captain Wilkes said. "While the Sierra and Sierra does its work. We'll be back for extract."

"Roger," Faith said. "Don't go down in Indian country. But if you do . . . We'll just come get you. I think that's a possible at this point."

"Assuming we come down somewhere you can get an amtrack to, Lieutenant," Wilkes said.

"If I can't get an amtrack there, I can get a tank there, sir," Faith said, grinning. "Gotta go."

"Force Ops, Ground Force, over," Faith said as soon as she was back to the track.

The Marines had swept the hangar and the surrounding buildings and now were moving on to the administrative and support buildings. So far, they were encountering no live infected. There was a pile of them conveniently off to the side left by the Sea Dragon's fire, but that seemed to be it within the perimeter.

There were more along the fencing, mind you. They were continuing to trickle in from throughout the surrounding area. That might be an issue at some point.

"Force Ops."

"Plan was to extract Marine contingent by water from main basin. Break. Are we changing the plan entirely? Over."

"Still looking at that. Main objective airfield. Once clear will look at breaching basin. Over."

"Copy. Ground out."

Januscheitis had gone into the hangar with the Survey and Salvage personnel so she walked over there to "discuss ongoing operations." And 'cause she wanted to see what they'd got.

"How's it going?" Faith asked.

"Incredibly, ma'am," the staff sergeant said.

"Hey, Harry," Faith added to the Survey and Salvage boss.

"Faith," the older man said. "You won't believe this. The birds in the hangar were prepped for long-term storage."

"Which means?" Faith asked.

"You know how we had to replace every seal and fix all sorts of... stuff on all the amtracks and Trixie, ma'am?" Januscheitis said. "Well, they took the time to rip all that out and cover everything that degrades or is susceptible to corrosion. Like they were going to put all the birds in a container and ship them. All the techs are going to have to do is reinstall everything.

Which will take time. But it's not *fixing* everything. And first going over and finding what needs to be fixed. Just . . . plug stuff back in. Then test it and if it's good you can just *go*."

"The guy who ran this place must have been OCD as hell," Harry added.

"How long?" Faith asked. There was a line of helicopters in the hangar with their rotors folded back. Three Sea Dragons and ten Seahawks. More than they had pilots for much less repair and support crews.

"A trained crew can get any of the Seahawks back up in half a day, ma'am," Januscheitis said. "The crews we've got . . . day or day and a half. The Sea Dragons maybe two. We worked for two *weeks* on your sister's bird, ma'am."

"We need this facility," Faith said. "I'm going to recommend that we just do clearance tomorrow. Although there's some question about the basin. We're going to need to get that breached at some point."

"We'll figure it out, ma'am," Januscheitis said. "This is really good news, though."

"I got that," Faith said. "Harry, you gonna call it in?"

"You got it, miss," the man said. "I'm going to go see what's up with the parts situation . . ."

"Force Ops, Ground," Faith said.

"Force Ops."

"For ForceCom: Sitrep. Birds in hangar quote prepped for long-term storage close quote. Break. Can be restarted with day to two days' work in most cases. Break. Per Sierra and Sierra then Marine aviation expert. Break. Sierra and Sierra boss wagging tail. Over."

"Roger. Will pass to ForceCom. Over."

"Plan and status basin breach, over."

"On hold pending full analysis of airfield. Break. May do full airborne extract. Over."

"Roger," Faith said. "Ground out. And there goes the plan out the window," Faith added. "Oh, well, welcome to another day in the Corps..."

CHAPTER 10

The man standing on the roof of the ranch style house was wearing a flight suit, survival vest, flight helmet and pistol in chest holster. He was carrying a flight bag.

"I guess I don't have to explain this to you, do I?" Olga asked as she hit the roof.

"Nope," the man said, stepping over and connecting to the line before she unhooked. "Let's hoist, Airman!"

"Gunner's mate," Olga said, tugging on the cable as she examined the man's patches and insignia. "Major?"

"Lieutenant Commander, Gunner's Mate," the man said, frowning.

"I'm sort of new at this, sir," Olga said. "Seems like years at this point, but if I see those sort of rank I figure major, sir." They fell silent then, as the rotor wash from the hovering Sea Dragon drowned out everything else.

"How long have you been in?" the lieutenant commander asked as they reached the door and were pulled in by Yu. "Were you pre-Plague?"

"No, sir," Olga said as she scrambled in after. "I was a model before the Plague. And our number three was an actress. You'll recognize her."

"Pilots?" the commander asked.

"Pre-Plague Marine captain," Olga said as they were pulled into the bird. "Post-Plague fifteen-year-old ensign. The flight engineer's old school, though. AFSOC MH-53 FE."

"Jesus," the man said, shaking his head and unclipping from the line. He set his flight bag down, walked over and hooked into the intercom system. "Pilot. Lieutenant Commander Greg Sanderson, former commander Helicopter Strike Squadron Forty. Permission to enter the cockpit?"

"Granted," Wilkes said. "Welcome aboard, Commander."

"Be right up," Sanderson said and unclipped. "Secure my flight bag," he said, pointing to it.

"Aye, aye, sir," Anna said, saluting.

"Are you . . . ?" Sanderson mouthed as he returned the salute.

"Yes," Anna said, nodding and grinning. She grabbed the flight bag and used a carabiner to hook it to a tie-down ring in the floor next to the bulkhead.

Sanderson shook his head and went forward. EZ handed him a spare comm cord and stepped back out of the way so that the commander could lean in and see the pilots as he spoke.

"Appreciate a sitrep if you have time," Sanderson said after he'd hooked in in the cockpit.

"Where to start, sir," Sophia replied. "Unit started as a scratch civilian effort at sea. Eventually was recognized as a military unit by the NCCC. Some became military, others remained civilian. We've been doing clearance and rescue for most of the time since the Fall, sir."

"Are you the fifteen-year-old, Ensign?" Sanderson asked.

"Yes, sir," Sophia replied. "That is a very long story, sir. Part of the story is that my father is LantFleet. Another part is that he's prior Australian Army and has never been Navy, sir. We're up to about eight thousand people, total, including the sub crews. Anyone who is competent to do something, or marginally in my sister's case, just throws in, sir."

"Faith is far more than marginal, Seawolf," Wilkes said. "I was the only helo pilot, sir. When I needed somebody to sit in the co seat, my first choice was Sophia, sir."

"Thank you, Tang," Sophia said. "I was a small boat commander, then a small boat division commander before this, sir. We needed small boats. Now we need helos. Seemed like a natural progression."

"Take this pick-up," Wilkes said as they approached the top of a Publix. The survivors were emaciated, indicating they may have had control of the back room but probably not the front area. "We'll do a ramp load."

"Roger," Sophia said. She tried not to sound nervous but she was sure the Navy commander was observing her every move.

"Ramp load, Wands," Wilkes said over the intercom.

"Got it," Anna replied.

"I'm afraid that one's going to have a stick up his butt," Olga said on the cargo compartment net.

"They tend to come around eventually," Yu replied.

EZ snorted, keying his mic so they could hear him do so, but he said nothing else.

"You said that there is a requirement for more helos, Ensign?" Sanderson asked.

"Yes, sir," Sophia replied. "The SAR reason is obvious, sir. But my father has hinted, for some time, that he has another use for them. I'm unaware of his plans in that regard, sir. But he generally has both short- and long-term reasons for his actions or needs, sir."

"You said something about the NCCC," Sanderson said. "Who is that?"

"Undersecretary Frank Galloway, sir," Sophia replied. "In the Hole and uninfected, so until we can clear a route to them and get them some vaccine they're stuck."

"We have vaccine?" Sanderson said.

"We have vaccine, sir," Wilkes replied. "Made in England, at the Tower of London, believe it or not, by an English/Pakistani biochemist from the spines of human infected. Which are mostly gathered by the Gurkha guards."

"I can see from that little statement there is going to be a lot of catching up to do," Sanderson said. "Have you done anything with the base?"

"Just got word that the field is cleared and the birds there were prepped for long-term storage, sir," Wilkes said. "If that was your plan, sir, may we say officially 'thank you.'"

"The admiral made the call," Sanderson said. "I was involved, yes. Last question for now. Any other pilots or crew make it out?"

"We've picked up two other pilots, although one of them was a female technical instructor..."

"That be Nicola Simpson?" Sanderson asked.

"Yes, it was, sir," Wilkes said. "Who, by the way, just got married but kept her own name. The other was Navy and I don't recall the name, sir. But he wasn't from HSM 40. Sorry, sir. And some of the maintenance crews have turned up here and there. You can check in on them when you get to the boat, sir."

"Roger," Sanderson said. "I'll just let you fly for now. I'll get out of the cockpit. Ensign."

"Sir?" Sophia said.

"You're doing fine for your background. No issues. That's an official statement as an IP on these and the commander of the squadron that trained people on them. That being said, at some point I want to ensure your full qual absent objections from higher."

"Da won't object if that's what you mean, sir," Sophia said. "Nor would I, sir."

"We'll schedule that when we have time," Sanderson said, getting up. "In the meantime, carry on."

"Whuff," Sophia said as soon as the commander left the compartment. "Not looking forward to *that* check ride."

"You'll do fine," Wilkes said. "Just remember not to miss any of the steps. I've got this one."

"Aye, aye, Captain Crunch," Sophia said.

"Or say anything like that . . ." Wilkes said, then keyed the radio. "Force Ops, Dragon."

"Dragon, Force Ops."

"Be advised. Recent pick-up, Lieutenant Commander Gregory Sanderson, former commander HelMarStrike Squadron Forty. Pilot and IP, Seahawk and Dragon. Over."

"Copy. Further, over?"

"Negative," Wilkes said. "Dragon, out."

"Figured the colonel would want a heads-up?" Sophia asked.

"Yep," Wilkes said.

"Survivors signaling," Yu said. "About ten o'clock."

"Roger," Wilkes said, banking to port. "Vector us in . . ."

"Dragon, Force Ops."

They'd been flying around most of the day, following a pattern that spiraled out in an ever expanding square, looking for survivors. And they were about full up. Hovering when loaded was a dicey proposition and between the time and the load Wilkes was about to call it.

"Force Ops, Dragon," Sophia replied.

"Romeo Tango Bravo. Change in plan. All personnel clearing base picked up airfield. Will take more than two lifts."

"Roger," Sophia said. "RTB at this time."

"Time to go do that voodoo that you do, so well," Wilkes said, pointing northeast.

"I suppose this means I have to talk to my sister," Sophia said.

"You should be grateful," Wilkes replied. "She's hard at work on getting you your birthday present."

"We'd all be grateful for that," EZ put in.

"Dragon, Force Ops."

"Dragon," Sophia said.

"Commander Sanderson to report ForceCom on arrival."

"Roger," Sophia said. "Further, over?"

"Negative. Force Ops out."

"You're ahead of me, Colonel," Steve said, smiling. "As usual."

"You'd planned on doing the mechanicals, sir?" Colonel Hamilton asked.

"Of course," Steve said. "I came up with them. I'd planned on moving Commander Isham to the chosen facility when we decided to start the program in earnest. He owned a small manufacturing company and has experience in setting up and managing line production. My original plan had been to use the commercial port of Miami. You think it's doable up there?"

"Yes, sir," Hamilton said.

"You want Isham?" Steve asked. "Be advised before you answer: I want hundreds of them within a year."

"Then I'd like Commander Isham if you can spare him, sir," Hamilton said.

"Done," Steve said. "I have a sufficiency of beached and extremely capable lieutenant commanders available to take over as chief of staff. Helicopters. Can you get the Mayport helo facility up and running?"

"Question is security, sir," Hamilton said. "There are still a bunch of infected running around the base and we're close to Jax of course. We can use the facility. It's useable at present. But if we start turning on lights at night, it will attract all the infected in Jax and sooner or later they're going to breach the perimeter. Which is what we're interested in the mechanicals for. Clearing Jax is the big issue. If we can get the infected numbers down . . ."

"Building the mechanicals at first will be an issue," Steve said. "Setting it up, right, will take time. This is always the problem, has been the problem, between creating the infrastructure versus other missions like, well, rescue. I'd suggest using alternate means for clearance if there are any available. So, the helos aren't going to be as much of an issue as they were here?"

"It doesn't sound like it, sir," Hamilton said.

"By the authority invested in me as Commander, Atlantic Fleet," Steve said. "If that lieutenant commander is functional and can work in the new world order, he's back as Commander HELMARSTRIKERON 40. Which is going to be a combination of training and operational. The fact that it's *called* the Air Wolves is, of course, a bonus."

"Yes, sir," Hamilton said. "I'll inform him as soon as he's aboard."

"We have one more helo pilot here, sort of," Steve said. "Civilian, older, and only trained on light helos. But he's a pilot. I'm sending Isham up, anyway. You want him?"

"Yes, sir," Hamilton said. "If this is going to be the primary helo base, then I'd like him, sir."

"Done," Steve said. "Not a change of mission but a change of focus. Get Jax cleared by any means necessary. At least reduce the numbers to the point the helo port isn't going to get swarmed. Clear the base to yellow-green. Get the helo port to the point it's useable. I'll send up the additional helo pilot and Isham as well as some additional machinist mates. Keep your primary weight on Blount for security reasons but we need to be able to use the facilities on Mayport day and night. When Mayport is up and going... Then head up the coast."

"Yes, sir," Hamilton said. "When can we expect them, sir?"

"Couple of days, max," Steve said. "We haven't been sitting on our hands down here. Gitmo out."

"Commander," Hamilton said when Sanderson was ushered into the office. "Welcome aboard."

"Thank you, Colonel," Sanderson said, looking at Lieutenant Simpson. "Nic, it's good to see you made it, too. Ahem, I'd heard you were recently married. Congratulations. And . . . Uh, are congratulations again in order?"

"Thanks, Greg," Simpson said. "Or I should have said 'Thanks, sir.'" She was in a Navy maternity uniform. "And, yes, congratulations on both are in order."

"When did you join the Navy?" Sanderson asked.

"As soon as she entered her social security number in our database, Commander," Hamilton said. "When she was automatically reactivated and automatically shifted in service. Time is a bit short for idle chit-chat."

"Yes, sir," Sanderson said.

"We have a priority need for helicopters and helo pilots," Hamilton said. "Assigned by LantFleet. The question is, can you adjust to war-time requirements, Lieutenant Commander?"

"I'm not sure what you mean, sir," Commander Sanderson said.

"The standards for pilot training pre-Plague were eighty-six hours ground training and one hundred twenty-eight hours flight training before being certified as mission capable," Hamilton said. "That's too long. And the training time on flight and maintenance crews is too long as well. So can you get your head around World War Two style training? Because that's all we're going to get."

"That . . . makes me uncomfortable, sir," Sanderson said. "I take it that's why there's a fifteen-year-old flying a Sea Dragon?"

"And because she read the manual on the float to England and when Colonel Kuznetsov stayed, Captain

Wilkes, who is about to be Major Wilkes, needed somebody to at least handle the radios," Hamilton said. "Her first solo was off the bobbing platform of the *Grace*, because that was where we were when Wilkes, reluctantly, agreed she was more or less ready to solo. Which pretty much says it all.

"LantFleet wants every Seahawk or Blackhawk and every Sea Dragon or Super Stallion on or near the East Coast with pilots for *all* of them. And he wants that within six months. Part of them will come from raiding every base within range of the coast and finding survivors like yourself. Many of them are going to be civilian refugees who meet minimum standards. Or even *below* if they are trained in the field.

"You've barely arrived, you don't know Papa Wolf, or you'd know that what he wants, he gets. He gets not because he is LantFleet, but because he *will* get it one way or another. He has been putting his own daughters on the sharp end since before the Fall. He's been on the sharp end more than once. And he has a total disregard for anything resembling normal procedures that get in the way of what he wants done. He actively encourages 'secondary sourcing' when there's no defined supply line. He's perfectly willing to do Montrose Toast over and over again to get the U.S., at least, cleared of zombies. So with that understanding, do you think you can handle that? If you can't, you're a pilot. We've got a crying need for same. But you're either with the program or you're not. And if you're not, you're not going to be involved in decision making on who is or is not a pilot. Period."

"I . . . understand, sir," Sanderson said. "I'll simply note that cutting the standards is going to cause losses, sir."

"I've been running like mad since I first got out of the warehouse in Gitmo," Hamilton said. "But I've had a few off-duty conversations. One of them was with a Coast Guard lieutenant, former petty officer and basically the Commandant of the Coast Guard at this point. He had the same reaction when Wolf told him that he had two days to put together a training program for boat captains. They had to be prepared, in no more than three days of training, to cross the Atlantic performing rescues at sea and doing underway replenishment. Of course, it was winter in the southern Atlantic, which isn't the worst of all possible worlds. But it was still too little training.

"And what he told me was that Captain Smith said: 'We're going to lose people because they're under-trained. I'm aware of that. And when we do, feel free to *not* say "I told you so" because I already know it.' And they did lose people. Boats sank, caught on fire, people fell overboard and there were always sharks. The net effect was more people saved and more materials recovered than lost. And that was 'good enough' for a zombie apocalypse.

"The mission is save people and free the world from infected. We're not going to get that done by crossing every I, dotting every T and screaming 'safety, safety, safety' the way that we did pre-Plague. Not in our lifetime. So if you're onboard, fine. If you're not, say you're not. And when, not if, we lose people because of undertrained crews, undertrained pilots, undertrained mechanics, feel free to *not* say 'I told you so.' We all know."

"Yes, sir," Sanderson said, taking a deep breath. "In that case . . . I'm onboard, sir."

"Very well," Hamilton said. "You are, once again, Commander HELMARSTRIKERON 40, which happens to be our only Squadron and one in name only. Since Kodiak Force is an off-shoot of Wolf Squadron, the name is appropriate as Captain Smith noted. In fact, it's what we were calling our air support, anyway. Your current manning is the lieutenant here, Captain Wilkes, Ensign Smith and the support personnel. There is an additional pilot coming up from Gitmo in the next few days. He'll need to be trained on the birds since his background is civilian. We're working on getting the heliport up and functioning. If you can handle not taking the three days off, you're going ashore tomorrow to start seeing what you have and what you don't."

"Ready to work, sir," Commander Sanderson said. "Hell, *very* ready to fly."

"Who flies what and when is up to you," Hamilton said. "We have an after actions review in about an hour depending on when we get everyone back. You're invited."

"Yes, sir."

"My one suggestion is don't under estimate Ensign Smith. I made that mistake, once, with her sister and I'm still regretting it. LantFleet has a bizarre and bizarrely competent family. They seem to positively enjoy this world we now inhabit."

"And we'll start with the standard institutional scab picking," Colonel Hamilton said. "Before we get into what others thought went right and went wrong, anyone want to fess up? Junior first. Lieutenant Smith?"

"Do not fire forty-millimeter auto-cannons at infected

at short range with undertrained gunners while bobbing in a basin smaller than their arming range, sir," Faith said. "That could have, and should have, gone really bad. The fact that no one was injured is a miracle."

"There were probably better ways to clear the basin for landing, admittedly," Colonel Hamilton said. "Off the top of my head, using the troops up and out as you did later."

"I think I should have used the fifties instead of forty mike mike, sir," Faith said. "Much more direct."

"And when you got bouncers, they could have hit the craft and sunk them," Hamilton said. "Fifty would have been an inferior choice to forty, Lieutenant."

"I'll keep that in mind if we have to do it again, sir," Faith said.

"Ensign Smith?"

"I'm getting better at flying, sir," Sophia said. "Just a matter of practice and hours, sir. But I'm still not . . . dialed in on recovery hovering. Especially in any kind of wind, sir."

"Just a matter of hours, as you said, Ensign," Sanderson said. "You were on the controls when you hoisted me, correct?"

"Yes, sir," Sophia said. "And I know you were all over the sky on the way up."

"While the Sea Dragon is a primary SAR platform for some services," Sanderson said, "it's got one hell of a lot of surface area. Also a bitch to maintain. I'm surprised you are using it, frankly."

"We left our sole Seahawk in England," Hamilton said. "Speaking of which, we're going to have to send some parts to the prince. There's a sub on the way and they're sending a list. They're also sending some prospective pilots and we're going to have to send them at least three birds."

"Any word on how clearing London is going?" Faith asked.

"Slowly is the best way to put it," Hamilton said. "Next . . . Captain Wilkes?"

"You're supposed to say something you're doing wrong," Wilkes said. "And . . . Not coming to mind. What is coming to mind is that we need better guns for the bird."

"Oh, yeah," Sophia said. "I don't suppose there are any miniguns in storage?"

"There are," Colonel Hamilton said.

"They mount those on Air Force 53s," Commander Sanderson said, frowning. "But we're not rated for them and the mounts aren't interchangeable. Also, they burn through their ammo fast."

"We should be able to do a battle box, sir," Sophia said. "And we've mounted stranger weapons on stranger stuff, sir. I'm pretty sure we can figure it out. Our flight engineer knows the mini. He'll be able to help."

"Battle box?" Sanderson asked.

"The primary clearance weapon for small coastal towns, or islands for that matter, is fishing boats converted to gun boats," Hamilton said. "They mount dual, water-cooled, fifty calibers. And carry about a hundred thousand rounds. The guns are fed from pre-prepared boxes, battle boxes, that hold five thousand rounds for each gun."

"Ah," the lieutenant commander said. "How many rounds were you planning on lofting, Ensign?"

"When we're doing air clearance, as many as we can, sir," Sophia said. "We have thirty-five tons of lift.

I'm doing the math in my head of how much seven six two that is, sir. All I'm getting is 'a lot.'"

"We're probably going to be shifting to primarily Seahawk as soon as they are up and running," Hamilton said, making a note. "But I'll have the mech guys look into it. And we may be able to mount gun pods on them."

"Could pick up some Sea Cobras, sir," Captain Wilkes said.

"We don't have limitations on how many airframes we have here," Hamilton said. "We do on the boats. And dual purpose is probably the way to go there. We're not going to be doing primary clearance from the air. Lieutenant Commander Chen is still on his away mission, which I hear is going well. Ah, tomorrow you're doing a long-range rescue mission. Chen's force spotted some survivors at the Jax NAS down the river. So tomorrow you'll loft the personnel for the base, then head down there to pick them up. We're sending Naval Landing Force as security for the airbase tomorrow. Marines will move to the airbase by air, then perform breach on the gates to the basin. Following that, clearance by fire of the base."

"Oorah," Faith said. "Sitting around watching people count parts is boooring."

"We're looking at ways, other than crushing all the cars on the 295 bridge, to get Trixie over to the base," Hamilton said. "If we can do so, over the next week or so the mission will be using Trixie to do clearance throughout the Jax area—"

"Oh, yes," Faith said.

"That is while we're working on getting the mechanicals up and going," Hamilton said. "The decision has been made that we need to use the base as is rather than moving the assets to Blount. So reducing the infected level in the area has just been increased in priority. We're not going to do even a yellow clear, just down to orange or so. But if we can get the numbers down to the point they don't breach the perimeter fences . . . that's good enough. Gitmo is sending reinforcements. Notably, Lieutenant Commander Isham is headed up. He's going to take over the mechanicals operations. LantFleet has stated that he wants 'several hundred' completed by year's end."

"Mechanicals are okay for clearing coastal cities, sir," Sophia said. "Not sure what we're going to do about interior. Except, possibly, helos with battle boxes."

"Trixie," Faith chanted quietly. "Trixie, Trixie . . ."

"We get it, Lieutenant," Hamilton said.

"Trixie?" Sanderson said.

"I'll let you catch up on that with others, Commander," Hamilton said drily. "Not in your bailiwick, anyway. But until we get Trixie across the river, just use what you've got to clear the base."

"Aye, aye, sir," Faith said. "Sir, point of . . ."

"Before you strain yourself looking for the latest word big-word, Lieutenant," Hamilton said. "Just say it."

"I've been looking at the map, sir," Faith said.

"Oh, dear," Captain Wilkes said.

"No, seriously, sir," Faith said. "There's a river to the west of the base, sir, between here and Arlington. South of the base there's suburbs stretching for just miles. But that river, sir, there are only four crossings within the range of probably infected closure. We block those crossings, sir, and they're not getting to us that way, sir. Basically takes Jax, per se, out of the equation."

"Interesting point, Lieutenant," Hamilton said. "What about the suburbs?"

"Well, sir, then there's Trixie, sir," Faith said, grinning. "But we close those crossings, sir, then do clearance just south . . . Base is as secure as it's going to get in this fallen world, sir."

"Use containers?" Hamilton asked.

"Yes, sir," Faith said. "But we can probably pick some up along the way. We'll have to sort of fight our way down, sir, but with Trixie . . . not going to be an issue. Probably wouldn't just with the amtracks, sir. And if we get in a London, we just egress to the beach and swim back. Except Trixie, sir, which I can't imagine getting in a London, sir."

"Trixie is the only M1 we've refurbished, Commander," Hamilton said.

"You're talking about the Chicopit, Lieutenant?" Sanderson said. "It's part of the Intracoastal Waterway. And, yes, there are only so many bridges. It is . . . was part of the fun of dealing with traffic on the way to the base. Rather than sending down land forces to drop containers, sir, it would be easy enough to do it with the Dragon. Empty or lightly loaded we could do it with a Seahawk."

"Satellite image," Hamilton said, bringing it up on the plasma. "You're talking about these bridges, Lieutenant?"

"Yes, sir," Faith said, standing up and going over to the plasma. "Block Wonderwood Drive, Atlantic Boulevard, Beach Boulevard, and Butler Boulevard and the only direction infected can approach is from the south, sir. And that's just suburbs, sir. Again, can probably do that with amtracks, at least to reddish orange. And if we get stuck, pull out through the beach, sir. Get some amphib training, feed a few sharks, sir. Oorah."

"Clearing the base, first," Hamilton said. "Keep the unit together or split up?"

"Split up, sir," Faith said. "If they get in a scrum, that gives us the ability to come in from the outside. And I don't see any scrums on the base, sir. There's a perimeter fence so we're only dealing with the personnel who were on base. And we've taken a good few out already, sir. Cover more ground as well. I'd estimate yellowish orange clearance in a day, sir. Yellow if we continue into night clearance ops, sir. Getting to green will require repeated sweeps. If we just sweep the base day and into night for three days . . . Could get it to chartreuse, sir. Combine that with external sweeps . . . A week or so we can probably turn on the lights at night and not have any issues with day and night operations in the secured areas."

"Tomorrow's missions," Hamilton said. "Move personnel to the Station by air. Survey and Salvage continue survey and getting the base up and running. Helo maintenance personnel to accompany and begin refurbishment of birds there. Navy Security teams for security on that. Marines: Breach the Basin for further eval and use. Sweep the station in individual amtracks. Check fence-line and gate security. Air: Transport personnel to the station, then pick-up for survivors at the NAS with further SAR after based on time. Usual extract begins at sixteen-thirty. I think that's a fairly full plate . . ."

CHAPTER 11

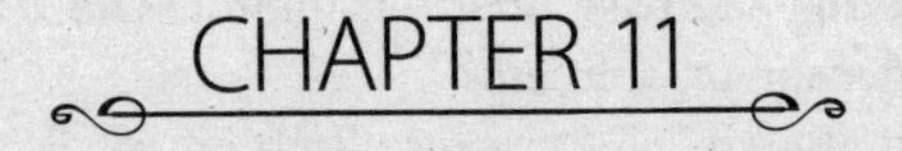

"Oh what a beautiful morning..." Faith said as her amtrack ran down the beach. Turned out there were no fences along the beach or the water-side of the base. There was a low wall designed to stop vehicular traffic, but no actual fence. There was a south perimeter fence, but it stopped at the shoreline. And infected *were* on the beach. Quite a few, all things considered. They were spread out until the amtrack came rolling along. Then they started to close in. Since the amtrack was barely rolling along, they were following in what had been dubbed "Pied Piper Marching Formation."

"Hold up here," Faith said. They were between a boardwalk, one of several, and a beached Panamax freighter that had listed so far over, the cargo containers on the deck had spilled onto the beach. It was still slowly leaking oil but the slick was nicely away from the amtracks so no fear of fire. And it gave them something at their back so all the zombies were in just a couple of directions. And most of them at range.

That was what .50 caliber was made for. Nice long ranges, lots of targets. They were closing by climbing over the low wall, as well. That triggered a long-dormant memory that Faith was having a hard time pulling out.

"Hooch," Faith said over the intercom. The squad leader had started wearing a crewman's helmet since they didn't really unload that much and Faith didn't have an issue asking questions.

"Yes, ma'am?" the squad leader said, pointing out a target to the SAW gunner.

"We've been together a while, right?" Faith said. She tapped Twitchell on the arm and pointed to a group of infected clambering over the wall.

"Yes, ma'am," Hooch said.

"Those zeds climbing the wall," Faith said. "What's that remind you of? Canary Islands somewhere? Crib?"

"Not that comes to mind," Hooch said.

"Damnit," Faith said. "I know I've seen it somewhere. Where, where, where . . . ? Okay, I think this cluster's done for."

The once pleasant beach was now scattered with shredded bodies. They just added to the debris of a fallen civilization, the small boats, garbage, discarded clothing and even picked bones. Seagulls were already starting to descend. In a few weeks, these zeds would just be skeletons to add to the piles.

"Move out," Faith said. "See if we can chum up some more . . . Where *was* that? Zombies climbing over a low wall. I don't think it was during the *day*, either . . ."

"You ever have one of those déjà vu all over again moments, sir?" Sophia asked as the survivors from the NAS were hoisted up.

NAS Jacksonville was a medium-sized facility that dated back to the First World War when it was a quartermaster training camp. Demobilized after the war, it was set back up for World War Two and had remained in operation ever since. Pre-Plague it had been host to a mass of fixed wing Navy aircraft including P-3s and the new P-8s. Besides having operational squadrons, it was, like Mayport, a major training command for them and a military airlift "hub" for the southeastern regions. It had dozens of hangars and support and maintenance facilities as well as over twenty long-range prop and jet birds on the pads.

Several of the birds had somehow burned. So had one of the hangars, a couple of the support buildings and about half of base housing. It almost looked like the security response was "use a flame thrower." There was a security vehicle, doors open, sitting on the pad with the remains of a body, mostly bones and a black security uniform, scattered around the rear hatch. Compared to Mayport, it was a wreck.

"Sort of looks like Northolt?" Wilkes said.

"That's the one," Sophia replied. The RAF base outside London had been, if anything, even more wrecked.

"Fuel state?"

"Seven thousand three hundred," EZ said.

"We're in and secure," Olga commed. "Seventeen. Not bad."

"We've got enough to do a rough clear of the base before heading back," Wilkes said. "Eyes out and let's see how many more we can find."

"Son of a bitch," Faith said as a sole survivor waved from the balcony of a two-story home along the beach. They'd slowed down to check since there was a line of surf-casting rods set up. That was a new one. Getting back and forth must have taken some balls. Or ovaries in this case.

"Helo missed one. Give some cover fire, people!"

The female survivor dropped off the balcony, carefully, then trotted towards the amtrack. She wasn't in the greatest shape and wasn't moving fast. A zombie coming around the corner of the house was moving faster.

"Unass," Faith said, pulling her M4 out of its rack. "Try not to scrum but do *not* let it get her."

Hooch's team opened up the rear personnel hatch and deployed. The 240 team stayed up and out, firing carefully past the survivor. They got the first zombie in pursuit, with rounds close enough the survivor hit the deck as they went past. But there were more coming.

"Hooch, move 'em up and get her into the damned track," Faith said. The survivor was now down on hands and knees doing a slow leopard crawl. "Check fire all weapons. Twitch, fire 19 *past* her and lay down suppressing on the right side of the house. Two-forty, lay down suppressing on the *left* side of the house. Hooch, get her into the track, *now*!"

Hooch's team ran forward to the woman and got her on her feet as the two heavy weapons poured fire to the sides. Faith looked up the beach and they had a few more infected closing from there. Glory.

The woman seemed to be struggling and saying something to the Marines. She was also pointing with her one free hand at the house.

"Ma'am, there's more in the house," Hooch said. "Kids."

"Stand by," Faith said. "Freeman, back us around. Twitch, switch to fifty, take the zeds on the south.

Two-forty, north. Hooch, you're going to have to cover the sides. *And* get the damned wood off the doors. I'm deploying."

The house had plywood over all the lower windows and doors. It was a fairly common preparation for hurricanes in the region and had clearly come in useful in the apocalypse.

Faith pulled herself up out of the hatch, then stepped nimbly down the side of the moving track. As it humped up on the dune in front of the house she almost lost her balance but corrected. As soon as it stopped, she jumped off the back, landing in a parachute landing fall, then rolled to her feet.

"Hooch, Quade, left side of the house. Curran, Randolph, right. Flip, survivor on the track. Haugen, Halligan tool. NOW."

"Aye, aye, ma'am," Haugen said, darting to the track as the Marines deployed.

"Hooch, status left?" Faith said, banging on the wood covering the main door. "Anybody in there, gather here and get ready to move!"

"Two children," the woman said, still not willing to leave.

"Get in the track, ma'am," Faith barked. "We have this."

"Got a few," Hooch yelled. "Handled."

"Randolph?" Faith yelled. "Status?"

"Quite a few, ma'am," Randolph replied. He'd just fired a 40mm from his 203 then switched back to 5.56. "Sort of hot."

"Moving right," Faith said, sprinting to Randolph's position. "Haugen, get that damned wood off and get those kids into the track!"

"Sort of hot" was about twenty infected closing the position. More were down on the ground from the fire from the Marines. Randolph had a 203 while Curran was using a SAW.

"Cover me while I reload!" Curran said, scrabbling for one of the box magazines for the SAW.

"Right about now is when some one hundred round mags would be nice," Faith said, firing at the oncoming infected. As they closed to within twenty yards she switched from multiple rounds into the chest to double tap, one to the chest, one to the head. She was hitting most of the head shots.

A few got through the fire just as she ran out of rounds in her M4 magazine. She let go of the weapon, letting it pull back on its slings, and drew her first pistol. A .45 did tend to stop the zeds when you center punched them in the chest. She fired off her whole mag, dropped the pistol, drew one from her chest holster and continued firing. Halfway through her second pistol, the wave of infected was on the ground.

Curran had just gotten his SAW mag seated.

"Your weapon, ma'am," Randolph said, bending down and picking up the dropped pistol. "I'm still having a hard time dropping training to just drop a pistol, ma'am."

"Hey," Faith said, grinning. "At least this time it was on sand."

She went back to the door where Haugen was levering at it with the Halligan just as he managed to pop one of the large plywood sheets loose.

She grabbed the edge of the plywood, put a boot into the bulkhead of the home and pulled it back.

"Can you get out?" Faith yelled.

"Yeah," a kid's voice answered.

Two children, boy and girl, slid under her leg, then stopped.

"What the hell are you waiting for?" Faith asked. "Get in the damned track!"

"Aye, aye, ma'am!" the boy said, grabbing the girl's hand and running for the track.

"Hooch, Randolph, can you break contact?" Faith yelled, letting go of the plywood.

"Roger," Hooch said.

"Can do, ma'am," Randolph replied.

"Load up!" Faith yelled. "Move to cover top as you load. Hooch, you're ass-end Charlie."

Faith got back in the track and stopped at the scene. The mother, presumably, of the two children had them in her lap and was crying. So were both of the children. But it was crying in relief.

"Thank you," the woman said, looking at her.

"Semper Fi, ma'am," Faith said. "Glad you made it. Hooch, we all in?"

"All present and accounted for, ma'am," the sergeant said, closing the personnel hatch.

"Let's roll, people," Faith said. "We got zombies to kill."

"Your lieutenant must have been right out of MOBC," the woman said as Hocieniec handed her and her children bottles of water. "She can't be more than twenty."

"She never went to MOBC, ma'am," Hooch said. "Post-Plague direct commission. And she's fourteen, not twenty. I'd say that this was a walk in the park for her but... The meaning of 'walk in the park' has changed. This was, in fact, what it means, a walk in the park. Fighting zombies. Were you a dependent or in service?"

"Dependent," the woman said. "Sherry Jackson. My husband was Captain Tyler Jackson. Navy."

"Daddy went to work and didn't come home," the girl said, her eyes wide.

"I don't suppose . . ." the woman said.

"Not familiar with the name, ma'am," Hooch said. "But you can check when you get to the base. We've picked up a good few survivors, ma'am." He waited until the children weren't looking, shook his head in the negative and shrugged. If a Navy captain had popped up on the radar, he'd have known.

The woman just nodded and held her children closer.

"Sergeant," Randolph said. "We got company."

"How's the survivors?" Faith asked as they cleared the latest concentration.

"Doing okay, ma'am," Hooch answered. "All things considered. Told them this was the new meaning of 'walk in the park.'"

"That's it!" Faith said. "That's where zombies climbing over a wall was from! Thanks, Hooch."

"You're welcome, ma'am."

"Nothing could be finer than clearing out a liner in the morrrning . . ." Faith sang. "Nothing could be sweeter than sending zeds to Peter in the morrrning . . . I wanna drive Trixie around. Amtracks are sooo last week . . . I know we're going to be clearing south, but I want to drive it down to Jax. Know why?"

"Why, ma'am?" Hooch said. "More zombies?"

"No, so I can sing 'Downtown,'" Faith said, grinning. "We're going *Downtown*! Where all the lights are bright. *Downtown*! You're gonna be all right! *Downtown*! Zombies are waiting for youuu!"

"Ma'am, with due respect and great admiration," Hooch said. "You are over the line of crazy and well into psycho."

"Yuh think?"

"Got survivors you missed," Faith said, making a horns sign at Sophia as she sat down to chow. "Two teams picked 'em up."

"We came back just about over max from Jax NAS," Sophia said. "Sixty people aboard. Lots of survivors there. They'd managed to hold the commissary."

"Sure, but *you* got to do it from the air," Faith said. "*We* had to *fight* our way in to the houses!"

"Which you enjoy, sister dear," Sophia said, grinning. "I prefer the easy way. Which I'm not getting tomorrow. Check ride on the Dragon with Commander Sanderson, then begin Seahawk cross-train. I'm curious to know where they found another pilot and how they're getting here. You hear anything?"

"Negative," Faith said, shoveling down her food. "And I've got an AAR in ten minutes. You?"

"I'm exempt to do homework," Sophia said, patting the manual she had open on the table.

"That'd be a hell of a choice," Faith said, standing up. "Homework or meeting?"

"Meeting," Sophia said, lifting the book and turning it to face her. It was a mass of mathematics.

"Ehhhh!" Faith hissed, throwing up one arm to cover her face and a hand out. "You shall not defeat me, Van Helsing!"

"Back, back!" Sophia said, jabbing the open book

at her. "Or I shall explain the math of weight and balance in aircraft operations!"

"The math!" Faith said, picking up her tray. "It burrrns! You are cruel! Evil, *vicious*, pilots!"

"Have fun in your *meeting*, Sis," Sophia said, smiling in triumph.

"Enjoy your *homework*, Sis," Faith said. "Here's hoping a quadratic bites you."

"Now that's just *mean* . . ."

"Ground Force, Force Ops."

"Ground Force."

A day and a half of clearance and the base was looking pretty good. Oh, there were bodies *everywhere*, but they weren't having much luck at this point finding zombies.

"Need you to bring all teams to the airfield for infected sweep and FOD walk-down, over."

"Roger, over," Faith said, mildly puzzled.

"Force Ops, out."

"Freeman, head for the airfield gate," Faith said. "Hey, Hooch."

"Ma'am?"

"What's a FOD walk-down?" Faith asked.

"Oh, no!" Hooch said. "We've got to do a FOD walk?"

Even over the rattle and rumble of the amtrack, she could hear the troops in the back bitching up a storm at the words.

"Infected sweep of the airfield and FOD walk-down," Faith said. "That's a problem?"

"Oh, you're just gonna *love* it, LT," Hooch said. "It's one of the main joys of being a Marine."

"We're supposed to walk down the runway in a line," Faith said, puzzled. "Looking for . . . ? Sir?"

"*Anything*, Lieutenant," Sanderson said. "And I do mean *anything* that is not the flat, plain, concrete. Foreign Object Debris. Which the runway is *covered* with. We have a P-8 coming in from Gitmo with some personnel and equipment. If it kicks up foreign objects and sucks them into its turbofans it's deadlined and cannot return. So there is to be nothing, absolutely *nothing*, on the strip. Is that understood?"

"Yes, sir," Faith said.

"Your gunnery sergeant and Staff Sergeant Januscheitis are familiar with the process, Lieutenant," Sanderson said. "I'd suggest you let them handle it."

"I keep finding things with which I need to be familiarized, sir," Faith said. "With due respect, sir, this seems like one of those things."

"Then carry on, Lieutenant," Sanderson said.

"Aye, aye, sir," Faith replied.

"So this is it?" Faith said, walking next to Gunnery Sergeant Sands. They were slightly behind the line of Marines who were stopping occasionally to pick up "debris." "We just walk along picking up trash?"

"FOD walk-down, ma'am," Sands said, looking around. "Curran! What the hell does 'pick up every damned thing' mean to you? *Bone*, Curran! You just *stepped* on it!"

The runway wasn't, exactly, covered in debris. But there was a hell of a lot of it. Winds had blown material onto the runway from the surrounding areas and infected had dropped stuff on it. Some of that was "biological" in nature, not just fecal matter but discarded bones.

There were even a couple of thoroughly decomposed bodies. The problem with those was picking up all the bits of the skeleton that were still around. Scavengers had scattered them far and wide.

"Question, Gunny," Faith said, putting her hand on his arm to slow him and separate from the Marines. "Why are my Marines doing this?" she asked, quietly. "We've got several hundred square *miles* of territory to clear. This would seem to be a job for . . . somebody else. Heck, refugees come to mind."

"Sector's still not ensured clear, ma'am," Sands said. "And it has to be done by people who will pick up every damned thing, ma'am. Which generally means someone military. You can bring it up with Force Ops if you want, ma'am. Probably a question for the AAR. But, if you will take your gunny's suggestion, bring it up as a calm question, ma'am. Not a bitch."

"Won't bitch, Gunny," Faith said. "That's the reason I wanted to have the question on the quiet. I get that. But . . . really does not seem like a good use of resources. Every sweep we find survivors. My opinion is we should be sweeping for zombies not . . . leaves."

"That's a question for higher, ma'am," Gunny Sands said. "And that *is* one of your jobs. To point out to higher that there might have been a better use of our time. But it is also true that this is important and has to be done by people who will . . . Moment, ma'am . . . Gawwwdamnit, Curran! Keep your head *down* and use your fucking *eyes* . . . !"

"That is . . . weird," Januscheitis said, looking up at the circling plane.

The P-8 was a variant of the 737 used by the

Navy for long-range reconnaissance and antisubmarine warfare as a replacement for the aging fleet of P-3s. There had been three of them on the pad at Gitmo, presumably used for drug interdiction, but Faith never expected to see them flying again. Apparently her da wasn't sitting on his hands.

"Yeah," Faith said, shaking her head. "It's like... That's probably the first jet anyone's got flying since the Fall. Maybe not the first plane. I hear there's a group down by Australia that's got an old amphibian flying. But that's the first *big* plane."

"I guess maybe we are coming back, ma'am," Januscheitis said.

"I wonder how far it can go," Faith said.

"They extended the range with inboard fuel tanks," Commander Sanderson said, walking up behind them. "After ripping out everything that makes it a real P-8. So it's trans-ocean capable. When PacFleet gets a field secure on the West Coast, it can get back and forth. Until we run out of parts."

"Are there any at Jax NAS, sir?" Faith asked.

"Yes," Sanderson said. "And, no, you're not going to be clearing it any time soon, Lieutenant. Too big, too far out."

"We can raid for parts, sir," Faith said. "If we know where they are in general."

"For an *engine*, Lieutenant?" Sanderson asked.

"We've done weirder shit, sir," Faith said. "If it's a critical item, we will get it, sir. One way or another."

"Please not London, again, LT," Januscheitis said.

"If we have to do an LRI, we do an LRI, Staff Sergeant," Faith said. "But next time we're going to use more firepower."

"LRI?" Commander Sanderson said as the circling jet lined up for landing.

"London Research Institute, sir," Staff Sergeant Januscheitis said. "It's where I lost my ear, sir. No KIA on the op, surprisingly. But people are already starting to try to figure out how to insert it into the Marine Hymn. Because it is this universe's equivalent of 'the Shores of Tripoli,' sir. From personal experience, made Fallujah look like . . . Well, a walk in the park in *peacetime*, sir."

"Good times," Faith said. "Good times. Which would you rather be doing, Staff Sergeant? LRI or a FOD walk-down?"

"FOD walk-down, ma'am," Januscheitis said instantly. "No choice. Zero."

"You disappoint me, Staff Sergeant," Faith joked.

"As long as that is not reflected on my eval," Januscheitis said, "I'm fine with that, ma'am. Even for a Marine, you have very odd ideas of fun, ma'am."

"I don't drink alcohol," Faith said, grinning as the plane landed. "Blood's the next best thing. Girl's gotta have a hobby."

CHAPTER 12

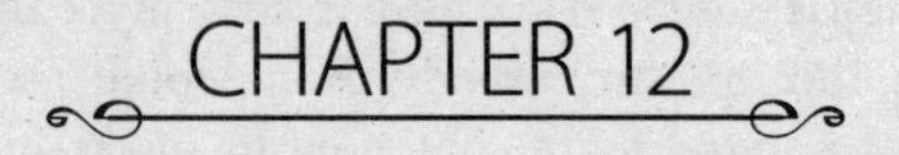

Once a ground crewman had the stairs up on the P-8, the passengers started to debark. Faith didn't recognize most of them but the gray haired man wearing a brand new Navy uniform was *widely* familiar.

"Is that . . . ?" Commander Sanderson said.

"Harold Chrysler," Faith said, grinning. He was wearing lieutenant JG rank tabs. "I'd guess that's the civilian helo pilot."

"I hope he passed a flight physical," Commander Sanderson said dubiously. "Do you know what he was rated on civilian?"

"No, sir," Faith said, walking towards the line of debarking passengers. "But I know he's a genuinely nice guy. Hey, Harold!"

"Lieutenant," the former movie star said, smiling. He looked momentarily unsure. "I'm not sure if I'm supposed to salute or not."

"Not me," Faith said. "Same rank. But you might want to salute your new boss," she added, thumbing over her shoulder at the lieutenant commander.

"Lieutenant Junior Grade Harold Chrysler, reporting in, sir," Harold said. He had a good salute, that was for sure. Very parade ground.

"Welcome aboard, Lieutenant," Sanderson said,

returning the salute. "I just wondered aloud if you're going to be able to pass a flight physical, Lieutenant."

"I did in Guantanamo, sir," Chrysler said. "Done by Dr. Price who is an astronautic and aeronautic specialist MD, sir. I may be a bit creaky but I'm in excellent health."

"What were you qualified on civilian?" Sanderson asked.

"Bell Jet Ranger, Lynx, Westland 139, MD 600 and variants, sir," Chrysler replied. "I owned, at one point or another, each of those. I have over ten thousand hours flight time including mountain rescue and harsh environment landing, sir."

"Okay," Sanderson said, surprised. "I'd heard you had a helo, I didn't realize you were *that* into it."

"I made *a lot* of money from movies, sir," Chrysler said, grinning. "And I spent a good bit of it on my one serious hobby. All that being said: I took a look at the grounded Seahawks in Gitmo and I've been reading the Dash Ones for those and Sea Dragons. Whoof! I thought *civilian* birds were complicated! Lots to learn, sir. Lots to learn."

"Good attitude," Sanderson said. "My attitude is that with that much civilian experience, I'm going to expect you to blast through the course. We need all the pilots we can get."

"Since being asked if I'd volunteer I've been reading, as I said, sir," Chrysler said. "I'm ready to take the phase one ground test. That was mostly basic helo and virtually the same as civilian. Mostly a matter of nomenclature. Seahawk . . . different kettle of fish, sir."

"We don't have the testing facility set up, yet," Sanderson said, frowning. "But I've got some of the tests on my laptop. I'll try to get that scheduled for tomorrow. How far along are you on the Seahawk and Sea Dragon manuals?"

"I've read them, sir." Chrysler said. "I won't say my brain shut down at points, but those are far more complicated than civilian. Mostly the peripheral systems, sir. I could probably drive one, now, sir. That's not . . ."

"No, got that," Sanderson said. "With that many hours civilian, assuming no emergencies, you could drive one. It's the emergencies that would catch you."

"Yes, sir," Chrysler said. "I'm not sure I'd be ready to command one, sir."

"We'll schedule you for the phase one ground test tomorrow," Sanderson said. "Then a test hop in the Sea Dragon, which is our only functioning platform, tomorrow afternoon."

"Yes, sir," Chrysler said.

"Um . . ." Faith said, gesturing with her chin to another older man wearing NavCam and rank for a full lieutenant. She vaguely recognized him but couldn't place where.

"Oh, Commander," Chrysler said, turning to the man. "May I introduce Lieutenant Jeff Malone, sir?"

"Reporting in, sir," Malone said, saluting. He had a Commonwealth accent.

"Welcome aboard, Lieutenant," Sanderson said.

"Jeff's from Oz, sir," Chrysler said. "He was a production manager down there."

"I started on *Lord of the Rings* as a gaffer, sir," Malone said. "Later went on to, well, a lot of movies and shows. I've been helping out down in Gitmo and they thought you could use a hand up here, sir."

"He's good, Commander," Chrysler said. "Getting production organized on site is a lot like being in the military except with more cat herding."

"Being able to say 'Do this' and know that if they don't I can hang them from a yardarm is *such* a refreshing experience I don't know why I didn't join the military a long time ago, sir," Malone said, grinning. "But I'd better go report in to S-1, if someone could point the way."

"You can either scale the fence and steal a boat, sir," Faith said. "Or you can try to swim the river. Note that the sharks and alligators have added humans to their standard diet, sir. Or you can wait for the rest of us to fly back over. If you take the steal a boat option, with permission of the commander we can provide cover fire, sir."

"How bad is the infected presence over the wire, Lieutenant?" Malone asked.

"Not bad," Faith said. "We've been clearing for the last two days, sir."

"I'll take the boat option, then," Malone said. "No rest for the wicked, ey? Take it the boats are that way?" he added, pointing towards the river.

"I doubt any of them will start, sir," Faith said.

"I'm a fair mechanic and there seem to be tools everywhere," Malone said.

"We're bringing in the Dragon to lift the whole group over to the Island, Lieutenant," Sanderson said. "Although I appreciate your enthusiasm. I'll take it that it includes competence?"

"I was the XO, *love* that term for some reason, of the team that got the P-8 up and running, sir," Malone said. "I did most of the organization so Lieutenant

Szafranski could concentrate on the technical details. I guess you'll just have to find out, sir."

"Again," Sanderson said. "Welcome aboard, Lieutenant. Now I need to go give an ensign a check ride..."

"Comments on the day's operations," Colonel Hamilton said. "Faith."

"We need a better plan for extracting refugees on the ground," Faith said. "I'm going to work that up with the staff sergeant and the gunny. Getting them out was sort of 'makee-workee' and we didn't take casualties either with the Marines or the survivors. But it was still a bit...chaotic. We need to reduce the chaos as much as possible."

"Plan?" Hamilton asked.

"We'll take part of tomorrow morning doing rehearsals on various methods, sir," Faith said. "Using buildings on the base. That would be my suggestion, sir. Then continue clearance ops."

"From reports, base appears as clear as it's going to get without night clearance," Hamilton said.

"Up to you, sir, if we're going to exit the base to continue, sir," Faith said. "I'm thinking that we can at least patrol down the beach, sir. We can bypass the pole line with the amtracks and if we get really in the busy we can just head out to sea. Also, we'd be staying together in that case for fire support. It would get some of the clearance going, sir."

"We'll bat that around in a bit," Hamilton said. "Next."

"On general security, the main opening is on the beach, sir. Suggestion?"

"Go," Hamilton said.

"There's a Panamax spilled on the beach, sir," Faith

said. "Deck cargo is in the water. If we can get one of those all-terrain container movers over to the station side, we can just pick those up and plop them down in the water, sir. Out into the surf. Maybe drag some farther out with the amtracks if it comes to that. That will force any infected that want to get around it out into the surf. And I'd guess that the sharks are patrolling for them, sir. At the very least, it's going to be a heck of a swim."

"We've got a barge ready to get Trixie across the river," Hamilton said. "The issue has been hoisting on the other side. I suppose testing that out first with a forklift would be useful. We'll put that on the schedule. Anything else?"

"I'm going to be careful with the last, sir," Faith said, looking at some notes. "During the first day's clearance, the platoon found nine survivors during ten hours of clearance. Rounding that's one survivor an hour."

"Which is good, Lieutenant," Hamilton said. "Any survivor is good but these were military and dependents. Pardon me for saying that is better."

"Yes, sir," Faith said. "Agreed, sir. Today, sir, we spent four hours doing security and FOD walk-down, sir. I am not bitching about that, sir. What I am saying, as an official statement, is that *I* do not think it was the best use of our time, sir. My Marines are specialists at clearance and killing infected, sir. I understand that FOD walk-down has to be meticulous, sir. My professional opinion is that we could have rounded up some refugees and have them overseen by Navy security with back-up of aviation ground personnel and achieved the same objective, sir. While my Marines were clearing zombies and saving people, sir. But I could be wrong. I'd like to . . . look at that, sir."

"Commander Sanderson?" Hamilton said. "You made that call."

"You were available, Lieutenant," Sanderson said. "And the security situation was still questionable. To get refugees over, assuming they'd volunteer, we'd have had to dispatch the Sea Dragon. Also a questionable use of resources."

"Last point first, sir," Faith said. "We've accessed the basin including the direct access from the field to the main basin. As secure a transfer point as you can ask. We have boats. We kept back two of the Navy light craft from Lieutenant Chen's flotilla. They could have been used as ferries. The area was secure, obviously, since there were no infected encountered and none had been observed in the area that day or even the previous, sir.

"On volunteering: That's a really complicated subject. I'm not getting into personnel resource use; over my paygrade. But experience shows that if you ask a group of refugees for help, you get some that respond immediately. And those tend to be your best people, ongoing. So just asking the question, sir, lets you start sorting the sheep from the goats, sir. Not always, of course. Sometimes the people who don't volunteer end up being very good. But it's a method, sir."

"You're very carefully not looking at me, Faith," Isham said, grinning. "But the lieutenant has a very valid point. That is the general experience. The counter is that people who have been . . . significant prior to the Fall often are initially resistant to menial tasks while having often high ability at more advanced tasks. I'll add that Ernest Zumwald's newsreels and radio shows have had a very positive impact."

"Well put, sir," Faith said, smiling thinly. "Very politic."

"Having a pistol shoved in the back of your neck can *make* you politic, Lieutenant," Isham said.

"On availability:" Faith continued. "That is the question, sir. And it *is* a *question*, sir. *My* professional opinion is that it was not the best use of resources. But I am very junior, sir. And I may be wrong, sir. I am aware that my professional knowledge base is not perfect, sir. However, sir, I would like to explore whether every time the runway needs to be walked down, are my Marines supposed to divert from their primary tasks? Is that a good idea or should we look at some alternative? 'Cause it will happen again. You gotta walk the line regularly. Is that our job? Or is our job killing infected and saving people?"

"When you put it that way, Lieutenant, the answer seems fairly obvious," Commander Sanderson said. "I'm man enough to admit it was probably a mistake."

"I don't know, sir," Faith said. "I wasn't even aware that the order had come from you, sir. I just did what I was told. Do what you're told and ask questions about it later when the time is right. So now I'm asking, officially, as is my job, if we need to be available on an ongoing basis, sir."

"No," Hamilton said. "I'm not going to explore whether it was a right or wrong call in this case. Receiving the P-8 was a snap-kick. Further, it was a snap-kick when the commander was just getting his feet on the ground. My gut is that it was not that big an issue in this case but it is not a primarily ground force Marine job. If there's a need in the future that cannot be filled by other resources, we'll address it. But the primary job of the Marines is outer perimeter security and clearance. Secondary is secondary. Subject closed."

"Aye, aye, sir," Faith said.

"Status of the aviation side of the Station," Hamilton said.

"One Seahawk will be up and running for testing purposes tomorrow, sir," Sanderson said. "We'll have a rate of about one per day thereafter. Working with survey and salvage on getting the training facilities back online. Notably the simulators, which is going to take some work. We could, possibly, do without them but having them will assist in reducing the training time. We'll have to have a round-the-clock ground training, including simulators if we have them, training schedule. And until we have more qualified pilots and airframe engineers, we're dying for instructors. It's going to be a matter of senior and experienced people staying as instructors and newly minted personnel going out in the field, sir. Once they get some field experience, they'll rotate back as instructors and so on and so forth. Anyone with serious experience will be a senior officer, sir."

"Got that," Hamilton said. "I'm going to say, definitively, and I'll point it out to LantFleet, that the more time you spend getting the basis right, the more efficient the program will be ongoing. Once we can turn the lights on at night on the base, for that matter get the lights *going* on base, we'll be pulling out to continue sweeps north. I really don't expect your training program to be hitting stride until that point, Commander. During the sweep, not as we leave. So get it right at the start and I'm confident that it will work out long-term."

"Will do, Colonel," Sanderson said. "One question."

"Go," Hamilton said.

"Am I also commanding the station, sir?" Sanderson asked.

"For now, you're station commander," Hamilton said, making a note. "Aware that doing that and the training program and squadron commander is a bit much to ask, I'll find someone to take over base command. It's not me. For one thing, it's a base command. Navy deal. For another, I'm the Force Commander, at least for present, and will be going forward with the Force. But as Captain Smith pointed out, we have a slew of capable lieutenant commanders, commanders and even lieutenants promotable who could handle it. We'll find a station commander from that group.

"Commander Isham, plans on mechanical production," Hamilton said.

"What we lacked before was resources, Colonel," Isham said. "Steve and I have been batting this idea around for a while. I've got a pretty good concept of operations on it and I brought along a couple of my people who have a clue. Like you said on the training operation, more time spent at the beginning getting it right means more efficiency as you go. But I'd say two weeks and we'll have the basics in place and start cranking out containers. Don't say 'One week.' When I say a time, I don't pad it. I could give you one in three days. Might have one in a week to at least test the concept. Getting people in place, trained and prepared to do all the tasks . . . Two weeks is a miracle."

"Two weeks sounds fine, Commander," Hamilton said. "Air Ops. Any points?"

"One more day's full ops and the Dragon is down for at least two days," Captain Wilkes said. "The question is, do you want us to do another day of ops or put it in for service now?"

"Can you service it at the airfield, Commander?" Hamilton asked.

"Yes," Sanderson said. "I was going to raise moving the helo support personnel to the station. We can do the work over there with them. And I may have to steal some for the training program."

"We'll need them back on the *Grace* when we leave," Hamilton said. "I get your point about experience in the trainers. We still need a solid crew on the *Grace*. We're going to be out on a limb, as usual. I'd prefer our air branch not be cut off. But they'll move over to begin work at the station tomorrow. Send the Sea Dragon over with one set of personnel, then get to work on it. The rest can, as the lieutenant pointed out, ferry by boats. Missions for tomorrow: Service the Sea Dragon. Begin work on mechanicals production facility. Continue work on the base systems. Closure of the beach to infected infiltration. Clearance operations down the beach. Air Ops at Commander Sanderson's direction. Setting up a regular ferry schedule. Now to the details . . ."

That evening in his quarters, Commander Sanderson turned on his computer, logged into WolfNet and typed a query: "London Research Institute."

There was already an "official history" of Wolf Squadron. The writer was a historian who had been tapped to write up "significant actions" post-Fall. Sanderson had already read the bios of the various senior officials and noted that Captain Smith's background was as a history teacher. So it made sense. It was from those as much as the, frankly, propaganda movies that Commander Sanderson had been getting caught up on this new world he'd entered.

"Operation Golden Lion: Airmobile insertion raid on the London Research Institute . . ."

Sanderson read the entry and realized that it was carefully crafted. "Stuff" had been left out. So he hit the links at various points and did some more research. Then he dug into additional information on his new ensign. It took some piecing together to see why she was inserted as a "technical expert" on the raid.

"Son of a bitch," Sanderson said when he was done. "I now get why the colonel said 'Never underestimate a Smith.' I knew where the vaccine came from but . . . that's double cold . . ."

"Permission to make a nonprofessional comment, sir," Sophia said as she banked the Seahawk around. They were staying over the cleared areas since her "check ride" was doubling as a test-flight of the newly refurbished bird.

"Your choice," Sanderson said.

"This is *so* much easier to fly than the Dragon, sir!" Sophia said.

"We try to use Rangers, which are about the easiest bird in the world, for first flights, Ensign," Sanderson said. "It would take a zombie apocalypse for anyone to have a person train and solo on a Dragon. They are, yes, a bitch and a half. Since we're having not-on-point conversation. Personal question."

"Sir?" Sophia said.

"You were sent to London in part to look for vaccine production materials?" Sanderson said.

"Yes, sir," Sophia said. "I worked in a corporate lab

making vaccine before the Fall if that's what you're tiptoeing up to asking, sir."

"That was what I'd gleaned," Sanderson said, nodding.

"I've got an official pardon from the NCCC, sir," Sophia said. "And I'm past apologizing, sir. Especially given that that is where all our vaccine comes from at this point. Thank God Dr. Shelley turned up or I'd be stuck in a lab instead of doing this, sir."

"It's inappropriate for me to ask something like this," Sanderson said. "But how did you feel about that?"

"When we were first clearing, sir," Sophia said, "there were still some child infected left, sir. And I occasionally had to shoot them, sir. That's about how I felt, sir."

"Ensign," Sanderson said. "Absent being unable to land this bird safely, your flying meets standards. My standards. You'd have been cleared pre-Fall, if you were, you know, old enough and went through all the right schools. I would prefer you to have more time as copilot and that seems to meet the mission plan. But you're a good, competent pilot. On the point we just discussed: I spent some time working with spec-ops. One of their unwritten mottoes is 'We do a lot of things nobody should have to do because they're things that have to be done.' Your . . . attitude on the matter was what I was looking for. And that fits that motto. I have no issues with you as a pilot, Ensign. I'm trying to figure out why you're still an ensign."

"Pretty much everyone up to the NCCC is okay with me being an officer, sir," Sophia said. "I've been working as an officer, effectively, since before I was sworn in. But there's a similar resistance, from just about everyone, to promoting me until I'm a little older. Either sixteen, which is coming up, or eighteen. They'll probably relent and promote me to JG when I turn sixteen. I'm not holding my breath but it's probable. I'm not really worried about it, sir. We really don't do this stuff for pay and I'm not zoned in on who salutes me or doesn't. I just want to do everything I can, to the best of my ability, to help, sir. Really don't care what rank I'm at doing that, sir. If I was a pilot and . . . I dunno, a petty officer, I'd be fine with that, sir. I just try to do whatever needs to be done even if some of it has been, yeah, pretty distasteful. And I don't really care what people call me when I'm doing it. Sir."

"'We just do what needs to be done, even if it sucks, to make the world a better place,'" Sanderson said. "Maybe we need a new squadron motto."

"Not many children infected anymore, sir," Sophia said. "And shooting up zeds gets to be . . . You just don't see them as people after a while, sir. At least I try not to."

"Bring her in for a landing, Ensign," Sanderson said. "The aircraft and the pilot seem to be functional. And we have promises to keep."

"And miles to go before we sleep, and miles to go before we sleep . . ." Sophia said.

"And she knows the classics," Sanderson said.

"Once more unto the breach dear friends, once more," Sophia said. "Or close up the stairs with our American dead!"

"That . . . is not a classic," Sanderson said.

"It will be, sir," Sophia said. "It will be . . . Tower, Hawk Three approach for landing . . ."

"Forth, Marines!" Faith called over the radio. "Forth and fear no darkness! Arise! Arise! Arise Riders of

Shewolf! Spears shall be shaken! Shields shall be shattered! A sword day . . . A red day . . . Ere the sun *rises*!"

With the decision to start clearance of the beach towns south of the station, some of the plan had been adjusted. The Marines had left before dawn, catching the outgoing tide, and swum their tracks out to sea. A large park extended south of the base for a mile and a half. When they were clear of the base, they'd turned on powerful spotlights and trolled down past the park to where the civilian houses started.

Now they were arrayed in a line with the sun rising behind them and facing them were a few hundred zombies.

"Death cried King Theoden," Januscheitis radioed. *"Charging the line of the enemy."*

"Open fire and let's roll!" Faith shouted, pointing to the shore. "Death! Death!"

It really was no contest. By the time the amtracks engaged their tracks and waded ashore, the entire group of zombies was shattered bodies from .50 caliber fire. Several were then ground into the sand by the tracks.

"You know," Faith said. "Few of these at the Battle of Minas Tirith and Sauron wouldn't have stood a chance."

"Sauron would have been the one using them, ma'am," Hooch argued. *"Or Saruman. Saruman was way more into machines, ma'am."*

"Wizards," Januscheitis said.

"Well, they were, right?" Faith said.

"I meant the movie, ma'am," Januscheitis said. *"From the seventies? The evil wizard had tanks. The good wizard didn't."*

"He had a Luger, though," Hooch radioed.

"Point," Januscheitis said.

"This is the geekiest conversation," Faith said. "I'm afraid of what I've started. Hey, there's a road off the beach. We're not getting many takers, let's go inland."

"We need to be able to extract, ma'am," Januscheitis warned. *"We're not getting hit heavy now. We may."*

"In which case, we drive back to the beach," Faith said, holding up a standard auto GPS. "Everybody remember where we parked. Looks like . . . Nineteenth Street."

"Staff Sergeant," Faith said over the radio.

"Ma'am?" Januscheitis said.

They'd hit some pockets of zombies. So far no survivors but the day was extremely young.

"In all seriousness, we need some big ass speakers on these things," Faith said, watching the fire. The infected weren't even getting close to the amtracks between the fire of the main guns and the fire from the up-gunned Marines in the back. "Zombies are attracted to light and sound. And loud as these things are, they're not loud enough."

"Psy-ops speakers, aye, ma'am," Januscheitis said.

"Which are?" Faith asked.

"Big ass speakers, ma'am," Januscheitis said. *"Big ass. Ever see Apocalypse Now?"*

"The ones in the helicopters?" Faith said. "That's exactly what I mean. But I'll let Sophia play 'Ride of the Valkyries.' I'm thinking . . . 'Immigrant Song'? 'Winterborn'? Hell, can we hook it up to a playlist?"

"We'll figure out a way, ma'am," Januscheitis said.

"Not to interrupt this planning session or anything," Smitty radioed. *"I think we got some survivors."*

"Where?" Faith asked.

"Couple of streets over, Shewolf," Smitty said. *"Over on Ocean Grove. Pretty sure somebody's waving something out a window."*

"Arise, Marines!" Faith radioed. "Fell deeds await! Now for wrath . . . Seriously, this time let's make sure we've got the situation controlled before extraction . . ."

"Where the hell have you *been*?" the man said angrily, as he boarded the track. "The base is right up the *road*!"

"You're looking at pretty much the *entire* surviving Marine Corps, *sir*," Smitty said, handing him some water. "So why don't you sit down, shut up, don't touch anything and don't *bitch*. We got more ground to cover."

"Shewolf, J, over."

"Hearin' you, J," Faith replied. They'd moved over to Seminole Road and were getting a lot more action. Both in terms of the occasional survivors and the infected.

"We're getting orange on ammo, Shewolf," Januscheitis said. *"Red on fifty and forty mike mike. Orange on everything else."*

"Roger," Faith said. She reached down and pulled out her laptop, then consulted the map on it. "Follow me. And hope I don't get lost . . ."

"And I'm lost," Faith admitted. "Hooch, get one of the locals up in the hatch. We're looking for the nearest beach access road . . ."

"Here," Faith said, ducking into the personnel compartment and handing over her magazines. "Have my mags."

The Marines were down to tossing grenades over the

side of the tracks at the increasing crowds of infected around them. They'd ended up going too far down Seminole Road and well inland. When they'd passed the Atlantic Beach city hall, and were out of fifty cal. and forty millimeter, they knew they'd gone wrong.

"There!" the local said. "Turn left!"

"And we're headed for the beach," Faith said as the amtrack bumped over something.

"Please tell me that was a speed bump," the woman closest to her said.

"That was a speed bump," Faith said. "For values of speed bump..."

"Run away, run away!" Faith radioed as the beach came in sight. "Full speed ahead and rendezvous offshore..."

They'd closed up all their hatches. First order of business in the AAR, admitting she couldn't map read for shit. Second order of business, amtracks should NOT be easy to climb. The things were ten feet high. If it wasn't for external climb bars and racks there was no way the zeds could climb on them. As it was, you could hear the scratching and banging from the zeds on the roof over the roar of the engines.

Faith ducked back into the personnel area as the track moved into the water. As it did, the refugees could feel the track begin to float, and the interior filled with eerie green light. So that might be why they were looking so green. Or not. The extra weight of refugees, who were packed in, and the zeds on top had them riding pretty damned low. If they'd had appliqué armor attached they'd have sunk like a stone. The bilge pump was working over time.

"We need to get these zeds off the track," Faith said loudly. "Take 'er down to fifty feet, helmsman!"

"Fifty feet, aye, ma'am!" Freeman responded.

One of the refugees fainted.

"... I definitely need to get better at map reading," Faith admitted. "In my defense, the roads down there get a little screwy.

"Second Item: We probably should have turned around before we were orange on ammo..."

There was a reason that AARs were referred to as "institutional scab picking."

"Third Item: We need to reconfigure the exterior of the AAVs," Faith said. "They're high enough that without the gear racks, there's no way zeds could climb on them. If they weren't on top, we could have just driven away from them. They can't keep up. As it was, well....

"Last item: We need to carry more spare ammo onboard. And it's been suggested we attach claymores to the sides although having the actual swords onboard in this case would have been useful. Put somebody up on top with a six-foot sword and the zeds aren't boarding...

"... The basic concept of approaching from off-shore works," Faith concluded. "Although if we're going to get swarmed, putting some grease or something on top would be useful."

"Yes," Colonel Hamilton said. "Although the gunny and I positively *delighted* in carefully shooting off the zombies you brought back with you, Lieutenant. And, of course, the alligators appreciated it."

"And we appreciated the care, sir," Faith said.

"Forty-five makes a really funny sound when it's pinging off the armor, sir . . ."

"Shewolf, Hawk Seven, approaching from your six."

"Nevada, that you?" Faith replied.

"Roger. You've got a bunch of tangoes clustered to your northeast. They're trying to follow you and getting hooked up on what looks like . . . Stand by . . . My GPS is saying Six-Zero-Two Selva Lakes Circle. That's Selva. Sierra, Echo, Lima, Victor, Alpha. Do you copy?"

"Selva," Faith replied. "Good copy. We'll head over there and make them good tangoes."

"Roger. Hawk Seven continuing mission. Out."

"He's just eating this up, isn't he?" Faith said, smiling. "I'm so glad we found him. Now . . . Selva . . . Selva . . . There you are . . ."

"Okay, not this Selva . . ."

"Or this one . . ."

"Selva Circle, right . . . ? No."

"Selva Boulevard?"

"Ah! *There* you are . . . ! Open fire!"

". . . in conclusion, suburbs, especially suburbs that use *the same damned name* over and over again, are *really* confusing, but the addition of more ammo and removal of all external holds has made the mission extremely effective. And it gave us the opportunity to make lots of good zombies. That concludes my report."

"Lieutenant," Hamilton said. "Remind me not to have you *ever* navigate in Atlanta."

"Sir?" Faith asked.

"So I say this with some trepidation," Hamilton said. "We have modified a barge, and tested it, capable of RO-RO of an M1 on any suitable landing point. Which does not, let me make this very clear, mean anything that has pilings under it. A *solid* landing point. This means we can move Trixie across the river."

"Oh . . ." Faith said, her eyes wide. "Oh . . ." She started to say something and stopped and frowned. "Sir, that is tremendous news. Really, sir. But . . ."

"But there aren't enough concentrations south of the base to warrant using M1028," Hamilton said. "Or a tank."

"No, sir," Faith said.

"The same barge, which is more of a landing craft at this point just not self mobile, will allow the amtracks to climb up onto it and cross it to land at otherwise inaccessible points such as wharfs," Hamilton said. "So tomorrow, what you are going to do is practice landing using the barge with Trixie, driven by Lance Corporal Condrey and not yourself, as well as using it to move amtracks from the water to the land. Crew of Trixie will be yourself as commander, Staff Sergeant Decker as gunner, Lance Corporal Condrey as driver and Private First Class Twitchell as loader. And if you drop it in the water, if you survive, you don't get another one. Understood?"

"Understood, sir," Faith said.

"The day following, if all tests are a go, you will proceed to the Bay Street Wharfs area of Jacksonville to perform a hard entry for clearance," Hamilton said.

"We're going downtown?" Faith asked.

"You're going downtown," Hamilton said. "There are survivors in some of the buildings who cannot or will not access the roof. Your mission, initially, will be clearance only. You will be covered by Hawk Three in the event that you run into a problem. The amphibs can, as you pointed out and proved, just drive into the water to get rid of most of their fleas. You cannot. You also are enjoined to avoid a repetition of LRI. If you get too in the busy, pull back. The barge will wait offshore for your extraction. Understood?"

"Yes, sir," Faith said, beaming.

"Last point," Hamilton said. "The point has been made, several times, that we need more noise to attract the infected. So Trixie has been further . . . accessorized."

"'In this episode of *Pimp My Tank*,'" Commander Sanderson said, "'we attach the largest speakers in the world to an M1 Abrams. I hope I like your taste in music, Lieutenant. I'm going to be able to hear it from the chopper . . ."

"We're going dooowntooown," Faith sang.

"'*These mist covered islands, are home now for me . . .*'" Montana sang quietly, watching more infected falling off the *Ronald Reagan*. It wasn't the zombilanche Lyons had faced but they were still coming. The Special Boat guys seemed to be having fun shooting the occasional survivor who made it to the SOC. Between their covered wheelhouse and maneuverability they were making sort of a game of moving in, getting a zombilanche, moving back. They were wearing respirators since there weren't enough sharks or giant squids in the ocean to clean up all the offal in the harbor. And the damned things just kept *coming*.

"I'd like to know where they're getting water," Captain Carter said stoically. He was watching the operation with arms crossed and a set expression on his face. Possibly because at least some of the falling infected were Navy personnel.

"I'd like to know how to turn off that damned light," Montana said. "At a certain level this is a perfect situation. Wolf would do something similar to draw infected to kill zones. But they would only do it overnight. This has been going on for months and has drawn a goodly portion of the entire infected population to one relatively controlled area. Viewed in that light this is a good thing. The problem is the *level* of infected. All we need is sufficient controlled firepower and at least half our problems in the San Diego area are solved. We can't just hit North Island with all the Tomahawks in the *Michigan*.

"Driver," Montana said, looking south in the bay. "Head south down the bay."

"Aye, sir," the kid said, starting the motor again and heading south.

"Sir?" Carter asked.

"Was it just my impression, or is there a long stretch of open area south of the base?" Montana asked.

"Technically it's part of the base, sir," Carter said. "Just unused except by BUD/S and runners. The locals have been petitioning for decades to get it opened up to development. But, yes, it is untenanted."

"Driver, you know where we're talking about?"

"Silver Strand," the coxswain said. "Yes, sir."

"Thataway."

"Aye, aye, sir."

The area south of the base was a long, narrow peninsula with beaches on both sides. Just north of the area was the BUD/S facility, parked on the seaward side of the stretch of beach.

"Scenic," Montana said, nodding. "Hell of a lot better than Camp McCall. I think one of the reasons there was always a rivalry between Special Forces and the SEALs was we were so damned jealous of where you were based."

"Beaches are kind of our thing, sir," Carter said.

"Having taken a close look at the situation," Montana said, "how would you rate the success likelihood of a mission to cut out the *Jimmy Carter* and take it under tow?"

"Low, sir," Carter said. "And that ignores what effect it would have on the reactor. They are very sensitive to temperature fluctuations."

"Pretty much my thought as well," Montana said. "We need a meeting. Gah. I hate it when I say that. . . ."

"We need to get the infected to move off North Island," Montana said. "At least the main base zone."

The meeting included Halvorson, Lyons, the COB of the *Michigan*, Captain Carter and Montana. If they needed more brainpower they'd expand but Montana was a big believer that the size of a meeting was inverse to its output.

"Specifically we need to get them to move to the uninhabited portion of the island south of the BUD/S base. To do that we need to either cover or turn off the light on the *Jimmy*. Then we need an alternate attractor set up alongside the open area. That can be something mounted on a barge with minimal crew. But it needs to be a lot of light. And that skips the part of turning off or covering the light on the *Jimmy*. Brainstorm time. Cutting the light on the Jimmy. The other is easy."

"Team of SEALs onto the *Jimmy*," Lyons said. "There's less of a zombilanche these days. Keep their heads up. Mount the sail. Cover it with a rubber mat."

"Problems," Commander Halvorson said.

"Wait on those," Montana said. "Alternatives."

"Hit the sail with a rocket launcher," Captain Carter said.

"Out of the box," Montana said, as Lyons made a note. "Good. Next."

"Slide something under it to block the water intake to the reactor," the COB said. "One way or another it'll shut 'er down. I don't think it's a *good* idea but it's an idea."

"I am going to formally protest if that one even gets a *mention*, sir," Halvorson said. "We don't know exactly how that reactor is still running and any attempt to futz with it without such knowledge has the likelihood of creating a meltdown. Strongly protest. Through channels."

"Duly noted. Now come up with something yourself."

"Rig up a boat with overhead protection and a crane," Halvorson said with a clearly unexpressed sigh. "Use that to install blocking material on the light. It can't be just a rubber mat. That light produces a fair amount of heat. Steel box?"

"That's the ticket," Montana said. "Keep going..."

"'*Seasons don't fear the reaper* . . .'" Montana muttered, watching the evolution of covering the light on the *Jimmy Carter*.

The "crane" on the end of the motorized barge was originally a boat lift found in "abandoned and inoperable" condition at the NALF. Four days of crack Navy nuclear engineering, "crack" being a variable term in this case, had created a "crane" capable of lifting a large steel box sixty feet into the air and forty feet sideways. One where the operator was, furthermore, covered in plates of corrugated steel taken from the same cargo container that had provided material for the "lights-out" box.

"The Beast" having already been taken, they called it "Franky" after Dr. Frankenstein's monster. Leuschen's suggestion of "Jaeger" had been ritually shot down in flames.

Leuschen and the barge driver had practiced maneuvering the box but it was still tricky. North Island had a more or less continuous wind from the sea that tended to push the barge off station. And the box was swinging on a single line which meant it wasn't always lined up to fit over the sail. Then there were the falling zombies hitting the barge, the crane and the box. The impacts of those falling from the flight deck could be heard a hundred yards away. However, after twenty minutes and what was clearly a good bit of swearing they had the box in place and the light at least muted.

"To the strand, driver," Montana said, pointing south.

Along the strand seven barges, previously cut out by SEALs and boat operators, were now arrayed along the shore. Each of them contained one or more generators and as many powerful lights as the remnants of Pacific Fleet had been able to find. They'd tried them the previous night and gotten some response. But with most of the infected concentrating on the light on the *Jimmy* the response had been muted at best. With that light turned off, hopefully they'd get more response over the subsequent nights.

There were crews on the barges, fixing light bulbs, reinforcing gear, fueling the generators. Despite the long trip down they'd put them in the bay. Less damage from waves that way. Alas, that also meant they were going to lose them. 'Cause it was *gonna* rain.

CHAPTER 13

"You okay?" Sophia said. Nobody had seen Faith since the meeting and she finally tracked her down in her quarters.

Faith was hunched in front of a computer, staring at it like a mouse stares at a snake.

"I'm fine," Faith said. She didn't move.

"Homework?" Sophia asked. Despite being "Officers and Ladies" with full-time jobs, they were both expected to keep up with school work. Faith was considered the "bad" student of the two of them and despite being a fourteen-year-old officer in a zombie apocalypse was up to eleventh grade work. Sophia, fifteen, was working on college courses.

"Sort of," Faith said.

"Need help?" Sophia said. She wasn't usually so nice but Faith looked . . . scared. She walked into the room and examined the computer. Faith was looking at an iTunes screen. "So, seriously, what's up?"

"I'm trying to figure out the playlist," Faith said in a small voice.

"Is that all?" Sophia said, laughing. "I did dozens of those!"

"I know!" Faith spat. "Okay, I know! I was there, okay? For shooting up a beach filled with infected on a *raid*, Sophia! I'm taking an M1 tank ashore in a *city*. You remember *London*?"

"Faith, calm down," Sophia said, sitting down next to her.

"I almost *lost* in London, Soph," Faith said, clearly trying not to cry. "I almost LOST. I almost *lost* all my *Marines*, Soph! 'Cause I was stupid and I thought . . ."

"Faith . . ." Sophia said. "I . . . You made the right call. The general backed you up."

"That's the *only* reason it was right," Faith said. "Because, Soph, you were *there*. If it hadn't been for General Montana, we'd be . . ." She stopped. "And I didn't *know* that, okay, Sophia? How could I? It was just Walker. It was wrong. *I* was wrong. And now . . . I've got to do *this*? Okay? And this is important, okay, Sophia? We're going into a *city*, okay? Just like God-damned London, okay? And this time there is no way that the fuckers are *getting* my Marines! I'm going to fucking SLAUGHTER them. Those fuckers need to *pay*! And they cannot *stop* me! They just *can't*, okay? This is where we *prove* we can fucking win, Sophia. So it's *important*! It's the most important thing I've ever *done*, okay?"

"Okay," Sophia said.

"And there's survivors, okay?" Faith said. "And they're going to *hear* this. And I want it to be right, okay? I have to have that *one* song. That song that I play when we go hot, okay? Like when you played 'Ready to Die' when we hit Gitmo. That was awesome! And I've never done this. The rest of the playlist . . . Doesn't matter really. Stuff. But that one song . . . That has to matter. And I'm sitting here and saying 'Has to be the Marine Corps Hymn.' But, let's face it, is that the right choice? I mean... It's *obviously* the right choice but it doesn't *feel* right, you know?"

"Wait, Faith," Sophia said, sitting down. "Just calm down. I get it. I really do. I didn't but I get it now. Just wait..." She said. She clicked on the Marine Corps Hymn and nodded. "That's... That's not right for opening fire with an M1 Abrams, you're right. You know how when we went into Gitmo, I played 'Homeward Bound' last before we opened fire?"

"Yeah," Faith said. "Sort of wanted to do that one, then I... Yeah."

"Okay," Sophia said. "That's the last one before you roll, okay? That's the last... *nice* one. Last one to draw them in."

"But which one do I play when we go hot?" Faith asked.

"That is up to you," Sophia said, holding up her hand. "And you're over-thinking it. What was the first song that came to mind when the colonel told you you were going in with Trixie?"

"'Immigrant song,'" Faith said.

"Oldie but a goody," Sophia said.

"But is that the *right* one?" Faith asked.

"Look, don't sweat it so hard," Sophia said. "Set up the rest of the playlist. That's what I'd do. There might be something that comes to mind that's better. Just let your back brain decide. You've got time."

"It's gotta be right," Faith insisted.

"It will be," Sophia said. "It will be..."

It had been decided, with some caution on Colonel Hamilton's part, to do the same thing that they did when clearing towns: Play music and make light the night before to draw in the maximum density of infected.

The "utility boat" yachts had, therefore, gone down the night before and shone their lights and played loud music. Added to them was a barge with a rotating spotlight system previously used to advertise a grand opening.

Then the barge containing Trixie was brought down before dawn. It was anchored, carefully, right up against the wharfs. There was a gap between the barge and the wharf. It was close enough the infected could jump had it not been for the *very* high raised ramp. Trixie had to be set up high on the barge due to the way she had to unload. The seventy-three ton tank going "up" to the wharf would have bent any conceivable bridge in half. So the bridge had to be long and thus high. Fortunately, they had some experts on Roll On-Roll Off techniques who'd designed the landing barge. It worked and doubled as a shield against the swarming infected.

Trixie was covered by a large canvas with the Marine Corps globe and anchor spray-painted on it. The canvas was propped up carefully, completely clearing the tank with some space underneath. Even an overhead observer could not determine what was under the canvas. There wasn't any tactical reason to cover the tank. Faith had suggested it without any logical reason and Colonel Hamilton had agreed, admitting that there was little or no logic. Zombies weren't going to be afraid of *any* tank, no matter how large. But having it covered just seemed . . . right.

When everything was in place, just before dawn,

Faith started her own playlist. It had a variety of tunes she'd chosen from pure gut to start off. "Winterborn," Cruxshadows. It would set the mood nicely.

"Vater Unser" by E Nomine, 'cause she was going to need some forgiveness for what she was about to do. She knew that blaming the infected for the way they acted was wrong. But she couldn't help herself. After London, she just purely hated zombies.

"He's a Pirate," the David Garrett version. She'd really wanted to meet David Garrett pre-Plague. If there was one guy on earth to lose her virginity to . . . That was, oddly enough, in honor of her dad who was a pirate at heart. Just with a conscience.

"Roland the Headless Thompson Gunner" 'cause she knew General Montana loved it. And if she had to choose another da, or a granda more like, it would be the general. She'd hardly known him before London and now she missed him as much as she missed Mum and Da.

"Meadows of Heaven." Someday she wanted to find a place that reminded her of that song and just . . . stop. Find someplace where she could raise kids. Buy a farm. A place. Just name it "Home." That was the future she was fighting for. That was why today had to happen. The road to home led right through the zombies gathering in the square.

"Danse Macabre" 'cause, well, it was appropriate to the current world. Long, but that would give them more time to gather.

"Miami 2017." Billy Joel was way before her time but . . . she'd *seen* the lights go out on Broadway. Close enough. She'd been there the night the lights went out in NYC, permanently. She hoped, someday, to see them turned back on. But from off-shore: NYC was not her idea of a fun time.

That was almost the last of the intro music. Time to get ready to roll.

"Start the engine," Faith said, then keyed the radio. "J. What's the status on land, over?"

"Remember that look we got out a window in London, ma'am?" Januscheitis said. The Marine NCO actually sounded nervous.

"Like that?" Faith asked.

"Worse. Shouldn't we . . . soften the objective, ma'am?"

"With what?" Faith asked. "I mean, we don't *have* B-52s, or napalm, J. What's bigger than Trixie? We're about to show gunboats how you do it."

She switched back to intercom.

"Condrey, when the gates drop, you are going to hit it on my command," Faith said. "You will obey that order unquestioningly, Lance Corporal. You are going to fucking floor it. Don't even look. Just do."

"Aye, aye, ma'am," Condrey said.

"We are going to bring hell and destruction to our enemies this day, Staff Sergeant Decker," Faith said as the final piano solo started. "We are going to retake our nation, Staff Sergeant. And we are going to lead the way in this beautiful iron monster, Staff Sergeant, you and Lance Corporal Condrey have returned to the service of our nation with your skill and dedication. Oorah?"

"Oorah, ma'am!" Decker said. "Semper *fucking* Fi."

They were closed up and Faith was in the compartment so she could see the staff sergeant's face.

"Are you going to be . . . okay, Staff Sergeant?" Faith asked as the Marine Corps Hymn started with a brassy flourish. He wasn't looking okay. "I need to know *now*."

"I didn't even *like* Lieutenant Klette, ma'am," Decker said, obviously trying not to cry. Marine Staff NCOs do *not* cry. *Especially* on the cusp of combat. Most especially with the Hymn playing in the background.

"He was one of the most *useless* fucktards Marine Armor Officer Course ever *produced*, ma'am. He was more useful to the Corps as a *zombie*! You think *you* get lost, ma'am? Motherfucker couldn't find his way out of the *mess*! And he was an ANNAPOLIS GRADUATE, not a fourteen-year-old girl! Useless as tits on a fucking boar HOG! But you couldn't *tell* him! Oh, NO! He was God's GIFT to the Marine Corps, ma'am! A more arrogant PRICK has never been produced by Annapolis, ma'am! Which EXISTS to produce ARROGANT, INCOMPETENT PRICKS! WHY THE FUCK COULDN'T *YOU* HAVE BEEN MY PLATOON LEADER, MA'AM? YOU'D HAVE BEEN *WORTH* MY SANITY, MA'AM! I am fine, ma'am. Finally. I am SEMPER FUCKING FI, MA'AM! I am fucking *UP*! READY TO *ROLL*, MA'AM! TANKER *UP*!"

Twitchell was pushed up against the side of the compartment, his eyes wide. Faith just smiled.

"Then let us roll fucking hot, Staff Sergeant," Faith said quietly. "Drop the ramp," she radioed just as the final flourish ended.

"Ramp down!" the operator called a moment later. "You gonna just *sit* there 'cause there's . . . ?"

"Lance Corporal Condrey," she said. "PUNCH IT!"

They couldn't see a *thing* till they cleared the canvas. As soon as the tank bounded forward, Faith popped the TC's hatch and took over the commander's gun.

The sight was . . . intense. The square by the wharfs was packed, side to side, with infected humanity. She couldn't even estimate how many. There was a solid stench of unwashed bodies mixed with offal and urine. The powerful speakers had actually been turned down for the intro songs. As the tank surged forward she hit the volume controls and "Bodies" by Drowning Pool boomed across the opening, echoing down the streets of the zombie held city.

"*LET THE BODIES HIT THE FLOOR*!" Faith screamed, triggering the TC's gun.

The ramp crushed a dozen infected. More boarded the craft in a tide but they weren't getting far. The tank filled the barge side to side. As the tank darted forward, the zombies were splashed up in the treads and the tank spun out, creating a massive rooster tail of molecularized infected, blood red mingling with the pink and purple paint of the pimped-out iron and depleted uranium giant. And those were just the first. The infected were packed tight. They couldn't run even if they wanted to. And the tank was no more slowed by them than by air.

"TARGET CONCENTRATION!" Faith shouted, firing the cupola machine gun with one hand and laying down a windrow of bodies on the square. It was spitting in the wind of all the infected in the square and the ones to the sides were trying to climb onto the track. They were mostly getting caught in the treads. But eventually one of the taller ones would get a hold, then the rest would swarm aboard. Not a problem, she could just close up and have the amtracks scratch her back. But she was about to fix the whole situation in her opinion.

"TARGET!" Decker screamed.

"FIRE!" Faith bellowed. They were having to shout. Even with the crewman's helmets, the music was so loud they could barely hear themselves.

"ON THE WAY!"

Then it turned out the gun was *louder*.

The M1028 was essentially a four point seven inch diameter shotgun round containing nearly twelve hundred thumb-sized ball bearings. The difference between it and normal shotgun rounds being a) size, it was more than ten times the total area and volume of a 12 gauge shell, b) the fact that instead of lead or steel shot, the shot was tungsten and c) it was driven at really *insane* velocity.

Tungsten is very dense, very massive and very hard. Besides being used as the filament in incandescent light bulbs, its other major uses were as tank armor and, not coincidentally, armor-piercing rounds.

Thus instead of just going through *one* body, the thumb-sized ball bearings went through *all* the bodies.

The advanced grapeshot turned a broad cone into red mush from just beyond the muzzle to the buildings a hundred meters away. And, in fact, penetrated the buildings' concrete walls. Blood flew into the air in a solid haze of crimson pea-soup fog that settled lightly over the charging tank.

The few infected who had survived to climb on the forward glacis were blasted off by the overpressure wave and driven under the treads.

"DRIVER," Faith screamed. "STOP! PIVOT PORT! . . . PIVOT STARBOARD!"

The pivoting tank solved the problem of infected trying to climb on from the sides.

"*FORWARD*!"

Faith slewed the turret to port with one hand, still firing the cupola gun to starboard with the other...

"Push *me* again..." Faith sang. "This is the end... *ONE* NOTHING WRONG WITH ME! TWO *NOTHING'S* WRONG *WITH ME*! *THREE* TARGET CONCENTRATION!"

"TARGET!"

"FIIIIIRE! PIVOT *STARBOARD*, TARGET CONCENTRATION... LET THE BODIES HIT THE FLOOR...!"

"Pick it up a little bit, Co," Commander Sanderson said. He *could* hear the music as it turned out and thought the choice was bloodily appropriate. "I'd rather not get splashed with the blood."

They were orbiting at five hundred feet. Blood wasn't really an issue. Bouncers from the canister might be, though. Really he just needed some space from the insane carnage below. The square along the river, a remaining undeveloped plot that was a good hundred meters wide and a half a klick long, was being traversed by the rampaging tank, the crowded infected churned under the seventy-three ton juggernaut and turned to sausage.

"Aye, aye, si—" the copilot said, then turned sideways and puked.

"My bird," Sanderson said, adding collective and pulling away from the carnage. "Chief, can you keep tracking?"

"Still on it," the crew chief said in a strained voice. "But I'm gonna have to ralph..."

"Fortunately, I don't have to clean the bird,"

Sanderson said, then paused. "Oh . . . craaa—" He couldn't release the controls so it went in his lap.

It was the middle of the night at the recently cleared San Clemente NALF. But General Montana wasn't going to miss this for worlds.

He grinned as the tank practically jumped off the converted barge and began laying waste to the crowded infected.

"There's my girl," the diminutive general purred. "There's my sweet, fell death. Damn, if I was just fifty years younger . . ."

"Did we have a count?" Galloway asked, setting his waste basket back on the floor.

The one real issue of an underground fortress was air handling. The Hole, with limited access to truly fresh air, always had a vaguely unpleasant smell of reprocessed humanity.

Everyone who had the access and the spare time, which was most of the base, had gotten up early to watch the landing. Faith's antics were generally good entertainment.

It now had a very distinctive odor of vomit.

They were getting "take" from the camera installed on the covering Seahawk. Long before the NRO had come up with a very good algorithm for counting crowds. Police and "organizers" might not have a clear picture of how many people were at a gathering, but the National Reconnaissance Office was about reality. The same algorithm could be applied to any overhead video. And it was not a "guess."

"Quarter million, sir," General Brice said. "They

were packed cheek to jowl. Don't have hard numbers, now, but figure ten percent survivors."

"The efforts to refurbish a tank no longer seem to be an indulgence," Galloway said. "Jesus wept."

"Let me revisit the issue of Buffs and cluster bombs, sir," Brice said.

"Noted."

"Jesus Christ," Sergeant Hocieniec said over the radio. "They're *running*!"

"Copy that," Januscheitis said. "They're fucking running!"

Zombies never ran. It was an axiom. Betas might hide, but the alpha swarms just kept coming. They'd waded through massed fire from the helos in London and never even slowed down except to feed.

Now the infected in the maelstrom of the square had had enough. They knew there were bigger and badder predators and they'd just met one. Much bigger and much badder. They were just confused by helicopters shooting them, the same with fire from gunboats. The M1, blaring music and bellowing fire, was something that even the most primitive primate brain could recognize as "Dragon." The beast that was beyond reality, supernatural in its power. The monster in the cave.

They had only the animal instinct and some vague understanding of past. They'd packed into the square, closing with each other in the belief that in numbers they could swarm the prey as they had so many times before and kill it and feast. Individuals were often lost. Which was food for the rest. But with enough numbers, they'd always triumphed before. Now they were trying to get away, prey themselves. But the iron and uranium giant would have none of it. They were crushing themselves, trying to get away, but it seemed there was nowhere to flee . . .

"There's not enough gators in the world to clean this up," Hooch radioed.

"Gators, hell," Januscheitis said. "I'm not sure the wash point operators are going to let her in till she at least rinses off."

"BEACHHEAD IS CLEAR," Faith radioed. "DO YOU COPY? MOVE FORWARD!"

"Roger," Januscheitis radioed. The square wasn't deserted, but the infected were trying to make it that way. Screw all the fresh carrion. There were better places to be. *Anywhere*. And it wasn't so much "carrion" as blood pudding. "Moving forward at this time . . ."

"We've got a following again," Faith radioed, watching the infected. "Slow it down; we need them to cluster."

They'd started off with Trixie in the lead of the formation, running down the zombies. That had worked for about an hour. But the problem was, the infected from the square had run while more were still trickling in. Some of their "trickles" were more zombies than you got in a liner. And they tended, because the unit was moving, to end up behind the unit. When they occasionally had to slow down to negotiate through the choked roads, the zombies caught up and fell on the less powerful amtracks. That wasn't a security problem but it was hard to kill the ones that were in close and even firing at the amtracks risked holing them.

So they had switched. Trixie was now trailing the unit with Staff Sergeant Januscheitis leading and, fortunately, navigating. And her turret was pointed to the rear. The light flow of infected they were running into as the tracks passed could be handled by the track guns or the Marines in the hatches.

While Trixie handled their "followers." In this case, several thousand infected in a mob. As the tracks slowed, the zombies charged, five thousand voices keening a discordant howl that even now sent a shiver down Faith's spine.

"*Where's the wonder, where's the awe?*" Faith crooned hoarsely as the infected clustered behind them. "*Where are the sleepless nights I used to live for? Before the years take me I wish to see The lost in me . . .*"

"Target concentration," Faith said. She'd turned down the music. She had to. Her voice was already going from screaming orders.

"Target!" Decker said.

"Fire!"

"On the way!"

The center of the mob was taken out. That wouldn't panic infected. It was only when the beast was in their midst that they panicked. There were more still coming forward. Faith slewed the turret to port, simultaneously opening fire with the commander's gun.

"Target concentration . . ."

"Target concentration . . ."

"Coax . . ."

"Concentration cleared," Faith radioed. "Roll it."

She ceased fire as Decker finished off the last few surviving infected with the coaxial machine gun. It was only then that she realized they were rolling at a walking pace past a burned-out church.

"Someday, maybe, God will forgive us for this, Staff Sergeant," Faith said.

"God already does, ma'am," Decker replied. "We are saving people by this, ma'am. And these fallen we send on are already forgiven. How could God condemn them for being victims of a plague, ma'am? Or for any actions before entering this fallen state? They are, too, forgiven by the Grace of Our Lord. We are just filling the choirs of heaven, ma'am."

"Duly noted, Staff Sergeant," Faith said as Trixie sped up.

The unit rolled on, leaving the One Hundred Block of Duval Street strewn with offal . . .

"I wish to see what's lost in me . . ." Faith sang to the music, clearing up a few last infected with the fifty, her face stone. *"I want my tears back, I want my tears back NOW!"*

Trixie rolled off the barge onto Blount Island as the sun was setting. She was still dripping. Not with blood, with water. Well, *and* blood. They'd stopped by Dames Island where there was a solid sandbar. Faith had taken the splattered tank down into the water and driven back and forth to get the worst of the mess off. The juggernaut wasn't clean by any stretch of the imagination. There was a biological purée of meat, bone, brains and internal organs in every niche on the exterior and the lieutenant was still covered. But it was clean enough to run through the wash point.

"That was quite a probe, Lieutenant," Hamilton

said. He'd decided it was appropriate for him to be present for the landing. Very appropriate.

The unit had never retreated as planned for the "probe." There'd been no need. They had swept through all of downtown Jacksonville. They couldn't cover the entire sprawling city but they'd covered a lot of it. They'd even rearmed Trixie from stores carried in the amtracks. They'd only stopped when the sun was going down. And there'd been very few surviving infected left behind them. The densely populated areas they'd swept repeatedly.

"Downtown Jax orange cleared, sir," Faith replied, saluting. "And Staff Sergeant Decker and Lance Corporal Condrey have something to report, sir."

"Yes?" Hamilton said curiously as the lance corporal and staff sergeant popped their hatches.

Decker climbed off the tank in a much less robotic manner than had been his habit and walked up to the colonel. He snapped off a parade ground salute.

"Sir!" Decker boomed as Condrey fell into formation beside him. "Staff Sergeant Decker with a party of one, reporting aboard, sir."

"Feeling better, Decker?" Hamilton asked, returning the salute.

"Sir, a Marine NCO should never publicly be disrespectful of the chain of command or superiors, sir," Decker said, almost conversationally. "However, in the case of Lieutenant Klette, may the Staff Sergeant be so bold as to state that the useless fucker should have been fragged immediately upon reporting aboard, sir. I would recommend turning him into vaccine, but his stupid might rub off, sir."

"Duly noted," Hamilton said, shaking the NCO's

hand. "I'm more than prone to overlook that public statement and I'd like to welcome you and . . . the Lance Corporal? Aboard."

"Feeling better, sir," Condrey said. "The staff sergeant's . . . When the staff sergeant went off about the fucking lieutenant, sir, I just . . . I used to dream, at first, about somehow strangling the damned lieutenant in his sleep, sir. Other than that, just hoping the wash point is up, sir. Trixie needs a serious wash down, sir. And I'm gonna need to go ever the systems real good. She's had a hard day for her first date, sir."

"Wash point is up, Lance Corporal," Hamilton said cautiously. Decker seemed better but Condrey had simply . . . changed. He had gone from robotic to wild-eyed. "We made sure of that earlier today. Why don't you two take her over and give her a nice bath while I debrief the lieutenant."

"I thought he'd cracked, sir," Faith said. "Decker, that is. Right before we rolled. Started *raging* about how bad an officer Lieutenant Klette was, sir. Almost crying. Then he was like 'I'm up, LT. Ready to rock and roll.'"

"Happens occasionally with severe situational neurosis," Hamilton said. "There will be after effects. He was functional for the mission?"

"Perfect, sir," Faith said. "Couldn't have a better gunner. Of course, he's a staff sergeant so you'd expect him to be superb, sir. Condrey is also an excellent driver, sir."

"The effect of the system was broadly noted," Hamilton said. "General Montana sends his regards. 'A Fine, Fell Day' was the message he wished me to convey. Various 'good jobs' from others. Another letter of commendation for your file from Undersecretary Galloway."

"Thank you, sir," Faith said. "I think that the... effort of getting Trixie into operation was useful. The major issue is getting sufficient concentrations of infected to justify the power, sir. I would recommend at some point doing night sweeps, sir. Possibly without lights, using night vision gear, sir. The sound will carry farther. And if we use some of the IR flares, we can engage the infected while their vision is limited."

"We'll discuss that at the full AAR, Lieutenant," Hamilton said. "Are you up for that?"

"I'm good, sir," Faith said. "Tired. Sort of... washed out, sir. But I'm prepared to do my duty, sir. What I'd really like is a shower and a drink, sir."

"You don't drink, Lieutenant," Hamilton said.

"I know, sir," Faith said. "And times like this it really bites, sir."

"Take time for the shower, Lieutenant," Hamilton said, reaching out and plucking a tooth off the lieutenant's shoulder and flicking it into the distance. "Definitely the shower..."

CHAPTER 14

"Your daughter has showered herself with congratulations again, Captain," General Brice said. "I'll add mine."

"It was certainly . . . riveting, ma'am," Captain Smith said.

"Tanks seem to be an effective urban renewal system," Brice said. "I'd prefer cluster bombs, but there are issues. Notably, getting the infected to . . . cluster."

"That is the problem, yes, ma'am," Steve said.

"You seem muted, Captain," General Brice said. "Does that mean you don't agree?"

"About tanks as an urban renewal program, ma'am?" Steve said. "No, I don't, actually."

"The Marines just did one hell of a job of clearance, Captain," Brice said. "I was going to recommend you start focusing on getting M1s up and going despite my own background."

"I'll let them continue," Steve said. "Until Colonel Hamilton has the conditions sufficient for the task force to move on. Far be it from me to harsh Faith's vibe. But . . . have you discussed this with Commodore Montana, ma'am?"

"Just in passing," Brice said. "We didn't really discuss mission focus."

"I suppose I could let him do the math, ma'am," Steve said. "In one day a group of thirty-seven Marines in tracks were able to say 'orange' clear a five square mile area, ma'am. The total urban area of the United States, alone, is one hundred and six thousand, three hundred and eighty-six miles. That works out to twenty-one thousand, two hundred and seventy-seven days or fifty-eight years, ma'am. Assuming, of course, only one platoon of Marines. That ignores transportation issues, which are serious given the weight of M1s and the number of bridges that are destroyed or damaged. Coastal cities are accessible, clearly. But even the Mississippi is currently questionable as a route. What Faith did was . . . fun for values of fun. And certainly morale raising. However, tanks and troops in armored personnel carriers are not going to get the cities cleared in any reasonable time frame, ma'am."

"What is, then, Captain?" Brice asked formally.

"Genocide, General," Steve said, sighing. "Pure and simple genocide."

"Are you ready to be specific, yet?" Brice asked. "You've indicated for some time you have a plan."

"There is one item missing, yet, ma'am," Steve said. "Well, two. One of them is some information I suspect Colonel Ellington will have in his remarkable brain. However, if you'd like the outline . . ."

"Please," Brice said.

"It involves what I like to call Subedey bots, ma'am," Steve said.

After Steve was done with the "brief outline" in no more than a few sentences, the general just looked at him for a long time.

"That is . . ." Brice said carefully. "My career, basically, has been thinking about ways to kill nations wholesale, Captain. And even *I* find that . . . cold as shit. Have you discussed this with anyone else?"

"Only General Montana, ma'am," Steve said. "After he broke cover and on condition of silence. I'm aware that the plan would make me a bigger monster historically than Hitler. Right up there with the developer of the virus, ma'am. But it is much more efficient than driving around in a tank. However . . . morale-boosting that may be. We will drive around in tanks and APCs, eventually, ma'am. We'll . . . clear major buildings. Get around to the remaining carriers. But only after the bots do their work."

"It will still take a big force," Brice said.

"Oh, enormous, ma'am," Steve said. "At some point, we'll stand the Army back up and that will be the main driver. And it will require lots of volunteers. I can't really see conscription working in this environment. Cross that bridge when we come to it, ma'am. But it will work. With one more piece, we'll be ready to start moving. And based on growth models . . . We should be able to clear the entire U.S. to, say, orangish yellow, maybe yellow, in five years. By which time we'll be working on Europe and Asia. People are already freeing themselves in the north, ma'am, and using kinetic activity to drop the infected level even more. Drop the infected level to yellow, hell, to yellowish-orange, and people will extract themselves. And definitely drop things to yellow, at least in the U.S. Lots of guns, lots of people capable of and willing to use them. We'll do it."

"Gunny," Nick said, shaking his boot. "There's movement."

"There's always fucking movement, Nick," retired Master Gunnery Sergeant James Robinson growled, taking his hand off the 1911 under his pillow.

"To be more precise, there's music and what sounds like armor," Nick said.

Robinson reached over, fumbled out a Marlboro Red, lit it with a Zippo that had the Globe and Anchor on the side, took two puffs, rolled over, sat up in his rack and put his feet on the floor. Oh-dark-thirty and his day had begun, God damnit. Waking up seemed to get harder and harder as he got older.

Back in the old days, soldiers used to say that when they retired they were going to buy a farm. It was so common it became the regular expression for dying: bought the farm. Robinson had grown up in rural Iowa. He knew how hard farm work was. The hell if he was going to bust his ass hauling bags of seed and picking rocks after thirty years in the Corps. He knew what he was going to do when he got out. Same damned thing he did for thirty years in: Logistics.

When—to the covert relief of Marine units all over the globe—he had retired, he looked around at Army/Navy stores. Like anyone who had an ounce of sense, he knew the world was a terrible place kept less terrible by much effort. If you were in a disaster, best possible place to be was sitting on a supply depot. Civilian equivalent was an "outdoors" or "Army/Navy" store. Pay for your supply depot by overcharging wannabes for cheap-ass tiger stripe made in Bangladesh out of finest, guaranteed-to-fall-apart-on-first-washing cotton, sell "disaster supply kits" at three hundred percent mark-up to idiots who thought the sky was falling when there was a hurricane, including corporate idiots—he'd made a *packet* off of that racket—and make sure your stock of critical items never fell below five years' supply. Just like in the Corps. Fuck the line. They didn't really *need* batteries. Night vision is for pussies. Let me tell you how it was back in the Old Corps. . . .

Ammo shortage? What ammo shortage? He had an FFL, and selling guns meant having plenty of ammo on hand. He bought all over the place, really got some cool ass shit in the nineties, and practiced a very strict program of "first in, keep most of it, let a *little* out especially if it was going out of date." He still had some of that Czech armor-piercing he'd bought at auction in '97 waaaay in the back. He'd been so miserly with his ammo, BATF finally insisted, with the rousing approval of OSHA and EPA, that he spend sixty-seven thousand one hundred and forty-eight dollars and seventy-three cents on a God-damned ammo vault. A God-damned "ammo vault." Made him pay some bastard to build a magazine "to Federal specifications." God-damned liberal Federal BATF assholes. Okay, so he had more ammo than Blount Island. Okay, so he was a certified holding point for civilian demolitions and if it all went off he'd take out the whole block. It still cost sixty-seven thousand one hundred and forty-eight dollars and seventy-three God-damned cents. Pissed him off.

Worst part? No matter *how* much ammo you had, there was *never* enough for a zombie apocalypse.

Good part was, a few of his regulars weren't total asshats. So when it was clear that the worm Oroborus was turning, they'd got together and activated Zombie Plan Alpha. First, get out all the metal screening that the City of Greater Arlington in all its glory had insisted he could not install in the first place. Took one morning for that to go up. Started right after he didn't turn around the "closed" sign. You want ammo? You want supplies? You want guns? Failure to prepare was preparing to fail. Fuck off. I'm bunkering up. Then plywood on top. Why plywood? Looked like they were just getting ready for a hurricane. More or less normal in Florida. What wasn't normal was when the gunny called in a favor and a pallet of concertina turned up in the back parking lot. They waited till it was a for-real shit-storm for that. Took one afternoon to string the concertina on the top deck of the building. Fuck the zoning commission. If they didn't like it, let 'em get a city inspector over and assess a fine. And zombies weren't getting over the wire.

That's when the families came in. Through the back. Some of the group had jobs they weren't willing to just drop. Nick was a cop. He had to stay out. They knew that would mean the zombie plague might make its way in. Decision would be made later whether they were in or out.

Plague came in, anyway. Probably from Dolores Sims. She'd been a teacher and she got sick first. From the reports . . . could have been any of them, honestly. And if it was Dolores . . . She paid the price. That was when there were still "infected care centers" and they'd hit Dolores with a Taser before she could bite anyone, then evacced her.

But a lot of them got it. He'd gotten the flu. He'd gotten over the flu. He hadn't turned. Shit was like that. Before he'd gotten the flu, he'd ordered everyone to rig up. Tie up that is. If they turned, that way thinking humans were in control. He hated that about zombie movies. People got bit or infected and nobody did *nothing*. Just sat around fucking crying like that ever did the world any good. And when things at the "infected care centers" went from bad to worse . . . They did what they had to do. Then Nick turned up when things just . . . toppled. They'd gotten him in using a ladder and just locked the fuck down.

They'd been locked down ever since. And the way things were going, the ladies who'd survived seemed hell bent on restoring the population. Not a one of them wasn't pregnant.

"All right," Robinson said, pulling on his wash-worn cammies and Altec tactical boots. "Let's see what we got here."

He got on some light battle rattle and took the ladder to the top deck. Sure enough, in the distance there was the sound of music, loud, and the rattle, rumble and squeal of tracks. You could barely hear the tracks over the music. There was also the occasional rattle of musketry.

"Amtracks," the gunny said. "M1 too, sounds like. Got that extra rumble and no engine noise from the front."

They'd seen the helos. They kept a top-watch twenty-four/seven. They'd even fired off flares to try to attract their attention. So far, the fuckers had failed to so much as waggle their rotors or whatever. This was probably the same group. But they'd never seen or heard the helos moving at night.

And these guys were blacked out. Sure as hell not for tactical reasons. The sound of the tracks reduced, they were slowing down. Then Nick jumped when there was a hellish, unholy, *Boom!* from up the road. *That* caused some light. A weird orange-purple glow.

"Heh, heh," the gunny said. "That there was the main gun on the Abrams. Somebody done raided Blount Island. I guess that group that says it's out of Gitmo."

"What do we do if they're not for real?" Nick said.

There'd been a lot of discussion of the radio reports. From the beginning, the radio waves had just been crazy. With no controlling authority anywhere to tell people they couldn't broadcast, even before the Fall, anyone who could get ahold of a transmitter was broadcasting.

Just a month ago, what were alleged to be "U.S. Government" broadcasts started. There'd been other people saying they were the U.S. Government but mostly you could tell the crazy ones. These guys were more professional. One stated it was the "Voice of America in Exile," another was "Devil Dog Radio," which interspersed news and commentary with heavy metal and rap, and "Anchors Aweigh," the Navy, which was mostly easy listening. All said they were broadcasting from Guantanamo, that there was a "continuity of government" in a secure facility in the U.S. and that there were plans to clear the U.S. mainland. But they also said they were keeping the plans confidential until action was taken. "To retake our nation and our world from the threat of the infected" as the VOA in Exile put it. "To render aid and comfort to the afflicted" was how Anchors Aweigh put it, pointing out that "afflicted" no longer meant "infected." Or "Put a hurtin' on the Gawd Damn Zombies" in the words of Devil Dog.

All three occasionally had discussed the formation of "Wolf Squadron" and notable actions. When the group in the store discussed the radio reports, which was most of the time, there being not much else to discuss, they'd all agreed that shit like clearing the *Voyage Under Stars* had to be double tough. And that the fuckers who ran Wolf Squadron were some serious dudes. Or chicks, in the case of the daughters of LantFleet, Shewolf and Seawolf. They never used the actual names of the people, just their handles.

Assuming it wasn't all made up. Paranoia was a recognized survival trait in the group. Nobody was taking the reports at face value.

There'd been talk about plans for Jax. The group getting the Station up might be Wolf Squadron or might be pirates. Or it might be the Plague was the work of space aliens and they were taking over now. There were books like that . . . Could be . . .

There were two more booms, a series of hammers from Ma Deuce and . . . the tracks started moving again.

"Nick," the gunny said. "Wake up Sheila if she ain't woke up from that, then go to shelf Two-Six-Four. Section Three. Chemlights. Box Seven. Bring three. Box *Seven* mind you. And two of the up FLIRS."

"Aye, aye, Gunny," Nick said, heading below.

Nick was back before the first amtrack came around the bend. They were moving slow.

When the gunny put on the forward-looking infrared night-vision goggles, it was clear the tracks were using light. Just not *visible* light. They had IR headlights on full and even an IR spotlight set up on the track. And they were moving very slow. Not much more than a marching pace.

The gunny cracked one of the chemlights and tossed it into the street. It began to glow immediately.

Then he pushed the call button on his radio.

"Approaching Marine unit," he growled. "You up on sixteen, over?"

"Up on sixteen. That your IR chemlight, over?"

"Roger," the gunny said. He was having to talk louder and louder over the music. They must have hooked up psy-ops horns.

"Are you prepared to exit, over?"

"Will be in ten," the gunny said. "This is a Marine unit, right?"

"First Platoon, Alpha Company, USMC," the man replied. *"Task Force Kodiak, Wolf Squadron. Being the only platoon, USMC. So far. We got less people than joined at Tun Tavern. Over."*

"Fast, what's the last stanza of the Marine Corps Hymn?" the gunny asked.

"If the Army and the Navy ever look on Heaven's scene, they will find the streets are guarded by United States Marines."

"Roger. Will be up and ready to egress from the roof in five," the gunny said. "We will be bringing weapons, over."

"You got to turn them in when you get to the ship," the Marine replied. *"Got an arms room. But you're welcome to weapon up for the ride. If your people know what they're doing, they can even pot infected. If they can do it in the dark, of course. Over."*

There were zombies trotting down the street, attracted by the noise. They ran right past the IR chemlight he'd thrown. They'd normally gather round any light source, which was why he'd thrown the

IR. The approaching amtrack took them under fire with the turret Ma Deuce. Now the street was littered with bodies.

They'd never shot any zombies from the roof. First of all, one shot and they descended in hordes from the noise and to feed. Second, he wasn't going to have the place surrounded by rotting bodies.

"Nick, get everybody up and ready to egress," the gunny said, frowning.

"Aye, aye." Nick ran below again.

The gunny was torn, though. He *knew* he had to egress. That was what made sense. But God-damnit, that meant leaving all his shit behind unguarded. And if they were clearing off the fucking zombies, first place looters were going to hit was his store.

Getting the civilians out, though, was a priority. Especially the ladies who hadn't popped yet. They'd managed the two deliveries they'd had, so far, pretty well he thought. But getting them some medical attention was a priority.

So he started making a hole in the concertina. . . .

The amtracks dispersed when they reached the chemlight, three going forward and taking up positions, firing their turret guns at approaching infected. The trail two spread out leaving a gap in the middle. They weren't firing because there was a tank in the way.

Even without the FLIR, you could see the mass of zombies following the Marines under the light moon. Thousands of them. Some of them were almost up to the tank and some on the sides were trying to climb on. It seemed like the wave would be unstoppable.

Then the tank with the psy-ops bullhorns pulled

into the gap. It was driving forward but the gun was pointed to the rear. And there was something weird about the color. It looked gray under the moonlight and had some weird camo along the base. Looked almost like flames or some shit. But you could see the Globe and Anchor in various spots. It looked like they weren't even subdued. On the side of the turret was written "Trixie" which was just... wrong. There were serious regulations against naming vehicles like that.

The horns were blaring some God-damned modern shit about "fury" and "darkest hour" so loud you could hardly think. Everybody on the roof had their hands on their ears or hearing protection on. You could still hear it clear. They hadn't had to wake everybody up. The noise would wake the dead. It was a good thing they did have something over their ears, because about the time it stopped, the main gun fired.

Canister. Mother *fucker*. They had 1028.

Three shots by the main gun and some coax and cupola and... there weren't any more moving zombies.

The music cut out and switched to the Marine Corps Hymn at a much lower volume.

"Y'all ready to get out of there?" a female voice asked over the radio. The tank TC took off her helmet and shook out her hair. *"Or you want to just stay? Seems like a nice position. If you're coming out, bring all your fucking guns. Shit is hot out here. Hey, you got any Altec in woman's size twelve... ?"*

"Of all the motherfuckers to survive..." Gunny Sands muttered as the unit rolled ashore. He'd already been informed by radio that Robinson had survived. He'd say he'd wondered where the bastard had gotten to but that would mean he hadn't tried to purge the memory of Master Gunnery Sergeant "Where's your authorization requirement form for a pencil, Sergeant? What do you mean you need a pencil to fill it out . . . ?" Robinson.

"Sands," Robinson said bitterly, as soon as he was out of the amtrack. "Of all the motherfuckers to survive . . ."

"I was thinking the same thing, Jimmy," Gunny Sands said, smiling. He knew that Robinson hated to be called "Jimmy" and he was taking the opportunity while he had it.

"Who the *fuck* authorized personalization of a military vehicle?" the master gunnery sergeant fumed. "And fucking *pink*? A Marine Corps vehicle painted *pink*? That's what we've gotten to? First God-damned DADT and now we've got PINK VEHICLES?"

"Guns, you need to lock it the fuck up," Sands said. "You're not in the Old Corps. I know you'd just casually flip off second lieutenants by not saluting 'cause you're a fucking prick that way. But if you fail to salute *Lieutenant Smith*, I and every remaining surviving Marine will fucking kick your fat ass. Even if, and I say *if*, they activate you at rank. And if *we* don't, Master Guns, the LT *will*. This is the new/old Corps, Guns. If the LT fucking *offs* you, *Master Guns*, for failure to provide her and her beautiful pimped-out tank proper and due respect, not one motherfucker from the lowliest wing-wiper to the NCCC will so much as bat an eye."

"Okay," Faith said, walking over to the two glowering NCOs. "I take it you two know each other?"

"Master Gunnery Sergeant James Robinson, *retired*," Sands said, his arms crossed, "Second Lieutenant Faith Marie Smith. Master Guns Robinson, Shewolf."

"Wait," Robinson said, knife-handing at Faith. "*You're* Shewolf?"

"Got a problem with that, Master Guns?" Faith asked, her arms crossed. The refugees had gathered around the confrontation by that time.

"You're Shewolf?" one of the women said. She was holding a newborn.

"Last time I checked," Faith said, unfolding then smiling and cooing at the baby. "She's beautiful. She, right?"

"Yeah," the woman said, beaming. "I can't believe… We heard about you on Devil Dog."

"Word gets around," Faith said, grinning. "The reality's not really up to the reputation."

"Not from what *I* saw," the woman said.

"Can I hold her?" Faith asked diffidently.

"I'd love that," the woman said.

"I love your tank!" one of the kids said. "It's totally pimped! Can I get a ride?"

"No," Faith said, taking the baby carefully and cradling her. "'Cause she's armed up. When you get a little older, maybe we can get you one of your own. Hey, baby, welcome to the world…"

"Can I get a picture with you?" the woman asked.

"Master Guns," Sands said. "You want to get your people checked in? And what the f— heck is this, some sort of fag— qu— *convention*?" Sands bellowed at the gathering Marines. "If you can't find something to do I will *find* something for you to do!"

"Could I get one with you in front of Trixie?"

"Better make it quick," Faith said, holding the baby and smiling at the camera.

"Sands," Robinson said.

"Guns?"

"Can I just get a ride back to my God-damned store?" Robinson said, shaking his head as the flash-bulbs popped in the dawn light. They really brought out the flames on Trixie's sides. "I'm not sure I'm ready for your new/old Corps."

"Gotta see the colonel about that one, Master Gunnery Sergeant."

"And it looks like rain," Robinson grumped. "Figures."

"*'Got on board a westbound seven forty-seven . . .'*" Walker half hummed as he watched the track.

The problem with cruise missiles is range. At least when you're a couple of miles from the target. They're not really designed to hit something in view of the launcher. In fact you can't really hit something closer than about twenty miles away. The choice was to either take the *Michigan* well out to sea and fire from there or fire from in close where the crew could watch the arrival.

In close just made more sense. Which was why twenty BGM-109E cruise missiles had been fired more or less at Miramar airfield with programming to turn around, come back and impact on Silver Strand. Twenty more BGM-109Ds were currently violating Mexican airspace and in the process of turning north over Tijuana. Those would arrive first.

The BGM-109D had been removed from production due not so much to violation of international law as violation of what some people thought was international law or should be international law. The BGM-109D carried "dispersal munitions," more commonly called "cluster bombs." Instead of one big explosion, a "unitary" warhead, the warhead consisted of 166 bomblets, more or less big grenades, that exploded over an area of about two hundred meters by seven hundred meters. The problem being they never all exploded. Therefore a large area was left with scattered undetonated munitions. Since they were a bit finicky they could explode if you kicked them, dropped them, etc. Not only had the occasional complete idiot soldier or Marine who should have known better found this out, so had various kids from developing countries with nothing better to play with. Thus the reason they were being removed from inventory. The *Michigan* only had sixty.

They were, however, just the ticket for infected in the open.

"TV breaks and movies . . ." Montana sang as the missiles arrived.

They'd been stacked nose to nose, headed north along Silver Strand Boulevard. There were thousands of infected roaming the strand looking for the source of the lights just off-shore in the bay. Lights meant people meant food. And there was food. Plenty of them had succumbed to dehydration. Those could be spotted by the huddles of feeding infected. Then they disappeared in a welter of red-cored explosions and dust.

Montana had been close enough to cluster strikes to fill in the sound of a million firecrackers from hell. He knew the screams the strikes produced. He'd heard them over half the Middle East at one time or another. He didn't have to see the shredded bodies in the dust. The wounded, bodies torn in half or limbs flying off. Been there, seen that.

Then the "unitary" warheads arrived from the east.

Spread over half a kilometer, twenty-one thousand-pound bombs detonated with near-simultaneity. Then the concussion reached the submarine. Even from sixty feet underwater and two miles away the massive submarine rocked.

"Think that'll do 'er," the *Michigan*'s Chief of Boat muttered.

"It pours, man, it pours . . ." Montana whispered.

CHAPTER 15

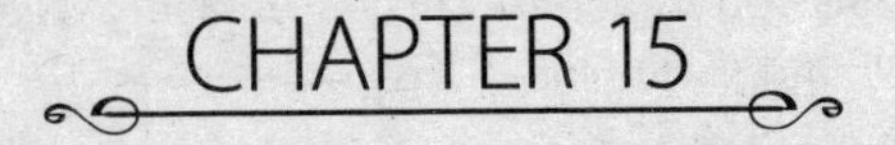

"Commander Daniel J. Wojcik, reporting aboard with a crew of sixty, sir," the commander said, saluting.

"Welcome aboard, Commander," Hamilton said. "Glad you're here."

The "crew of sixty" was unloading from the USS *Florida*, another OMFG class.

One important aspect of the OMFG class, post-Plague, was that it had additional berthing and thus could be used for moving personnel around. Two OMFGs had carried the core of PacFleet to the Pacific and now the *Florida* had brought the Base Operations group up from Gitmo to take over running Mayport.

Some of the arrivals had clearly not enjoyed the experience of speedy travel in the ocean's depths. A few were being carried out on stretchers.

But the base operations force was here. Just in time, too.

"We've got two days to do hand-off," Hamilton said. "Then payday activities for my crews, day and half off and we roll north. Official turn-over and stand-up of Mayport will be a ceremony involving turning on the exterior lights. We've refrained both there and on Blount until we had the infected in the zone reduced. Our electrician's mates say that we're ready and the security situation is getting to the point it's doable. We've got two of the barracks being cleaned and prepped for more arrivals and we've informed the refugees that they're going to be moving from the *Bo* and temporary space on Blount over to the Station. As usual, they're handling most of the cleaning. The main issue unresolved is the damaged POL point which is on your plate. Questions?"

"No, sir," Wojcik said. "We've got plans in place to begin rebuilding of the POL point. The *Eric Shivak* is a day behind us with POL resupply and we should be good until we can get it up and going. Two days should be about right."

"Then as fast as your people can get recovered from their voyage, they need to link up and start turn-over," Hamilton said.

"We're ready when your people are, sir," Wojcik said. "Well . . . most of them are. The rest it's going to take a few hours for the tranquilizers to wear off. Some people, sir, are ill-suited to the sub service . . ."

"King's Bay, Georgia," Colonel Hamilton said, pointing to the overhead.

Hand-over was complete. They were waiting for that evening to turn the lights on at both bases. The last ground sweep had been completed and now it was time to talk about the next mission.

"Home of every boomer in the Atlantic," the colonel continued. "And quite a few of the fast attacks. Which in strategic terms means . . . Gunny?"

"Big stash of special weapons, sir," Gunnery Sergeant Sands said.

"Master Guns" had found his niche. He'd remained

"retired" and had settled into an office on Blount Island like he was born there. They were never going to be able to get another round out of the place. They'd have to scrounge for pens and pencils for the rest of the war.

"Special weapons storage facility is here," Hamilton said, pointing to the magazines. "No infected have been detected inside the facility. Indications are the roving guards all succumbed, were eaten or died of starvation and thirst, unable to break out. Lots of infected on the outside, fortunately. I say 'fortunately' because there are other groups starting to move around. And whatever your beliefs in the Second Amendment, nuclear weapons are not something we want getting loose."

"Oh, God, no," Faith said. "And I say that as a born, bred and trained gun-hugger, sir."

"So the first and overriding priority is to secure the special weapons," Hamilton said. "The second priority is destruction of all heavy weaponry in the other magazines with the exception of some that we will extract for later use. By direction, LantFleet, with concurrence JCS and NCCC, small arms magazines will be left intact except for what we extract for our own use."

"LantFleet wants any survivors to have access, sir?" Gunnery Sergeant Sands asked.

"That is the Atlantic Fleet commander's intent," Hamilton said. "When I asked the same question, not particularly surprised, he pointed out that they would most likely be accessed by American tax-payers who had paid for it in the first place and have an obvious need. On a purely legal basis, it's the Federal

Government arming the militia. On the other hand, the militia does not necessarily need to be playing around with W-88s, Tomahawks and ADCAPs."

"Sir?" Faith said.

"Nukes, cruise missiles and torpedoes, ma'am," Gunny Sands said.

"Thank you," Faith said.

Hamilton paused for a moment and looked around the room.

"The submariners are, obviously, critical to all ongoing operations. And they, like many of the rest of us, are wondering and worrying about whether their dependents survived. In addition, the boomers had a dual crew system so half the crews were ashore when the Plague broke out.

"Most recent satellite sweep has detected multiple survivor groups. Looks like every building that had stash has survivors. A couple of homes have been spotted as having probable survivors. Therefore, due to both morale and personnel value issues, over and above *any* other base, including Marine bases, Marines will perform *intensive* search and rescue sweeps of the base housing areas as well as nearby town areas. To give you an impression of what I mean by 'intense,' we have allotted seven days of SAR and clearance of an area that is a fraction of the size of Jax. By contrast, I've been reliably informed, we'll have only *two* days on Lejeune."

"Son of a bitch," Gunny Sands said bitterly.

"Are we taking Trixie, sir?" Faith asked.

"On reflection, yes," Hamilton said. "It was discussed and we came to the conclusion the value was obvious."

"Then there are two ways of looking at this, Gunny," Faith said. "One way is Da doesn't care about the

Marines so he's leaving them and their dependents to die. Care to think about that for a second, Gunny?"

"I know your father cares about the Corps, ma'am . . ." Gunny Sands said.

"The other way to think about it is this:" Faith said. "With submariners, you're obviously going to have to drive up to their house. They like to hide. They're shy. And they scare easy. We'll probably have to coax them out with treats. We'll need to lay in some pogie bait. Drive Trixie around the Lejeune area for two days straight, drop some caches behind as we go and the Marines will rise up in an *unstoppable tide,* Gunny. We ain't takin' two weeks on Lejeune 'cause Da figures we ain't gotta. Just leave 'em a note the assembly area is Jax. Marines'll canoe down."

"That is a point, ma'am," Gunny Sands said.

"And my first op-order on Lejeune, Gunny," Faith said, "I've already written the opening line: 'We're rollin' hot to the gunny's for some cold-beer.' Oorah?"

"Oorah, ma'am," the gunnery sergeant said. "Semper Fi. Power's been out. Beer might not be cold. And knowing my wife, probably ain't but the one can left."

"Well, then, Gunny," Faith said. "That can will be waiting for you. Discussion closed. Sir?"

"We are taking one Seahawk," Hamilton said. "We've reconfigured so it can operate solely off of the *Boadicea.* No more perching like a . . . Seahawk on its nest."

"Hoowah or oorah or whatever you're supposed to say in the Navy," Sophia said. "On behalf of the mechanics who had to work on the bird up there, thank you, sir."

"I think it's hooyah or ooyah or something," Captain Wilkes said.

"I think that's just SEALs, sir," Gunny Sands said.

"And on the *subject* of Navy," Hamilton said, cutting off the discussion. "Captain Wilkes?"

"Sir?" Wilkes said cautiously.

"Congratulations are in order," Hamilton said. "And possibly condolences. You just made Lieutenant Commander."

"Agh," Wilkes said, clutching his chest. "What's that psychological term, Colonel?"

"Conflicted?" Hamilton said.

"That's the one, sir," Wilkes said. "I thought that might be coming, but . . ."

"Marines are, for the time being, pure amphibious and boarding combat arms," Hamilton said. "The current split, and I'm told it may change back and may not, is Navy handles *all* support including *all* aviation. Which means our mechanics will be Navy, our cooks will be Navy, our clerks will be Navy, our *armorers* will be Navy and most notably our *pilots* will be Navy. For the immediate future, if you were pre-Plague Marine, you are driving something with a primary gun system, holding a weapon or commanding same. Period. In the event that we recover aviators from Cherry Point or New River . . . They just became either Navy flyers, if rotary, carrying a rifle, commanding a company of armor, et cetera, if fixed. Possibly aviators if we have more fixed wing needs or possibly cross-trained to rotary. In which case they'll also be transferring services."

"Pretty much how it went when the Marines first started out, sir," Gunny Sands said. "I'm not even sure when we started having things like our own cooks and mechanics, sir."

"When we started having expeditionary forces,

Gunny," Hamilton said. "It was Nicaragua and the World Wars that forced us to change and grow into an independent service. Which was the point that Captain Smith made. We're not currently mounting those nor does he intend to do so in any conceivable time-frame. All 'inland' operations will be Army when it is reactivated. Marines are hereby entirely littoral and thus can draw upon the Navy for support personnel. We're not even bivouacking ashore in case you haven't noticed. When we have enough Marines for a company, we'll probably have a Marine company clerk. Unit armorer will probably be Navy. Anyway, congratulations on your promotion, Lieutenant Commander. Well deserved. And once a Marine, always a Marine."

"Yes, sir," Wilkes said.

"One aspect of this general 'support' subject that has always held true is the assignment of corpsmen to the Marines from the Navy," Hamilton said. "We're hoping that the same rubbed off esprit de corps that corpsmen have will work for the rest of the rates. However, again as people may have noticed, we have yet to have a corpsman actually assigned to the ground unit. That is because they are all assigned to other duties, notably the baby-boom we're currently experiencing. I discussed this with higher and we have been assigned a corpsman."

"Hallelujah," Faith said. "About damned time."

"Volunteers were solicited and several of the former sub corpsmen have volunteered," Hamilton said. "Gunnery Sergeant Sands, I'm putting you in charge of selection. I'd recommend running them through a PT and marching test, then interview. Anything else they'll have to pick up OJT. Oh, and a range qualification. Zombies really have no regard for the Geneva

Convention and thus the corpsmen will be armed. It's a pity, but that's life."

"Yes, sir," Gunny Sands said. "When?"

"Tomorrow," Hamilton said. "We're on short time."

"Yes, sir," Sands said.

"And that is the outline," Hamilton said. "Now to wrestle the devil . . ."

"Moment of your time, sir?" Faith said as the meeting broke up.

"Of course, Lieutenant," Hamilton said, gesturing with his chin.

The gunny took the hint and left. Officer talk.

"It's not a big deal, sir," Faith said. "It's about Trixie, sir."

"Tiring of your toy, Lieutenant?" Hamilton said wryly.

"Not a bit, sir," Faith said, grinning. "And I love every bit of it. I think, given that there's no threat from enemies with anti-tank systems that we're fighting, pink is an awesome color and it was, absolutely, the best birthday present ever, sir."

"That being said?" Hamilton said curiously.

"She needs to be a regular color, sir," Faith said. "Some people were great with it but it causes a lot of consternation, sir. When it was just the greatest birthday present, ever, and, yes, a toy, sir, that was one thing. But we're using it as a vehicle of war, sir. I don't go fighting zombies in a mini-skirt, sir. Trixie needs to be in uniform if she's going to war, sir."

"Concur, Lieutenant," Hamilton said. "We'll have to do the paint-job on the float. And we're not going to be floating long. Get with the gunny and Staff Sergeant Decker on the particulars."

"Aye, aye, sir," Faith said, then grinned. "She's going to miss the paint-job, sir. But Trixie's really excited about going to war, sir."

"Glad to hear that, Lieutenant," Hamilton said delicately, then sat down. "However, I have to ask... Did Trixie *tell* you that, Lieutenant?"

"Sir," Faith said, shaking her head and grinning. "I know that you're a great psychologist. And crawling into the head of an Islamic terrorist was probably worse than crawling through rotting bodies in the bowels of the *Voyage*, sir. But I can guaran-damn-tee you, the one head you *don't* want to troll through is mine, sir."

"Who decided a swamp was a good place for a Navy base?" Faith asked.

King's Bay was, unquestionably, a swamp. It was surrounded by swamp. It looked like a swamp. And it was slowly turning back into swamp.

The waterside portions of the base were nothing much to look at. There were a few "covered" submarine pens, more or less hangars built on the water. They were already falling apart due to lack of maintenance.

The one thing going for the base was it didn't look like much had burned. And several of the buildings had survivors on them, checking out the flotilla.

The civilian ships had been led in by the *Alexandria*, so the people on the base could have some reasonable expectation that the people in uniform on civilian ships were, in fact, Navy and not pirates come to steal their lucky charms. Or nuclear weapons as the case might be. The *Alex* had previously taken a run up to the base to check out the channel—it was clear enough for the *Grace*, and signal to the survivors that, yes, there was help coming. They'd also gotten a list of known survivors. For good or ill, the base commander, a vice admiral who also commanded most of the boats in the Atlantic, had succumbed to H7D3.

Ill because any loss was a tragedy. Good because the one thing they didn't need any time soon was a split in the chain of command. The first admiral or general they ran across was probably going to throw a shit fit about "Captain Wolf." Undersecretary Galloway was the NCCC and that was a trump card. Didn't mean someone who had the "advice and consent of the Senate" in their appointment to stars was going to just salute and say "Yes, sir" to a jumped-up civilian "playing" at being LantFleet. General Montana had been an aberration in that regard as in every other human trait.

"I'm wondering who's going to file the environmental impact statement," Sophia said, pointing to the docks.

The *Nebraska* had been alongside when the Plague hit. It had suffered some sort of catastrophic malady, listed hard over and basically sunk. Barely ten percent of it was above water level.

"Just what we need," Faith said. "Two-headed alligators."

"Ensign Smith to the ready room . . ."

"Here we go again," Sophia said.

"Try to keep it in the air, Sis," Faith said.

"I'd say 'stay out of trouble' but there's no real point, is there?"

"Lieutenant Smith to the armory. Lieutenant Smith to the armory . . ."

"Probably not," Faith said, grinning.

"Think we got enough guns this time, sir?" Sophia asked as she spun the barrels on the minigun mounted on the weapons sponsons. It *was* part of her preflight, after all.

Besides the dual miniguns mounted on each sponson, each of the two door gunners had the same system for a total of six of the insanely powerful weapons. And at the insistence of the various personnel involved, the ammo supplies for all guns were five times those normally lofted by helos. The bird was basically a flying ammo dump of 7.62 NATO.

"Aren't you the one that insists there's no such thing as overkill?" Wilkes asked as he climbed into his seat.

"I think you're mistaking me for my sister, sir," Sophia said. "Bit taller? Wears an ugly camouflage uniform, not a really cool flight suit, sir?"

"Just twitting you, Seawolf," Wilkes said.

"We used to get mistaken for twins when we were younger," Sophia said. "Now everybody thinks she's the older one. It gets old."

"Understood," Wilkes said. "Port, starboard, you up?"

"Intercom set and checked, Port," Olga replied.

"Set and checked Starboard," Anna said.

"They ever switch me out for Lieutenant Simpson and there's no stopping this crew," Wilkes said.

"Feel the estrogen, sir," Sophia replied. "*Be* the estrogen, sir."

"Your cycles start syncing and I'm putting in for a transfer," Wilkes said, as he started the engines. "You all have guns..."

The helo coasted low over the ground, followed by infected.

"Watch your forward speed," Wilkes said. "This loaded, we don't have a lot of power or ground clearance to spare."

"Aye, aye, sir," Sophia said, speeding up.

"Permission to engage, commander?" Olga said. "I've got some nice concentrations."

"They'll stop and feed, port," Wilkes said. "We want them in the killbox first."

The "killbox" was designated as a large open area by the port. It was in firing range of the amtracks that were preparing to plop off the back of the *Grace Tan* and was nicely away from anything they were interested in.

"Those are interesting," Sophia said, pointing to two ships alongside the pier. They were platform supply ships with their back decks covered in containers. "Are those sub tenders?"

"No," Wilkes said. "I'm not sure what they are."

"We can use them," Sophia said. "Especially if that's military cargo."

"Save it for later," Wilkes said. "Port, starboard. What's the concentration looking like?"

"Most of the infected close to the port seem to be swarming, command," Olga said. "Getting to the killbox."

The helo couldn't continuously hover over the infected and slowly lead them as the Marines did. It was having to pull in, lead them for a while in a certain direction, then pull up and around. It was tedious. On the other hand, the Marines weren't off the ship, yet.

"There they go," Sophia said as the first amtrack, commanded by her sister, plopped off the *Grace Tan* and, unfortunately, didn't sink. One of these days . . . "Bet she's pissed she has to wait to use Trixie."

"At least the colonel finally ordered it painted a decent color," Wilkes said.

The tank was now back to its original desert sand. On the other hand, it still had TRIXIE written on both sides of the turret. On the front glacis and the track shields was MARINES with a globe and anchor to either side. The deck of the *Grace Tan* had been reinforced to hold it and the crane significantly upgraded. The tank, alone, had cut the *Grace Tan's* cargo capacity and was one of the reasons the helo had been moved semi-permanently to the *Boadicea*.

"I think we've got enough in the killbox," Wilkes said. "Ground Team, Air. We're preparing for our first run."

"Roger," Faith said. *"We'll be there as soon as Freeman gets his act together."*

"Air, out," Wilkes said. "So . . . let's see how these work . . ."

"Oh, that's sweet," Faith said as the Seahawk dove. The four GAU 17/A miniguns slung on the weapons sponsons put out individual streams of two thousand rounds of 7.62x51 per minute. Olga and Anna had slewed them full forward. Every fifth round was a tracer. With the MG240, the tracers were clearly separated even at highest rate of fire. With the miniguns, they were one continuous stream that looked like a red laser.

When they hit the ground they bounced, and created a small volcano the color of blood.

Since most of them *weren't* hitting the ground, they were hitting infected, this time much of it *was* blood.

"Let's join the party," Faith radioed. "Open fire, forty millimeter."

The 40mm grenades pumped out of the tracks and soared, slowly, over to the mass of infected a hundred meters on shore. If they were having any effect, it wasn't apparent. The helicopter, on the other hand, was devastating.

"Okay, so it's cool," Faith muttered. "Trixie's totally cooler..."

"Do this very slowly, Lance Corporal," Faith said from the TC's hatch of Trixie.

With the inner port zone cleared of infected and the survivors picked up by the amtracks, the *Grace Tan* had been pushed in by tugs to butt stern-first to the wharf. Then a large ramp, borrowed from one of the MPF ships, had been lifted into place. Now all they had to do was drive Trixie off the ship and onto the land.

Trixie was a significant percentage of the cargo weight of the *Grace Tan*. And although her cargo deck had been reinforced, it wasn't really designed to support seventy-three tons of tank. Last, when Trixie moved, she was going to throw the balance of the ship off. She was midships, so it shouldn't list. But it was going to go down by the stern. How much had been an interesting and still theoretical calculation. Which was why only Faith and the lance corporal were in the tank and both were wearing just their uniforms and PFDs. If the tank went in the drink, they'd have some chance of survival. Not much, given sharks and gators, but some.

Condrey rolled forward slowly. As he did, Faith could see the stern of the ship start to settle.

"We're gonna need a bigger boat," Captain Gilbert radioed. *"She's pretty darn heavy."*

"Should we stop?" Faith radioed back. "And she's not fat, just big boned."

"Got it," Gilbert replied. *"She'll take 'er. Just take it slow."*

"Roger," Faith said.

The ramp wasn't all that wide and Faith was taking it on . . . faith that it was really rated for a tank. It didn't look rated for a tank. Occasionally in Jax, Trixie had almost got stuck when portions of the road crumbled under her from sewer collapse. Then there was the time Condrey "accidentally" ran into a bank and cracked the vault. At this point, Faith had a very firm appreciation for Trixie's mass.

Finally, they were up on shore. On a, fortunately, very solid wharf.

"We definitely need a better way to do this," Faith said.

"Landing craft, ma'am," Condrey replied.

"I'm sure we'll get them eventually," Faith said. "Now to get the rest of the crew and our battle rattle. And show my sister who's boss . . ."

CHAPTER 16

"You do not have the clearance to enter this facility, ma'am," the staff sergeant said, staring at Faith over a pointed and locked M4. Actually, he was staring past her into the distance with "thousand mile eyes."

They'd found Marine survivors. Five members of the FAST unit securing the special weapons site had managed to hold out in the main guard shack at the entrance. They were currently spread out trying to cover a platoon of Marines in armor with M4s. They did not care if Faith was a Marine lieutenant. She did not have clearance to enter the facility.

"My clearance comes from the National Constitutional Continuity Coordinator, Staff Sergeant," Faith said. If she was nonplussed by having a weapon pointed at her, she wasn't showing it. Of course, if the Marine pulled the trigger, he and his companions had the survival time of a paramecium in a jar of acid. The Marines didn't seem to care. Semper Fi. There was a reason that Marines secured Navy special weapons.

"The mission of my platoon is to secure special weapons and destroy the heavy weapons on this base. What are your special procedures in the event of complete breakdown in communication with chain of command, Marine?"

"Those procedures are classified, ma'am," the staff sergeant said. "You do not have clearance for those procedures, ma'am."

"Stand by," Faith said. He had a point. She didn't even have an ID card. She'd thought about pointing out her authority was a tank and declined. She could tell a Decker when she saw one. "Force Ops, Ground Team One."

"Ground Team, Force Ops."

"Surviving FAST on site. Refusing entrance to facility. States do not have authority to know special security procedures in the event of breakdown in chain of control of special weapons. I think we need the Hole on this one, over."

"Roger, Ground Team. Stand by."

"We're getting higher in on this, Staff Sergeant," Faith said. "I'm going to ask you to take a deep breath. I'm not taking another step forward. But your weapon is armed, your safety is off and your finger is on the trigger. If you so much as breathe wrong, you're going to be turned into paste by my platoon, right or wrong. So would you like me to step back or what?"

"Step back five paces, ma'am," the staff sergeant said.

"My tank is three paces behind me," Faith said. "Would you prefer I back it up as well?"

"Step back five paces, ma'am," the staff sergeant repeated.

"Condrey, back Trixie up so I can step back five paces."

"Aye, aye, ma'am."

She could hear the chopper approaching. She didn't need that.

"Air Team, Ground, over," Faith radioed.

"Air," Sophia said.

"Recommend avoid special weapons site air space," Faith said. "Surviving very twitchy guards. Little tense at the moment. Would prefer you keep your distance, over."

"Roger," Sophia said. *"We'll circle outboard and keep your back covered for infected."*

"Thanks," Faith said. "Ground, out."

When Trixie had backed up, she took five steps backward.

As soon as she backed up, all five FAST members went to tactical carry while keeping an eye on the entire unit.

"Ground Force, Force Ops."

"Ground," Faith said.

"Stand by for transmission from higher."

"Roger."

"Shewolf, Colonel Ellington."

Ellington had recently been promoted to full colonel and was the acting commandant. He was also a former nuclear weapons maintenance officer at King's Bay.

"Yes, sir!" Faith said.

"I'm going to have to negotiate this directly with the guards," Ellington said. *"Give them your helmet."*

"Aye, aye, sir," Faith said, unbuckling it. "Anything before I take it off, sir?"

"Just let me handle it," Ellington said.

"Aye, aye, sir," Faith said. "Staff Sergeant!"

"Ma'am," the staff sergeant said, still not looking directly at her. His wide-opened eyes were for detecting any hostile movement on the part of her force.

"Acting commandant on the horn," Faith said, holding up the helmet. "How do you want me to do this?"

"Take five steps forward, ma'am!" the staff sergeant barked. "Place the helmet on the ground. Return to your position. If you please. Ma'am!"

"Right you are," Faith said, stepping up and placing the helmet on the ground. Then she backed up.

"Kay," the staff sergeant said. "Retrieve the device."

One of the other guards stepped forward warily and retrieved the helmet, then handed it to the staff sergeant at a gesture. The staff sergeant waited until he was back in position, then unbuckled his own helmet and donned Faith's. It didn't fit very well but he could hear. He nodded for a moment then said: "Stand by, sir."

"Remain on post," the staff sergeant said, then returned to the guard shack.

He was in there about three minutes, then came back out buckling on his own helmet.

"Stand down," he said, then walked over to Faith. "Your helmet, ma'am."

"Thank you, Staff Sergeant," Faith said warily, then put it on. "Anyone up?"

"I have cleared you and your group for entry," Colonel Ellington replied. *"What you have to say right now is: 'I relieve you, Staff Sergeant.' Got it?"*

"Aye, aye, sir," Faith said. "I relieve you, Staff Sergeant."

"I stand relieved, ma'am," the staff sergeant said.

"What's next, sir?" Faith asked.

"The guards will assist your personnel in removal of the weapons. Let the gunnery sergeant handle that. He has the background. Listen and learn but do not get in the way. Sergeant's job, anyway. What you are going to have to do is inspect each weapon,

personally, and verify the serial number. Then sign for it."

"Oh, joy," Faith said. "I'm about to legally own enough firepower to level the Earth." She keyed her radio. "Inspect each weapon for serial number, aye. Verify serial number, aye. Sign for each weapon, aye."

"Has to be a commissioned officer, Faith," Ellington said. *"You'll later sign over the inventory to Colonel Hamilton. Then we'll figure out whether to keep them or dispose."*

"Roger, sir," Faith said.

"Questions?"

"Negative."

"Good job on handling this, Lieutenant," Ellington said. *"I'm glad you didn't shoot first and ask questions later."*

"These are about to become my Marines, sir," Faith said, looking at the staff sergeant. "And we need every Marine we can get. I'll just have to get them dialed in on boarding and clearance, sir."

"Roger that," Ellington said. *"SAC, out."*

"Gunnery Sergeant!" Faith bellowed.

"Ma'am," Gunny Sands said a moment later. He'd been in the trailing track.

"These Marines are to assist in the removal of all weapons, nuclear equipment, encryption gear, codes, data, materials, paperwork, doodles and anything else that can give anyone the vaguest indication of how the United States manages, maintains, stores or uses nuclear weapons. Is that clear?"

"Clear, ma'am," Sands said.

"You and I will verify each serial number against the inventory," Faith said. "I will *sign* for each weapon but I am damned well going to have a cross-check. Clear?"

"Clear, ma'am."

Faith looked at her watch and set the timer.

"You have five hours, Gunnery Sergeant."

"Oh, no," Faith said breathily. She flipped the pages back and forth several times, counting under her breath. "Gunnery Sergeant..."

"Seem to be missing ten warheads, ma'am," Gunny Sands said.

Januscheitis and the new staff sergeant, FAST Team NCOIC Dave Darnall, were overseeing the process of removing every scrap of support material. There was a lot of it and it was going slow. Which was sort of good since they were definitely missing some warheads and were not going to make the deadline unless they found them.

"Jan, Shewolf," Faith radioed.

"Jan," Januscheitis replied.

"Ask Darnall if he has any clue where ten warheads went," Faith said. "'Cause they ain't here. Or something."

"Freeze," Gunny Sands radioed. "Ma'am. The easiest way for ten warheads to go missing is if the guards were the ones that removed them."

"Jan, countermand," Faith said. "You there?"

"Roger," Januscheitis said.

"Orders from higher. FAST team is to disarm. Draw down, then tell them that's an order. Then ask them where the hell enough firepower to level a couple of cities went. Stand by on that."

"Roger. Standing by."

"Issues?" Darnall said.

"Fricking lieutenants," Januscheitis said, shaking his head. "Especially split lieutenants. I think it's her time of the month."

"Can you draw down on them successfully?"

"Roger," Januscheitis said.

"Do it."

"TARGET!" Januscheitis shouted, lifting his M4 and pointing at Darnall. "STAND DOWN, FAST, STAND DOWN!"

"Son of a bitch!" Darnall said, raising his hands. "You fucking traitors."

"Where are the other ten warheads, Darnall?" Januscheitis said. "There are ten missing. And the only people who had access were you and your men."

"We did not remove any warheads," Darnall said angrily. "Fucking jackers."

"We're not jackers," Januscheitis said. "But it looks like you're thieves. Who'd you sell them to?"

"Sell them?" Darnall said. "We've been stuck in that fucking guard shack for months, you dipshit! Who the fuck would we have sold them to?"

"We'll figure this out back at the maintenance shed," Januscheitis said. "This is an order. Place your weapons on the ground and kick them away. You may think we're jackers. But the paperwork says you're thieves. And we're going to find out where the fucking weapons went. Every guy here has had a master's level class at killing over the last few months. You may be tough, but you are not going to survive."

"Neither are you," Darnall said hotly.

"My life is my country's," Januscheitis said.

"So is mine," Darnall said, his hand on his weapon.

"Jan."

"Go," Januscheitis said, without taking his eyes off the other staff sergeant.

"Status?"

"Mexican stand-off they're going to lose," Januscheitis said. "They claim they didn't take them."

"Which means we have a paperwork problem," Faith said. *"Tell them they are to stand down. That is an order."*

"They think we're jackers," Januscheitis said.

"Christ," Faith said. *"Tell them to keep their weapons and wait. Do not get into a firefight."*

The tableau was being held outside. Faith took a walk.

There was a rumble and a squeal of treads. Then Trixie came into sight.

Faith directed the tank over to the tableau and had Decker point the main gun right at the FAST staff sergeant.

"Just so we understand the situation," Faith said, walking over with the clipboard in her hand. She held it up and started pointing. "Missing weapon. Missing weapon. Missing weapon. Now, Staff Sergeant, I may be a kid, and a girl, and look like fucking Barbie. But I am A COMMISSIONED OFFICER OF THE UNITED STATES MARINE CORPS. And when I am given a mission, I fucking PERFORM IT. Oorah? I have PROVEN I will sacrifice myself, I will sacrifice my Marines, to perform that mission! Oorah? And I will happily kill ANYONE or ANYTHING that gets in the way of performing my mission! Oorah? My mission is to find every fucking nuke, then let someone else figure out what to do with them. Oorah? Because we can't HOLD THIS BASE! Oorah? That should be fucking OBVIOUS! WE ARE NOT STEALING THE NUKES! We're MOVING them! Someplace we can keep an *eye* on 'em! Someplace NOT HERE! And I'm missing ten, *TEN* NUCLEAR FUCKING WEAPONS. So, Staff Sergeant, WHERE THE FUCK *ARE* THEY?"

"No weapons! Have been removed! From this site! Since I went on duty NINE MONTHS AGO, *MA'AM*!" Darnall bellowed. "We sure as HELL didn't take them, ma'am! And we didn't fucking steal them!"

"Jesus Christ!" Faith shouted, throwing the clipboard on the ground. "This is an order, Staff Sergeant. *Stand down.* Stand down," Faith said, walking up and putting her face right into his. "Stand down *right now*. That is a direct order. Or this is your last day as a Marine alive or dead. You will stand down or never ever be a Marine again."

"Aye, aye, ma'am," Darnall said, his jaw working. But he unclipped his weapon and set it on the ground.

"*Everybody* stand down," Faith said waving her hand. "Weapons down. Weapons down! FAST. Pick *up* your weapons. If you were willing to stand down you're not thieves. My personal and professional apologies for doubting you. But we gotta get this unfucked. Where could they have gone?"

"We'd have to go back over every piece of paper on them, ma'am," Darnall said, cautiously picking up his M4. "And we just packed that all up."

"Mother*fucker*," Faith said. "I *hate* fucking paperwork. Close the gates, transport the truck drivers back to the port on the amtracks. We're going to be here after dark. Gunny!"

"Ma'am," Sands said.

"Get with the *Grace* on getting us some MREs or something," Faith said. "We're about to pull an all nighter. I'm going to call the Hole and see if the acting commandant has any suggestions . . ."

"Son of a bitch . . ." Darnall muttered. "I completely forgot about that."

"Forgot what?" Faith said fuzzily. It was three AM and they'd been poring over paperwork looking for the missing nukes for hours.

"There was a transfer," Darnall said. "Post-Plague announcement. They were transported to Canaveral for loading."

He handed her the receipt he was reading.

"*Cape* Canaveral?" Faith said. "What?"

"The actual missiles are loaded at Canaveral, ma'am," Gunny Sands said, taking the receipts and examining them. "They have the facilities to attach the nukes to the missiles. And those are the missing serial numbers."

"It should have been logged with us, Lieutenant," Ellington said.

"Can you see what I'm looking at, sir?" Faith said, holding the paperwork up to the camera.

"Roger, Lieutenant," Ellington said. *"If you hold it back a bit I can see it better. But hold the signature block right up to the camera . . . That's the right signature. I know the officer. We don't have the transfer logged. Wait one . . . Son of a . . . We have the receipt for the aircraft used to transport nuclear weapons*

and . . . the manifest that they were transferred. And they were logged in at Canaveral. It's valid. We just didn't get the data from King's Bay."

"So we know where they're at?" Faith asked.

"Presumably," Ellington said. *"Until someone puts their hands on them I'll only say that. They shouldn't have been transferred at all with things they way they were going. But . . . water under the dam. They're probably in the temporary magazines in Canaveral. Hopefully in the magazines in Canaveral."*

"Does that mean we have to clear *Canaveral*?" Faith asked.

"Looks that way, Lieutenant," Ellington said. *"Lieutenant, this is an order. Get some sleep. You're punch drunk. We'll deal with this later. Your devotion to duty is well understood but this is not going to get solved tonight."*

"Roger," Faith said. "Just need to check in with the colonel and make sure the guards are posted, sir."

"Then get some sleep," Ellington said. *"SAC is out."*

"I'm not even going to ask if this happens often," Steve said during the conference call the next morning. "I really don't want to know."

"The transfer was well into the down spiral of the Fall," Brice said, looking at the copies of paperwork they'd received. "Looks to me like there's an order somewhere, we don't have it, to go to 'max load' on every boomer in the event we, well, had to nuke cities. And this sort of thing, bad inventory, was *why* SAC was stood back up. Really shouldn't have been done at all. Not my call at the time. The miracle is that the bird seems to have arrived. One reason not to have done it was I'd be surprised if the pilots were vaccinated. I'd have anticipated losing the bird."

"We need someone to put their hands on those weapons," Undersecretary Galloway said. "Which means clearing Canaveral."

"I've slated seven days of clearance on King's Bay," Steve said. "There are valid reasons for that. Do I order them to proceed immediately, continue clearing King's Bay, then Canaveral, or complete some or all of their planned missions then hit Canaveral on the way back? I'll note the obvious that this is not the only such facility on the east coast alone."

"We're going to be a while getting to the ones out here," Commodore Montana said. "The good news being that it's because you wouldn't *believe* how many God-damned infected there are on the West Coast. And if *we* can't access them, nobody else can."

"Going slow I take it, sir," Steve said.

"We've got North Island," Montana said. "But every other base, town and city is just as chock full. And I'd rather not shoot the full load on the *Michigan*. Cruise missiles are somewhat hard to build in the current climate."

"Can you do a Mediterranean at any of the ports in Diego?" Steve asked.

"Possibly," Montana said.

"Mediterranean?" Brice said.

"Pulling in to the dock aft-in, ma'am," Steve said. "If you can get a big ship alongside Mediterranean . . . We have *Blount*, Commodore. We can send you . . . *Anything* you need. Ammo, tracks, guns . . . Do a Med, then roll out an M1. Of course, most of it needs work but we can send crews along to work on it on the way. And the ships are capable of going around the Horn. Especially since it's still summer down there."

"I graciously accept," Montana said. "Some Abrams is what this calls for."

"You're going to owe me some M1028," Steve said. "I'll have them start prepping the ship right away. May be a couple of weeks before we can even get it going."

"Works," Montana said. "And thanks, Steve."

"Thanks for saving both my daughters' asses in London," Steve said.

"Back on the subject of the *missing nuclear weapons*," General Brice said.

"They're in Canaveral, Shelley," Montana said. "Ninety-nine to nine nines percent chance. Assuming that Canaveral has the same security issues the rest of the world seems to have. And if they're not . . . They're gone. They could be in some building to be installed, or some kid playing Zombie Apocalypse The Rising could have found them and gone 'cool.' Which is not a huge issue. The combination of someone who can override a Positive Action Lock and is crazy enough to do so was *likely* in the pre-Fall world. You could find that person if you had enough money. Losing a nuclear weapon was devastating. Literally. In this one . . . Highly unlikely."

"So we should just consider them lost?" Undersecretary Galloway asked.

"General Brice is your primary advisor on all things military, sir," Montana said. "She is the acting CJCS and also a specialist at this field, which I am not. But my nonprofessional opinion is to not lose sleep over it. We had no firm knowledge of the situation with the nukes at King's Bay until yesterday. They were *all* in this condition. This changes little if anything about the overall security situation. Especially given the difficulty of bypassing a PAL. What to do about it, to divert the Force now, or later, or not at all, should be a recommendation from General Brice, sir.

"My only counsel is psychological. This would be something to definitely freak out about pre-Plague. These days, it falls into a minor peccadillo. The conversation the captain and I just had was more useful to the needs of the nation than where ten nuclear weapons happen to be. That may seem absurd, but it is not, sir. They affect nothing. They are expensive toys that are useless to our needs and are going to have to be disposed of soon enough since we're not going to be refurbishing them any time soon."

"Captain, do you wish to input, since this is your Command?" Brice asked.

"Yes, General," Steve said, looking at the view of Canaveral. "I'm going to request to split the difference and add a mission."

"Go on," Brice said.

"There were a number of defined and potential missions on this sweep," Steve said. "The defined were thoroughly clear King's Bay, and recover what nuclear weapons were on hand. Note, *on hand*. Clear and perform SAR on Parris Island and Lejeune and perform SAR on the Hampton Roads region. If possible, remove any special weapons from Hampton Roads.

"Could we cut out one of the LHDs? We need a better platform than the *Grace Tan*. Can we get some landing craft? Well, that depends on what we get elsewhere, as usual. How many Marines are we going to get at Lejeune? What shape are they in?

Can we turn them into a cohesive fighting force in any short time frame?

"We're starting to get some reasonable statistics on survival at this point," Steve said. "Horrible statistics, but reasonable for planning. Active duty military and dependents seem to have one of the highest survival rates if they were on bases. Not *high*, mind you. Just higher than normal, ranging from five to possibly in some cases as high as ten percent. We are used to a trickle of survivors in the areas we've cleared. Even in London they're looking at one percent or less. In the Mayport area we're looking at possibly five percent of the base personnel and dependents surviving. Which isn't a lot but if you've been out here finding God-damned *nobody*, it's a bloody miracle.

"If it runs the same in and around Lejeune, say, we're looking at *ten thousand* survivors."

"I hadn't done that math," Brice said, nodding.

"Now, all of those won't be active Marines," Steve said. "But quite a few of them, virtually all, will be military oriented. Very useful people to have around in a zombie apocalypse. Which is *why* we're clearing the bases. But we'll need to do something *with* them. Move them. Some, if the clearance is thorough enough, will wish to, or be ordered to, hold the area. Most will wish to move. If for no other reason than their services are needed. At which point, we face a logistics issue: How do we move several thousand people from these bases to Mayport or Blount or Gitmo or, indeed, all three? At which point, we get to what else is at Canaveral."

"Rockets?" Brice asked.

"Festival Cruise Lines has four," Steve said, holding

up his hands with fingers up. "Count 'em, four, cruise liners alongside at Canaveral. Two fall into the mega-cruise category. Each of the four is larger than the *Boadicea*."

"And they won't need much clearing," Montana said, nodding.

"And they should be virtually clear, Commodore," Steve said, nodding. "Very few of the infected will have survived and they wouldn't be packed with crew or passengers. That's where they load, not a destination. Getting them up and going is another issue: they won't just start at the turn of a key. We've been training Navy crews on other ship types. So . . .

"My recommendation as LantFleet, is to clear King's Bay, clear Parris Island, clear Lejeune, establish a safe point at Lejeune, which shouldn't be hard with Marines, shovels and concertina—then take a larger Marine force to Canaveral. Clear Canaveral, which is functionally an island and has several extremely convenient drawbridges and fence lines, then return to Lejeune with sufficient lift to pull out all the survivors who are going to join the effort. Oh, *and* that way we'll have more Marines along in case it turns into a nuke hunt. Then Hampton Roads. Then, assuming we have an LHD at that point, all the other bases within close range of the water. Hunter, Groton, Stewart, some of the D.C. area bases, even Bragg and possibly Bragg sooner.

"My estimate is that with the clearance of Lejeune alone, we'll have so many survivors plus equipment we can really get started on serious continental clearance. We will also be exceeding my competence level. If we find an admiral or general, at least one who has the right feel for the zeitgeist, I'm going to recommend turning over LantFleet to him. Or her."

"We'll discuss that if the time comes, Captain," Galloway said. "And I see your reasoning on the mission strategy."

"Concur," Brice said. "And don't you quit on me, Wolf."

"Oh, not going to *quit,* ma'am," Steve said, grinning. "But there's a mission I don't have the right person for. I'd just ask to take that one. If General Montana wasn't so obviously the choice for PacFleet I would have asked him to take it. He'd have loved it. Or gladly switched places. I hate being chained to a desk. Did it for too many years as a teacher."

"What's the mission?" Montana said.

"Gulf Coast Irregulars, Commodore," Steve said instantly. "Bunch of small boats and airboats clearing the Gulf Coast. Basically a barely disciplined littoral militia. Just feed them ammo, guns and vaccine and let them rip a new asshole through the infected while screaming 'Yahoo!' Think Florida rednecks and Cajuns with Ma Deuce and maybe some miniguns if they find them."

"God," Brice said, shaking her head. "You really are a pirate at heart, aren't you?"

"Hoist the black flag, mateys," Steve said, grinning. "I'm still looking for the right guy. Besides me, that is. I mean, the *Keys* haven't been cleared and they're just sitting there, low infected numbers and easily securable. Maybe Chen. He's gotten fairly irregular. I digress. That is my recommendation, ma'am, sir. King's Bay, Parris, Lejeune, Canaveral, figure it out from there."

"And we concur," Galloway said. "Sounds like a plan."

"I'll pass it to Colonel Hamilton," Steve said.

"SAC, out."

"Now you make me sorry I took this job," Montana said, grinning. "That does sound like fun."

"Biggest problem for me would be no wenching," Steve said. "Sure you want CINCPAC?"

"No," Montana said. "But a ship full of gear and ammo will probably change my mind. You can spare it?"

"We're about to take Lejeune, sir," Steve said. "And we're in the process of pulling in the *Iwo*. Even with worst case scenario in the mid-Atlantic bases, we can spare it."

"As soon as possible, then," Montana said. "CINCPAC, out."

"LantFleet, out," Steve said to himself, then keyed another icon. "Get me Kodiak."

CHAPTER 17

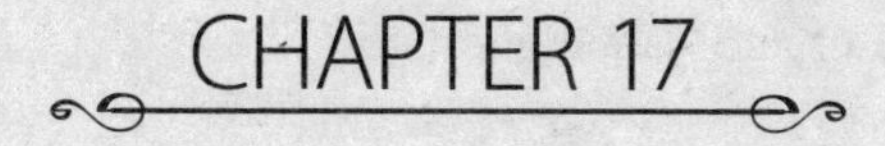

"Current mission remains the same," Colonel Hamilton said. "Destroy the heavy weapons in magazines today. Don't worry about the nukes for now."

"Yes, sir," Faith said, still a bit muzzy. "Are we supposed to eventually?"

"Eventually," Hamilton said. "And our mission for Lejeune and Parris Island has changed. We're to do a thorough ground level clearance of both. But for today, just take care of the magazines."

"Aye, aye, sir," Faith said.

"Oooh!" Faith said as the first torpedo magazine erupted. The blast doors had been left open and the blast went halfway across the massive magazine area. "That gives me an idea. Wait on the next one . . . Seahawk, Ground."

"We saw that from way over here," Sophia said. "Felt it, too. We'd appreciate some warning next time."

"Sure," Faith said. "But any chance you can pied piper some infected over here . . . ?"

"Oooh," Januscheitis said as the blast ripped through the group of infected. The center of the group simply evaporated. Those on the edges were . . . well, some of them were almost intact. "That's *vicious*."

"Glad that the bird was far enough away," Faith said. "But that's it for fun today. Next magazine . . . Wait . . . Let me call higher . . ."

"It's an interesting suggestion, Lieutenant," Hamilton said. "But I think the normal clearance methods work well enough."

"There's only so much 1028 left in this fallen world, sir," Faith said. "And we've got a lot of power, here, we're just throwing away. Waste not, want not, sir."

"I'm thinking about the safety issues and have to reluctantly say no, Lieutenant," Hamilton said. "Reluctantly. Your point on 1028 is valid. But the thought of our few amtracks rolling past an open and rigged magazine acting as pied pipers is . . . No."

"Well, at least there's a buttload of forty and fifty in the small arms magazines, sir," Faith said. "But somewhere in the world there is a reserve of 1028. A true treasure trove, sir. And I make it my personal quest to find it, sir."

"That's the spirit, Lieutenant. Eventually we will clear Fort Hood."

"Where's that, sir . . . ?"

"Check fire!" Olga shouted over the intercom. "Check fire!"

The helo had been doing pure clearance while the Marines were blowing up bunkers. There were a lot of infected between the outer perimeter fence and the pier fences. The base had had a population of fourteen thousand on-site military and dependents at the Fall. At this point estimates of infected populations were thirty percent of pre-Plague population, skewed almost entirely to prime age males, most of whom lived on base. That was a lot of infected. They'd seen survivors waving but the plan this time was to do a "yellow" clearance, then pull out the survivors.

"Check fire, aye," Anna said.

"Status?" Wilkes said.

"Command, have civilian SUV moving south on... hell, that double road down there..."

Apparently at least one group thought "orange" was good enough.

"Roger," Sophia said. "Got it. Command, heading for infected concentration."

"Then let's get down and plow the road for them," Wilkes said, banking the bird around.

"They're taking the turn towards the piers," Olga said over the sound of firing. "Command, gate closed. Say again, gate closed."

"Roger," Wilkes said. And there was a solid mass of infected sitting right on Henry L. Stimson drive. "Sophia, handle the phones."

"Force Ops, Seahawk Four..."

"Ground Team, Force Ops."

"Ground Team," Faith replied, signing another sheet of damned paper. Like someone was going to check the inventory of ammo? They were leaving most of it behind, anyway.

"Discontinue evolution. Respond group of survivors attempting self-extraction."

"Roger, Ops," Faith said, grabbing her helmet. "STOP THE LOAD. WE GOT A MISSION!"

"Damnit," Wilkes said, looking out the side window. "They're panicking."

The SUV had skidded to a stop when it saw the mass of infected on the road, then tried to do a three point turn and gotten at least temporarily stuck in the median.

"Time to start plowing," Wilkes said, dropping the bird down over the struggling SUV. "Fire."

The four miniguns opened up in their laser lines, shredding the group of infected. Until the fire slowed, then stopped abruptly.

"Looks like a jam on four," Sophia said. "The others are out."

"Starboard has rounds," Anna called.

"Port is low," Olga said.

Wilkes pivoted to bring his starboard side around and Anna finished off the last of the infected in the group.

"I've got more closing port," Olga called over the sound of fire.

"Check fire," Wilkes said.

"Check fire, aye," Olga and Anna said simultaneously.

Wilkes spun the bird, again, dropping down to almost ground level. The SUV had gotten freed but the female driver was looking wide-eyed. There were kids in the car.

"Stay here," Wilkes said, making standard hand-and-arm motions. "Stay here!"

The woman nodded at him, still wide-eyed.

"Go hot," Wilkes said, picking it up. "Freaking *dependents*! You couldn't wait a *day*? Ground team, Air. Where are you?" He started moving the helo around in an out-of-ground-effect hover to allow the door gunners to engage the closing infected.

"Moving to your location," Faith responded. *"In sight of the gate at this time, over."*

"Hurry," Wilkes said. "We're clocking out and there are closing infected, over."

"Roger. Will comply. Make sure the vehicle is clear of the gate, over."

"They are two hundred meters beyond the gate," Wilkes said.

"On the way."

"Force Ops, Ground, emergency, over. Condrey, *punch it*."

The M1 was in the lead for a change and it was *much* faster than an amtrack. It quickly left the rest of the Marines behind.

"Force Ops."

"Need permission to breach the main gate, over."

"Stand by."

"You have twenty seconds and I'm making a command decision," Faith replied. She could *see* the car. She could also see the infected closing on it in a wave. The helo was down to spitting fire from one gun. Then that stopped.

"Just stand by."

"Ain't happenin'," Faith replied. "Condrey, we're going to have to rebuild the gate. You got that?"

"Roger, ma'am," Condrey replied.

Faith reached down and keyed on the still installed speaker system. The Marine Corps Hymn started to boom across the area in a brassy flourish.

"RAMMING SPEED!"

When Trixie hit the gates, she was going "in the region of 45 miles per hour." That was what the after action report stated. "In the region of 45 miles per hour." Why? Because the M1 Abrams had a governor that limits it to 45 miles per hour and there were stiff regulations against removal of same.

The guys doing most of the detailed mechanical work on Trixie were nuke mechanics, mostly from fast attack boats. There's a reason they're called "fast attack" boats. They're attack boats and they're fast. Very fast. Why? Because in submarine warfare, there are two main prerequisites, silence and speed. They couldn't figure out a way to make Trixie stealthy but the hell if they were going to let her be slow. The governor was the first thing to go flying out of the engine compartment. They'd ended up with a lot of "excess" parts, which is a common characteristic of engineering in the nuclear submarine service.

Thus Trixie was going well in excess of 45 miles per hour. Which, coincidentally, was the posted speed limit. She would have definitely been ticketed were there any remaining Shore Patrolmen because she was going closer to sixty. Okay, *over* sixty.

The gates of the nuclear submarine facility were very heavy. They were designed to stop a suicide truck bomb.

They didn't stand a chance against something weighing as much as a train locomotive that was made out of steel and depleted uranium and doing better than sixty miles per hour.

They might as well have been tissue paper.

"Gun up on canister!" Decker said as the gates and part of the gate house flew in every direction.

"Not a chance," Faith replied, straightening back up. One of the speakers had been ripped away but The Hymn was still booming. "Coax and treads only. Condrey, if you hit that car I'll have you up on charges."

"Aye, aye, ma'am," the Lance Corporal replied.

The behemoth plowed into the crowd of infected surrounding the car, splashing the blue SUV with body fluids and offal like a car passing through a puddle. While the tank technically missed the SUV, the impact on the crowd of infected caused a ripple effect of bodies crushed between seventy-three tons of tank and a half a ton of SUV. The SUV lost, to an extent, being pushed nearly over by the impact of thirty human bodies that were more or less jelled by the physics.

The windows held, though, and that was the main thing.

Then Trixie was past and still going *way* too fast in the wrong direction.

"Condrey!" Faith said, spinning around the cupola gun and giving the most boneheaded order she'd ever given in her short life which had already included more than a few boneheaded orders. "Turn around! NOW!"

Lance Corporal Steve Condrey was an experienced tank driver. He knew full good and well that you *did not* attempt a radical turn of *any* tracked vehicle, much less an M1 Abrams, when going "in the region of 45 miles per hour." You were bound to throw a track.

But he had also spent waaaay too long being capable of only cadaver obedience to orders. So despite his understanding of all the bad things that happen when you try to pivot a tank going "in the region of 45 miles per hour" he turned the wheel hard over...

"JESUS MARY AND JOSEPH!" Decker bellowed, holding onto the gun as the tank seemed to be headed for who knew where. Sideways.

What should have happened at that point was the

tracks should have popped off like tiddlywinks whereupon the tank would grind to a halt in a shower of sparks. Then the crew, including Faith by order of Colonel Hamilton, should have had to put the tracks back on, an incredibly tedious, time consuming and back-breaking business, while the amtracks covered them from raging infected. Seahawk Four should have had to return to base to rearm. There should have been a spectacular and tense battle as the gallant, if somewhat ignorant of tank driving, young female lieutenant led her crew in heroic tank tread reattachment while under attack by waves of howling zombies well into the night, as the helo repeatedly screamed by overhead, laying down masses of fire, possibly having some catastrophic malady to add to the drama, requiring the Marines to rush to *their* rescue and possibly starting up a star-crossed love affair between Januscheitis and Anna and by the end of the long night of tense, dramatic and heroic battle, much of the base would have been cleared by default. Or, possibly, the situation might have forced them to tearfully leave Trixie behind until they could clear the base enough to repair her, leaving Faith despondent and remorseful for all of, say, three minutes or several paragraphs of exposition.

That's what *should* have happened. What *would* have happened in any *sane* universe.

But then we get to the subject of... lubrication. And friction. Much about friction.

Patton once famously remarked that his forces were going to "use their (Germans') guts to grease the treads of our tanks." That is because, well, the human body is not actually *good* grease, it's not something that you'd want to, for example, pack a wheel bearing race with, but it has, at molecular level, some of the same constituent elements. Even in a slender body, there are a fair amount of lipids, the basic component of lard. And the human body is ninety-five percent water. Which is slippery. Ask anyone who's ever driven on a wet road. Wetness, to a certain degree, decreases the force of both static and mobile friction. Huh?

The reason that tank tracks pop off like tiddlywinks when you try to turn too fast is static friction. All tank treads work on that basis. It is, at the quantum level, the stickiness between two dissimilar substances caused by photonic interaction. It is increased by the nature of the two substances and pressure. A tank tread drops down, sticks to the ground due to pressure and static friction, which is increased by pressure, then is lifted back up to be brought around again. Ah, the miracle of caterpillar treads. Thank you, George Cayley. Your invention led to all modern civil engineering *and* the ability to kill your enemies from inside a mobile castle. Go you, George.

The coefficient of static friction is higher than that of mobile friction. Mobile friction is when something is rubbing on something else but still moving. A belt sander works by mobile friction and car pistons experience it. It produces much more heat than static friction. By the same token, it has a much lower coefficient. That's the reason that cars slide so far on ice. They're operating under mobile friction not static friction until they get a grip again.

Very rarely do tanks encounter a situation of mobile friction. They are very heavy, thus increasing the coefficient of static friction, and their treads have rubber soles which increase it more. They occasionally slip in mud, but that's something different. You generally have to have ice to have mobile friction conditions and even then with an Abrams it has to be black ice on a very solid road. Or, occasionally, they can slide on a road that is, say, covered in oil and water. Lube.

In this case there was not "black ice" but . . . call it "red lube." Lots of red lube. There were the infected they'd already been using to "grease the treads of our tanks." There were the piles left by Seahawk Four. There were the infected trying in most cases very hard to get out of the way. There was the pile they'd just greased.

Greased. All of them were greased. Flat. To molecular level . . . They were, in fact, lube.

Lubrication acts to reduce the coefficient of static and mobile friction by . . . Oh, enough.

In short, the seventy-three-ton tank did not slide to a halt in a welter of sparks. It instead started to spin.

Trixie was in a flat spin, as if she was on ice, going "in the region of . . ." oh the hell with that, sixty-five or so and completely out of control. Like the beginnings of a spectacular NASCAR wreck but much, *much* larger and the dirt flying up on the infield wasn't dirt. She looked like a Brobdingnagian sand-colored top that had been filled with red food coloring that was spraying in every direction like crimson snow in a spin-out in some insane Dante's land where snow was red instead of white. She looked, in fact, like nothing any of the observers had ever seen or hoped to ever see again.

Fortunately, the road was flat, straight and there was nothing but more infected and piles of bodies or wounded zombies to get in her way. Most of the hale infected were diving away as fast as they could, generally not fast enough. Many were frozen in the road like possum and ended up much the same. But road-killier.

She finally stopped, pointed at an angle to the road, more or less in the direction of the SUV, in the intersection the SUV had taken, four hundred meters from where she'd *tried* to turn. The engine had automatically shut down so there was only the sound of the fading Marine Corps Hymn and a plinking of hot metal.

"Condrey, don't do that again," Faith said quietly. "*Ever.*"

"Aye, aye, ma'am," Condrey said, restarting the tank.

"Now go back to the car," Faith said. "Carefully."

The Marine Corps Hymn had been a brief instrumental, the sort of thing played by the Navy band when a cadet who stated he wanted to be a Marine armor officer made the winning touchdown against Army, which gave him a sense of superiority and perfectly incompetent arrogance that lasted right up until turning into a zombie.

It was, in fact, a mere forty-four seconds long. Which told Faith exactly how long she'd spent with her entire life flashing before her eyes. All things considered, the replay hadn't been much better than what was happening. She was forced during the replay to reevaluate her choice of lifestyles and came to the conclusion that one of these days she really needed a change of scenery. Some gentle Eden was looking better and better. Or maybe she'd put in for a desk job at Blount Island. Work with the master gunnery sergeant and learn the intricacies of saying "No, you can't have them, I need a minimum inventory to count . . ."

Faith had forgotten, what with one thing and another, that "Bodies" followed the Hymn. But it was appropriate. The road was now one gigantic smear. And Trixie was pink again. So, for that matter, was Faith.

Once again, the monstrous, and very, very scary, pink dragon in their midst got through to the normally insensate infected. They'd had enough. They were scattering in every direction.

"Pull up next to the car to cover until the amtracks get here," Faith said, targeting the runners. Waste not want not. "And *you're* going to have to figure out how to clean her."

"Ground Force, Force Ops. Permission to breach main gate, aye. Try to do minimum damage."

"Roger, Force Ops," Faith said, looking at the demolished gate area. The gate house had been torn apart like a trailer in a Kansas tornado, the gates themselves, what she could find of them, were fifty meters away and a section of fencing and fence poles was ripped out for at least twenty meters on either side. "Copy that. Breach already performed. Damage appears minimal and easily repaired. Probably should get a couple of containers up here to do a temporary patch. Oh, and in the words of Viscount Field Marshall Sir William Slim: There has been a good killing."

"Now hear this! Now hear this! Stand by for a transmission from LantFleet, subject: Survivors, MIA and known KIA, King's Bay Submarine Base."

"Under orders from LantFleet, Navy and Marine Forces have completed a thorough sweep of the King's

Bay Naval Submarine Base in Georgia. Rather than send the information piecemeal, the decision, by me, was to wait until all the lists were compiled. Marines swept every housing area up to and beyond Kingsland, and with additional care swept every home-of-record of active duty and dependents who had not checked in. General reaction: Survivor level at King's Bay was five percent. That is high compared to past experience but clearly not good. Task Force Kodiak found every survivor in the area and in a few cases were able to identify noninfected KIA. Infected were, obviously, unidentifiable. All others remain MIA, PI—missing in action, probability infected.

"All the information is now being loaded to your boats. If a dependent was a known KIA, that will be transmitted by your chain of command. I am sorry for your loss. The mission remains. Wolf, out."

CHAPTER 18

"Parris Island, to an even greater extent than King's Bay, is surrounded by swamp," Colonel Hamilton said, pointing to the overhead. "It is, let's face facts, the Devil's Island of the Marine Corps, designed to keep recruits from escaping until they can be properly brainwashed."

"Oorah, sir," Gunny Sands said. "Makes better Marines than Hollywood, too, sir."

"The point to this being it is actually *hard* to perform an amphibious assault on the island," Colonel Hamilton said. "The majority of the strand zone is mud, which is impassable by the amtracks, much less Trixie. Gunny, you're going to have to check me on this: the only solid point is here," the colonel said, pointing to a spot on the southwest of the base near some ranges.

"That is my recollection as well, sir," Gunny Sands said. "I don't know of anyone we have who was stationed at the base and would have more information."

"I asked Colonel Ellington and he concurred," Hamilton said. "But we're going to have to recon it. And given . . . all the animal interaction with infected, that may be problematic."

"Gators?" Faith asked.

"Oh, God, yes, ma'am," Januscheitis replied. "Big ones. At one point they had to shut the confidence course down 'cause of gators in the water hazards."

"And probably well fed at this point," Colonel Hamilton said.

"Not a real issue, sir," Faith said. "You can take out a gator with a Barbie gun, sir. Now, if they're swarming on infected piles, different issue. But if we've got to jump off a Zod to check the beach stability... Da swam through a feeding frenzy to release a boat at one point. You just have to act like you're supposed to be there and they don't want to mess with you, sir. Last but not least, they're not salties, sir. Gator gets ahold of you, it's going to be a bad day. It's not your *last* day, sir. Not if you have mates, sir. I recognize that checking the landing point will be a PFC job, sir. I respectfully suggest the platoon leader handle it, sir. 'Cause I really don't care about gators. Unless they're swarming a zombie pile, sir. And if one gets ahold of me, sir? That'll be a scar to tell the grandkids about."

"I'll take that under advisement," Hamilton said. "With the Seahawk, clearing the base should be possible without Trixie—"

"Sorry, sir," Faith said, raising her hand.

"Yes, Lieutenant?" Hamilton said.

"Other than a beach clearance somewhere, may I request amtracks and amtracks only, sir?" Faith said.

"Rationale?" Hamilton said.

"Gunny?" Faith asked.

"It's Parris Island, Colonel," Gunnery Sergeant Sands said. "Possibly Seahawk to provide top cover only *after* the Parade Field is cleared, sir."

"Duly noted," Colonel Hamilton said. "Which leads

to the next point. Lieutenant, you will *not* be leading the landing."

"Sir?" Faith said. "I know I'm not . . . I know I've never been to a real Marine officer's course . . ."

"That is not the reason, Faith," Colonel Hamilton said. "If you think I'm going to let *anyone* else be the first Marine to touch down on Parris Island, you've got another think coming, Lieutenant. And you've been having all the fun."

"Are you sure I shouldn't do this, ma'am?" Staff Sergeant Januscheitis asked nervously.

The Zodiac, what the Navy called a "RHIB" for "rigid-hulled inflatable boat," was puttering along a small strand of beach by the Known Distance Ranges. The objective had been used as a launch point for small boats from the looks. The otherwise solid scrub along the waterline was broken and there was a small sandy trail leading away from the water.

For a change, there was very little indication of an apocalypse other than the almost perfect silence. There was a call of seabirds and a buzzing of the ubiquitous sand flies. Other than that, it was quiet, peaceful and deserted.

Except for a couple of alligators pulled out on the shore, sunning themselves. One thing Faith thought she had going for her was that the water was extremely cold and the gators were going to be sluggish. They also didn't like cold water.

"I'm sure you should, Staff Sergeant," Faith said quietly. "Just as I'm sure I'm gonna. We sent our only disposable SEAL to the Pacific."

SEALs had been formed from Navy underwater

demolitions teams but their progenitors had been the beach reconnaissance units of World War Two. Although the Marines were famous for taking island after island away from the Japanese, with the exception of Guadalcanal, Navy frogmen had been on every island before they got there. In fact, an entire BRU unit had landed in Japan before the First Marine Division arrived, and had greeted them, for once, with a banner proclaiming "United States Navy, welcomes the United States Marine Corps to Japan." Since they were a top secret unit, the pictures had been quickly suppressed.

However, the primary mission of the SEALs remained reconnaissance of beaches for Marine landing forces.

"Maybe we should have swept Virginia Beach first, ma'am," Januscheitis said. "Just look for the guys taking pictures of themselves flexing their pectoral muscles."

"I'm sure there's a joke there somewhere, Staff Sergeant," Faith said, concentrating on the plan. "I'm not sure what it is."

"Yes, ma'am," Januscheitis said.

"Bring it in right over there," Faith said, knifehanding to the left of the opening. Most of the gators were to the right.

"How hard can it be?" Faith said. All she had to do was collect five samples of sand off the short strand between the water and the vegetation. They'd already pulled the samples from in the water with a pole device. Take them back to the ship, get them checked out and they were golden. Assuming the sand would take the weight of the amtracks.

"Don't jinx it, ma'am," Januscheitis muttered, covering the shore. All the Marines were wearing FLIRs, forward looking infrared monoculars, so they would hopefully see any infected before it took down the skipper.

As it turned out, alligators didn't show up well on infrared.

"SON OF A BITCH!" Faith screamed as her right leg was taken out from under her. She found herself being dragged into the water before the surprised Marines could react.

"Don't let it ro—!"

Faith's yell ended in a gurgle as she was taken under and the beast began a death roll with her leg clutched in its jaws.

"Motherfu—" Faith snarled as she briefly surfaced. "That HURT!"

Faith hadn't survived this long by standing idly by while being killed. She'd dragged one of her .45s out *while* being rolled.

Alligators roll, check to see if the prey is still struggling, then roll again. Faith knew this. Which was why she didn't struggle. She just leaned sideways and shot the gator in the head.

Alligators have very hard heads. And while the .45 ACP round is quite good at killing anything alligator size that is not armored, it's not so good at penetrating crocodilian craniums. What it does do, however, is sort of throw them for a loop.

The gator started thrashing like a snake with its head chopped off. Still holding onto Faith's leg.

Faith reached down with her left hand and managed to get the gator's jaws unclamped from her leg. This was aided by the fact the gator was opening and closing its jaws spastically due to being shot in the head by a .45.

She held up her now somewhat mangled hand and shook her head in disbelief.

"When am I ever gonna learn?" she muttered.

Januscheitis was already in the water dragging her to the RHIB.

"You're gonna be okay, ma'am," the staff sergeant said, half desperately.

"Oh, I'm gonna be fine," Faith replied, holding up her hand. "But I still gotta get those samples."

"Got it under control, ma'am," Twitchell said. "Five samples."

"I'd say you should have done this in the first place," Faith said as Janu pulled her into the boat. "But you gotta admit this is gonna be one hell of a story."

"One I'm not looking forward to telling your father, ma'am," Januscheitis said. "Jesus, that leg don't look too good..."

"'Granma! Tell us again about when the alligators tried to eat you!'" Faith said, holding a thumb on her wrist artery to control the bleeding. "I swear to God I am going to find a better line of work."

"Hello, again, Reginald," Faith said as the amtracks approached the objective. The alligators were sliding off the bank into the water to avoid the loud things approaching from the water but even in the pre-dawn light she could spot Reggie. He had a distinct wound on his forehead.

"Should I take care of them, ma'am?" Twitchell said.

"No," Faith said, switching to radio with her good hand. It had only taken a few dozen stitches to sort of fix. The corpsman was pretty sure she'd get almost full use again someday. The leg was also pretty mangled. It had been suggested she sit this one out. She'd pointed out all she had to do was sit in an amtrack and look important.

"Kodiak, Shewolf," Faith radioed.

"Kodiak."

"Request no fire on local wildlife," Faith said. "They were just doing their job, protecting the base. Over."

"Roger," Kodiak responded. He'd taken Sergeant Hoag's place as TC of Track Two. And had the psy-ops speakers loaded on the track. *"All tracks. Shewolf likes the gators 'cause they're family. Do not fire on the gators. Now line up and get ready to hit that beach."*

The music started and Faith grinned. Even she would admit that there was only one choice for this landing. And it was a longer version than the one she usually played: The Irish Grenadiers version.

Alas, since it was a fairly deserted part of the base, there seemed to be no one to hear it. But they were on the land on Parris Island. Check that, there seemed no one sentient to hear it. They were definitely getting customers. Track Two had already opened up with fifty cal.

As her track cleared the bushes along the shoreline she could see what they were firing at. Dozens of infected in this part of the base had apparently not headed over to the Navy fire zone.

"Twitchman," Faith said. "Free fire, forty, on all infected."

"Free fire, forty, aye, ma'am," Twitchell said, opening up with the Mk19.

"Sergeant of the Guard to Post Four!" Recruit Private Gina Swanson called, continuing to observe her sector.

"Report, Recruit!" Gunnery Sergeant Annette Brown barked as soon as she'd reached the post.

"Ma'am, firing from the southwest, ma'am!" Swanson barked. "Also . . . music, ma'am!"

The plague had swept Parris Island just like the rest of the world. The response had been to fall back on food stores for a siege. The process had been as strict and orderly as possible. No attempt was made to hold any portions of the base except the food stores. All recruits who had completed basic rifle marksmanship were armed. Recruits who had not completed rifle marksmanship or who had failed their first time through were put on non-armed duties including maintaining control of and security for dependents.

As per Marine Corps doctrine for trainees, all females were located in one facility, separate from males. They had dependents as well, but not so much as one teenage male.

Which was lucky, because from what Brown was getting about the other facilities, pregnancy was endemic.

Holding things together had been hell for a while. They'd lost one of the facilities to infected getting loose. But the rest had held. Huge death rates as well as "turning," but they'd all held. The infected had either been terminated or turned out. In retrospect, the initial orders to turn them out were probably boneheaded but that was then.

There was an increasing issue about the food stores. They had not anticipated a ten-month siege. If they weren't relieved soon, it might become necessary to attempt a breakout. If the force could access the remaining ammunition on the base, it might be possible to take it back. However, the infected level remained high and the nearest magazine to the food stores was nearly two miles away.

Probably the only bright spot was that all the recruits were trained up with the exception of marksmanship. There was insufficient remaining ammunition to do proficiency training. On the other hand, someone had brought in pugel sticks. Given that it was one of the few forms of entertainment, they might be able to fight their way through with some rebar.

They'd seen a Seahawk in the distance yesterday and there'd been a report of shots from the southeast last night. It looked like relief forces might have arrived.

The sound of the Marine Corps Hymn changed that from "might" to "likely."

"Signaler! Signal Building Sixteen that we hear heavy fire, the sound of tracks and the Marine Corps Hymn from the southwest, vicinity of the Known Distance Range!"

"Aye, aye, ma'am!" Recruit Private Tami Bishop replied. Her planned MOS was communications and she already knew International Code when she'd joined. Which was fortunate, since that was what they were using for signaling between the buildings.

"Runner! Pass the word to Staff Sergeant Warren. All recruits up and in gear! Reinforcing forces have arrived. We will be ship-shape when they get here."

"Aye, aye, ma'am!" Recruit Private Christy Brooks said, hurrying below.

Brown could see the Seahawk was up again, circling up from a ship against the rising sun. It seemed to be patrolling back and forth to the southeast. Through the binoculars she could see it was armed. Heavy. Bunch of fucking miniguns. So why was it holding off?

There was a shit load of fire approaching, though. She could spot the fifty caliber and Mk19 by ear. Machine guns, probably 240 and M4s. SAW. You could tell by the way it sounded like one. Several tracks, probably amtracks.

Shitload of fire. They were rolling hot.

"Randolph!" Faith yelled, sticking her head into the crew compartment.

"Ma'am!"

"Reloads on the fifty!"

"Reload the fifty, aye, ma'am!"

"And just *keep* reloading!" Faith yelled. They were burning through fucking ammo. Good thing the back of the amtrack was filled with it.

"Seahawk Four, Kodiak, over," Colonel Hamilton said. His inexperience at infected ground combat was showing. He'd done the landing with zero prep, on the assumption that infected levels on the island were bound to be low. And they were getting absolutely swarmed. On the other hand, most of the infected were trotting behind, trying to keep up. The "pied piper" maneuver.

"Seahawk Four."

"Swing to the north, opposite the parade deck," Hamilton radioed. "We have massed infected in pied piper. Unit will continue to parade deck and draw them onto it. Engage on parade deck on orders. Seahawk will not cross onto land zone proper until ordered to engage."

"Attack from north on parade deck, aye. Avoid island proper until ordered, aye. Good news, sir. The pilot at least is a Marine."

"Roger," Hamilton said, smiling. "Kodiak, out."

The Seahawk was moving. Heading north. It seemed to circle around the island and ended up north of the parade deck. Why it hadn't just crossed she wasn't sure. It wasn't like the infected used MANPADs. The miniguns were clearer now that it was closer. It had four under-slung and two door guns. Flying fucking gunpoint. Why it wasn't attacking was the question. There were infected moving around. Mostly swarming towards the approaching tracks.

"Ma'am!" Swanson barked. "Permission to report, ma'am!"

"Report, Recruit!"

"Armored vehicles in view to the southwest!"

They were amtracks. The lead one was flying a large American flag and the trail was flying the Marine Corps flag. They were modified, too. The external cargo racks and all other handholds had been removed as had the appliqué armor. They were just fucking laying waste to the infected closing on them but that was less noticeable than the huge fucking *mass* of infected following them. It looked like half the base was on naked parade. The tracks were moving at a jogging pace and the infected were just trying to keep up.

She looked at the tracks, looked at the Seahawk doing figure eights, then looked at the parade deck.

"You are *not* going to fuck up my parade deck!" she said. "Oh, *tell* me you are not going to fuck up the parade deck."

"Spread as we cross the parade deck," Hamilton radioed. "On my command, speed up. When we reach the end, stop, then pivot. At that point, all tracks engage the infected with fifty caliber. We are under observation. We *are* going to do this by the damned numbers . . ."

"Ahhh," Gunnery Sergeant Brown said as the amtracks started tearing up her parade deck. Okay, so it was overgrown and filled with weeds. Some recruits with brush hooks and mowers and they could fix that. What the amtracks were doing to it . . . It really made you want to cry.

On the other hand, it was clearly about to be well nourished. And they might be able to roll out the track marks. After they got the bodies cleared.

The tracks spread out, pretty evenly, then sped up to get some distance between themselves and the following zombies. There were more coming from the direction they were driving but they either shot 'em or ran 'em over.

She looked around for a second.

"Recruit Reed! What the fuck are you looking at? Is the parade deck part of your sector of observation?"

"Ma'am, no, ma'am!" the recruit shouted.

"Keep an eye on your sector, Recruits! The next one I see looking around is going to be cleaning toilets with a toothbrush for a *week*!"

"No, no, no . . ." Brown said, going back to watching the tracks. They'd sprinted across the field, throwing up a welter of grass, weeds and dirt and just totally screwing up her parade deck. "Aaaaah! Not a pivot! Not a pivot!" she yelled as the tracks stopped, then . . . pivoted. "You *bastards*! You inconsiderate bastards! That's my *parade deck*!"

But then the Seahawk descended and she forgot about the damage the tracks had done.

The laserlike lines swept through the infected, leaving windrows of bodies, then it swept back up and around as the tracks laid down all the infected between the gun-sweep and their own position. It was really fucking glorious. The only thing that would make it better was if it had been a Marine gunship.

"Ma'am, permission to report, ma'am!" Post Two barked.

"Report, Recruit!" the DI replied.

"Ma'am, signal from one of the tracks, ma'am!"

"Signaler!"

"Lieutenant Colonel Craig Hamilton, USMC, Task Force Kodiak Commander. Seeking senior survivor. Over."

"Post Commandant, Colonel Locky Downing, USMC, Building Fourteen, currently out of view. Will retransmit."

"Request remain redoubts pending clearance and blockage of bridges. Will extract all survivors to ships off-shore. Orders LantFleet, NCCC, Parris Island to be evacuated, all Naval services personnel to be placed under command Task Force Kodiak to assist Operation Swamp Fox East Coast Sweep. Will clarify command structure on basis Commandant superior officer to Task Force Commander."

"Transmit 'Stand by,'" Brown ordered. "Then send that to the colonel."

"Aye, aye, ma'am," Recruit Bishop replied.

"To Commander, Task Force Kodiak, from Commandant Parris Island Marine Base. Will comply. Personal: Glad you made it and very glad to see you. End personal."

"Query: How many survivors?"

"One thousand eighty-six. Five hundred twenty-three Marines, all ranks, most boots. Twelve Navy, all ranks. Other dependents and other civilians."

"Congratulations. Highest rate of survival found. Will require hot bunking. Very good to hear. Previous total known manning, USMC, sixty-three."

"Jesus Christ," Brown said quietly. Those Marines clearing out the last few infected were pretty much the entire Marine Corps.

"Primary mass infected cleared. Will continue sweep. Moving your position this time. Kodiak, out."

The parade deck was a fucking mess, pretty much covered with dead infected and, of course, 7.62 rounds. She could even see where the brass had cluttered it up from the Seahawk passes.

On the other hand, wasn't going to be her problem. They were pulling out.

CHAPTER 19

"Gunnery Sergeant," Januscheitis said as the doors of the building were cracked for the first time in ten months. "Staff Sergeant Januscheitis, Platoon Sergeant, Platoon One, USMC."

It was barely midday and the base was mostly clear. Parris Island wasn't particularly large.

"Gunnery Sergeant Brown, Senior Drill Instructor, Platoon Four, Delta Company, Battalion Four, USMC," Brown said.

"Here's how we're going to do this, Gunnery Sergeant," Januscheitis said. "All Marines absent movement issues are going to walk. Dependents with movement issues, including babes in arms, will ride in the track. We only have one. The others are at the other buildings. All others will walk. Phase Three Marines, only, will carry weapons with loaded magazines inserted but not locked or loaded and on safe. They and the rest of the team will take outer perimeter security for the extraction. Movement will be from here to the beach by the KD ranges where evacuees will be picked up by RHIBs and transported to the ships. Last people off from the local command will be instructors and phase three Marines. Then the Wolf Marines will evacuate in tracks and we're done with this clearance. Roger?"

"Roger, Staff Sergeant," Brown said. "No babes in arms. Some young babies but . . . most of them didn't make it. Toddlers is about the youngest we've got."

"I have seen damned few toddlers at all," Januscheitis said. "Lots of babes in arms. No pregnancies?"

"No males," Brown said.

"Well, that's a change," Januscheitis said. "Very well. Let's get them sorted out and loading."

"Anything I need to do here, Jan?" Faith radioed. She was still up in the TC hatch, placidly watching the boots get organized.

"No, ma'am," Januscheitis replied.

Unsurprisingly, getting the boots organized was going well. They'd had boot camp extended for ten months. They were nearly as wound tight as Decker when he was first found.

"I've got this," Januscheitis continued. "I'm still unsure how to break it to Senior Drill Instructor Gunnery Sergeant Annette Brown that her new LT is younger than any of her boots. Over."

"Maybe I should walk around with a swagger stick. That way she knows I'm the boss, over."

"She's probably spotted the bars, Shewolf," Januscheitis said as Gunnery Sergeant Brown marched over.

"The unit is assembled, Staff Sergeant," Brown said.

"We're ready to roll, ma'am," Januscheitis radioed.

"Let's get this wagon train a rollin'."

"Yo, boot," Curran said to the private next to him. "Chill. Relax. First of all, these things kill pretty easy. Second, we laid most of 'em out on the parade deck, which was, by the way, *awesome*! We made *sure* we tore that motherfucker up, too. I'd been wanting to do that since *I* was a boot. Third, if you're all wired the fuck up, you're not really seeing what's there. Stretch out the kinks. Just chillin' in the hood..."

The platoon had been spread out with the boots and their drill instructors to lend some experience and stiffening. The phrase about buckshot was appropriate. On the other hand, there had been very little in the way of action.

Which had its own difficulties.

"'Chillin' in the hood,' Private First Class?" one of the drill instructors said. "You'd better be on your God-damn sector, not *chillin'*, Private First Class!"

"Staff Sergeant," Curran said. "With due respect, when you've been killin' zombies as long as I've been killin' zombies, you can tell me how to kill zombies, Staff Sergeant."

"Get your ass over here, Private First Class," the staff sergeant snapped. "Right the fuck now!"

And Faith just *had* to take a walk...

"Excuse me, Staff Sergeant," Faith said as she limped up to the twosome. Curran was locked up with a staff sergeant drill instructor doing the full head tilt with the brim of the hat on Curran's nose.

"And furthermore, you *shall* show proper respect to your superiors..." the staff sergeant said, knife-handing Curran's chest.

"Excuse me, Staff Sergeant," Faith barked, tapping him on the shoulder.

"Yes, ma'am," the staff sergeant said, his face tight.

"What the *fuck* do you think you are doing?" Faith asked.

"*This* is an *NCO* matter, ma'am," the staff sergeant said, not looking at her. It was in a "proper" tone but there was more than a bit of "instructor" tone. The staff sergeant drill instructor knew a very junior lieutenant when he saw one. "It is something to let NCOs *handle*, ma'am."

"Oh, you did not just go there . . ." Curran muttered.

"Curran," Faith said, very quietly. "Fall out and return to your post."

"Aye, aye, ma'am," Curran said, running away.

"Assume the position of attention, Staff Sergeant," Faith said.

The staff sergeant popped to attention and Faith leaned in to whisper in his ear.

"Do you know who I am, Staff Sergeant?" Faith whispered.

"No, ma'am!"

"Do you know *what* I am, Staff Sergeant!"

"You are a Marine Officer, ma'am!"

"True, and beside the point," Faith hissed. "I am a fucking psychotic bitch so far over the redline I can't see it with an Abrams gunsight. I am a zombie-killing *monster*. All my Marines swear I have to drink a pint of zombie blood a day to wake up in the morning. What were *you* doing last night, Staff Sergeant?"

"I was off duty, ma'am," the staff sergeant said. "I was in my rack, ma'am."

"I wish I knew what off-duty meant," Faith said sorrowfully, like she'd lost something she loved and didn't even know where to start looking. "*I* was up to my ass in alligators. Literally. The reason my hand is torn up and I'm limping was I was attacked by gators while hip-deep in water doing the fucking beach recon for the assault, Staff Sergeant! And what were *you* doing? You were 'off-duty.' I haven't been off-duty in ten God-damn *months*! I've been weeks in the pitch black holds of carriers and liners and freighters and tankers killing fucking zombies while you've been whacking off to how *great* it is to march the fucking *boots* around on your fucking quarterdeck! And Curran, who is sort of a ragbag but *my* ragbag, has been right there with me. And you're going to give me, *me*? *Shewolf*? The fucking *monster* that makes fucking monsters *run* at her NAME! *You* are going to give *me* that 'I'm a Marine Staff Sergeant and she's just some Barbie with a bar' *attitude*? You completely useless piece of *alligator shit*? And you, you, who has spent the last ten months doing fucking NOTHING! ARE GOING TO DRESS DOWN ONE OF *MY* MARINES, STAFF SERGEANT? YOU? WHO THE FUCK ARE *YOU* TO TELL ONE OF *MY* MARINES ONE *GOD-DAMNED* THING?"

"Excuse me, ma'am!"

Faith turned around and looked at the new NCO who had approached. She'd heard him coming up from behind her and checked the tendency to just turn and fire.

She looked him up and down and looked at his rank. She was too furious to try to figure it out.

"Lots of stripes!" she said angrily, knife-handing at his rank. "Lots of stripes. That's all I got. Tell this *fucker*, and all your other *fuckers*, that they do NOT tell my troops what to do and they do NOT dress down my sweet vicious devil dogs, *WHATEVER YOU ARE*!" Faith bellowed. "THAT'S A FUCKING *ORDER*! ALL I WANT TO HEAR FROM YOU IS AYE, AYE, *MA'AM*!"

She spun around and limped back to her track without waiting for a reply.

"Is there a female lieutenant in this track?" a male voice bellowed from somewhere in the crew compartment.

"Freeman, Twitchell," Faith said. "Bail."

"Aye, aye, ma'am!" Freeman said, bolting.

Faith laboriously made her way into the crew compartment where a guy wearing the same rank as her dad was standing with his arms crossed.

"Second Lieutenant Faith Marie Smith, sir," Faith said.

"Colonel Locky Downing, Lieutenant," the colonel said. "Sit."

"Aye, aye, sir," Faith said, sitting down.

"How long have you been an officer, Lieutenant?" Colonel Downing asked.

"Lemme see . . ." Faith said, looking at her fingers and counting. She had to hold up the bandaged hand. "*Six* months, sir? I think? Maybe? What month is it?"

The colonel paused for a moment in thought.

"That's post-Plague," the colonel said.

"Ah," Faith said, nodding. "Direct commission, sir. From civilian, sir. I'm sort of a mascot, sir."

"Well, since you haven't been around the Marine Corps very long, Lieutenant Mascot, let me explain something to you. While you are, technically, senior to the post sergeant major, and the sergeant major will and should respect your rank, that does NOT give you the right to dress him down publicly *nor* to order him to perform actions, especially related to his NCOs! The *only* person who might dress him down or give him orders is *me*! Do you understand me, Lieutenant?"

"I heard the words, sir," Faith said after a very long moment.

"Lieutenant, you had better have *understood* them as well," the colonel said, frowning.

"I understand them quite well, sir!" Faith said. "I don't talk real good but my comprehension is fine, sir! However, there is . . . just a bunch of shit you don't know or understand, sir!"

"Care to enlighten me, Lieutenant?" the colonel asked sarcastically.

"Not the job of a fourteen-year-old lieutenant to relieve a colonel's ignorance, sir!" Faith said just as sarcastically.

"Fourteen?" Downing said incredulously.

"Just turned, sir," Faith replied. "About a month ago."

"I don't know what moron armed a fourteen-year-old 'mascot,' much less gave her command of troops," Downing said, holding out his hand. "But it's going to be the first thing I discuss with Colonel Hamilton when I reach the boat. For now, turn over your weapon and rank. I am not going to have an untrained child commanding Marines in combat. That goes against so many regulations . . . I really cannot count."

"You're *serious*, sir?" Faith said calmly.

"Your supposed commission is hereby rescinded, Lieutenant Mascot," the colonel said. "Give me your bars. And take off those guns. I don't know what maniac allowed you to run around armed up like Rambo but it stops here."

"Colonel, I will give you one warning that this is an unwise decision," Faith said. She'd always wondered about how Da got calm at certain times. Now she knew what a *real* killing rage meant.

"Duly noted," Downing said. "And I repeat: turn in your arms and join the civilians."

"You can have the M4, sir," Faith said, unclipping it and setting it on the deck. "But all the pistols are mine." She reached up and yanked off her rankplate. "So does this mean I'm out of the Marines?"

"You never were a Marine," Downing said, shaking his head. "You don't direct commission a thirteen-year-old. Whoever did so is clearly in violation of both regulation and good order. Not to mention sense. Being a Marine officer, child, is far more than being a mascot."

"Okay," Faith said, standing up with tears in her eyes. "Good. Great even. That means I don't have to take my troops on another *suicide mission*. That means I don't have to put up with any more NCOs and assholes like you that can only see the Barbie with a bar! That means I don't have to let another ignorant 'I know what I'm doing because I've got fucking rank' fucker like you get them killed! That means I don't have to take shit from *anyone*, especially *you*, DICKBREATH! SO FUCK YOU, ASSHOLE!"

With that she stalked out of the track, passed through the lines and was out of sight in seconds.

"Oh, Jesus Christ," Hamilton said, looking at the radio. He'd gone back to the ships to arrange for berthing and support leaving Colonel Downing in control of the extraction. He realized, too late, that he probably should have ensured a more complete briefing. "Oh, no, no, no, no . . ."

"I'm uncomfortable with leaving the kid on the island," Colonel Downing radioed. *"Both in terms of her personal safety and the fact that there is Federal military equipment on the post."*

Hamilton just looked at the radio. He really didn't know what to say in reply.

"*Her* safety is not an issue," Hamilton replied, speaking very slowly. "Lieutenant Smith is—"

"This is Brigadier General Brice, Acting Chairman of the Joint Chiefs. Who the fuck *drove Shewolf off the reservation, over?"*

The subs, as usual, were monitoring communications. And the commanders knew a shit-storm incoming when they heard one.

"Shelley, this is Commodore Montana. What's this I hear that Shewolf deserted?"

"She didn't desert... Commodore," Colonel Downing said. *"I accepted her resignation based upon her failure to maintain proper military decorum and insufficient age for enlistment much less a lieutenancy. I'm not sure why a fourteen-year-old was commissioned in the first place. Combat leadership is no place for mascots."*

"LantFleet. Where is my daughter at this time, Colonel?"

Captain Wolf *sounded* mild. He often did when he was about to explode. Hamilton hadn't heard him sound *that* mild since the bad moments of London.

"Not understood, LantFleet," Colonel Downing replied. *"Who is your daughter, over?"*

"This is Commodore Montana. I am hereby assuming control of this communication. For the colonel's information, I was pre-Plague retired Lieutenant General Carmen Montana, former commander Delta,

Fifth Group, Joint Anti-Terrorism Task Force, Joint War College, Joint Special Operations Command. I hold three Silver Stars and two Distinguished Service crosses for classified operations in very bad places. I am currently CINCPAC. Lieutenant Faith Marie Smith, handle Shewolf, is the daughter of LantFleet, has been awarded TWO Navy Crosses since she was commissioned for shit that would have your hair stand on end, and I'd personally have her fucking children, you pimple on a Marine's ass! What could anyone possibly say to that psychotic little zombie-killing machine that could make her give up her commission to her beloved Corps? Colonel, if I have to get in a fucking fast attack and come over there to find her, the first zombie I will kill is you. *And I am absolutely serious. Don't bother to run 'cause you will only die tired!"*

Like Faith figured, there was gear.

The Marines hadn't just given up Parris Island. They'd fought a bit, covering for the retreating dependents and early phases. And, of course, zombies threw their clothes and gear away like Swedish nudists. There were remaining rations in the facilities the boots had evacced. She'd found an M16A4 pretty quick. It wasn't fireable, of course. You had to keep Barbie guns pristine, another reason she didn't like them. If it had been an AK it would be good to go. Ammo in mags, check. Need to cross-load. Infected level, low. She'd only gone pistol a couple of times so far. Hadn't even gotten in a scrum.

Sand fly, black fly and mosquito level, on the other hand, high. She really needed to find some cover from the sand flies and some Off. There'd be some in the cadre quarters. And a good solid place to hole up in the dark. And someplace to do some work on the . . . oh, there's another M16 . . . *Maybe I can Frankenstein one functioning Barbie gun. There are probably better ones on the base somewhere. Wish I had my AK . . .* Somewhere there would be magazines. Their location would be on a map at the headquarters. She was a past master of scrounging and salvage at this point and no more meetings, no more paperwork, no more new-join assholes who only saw the Barbie . . . Frankly, she still hadn't forgiven Colonel Hamilton for shoving Staff Sergeant Barnard down her throat. She wasn't going through *that* again . . .

No worries, mate. No worries . . .

The roundhouse came out of nowhere.

A gunnery sergeant does not hit a sergeant major. It's a court-martial offense. Of course, if it's in anything like private, "it never happened." Usually.

When it's in front of a company of boots, it happened.

The post sergeant major was flat out on his back.

"Colonel," Gunnery Sergeant Sands said through gritted teeth. "You will walk away or you will be next. Choose."

"Sir, we have over three thousand personnel in space for barely a thousand," Colonel Hamilton said. "We have priority missions. What are our orders?"

"Return to Mayport," Steve said. "Faith's not going anywhere and she's not in any real danger absent her wounds infecting. I'm not getting involved in this one. Conflict of interest doesn't begin to describe it. I'll be putting it on higher and letting them make the decisions. We've got missing nukes, a coast to clear... I'm putting it on higher."

"Aye, aye, sir," Hamilton said. "Sir... I'm sorry about this."

"Faith has been redlining since before you met her, Colonel," Steve said. "We should have... *I* should have found some way to bring her down before this. Honestly, I'm so bloody pissed right now, I'm tempted to just throw my *own* rank on the deck and go look for her myself. I'm not pissed about losing Faith. We haven't. Not permanently, whatever she's thinking right now. I'm pissed because I was looking forward to having another trained senior officer to throw details on. Right now I'm trying to convince General Montana and General Brice that he doesn't need to be busted to private and handed a rifle. On the other hand... I'm not sure he's useable given... I'm tempted to give him a rifle and drop him off at King's Bay to tell you the truth."

"Say the word, sir," Colonel Hamilton said. "Say the fucking word."

"No," Steve said. "I'm sure I can find something more unpleasant for him than that. I assume he enjoys command. Tell him that absent some global change in command structure, which is possible at some point, he can assume, as he made assumptions already, that he will never have a position of any sort of authority, again. Probably the best choice is to bust him but, again, will not be my call. Conflict of interest and all that... Get back to Mayport. Sail out tonight. Faith can have her shore leave. We'll figure out what to do later."

"Lieutenant Lyons," Montana said.

"Sir," Lyons said. He'd been acting as Montana's aide and was, thus, filled in on the situation.

"The USS *Hampton* is in harbor," Montana said. "You will board her and proceed to Parris Island. You will find Shewolf. You will bring her back. You will return with either Shewolf or her body. Is that clear, Lieutenant?"

"Clear, sir," Lyons said, standing up.

"Go." He sighed angrily and keyed his computer. "Get me the Hole and LantFleet…"

CHAPTER 20

"You're about to clear Lejeune, Steve," Montana said. "You'll find more colonels and sergeants major. So we've learned their putative 'help' is a myth. People who have long-term careers in training commands tend to be of limited utility in actual operations. There are options: Exile Downing somewhere like the Indian Ocean. Bust him to private and hand him a rifle. Make him something unimportant in an unimportant spot. I suppose we could send him to stand up the base on Greenland, again. Since there are options, my suggestion is to table it and figure it out while he steams to Mayport.

"As to Faith, once we get her back I'd be more than happy to have her as my junior aide. Being a commodore's aide carries with it an automatic cachet. People won't tend to look down their noses at her. As much. And when our only remaining SEAL and a former astronaut says 'She scares me. And I'm not joking . . . ' people will tend to pay attention. And it will give me an opportunity to train her, and from me she'll take the training."

"Thank you, sir," Steve said. "I'd like to ask to hold on the aide thing until she is back. I'd like to give her some down time so she can make a rational judgment. The one question is can we find her?"

"Lieutenant Lyons is on the way to Parris Island on the *Hampton*, Steve," Montana said, smiling. "He's a SEAL. They're occasionally good for more than swimming long distances and carrying heavy weights. He'll find her and bring her back. Or he's not *coming* back. Give Stacey and Sophia my regards and tell them not to worry. Situation under control. CINCPAC, out."

"Colonel Hamilton," Steve said. "Here are your orders. The colonel, the sergeant major and the staff sergeant involved in this incident are relieved of all command and authority and confined to quarters during the float. The *same* quarters. They are to be served MREs in quarters. The TV, which they are ordered not to turn off, is to be set to a selection of news reels and other videos, subject: the history of Wolf Squadron. Start with the night sky video, then run all those propaganda news reels Zumwald has been producing as well as the better mashes. You won't have to select for ones about Faith, obviously. They are to view those videos, which will run in their quarters from zero six hundred hours until twenty-one hundred hours when they are to have lights out. Just cut the power to the damned room.

"Upon arrival at Mayport: The colonel, sergeant major, the staff sergeant DI, all officers and staff NCOs associated with the Phase Three trainees will be separated. Phase Three trainees will be placed under the training direction of Gunnery Sergeant Sands. Training will be conducted by the Wolf Marines. They are to begin active training for post-Fall combat techniques, then organized, sans officers and staff NCOs, into a unit of the appropriate size for their numbers. All the junior

NCOs will participate in training *as boot privates*. They will act as boot squad leaders in every way including living with the trainees. They're going to be the cadre for the unit in combat. That should take very little time, two weeks at most. Their final exam, the Crucible if you will, will be active clearance of closed space environments and towns in small teams, including night ground clearance as a final test. If you have to put some of them in small boats and send them down to the Crib to clear liners and towns, do it. But just send along one or two Wolf Marines to evaluate, not participate.

"Phase One and Two trainees, who should all be at Phase Two, shall go through an abbreviated training schedule to bring them up to Phase Three. At that point, those officers and staff NCOs will be similarly separated and the same thing is to be done with those trainees and junior NCOs.

"Those officers and staff NCOs, with no additional training other than their common knowledge of combat tasks, shall be given a mission similar to the following:

"Upon arrival at Mayport, the colonel, sergeant major, the involved staff sergeant and all staff NCOs as well as surviving officers associated with current Phase Three or supernumerary of a size less than a platoon shall be given one gunboat division and such weapons and equipment as they wish and sent to Canaveral. Their mission is to clear the Cape Canaveral base, close every bridge, find and recover the missing nuclear weapons and clear all the liners alongside to the point that survey and salvage can come in and recover them. We need everything on that island including the POL point intact. You have the requirements for that mission.

"If they are unable to complete the mission in three days, the colonel, sergeant major and staff sergeant are to be stripped of all rank. The remainder of the force shall be reduced in rank to a level to be determined by their actions on the mission. Officers can assume they are going to be starting over as second lieutenants, gunnies will be sergeants and staff sergeants will be PFCs or lance corporals.

"On the way to Canaveral, in addition to their other duties, those who have not seen the various news and propaganda videos should avail themselves of them. Have a class where you, personally, specifically instruct all senior Marines on the reality of the new world. We're in a zombie fucking apocalypse. People have a hard time getting their heads around 'no matter how this looks, this isn't the pre-Fall world.' This isn't about a girl's dad having a hissy fit. I've been the voice of *reason* in this.

"Tell the colonel that his actions in keeping so many people alive on Parris Island is the *only* reason he is not being stripped of rank immediately. Again, her 'Daddy' has been the voice of reason. The same goes for the sergeant major.

"The point being that the persons involved should have had the good sense to recognize not a 'salty' young Barbie lieutenant who was drunk with sudden power but a combat-proven officer who had both the authority and gravitas—and was in the legal and moral right—to dress down the original NCO involved. They assumed. They would make others pay for similar assumptions. They are paying for this one.

"Faith has done similar missions with much less in shorter times. If they can prove that with many

many more years of training and experience they're as good as a *seventh grader*, I'll give them a pass. If not, none of them deserve their current rank. That goes for all the senior NCOs and officers at Parris. If all they're good for is being training cadre, they're no good to anyone in this world. We're not standing up the equivalent of Parris Island again. Not for a century most likely.

"Pass to everyone that Lieutenant Lyons, former SEAL platoon leader, is on the way to Parris Island to find and hopefully recover the lieutenant. And that whatever the colonel might think, Faith is still a Marine lieutenant. When she returns to Mayport she is to have thirty days' leave. She can go salvaging and zombie hunting in Jax if she wishes and have someplace to sleep that's in the cold. She's owed: She and her Marines cleared it.

"We're taking something resembling a pause. Clearly everyone needs one. Take the time to get more equipment stood up, more people trained, get all the Marines trained in on the Wolf Way and try to give the Wolf Marines as much down time as possible consonant with getting the Parris Marines trained up and dialed in. Tell them that Faith may be going to the Pacific, General Montana wants her as his aide, or she may come back and take a command on this side. That will be determined at a later date. She's not going to stay in the wilderness. Among other things, she has friends here.

"If the colonel succeeds in three days, good. I'll send him to the Pacific since he's massively *fucked* the politics of the Atlantic. Montana has all sorts of nasty jobs for him. If not, send down some, fewer, Wolf Marines and Lieutenant Chen to get the job done. We can't let nuclear weapons go missing forever and we need the boats. The personnel there are to be temporary privates, whatever their rank, under the direction of the Wolf Marines who will be instructed to treat them like untrained privates. For the sergeant major, colonel and staff sergeant, that will be their permanent rank. They will be transferred to the Navy and assigned as stevedores.

"This matter is closed. Wolf out."

"This is fucking insane," Gunnery Sergeant Brown said. "All this . . . She's a God-damned *lieutenant*, Gunnery Sergeant! Just some salty newbie. You don't fucking break a colonel and a sergeant major over a *lieutenant*!"

"So was Presley O'Bannon," Gunnery Sergeant Sands said coldly. "So was Chesty Puller at one point. And I'm not exaggerating. You got no fucking clue what's been going on in the world, Gunnery Sergeant. If you don't want to step in the same steaming pile of infected guts your boss did, you'd better bone up. Fast. I'm not going to hold your fucking hand . . ."

"Oh . . . Jesus Christ," Gunnery Sergeant Brown said, watching the videos. "Oh . . . Fuck me. *And* a split? Fuck me . . ."

"This is at least a company objective, Colonel," Colonel Downing said, looking at the mission requirements. "Certainly to do it in three days."

"You are not being asked for your opinion, Colonel," Colonel Hamilton said. "Similar missions have been completed, in less time, by the young officer you castigated then relieved of her commission. Clearing the liners should be simple; they indicate low infected presence and there's a possibility of survivors. Nine Marine officers and staff NCOs should have no issues. If the special weapons are not in the magazines, you are not required to find them. They're just gone for the time being.

"You are to clear all the boats and prepare them for survey, salvage and recovery teams from Gitmo, raise the bridges for which you have equipment and supplementary trained personnel who can figure out the bridge systems, and clear the island to chartreuse. This is a *simple* mission, post-Fall, Colonel. You're not trying to do it with gear stripped off of boats, boarding the liners at sea and in a storm. You have one day to requisition anything you need from the base for this mission. That, right there, makes this so easy it's insane. This is *baby* steps, Colonel. Lieutenant Smith would do this mission in her sleep, having completed ten *harder* missions in the previous week, while singing the 'Star Spangled Banner' to the zombies, Colonel. As LantFleet put it, time to prove you're better than a seventh grader."

"Very well, Colonel," Colonel Downing said, standing up. "I'd better get started."

Lieutenant Lyons shook the can of spray paint and started spraying the wall.

He'd considered being an artist growing up. He was one of those kids who was always getting in trouble in school for drawing artwork in class instead of paying attention to the teachers. Of course, that was because he was bored: He was generally ahead of the class.

But he also was physically active and athletic. Which had stood him in good stead during his teenage years when you could often find him in dark clothes in an alley with a bag full of spray paint. When he'd gone through his poly for his TS they'd asked him not only had he ever been arrested or convicted of a crime but did he ever commit one. You got a free pass on most of those. This was the only crime he'd ever committed and he'd done it quite a bit over the years. Even after becoming a SEAL officer. Many an alleyway in foreign countries had his art on the walls. And NASA had even let him do so "officially" a few times, doing murals on some of their walls. Having an astronaut who was a known graffiti artist was sort of a cachet. Showed NASA was hip or something.

In this case, all he was writing was letters...

Faith took a step, paused, took a step, paused, rustled the undergrowth at her feet for a moment, took a step...

It was the way that animals moved. They weren't silent. They made a little noise. Unless startled, they didn't move fast. She could move so carefully and so naturally that the birds didn't do alarm calls when she approached. And they generally were her first warning there were infected in the area.

She stayed in the open. Moving around corners kept you out of observation for a longer time but limited your own views. Deer do not sneak around corners. Rats do, but she wasn't a rat. She was a hunter.

There were, alas, damned few alpha infected left on the island. Birds alarmed for alpha infected. That was how she'd tracked most of them down. She'd spotted, she thought, most of the betas and figured out their territories. She felt sorry for the betas. They were like naked, harmless, homeless people.

She'd actually been learning more about infected in the last week than she had in the last ten months. They nested. She'd seen one nest in Anguilla, and more than a few on boats, but hadn't really understood them. Humans were, apparently, innately acquisitive, primate magpies. But what they acquired was odd. There was always the mess of discarded food, bones and skin. One way to find them was to look for flies. But there were little things. Bright things, mostly. Jewelry, broken glass, bright clothes, toys. She'd found one beta nest she could covertly observe and watched the female playing with a doll. The female had the signs of having given birth but there was no baby. Just the doll.

She always watched her surroundings. Not focusing, staying open, her eyes drifting, looking for signs of change.

Which was why she spotted the trail. It was faint, but they generally were. Something had moved through the area. Just a few strands of bent grass but it was enough. It was human sign. It wasn't infected, either. Their trails were subtly different. It was moving in a straight line. It was a sentient.

She paused and thought about it. Da always said the most dangerous thing in a zombie apocalypse was the most dangerous thing in the world: Humans. Forget the zombies, the lions and tigers and bears. Humans were the most deadly predator on the planet.

She'd been on the lookout for humans. Any cleared area was eventually going to attract human predators.

Scavengers, anyway. And they'd probably love to scavenge a nice ripe female. The good part was that they probably wouldn't shoot first. They'd want to capture her. That would be a mistake.

She knew the betas' territories. She'd left them alone. But other territories...

The scavengers would know they were in someone else's territory when they hit the tripwires...

Lieutenant Lyons stopped as he was about to cross between two buildings. There was something subtly wrong. He wasn't sure what, but *something* was screaming at him.

He looked around. There were various places people could observe him from. But it wasn't that. He wasn't sure *what* was wrong.

He started to step forward and it was like his leg had a will of its own. "Uh, uh. Not gonna."

He closed his eyes for a moment in thought, then grimaced. He'd had this feeling before. He reached into his messenger bag, pulled out a can of silly string, shook it vigorously, then squirted it on the path. The sting landed on a nearly invisible wire placed across the concrete walkway. Following the difficult-to-see wire he finally spotted the claymore covered by a piece of junk cardboard his subconscious had detected. The cardboard must have slipped down a bit and the arming point was just visible.

"Clever girl," Lyons muttered.

That was enough graffiti art. He headed back to his hide. Give it a few days.

And stay off the trails, Lieutenant.

Faith paused at the faint remnants of another trail. It wasn't recent. Yesterday, probably. She knew there was another human on the island. But he or she was staying very covert, just as Faith was.

She continued on, cautiously. Infected didn't scare her. Humans scared the shit out of her.

She was always looking for a change. But she was primarily looking for threats. It was the smell that drew her attention, not the writing. Graffiti was not a threat. Then she realized that the human on the island probably wasn't, either.

The graffiti was professional quality. Beautifully written and drawn. A giant porcelain toilet with a rack of toilet paper next to it. And a gorgeous caption:

"FLUSH TOILETS!"

"Oh, you're not getting me back *that* easily..." Faith said. She kept the chuckle down and wondered whom they'd sent. Someone with a sense of humor at least.

She thought about where her nearest claymore was and headed that way, a bit more openly. Time to strip out some of the defenses.

The claymore was gone. He had to check. So she'd gotten at least one of his messages.

He sprayed some silly string just to make sure, then walked over to the wall where the claymore had been and started painting.

Faith had spent the afternoon the day before clearing her claymores. She didn't want a friendly to accidentally hit them. But she wondered if the unknown actor had noticed.

At the third point there was another graffiti painting.

She'd seen two more at this point. "Running Water" and "Hot Showers." That one was a little, ahem, graphic. The faces of the two people in the shower as well as naughty bits were obscured but . . . She'd gotten kind of hot. It was, okay, very soft and very well done porn.

This one, though. The guy had really taken his time. And he was, yeah, one hell of an artist.

It was a tableau: Her mum and da. Sophia in her flight suit. Gunny Sands, Januscheitis, Hocieniec. And General Montana. All of them with a hand outstretched as if asking her to join them in heaven.

"You got me," Faith muttered.

And the trail, for once, was very clear.

Lyons heard the whistle and just kept stirring the stew.

"HALLO THE CAMP!"

"Come on in!" he called, waving for her to come to the fire.

"You know, you really missed your calling, Lieutenant," Faith said as she plopped on the ground by the fire.

"You haven't, Lieutenant," Lyons said. "You damned near got me with one of those claymores."

"Sorry about that," Faith said. "I was expecting scavengers. Human scavengers. Deer step right over them."

"Animals are like that," Lyons said. "You gotta be the animal."

"Yep," Faith said. "I can't go back."

"You know how common teenage runaways were in the pre-Fall period?" Lyons asked. "I was a spokesperson for a group that helped teenage runaways. Knew a bunch of them growing up from the graffiti movement.

Which was, face it, what you did. And for all the same reasons. And they always say 'I can't go back.' They're too embarrassed even if they won't admit it.

"Faith, General Montana sent a *fast attack boat* from the Pacific. A nuclear submarine dispatched for one reason and one reason only. My orders are bring you back or your body. If I go back and say, 'She needs more time' that's fine. I'll do that. But you're wanted. You're loved. Hell, you're *beloved*. Everybody gets this. They really do. And if you want to spend some time, or the rest of your life, playing lone zombie hunter, okay. But for God's sake, you can do this in Jax and have a place to sleep with flush toilets and security. And, you know, friends.

"There is one bit of paperwork. You have to sign a form to officially withdraw your commission. Currently you are on an unscheduled 'reconnaissance of the island to gather intel on infected.' And when you get back to Jax, you're on admin leave for thirty days. Which means you can decide to sit by the pool—it's up and going again—or go salvage in the ruins or . . . read a book or something. Then decide if you really want to withdraw your commission.

"If you don't, General Montana wants you as his aide. Your da would prefer that you take over one of the new platoons that's training up in Jax. The officers and NCOs are being trained by your Marines and are, well, I'd say 'starting to realize' what a fuck-up this was but they're *past* starting and on to realization. Colonel Downing, by the way, was ordered to take his officers and senior NCOs down to Canaveral and clear it. He had three days. And he failed. He's now a stevedore in Gitmo. Your da took pity on the sergeant major and he's a sergeant. His officers were reduced to your rank and the senior NCOs were reduced to sergeant or privates."

"Waste not, want not," Faith said.

"Then they sent down Januscheitis and Hocieniec," Lyons said, grinning. "Everyone was reduced to the rank of private, temporarily except for the colonel, and put under their command. They had the island cleared and the bridges up and the liners cleared in *two* days. Oh, and they found the nukes. Right where they were expected to be."

"That's good news," Faith said. "And of course they cleared it in two days. I'd expect nothing less from my sweet devil dogs. I'm sort of... How fucked up did they have to be to *not* clear something that easy in three days?"

"Trainers often have a hard time readjusting to regular units and actual action," Lyons said, shrugging. "I had a guy come to my platoon who had been a trainer for years. He was one of *my* trainers. I really looked up to the guy. Then when he got to the teams he just could not cut it. Good operator, no leadership skills for teams. Got cut then got out of the Navy. The training cadre has operator skills by the same token. They just have to relearn the leadership for a combat, hell, post-apocalyptic, environment. So, yeah, waste not, want not.

"You can do anything you want, Faith. Stay here, go to Jax, go to Gitmo and start clearing Cuba. You can have your own island and a boat so you can come visit. But, *here*? These sand flies really *are* killer."

"And the mosquitoes at night," Faith said. "Jesus. I'm spending most of my time looking for Off."

"No harm, no foul," Lyons said. "What this . . . kerfuffle exposed was that the training cadre was not prepared to take control of combat units. That's a good thing. Some of them will be okay, some won't. We'll let the usual process handle that. If you come back, what you do after that is up to you. But you have thirty days' leave before you decide whether to actually resign your commission. Administrative. Not counted against regular leave time. It's a pre-Plague standard when you calculate your combat time and nature of actions. Not 'Daddy being nice to his poor daughter.' I've had admin leave based on stuff that's nowhere *near* the level you've done. You end up back of beyond for extended periods you get admin leave to get your head back. Normal and standard. Should have been done months ago. Just now we have enough people we *can* take the time."

"What about my troops?" Faith said. "Hocieniec has been through as much as I have. Januscheitis and the *Iwo* Marines nearly as much. They need time off, too."

"They're training the Phase Three Marines and their junior NCO instructors and having boatloads of time off while doing so," Lyons said. "And they sort of own the NCO club at Mayport. I don't think any of them have bought their own drinks since the landing. And what they're mostly doing is telling 'Lieutenant Faith' stories. Faith, can I at least get you off of this horrible little patch of swamp? Figure out what to do later?"

Faith looked around. The island was hers, all hers. But it was not the gentle Eden she was looking for. There were no horses. There were no friends to have her back. And it really was a horrible little patch of swamp.

"How are we getting out?" Faith asked.

"The *Hampton* is right off-shore," Lyons said. "And I've got a RHIB."

"Gah," Faith said. "Subs. I'm terrified of subs."

"Faith, you're terrified of *everything*," Lyons said. "You're terrified of failure and strangers and new people and public speaking and infected. A very short sub trip is minor."

"Are you saying I'm a coward?" Faith asked angrily.

"No," Lyons said, looking honestly puzzled. "But did you think that people like myself and General Montana and . . . well, everybody that was on that painting don't know that? You react to fear by being angry. It's your gift. So do all the people on that painting except maybe your mom. I don't know her at all. Did you think we didn't get that? We're the same way."

"I . . ." Faith said. "No. I thought . . . Seriously?"

"Ready to go?" he asked.

"What about the stew?" Faith said.

"It's raccoon," Lyons said. "Which tastes really horrible. On the other hand, the galley on the *Hampton* is pretty damned good. And they've got flush toilets. I'm dying for a Hollywood shower and a flush toilet. And I understand the first meal back is steak and lobster."

"Steak?" Faith said, her mouth starting to water. Lobster in the Caribbean had become something of a staple. But steak was a new one. She couldn't remember the last time she had fresh beef. "Where'd they get steak?"

"Florida turns out to have more cows than Texas," Lyons said. "And Lieutenant Chen had rifles."

"What are we waiting for?"

"How did your reconnaissance of the island go, Lieutenant?" Colonel Hamilton asked when she reported in.

"Fine, sir," Faith said. "I discovered some interesting things about infected lifestyles which I'm not sure how to apply, sir."

"After you get off your thirty-day leave, I want a detailed report," Hamilton said. "We'll add it to our general intelligence summary. That is *after* you get off leave."

"I'm not sure I need thirty days, sir," Faith said. "I'm not sure what to *do* with thirty days' leave, sir."

"Persons on leave can travel space available on any vessel in the U.S. military, Lieutenant," Hamilton said. "We have a regular ferry flight to Gitmo leaving and returning every three days so feel free to visit your parents. You can grab a boat from one of the cleared marinas and go travelling around. You can sit by the pool and read. You can go scavenge in Jax. Hell, if you found that you are evolved for submarine travel, we have a regular run to England and you can go visit King Harry. I'd say you could take the *Hampton* to the Pacific but that bastard Montana is trying to shanghai you. World is your oyster, Lieutenant. Then I need you back with your headspace and timing in place. Since we have all these Marines, gear and transport, our mission creep has gotten extensive. We've got multiple missions coming up and I need good officers for them. Oorah?"

"Oorah, sir," Faith said.

"Welcome back, Lieutenant."

CHAPTER 21

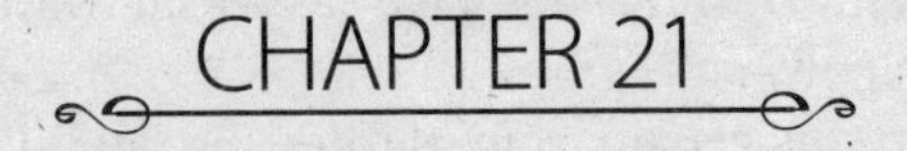

Retired Master Gunnery Sergeant Evan Walters was up on his roof waiting for the Wolf Squadron relief forces. Two days ago, there had been an announcement on the FM band that "Forces of the U.S. Naval Services" were beginning clearance in the Lejeune operational area. Starting yesterday, there'd been a rattle of fire for most of the day, occasionally punctuated by the *boom* of either a 155 or an Abrams. He was guessing Abrams. From the sound of the fire, 40mm, Ma Deuce and small arms—he'd guess amtracks with the troops up and out giving cover fire from the side. And that might mean he was going to get a chance to meet Shewolf.

Master Gunnery Sergeant Walters had heard a lot of fire in his time. Twenty-five years in the Corps in every fucking shithole in the damned world, he got out, got a good civilian job on the Post and there's a fucking zombie apocalypse. Wouldn't you know it.

He'd figured that if there was one place that wouldn't fall, it'd be Lejeune and the surrounding areas. There might be a Marine in the world that when he got out put away all his guns. There were fuckers who got out then went on TV sobbing about "give peace a chance." Happened. Didn't personally know any, and every dude he knew had an extensive gun collection as well as beaucoup ammo.

Not enough for this shit. Naked zombies were fucking *everywhere*. Half of them sporting moto tats. Turned out that having a base area full of really in-shape fuckers turned into zombies was the worst of all possible worlds.

He'd never even gotten sick. Wife three, and the best of the lot by far, not so much. Gladys had just died. He'd buried her out back. By then it was pretty apparent calling a funeral home wasn't much use.

The last act he'd performed in his civilian double-dip job was the only act he'd ever performed of which he was truly ashamed. He worked in a logistics job. Hell, he knew where stuff was stored from just being a master gunnery sergeant. So he'd gone over to one of the warehouses, loaded his truck with MREs to the top of the cover and driven home. That was shortly after Gladys passed away. He'd told Colonel Adams, his boss, who had just nodded and said: Good luck, Gunny. He couldn't approve it, obviously, and it felt a lot like stealing. But the MREs weren't going to do anyone any good sitting in a warehouse.

The base had finally gone free-fire. Too late and, with everybody fucking turning from the little intel he got, there was no way to maintain control. Then the whole area had settled down to mostly quiet. There was fire for the first week or so. He could hear the mobs of zombies any time someone fired. Then the fire would stop. You could crush a house he supposed with enough bodies. He conserved his rounds and laid low.

He had some seeds. He knew that they were hybrids and would only be good for one planting. But they were potential food. The house had a privacy fence in the back yard. He snuck out, quiet like, and did a good solid garden. Gladys had been the gardener but he'd worked on it enough with her he knew the drill. He put out snares and got some rabbits for stew.

Water. Cistern system hooked up to the gutters in the back. Cistern was a design he'd seen in Africa doing one of those fucking "hope and change" missions. Pretty good system. Needed some TLC but he had water. As long as he was quiet.

Then all he had to do was wait. The zombies had to die off sooner or later, or somebody would be able to break out. Somewhere.

The zombies didn't die off. Figuring at some point there'd at least be helos he chopped a hole in the roof in the garage and went up to stand sentry from time to time. Build some intel.

Zombies ate fricking *everything*. Humans were omnivores. They ate rats. They ate cats. He saw one get into a tussle with a coon and win. The rats should have been bad. No traps and all that food and dead bodies and shit. Nope. Because they were all getting eaten by the zombies.

He had a wind-up radio. And it kept working. All the "official" bands went silent, fast. Then it was just ham radio operators and crazies all over the place. Most of the crazies didn't last. You couldn't be entirely bughouse and keep up a generator and security to keep broadcasting. Some of them held in there. He was a personal fan of the dictator of CUBAFLORATAMP. Fucker was bughouse in a funny sort of way.

Then, one day in January, bored and sort of scanning around he heard the words "Devil Dog." So some Marine . . . what the *fuck*?

It was, allegedly, an official radio station of the United States Government. Devil Dog radio, broadcasting out of Gitmo. And it had news, at least if you believed it. Lots of news.

Devil Dog, Anchors Aweigh and Voice of America. Voice of America was like listening to PBS crossed with conservative talk radio. It had the voiceovers from "news reels" as actions happened. And they'd apparently gone back and made ones covering the creation of "Wolf Squadron."

If *any* of this shit was for real, he wanted to have Shewolf's babies. And her sister sounded like a badass for being Navy.

Then one day they had an interview with "Gunnery Sergeant Tommy J. Sands." Son of a bitch. Gave his background, which was right, and it sure as hell sounded like Tommy.

It became his regular schedule. Devil Dog did a Marine and combat-clearance news focused broadcast at 1700, very "Oorah! Oorah! Target rich environment! Oorah!" Anchors Aweigh was Navy focused—logistics, supply, sea-lanes, heavy fire power—at 1800. Then VoA at 1900 covering mostly the civilian side and international news. It was like the 1940s in a lot of ways. He was pretty sure that was deliberate on the part of whoever was running the radio stations. What was happening with Wolf Squadron and in the world as they spread out. There were other groups sort of organizing. Once Devil Dog started broadcasting, the ones on coasts were reporting the arrival of U.S. subs with vaccine and other supplies. Shit was happening. They were coming back, finally.

But for a long time it hadn't at Lejeune. He got that.

They were having to build up forces. They reported that they'd cleared Blount Island and were getting equipment into gear. Smart move. Right on the water, full of gear, probably low infected density. He grinned when they had a radio show about Shewolf's fourteenth birthday party. Fourteen, man. Fucking *fourteen*. Hell, *he'd* have turned a wrench to get that girl a tank. And Seawolf was interviewed. All she wanted for her birthday was to have a good repair and support facility for her helo. Just like her. Focused, dedicated, smart. If this was a scam, somebody was being very consistent.

Then the word that they had cleared King's Bay and secured the special weapons. No more on those than that but he'd been sweating all the SWs lying around. Most people couldn't get them to work but some crazy fucker had started this whole thing. Could happen. And if he was trying to ensure the U.S. didn't come back, he'd nuke Lejeune right after Mayport.

Parris Island, working north. The announcement had given survivor numbers, high, then, curiously, announced a change in how survivors were handled. "In all future cases where military personnel are recovered, they will be subject to evaluation and/or retraining to determine competency for exercise of rank in post-Plague conditions prior to being given any authority over personnel or units of the United States Armed Forces. Until such evaluations shall be completed, all such persons are to be treated with the respect due their rank but as civilians in terms of authority. This holds for civilians, officers and NCOs of any rank, service or position pre-Plague." There was also exactly zero mention of Shewolf or her pack.

Then the announcement that Wolf Squadron would

be conducting "retraining, small scale clearance and local operations in the Jacksonville area" "for a minimum of thirty days."

What the fuck had happened at PI? It sounded like a shake-up in the chain of command. But Wolf was still doing weekly fireside chats. In one of those he'd specifically stated that as a person born in Australia he was ineligible to run for President and "in the words of General Sherman, if nominated I shall not run, if elected I shall not serve."

The radio shows always came after the action. So now it looked like the action was starting at Lejeune. Nearly a month and a half after PI, which was odd. But he was willing to take it.

He was up on the roof scanning by Mark One eyeball when he spotted the helo. Armed up Seahawk, armed up more than any Seahawk he'd ever seen, flying fucking pillbox. The nose was painted with shark's teeth. Which was nonregulation as hell. And it was one regulation he'd always found stupid.

Then the tracks finally came into sight, the music blaring. And they were . . . Jesus. The lead was electric blue with a dragon eating zombies on the side. Big "USMC" on the front and "SEMPER FI" on the side. The others were pimped as well. American flags. Eagles. One of 'em had "Visualize World Peace" with a belching cannon firing at zombies.

The troops, who were, in MarCam at least, saw him up on the roof and waved. He waved back. He figured they were doing clearance and as long as they weren't shooting at him he could wait till the zed density dropped a bit then break out himself.

He'd hardly noticed the zombies gathering around.

They were swarming in, drawn by the sound of the music and the tracks. The tracks didn't even slow down. They were moving at about six, seven miles per hour, fast jogging pace. They'd fire up some of the infected but mostly they just kept moving, running over any that got under their treads but not even maneuvering for that.

Then he saw the Abrams. It was pink with purple tiger stripes. On the side of the turret was "Trixie," which was right, and a snarling teddy bear. Jesus. And the TC, who was turned to the rear with the turret covering their six, looked like she might be a teen. But, hell, all the troops looked that way when you were his age.

That's when he realized why they weren't stopping. They were being chased by all the fucking zombies in the world.

Then they stopped, laagering up in a formation they'd clearly used before. He figured he knew what was about to happen and put his hands over his ears.

The main gun belched canister down the road. He hoped they had checked for survivors in that direction. But it pulped the zombies. Pulped hell out of them. Staying was no longer an option. It was about to get hellish around the house when those decomposed.

Then it fired again. More pulped zombies. Cupola and coax. No more zombies. The music finished and the speakers cut out.

A guy got out of one of the amtracks, looked up at him, then gave him a thumbs up. Son of a bitch. It *was* Tommy. And the master gunny knew what was waiting for him at home. Better or worse than normal was the real question.

Fuck this. Area was clear and they were stopped. He wasn't waiting for an invitation.

Gunny Sands had gone into his house, stayed about three minutes, then come back out carrying a single can of Pabst Blue Ribbon. He paused on the doorstep on the way out, pulled out a thermite grenade, armed it and tossed it through the door. There'd been a light rain the night before and they were due for more. Nothing should burn but the one house and if the gunny wanted to burn his own house, let him.

Faith had seen the guy on the roof and that he'd come down. Before Gunny Sands was out of the house, the guy came out his front door, left it open, in uniform and battle rattle, M4, assault pack over his back, "civvies" bag in one hand and buckling on his helmet. Fuck, another master gunnery sergeant who was probably going to go on and on about the fucking "unmilitary" fucking vehicles.

Sands saw him as he was coming out, the house already going pretty good, and walked over. The gunny popped the beer, took a sip and offered it to the former neighbor. They talked a bit, then walked over to Trixie. So maybe this wouldn't be a disaster.

"Lieutenant," Gunny Sands said, holding up the can after climbing up on Trixie.

He knew she hated carbonated beverages and alcohol. Beer was both. This was important. She took a swig and handed it back.

"Thank you, ma'am," Sands said quietly. "Ma'am, this is my old boss, Master Gunnery Sergeant Evan Walters. Who is *not* a shit-head."

"Glad to have you aboard, Master Gunnery Sergeant," Faith said.

"I'm pleased to be aboard, ma'am," the master gunnery sergeant said. He almost sounded nervous. "Ma'am . . . I had a radio. I've been keeping up with Devil Dog. I just want to say it's an honor to meet you, ma'am."

"They exaggerate," Faith said, grinning. She wasn't sure which was worse; the people who couldn't get their heads around her being a lieutenant or the fans. She hated attention. And liked it at the same time. "But thanks. Way better than the alternative."

"I'd guess y'all'd be moving out about now," the master gunnery sergeant said. "Mind if I catch a ride?"

"Load up on my track, Evan," Sands said. "We can catch up."

"When the gunny's loaded we're rolling," Faith radioed, firing at an infected that was poking its head around a house.

The rolled out and left the house burning behind them.

"Tommy, I'm sorry about Charlotte," Evan said.

"No, you're not," Gunny Sands said. "But I *am* sorry about Gladys. I take it she didn't make it."

"Died of the fever," Evan said. "Buried in the back. Deep. The zombies never smelled her."

"That's good to hear," Sands said. "She was one in a million. It's a damned shame. It really is."

"Yeah," the master gunnery sergeant said. "Changing the subject. Which one, though. First, what's up with the paint jobs? Second, what the hell happened at PI? Something happened. But it wasn't reported. Wolf

Squadron had been rolling hot to PI, then 'thirty day plus stand-down.' What the hell?"

"Did you get the announcement that military personnel do not have authority until evaluated?" Sands asked.

"Yeah, and that was another thing," Evan said.

"The DIs had been locked in with their recruits for ten months," Sands said. "You know that nightmare you have when you first get to your unit and you're back in PI and it's hell and it's never going to end?"

"I had that nightmare as recently as two weeks ago," Evan said. "Hell with when I first joined."

"Well, it was like that," Sands said. "They'd just been doubling down on boot camp for ten months. Some of the recruits were around the bend. So were some of the DIs in a way. One of the DIs went off on one of our troops. I wasn't there or I'd have handled it. Guy is a ragbag, admittedly, but the DI was out of line. Faith locked him up. Acting post sergeant major got involved. Faith was having a bad day. She'd gotten half eaten by a gator reconning the landing the night before. She went off on the sergeant major. Colonel decided this salty young officer drunk on power needed 'counseling.' When he found out she was fourteen he ordered her to turn in her rank and weapons. She was out. So she went bush on PI."

"Jesus," Evan said, shaking his face. "Do I get to punch out the sergeant major? I'm retired. They can only charge me with assault."

"They didn't even charge me with that," Sands said. "Past issue. That was the stand-down. Getting them all back in shape, the ones that were recoverable. Colonel Downing might have been, might not. Wolf gave him a task and more or less the standard we'd have for ourselves. He failed. Then we sent down one of our good staffs, put him in charge of the colonel and his team and showed them how you do it the Wolf Way. Colonel's now a stevedore. Sergeant major was reduced to sergeant. He's on the West Coast. And that's the reason for the 'unmilitary vehicles' to answer your other question."

"That I don't get," Evan said.

"You said 'what's with the paint job,'" Sands said. "Part of that is you know me and you've been on a radio. But you could handle it."

"Paint's fairly ship-shape," Evan said. "Just seems weird. Looks more like a militia."

"There is that issue," Sands admitted. "It's why Trixie was pink, then sand, and now pink again. And when we go back to clearing civilian areas, we may switch back to regular paint jobs. But the bigger issue is people who cannot handle the fact that we're not *hiding* from enemy forces, we're trying to *draw them out*, cannot handle command or authority in this world. They're useless to us, at least as combat officers and NCOs. So we get to test them right away. And if they don't pass, they don't have any real authority. And until they're evaluated, they *definitely* don't have any authority. They try to lock our people up for unmilitary vehicles, we just log that and they have a long road back to ever being able to give an order."

"That makes sense," Evans said. "I guess. Are we evacuating the base?"

"No," Sands said. "We're pulling most people off shore until they're evaluated. You're already evaluated by the way. Pass. If you want back in, you're onboard. If not, we're picking up enough people these days it's not an automatic reactivation. Up to you."

"I think I got one more war in me," Evan said.

"We'll get you cleared immediately, then," Sands said. "Can I tell you the truth?"

"Sure," Evan said.

"I'm glad you made it," Sands said. "Sort of. If Charlotte was dead and you didn't make it, I was going to propose to Gladys. So . . . sort of."

"Bastard," Evan said, grinning.

"Second finest woman I ever met," Sands said.

"Second?"

"Okay, so Shewolf is crazy as a bedbug," Sands said. "And way too young for me. But, yeah, second."

"Going for the crazies was always your problem, shipmate."

"Who the hell authorized personalization of vehicles!"

The major was a little wild-eyed and clutching an AR15. This one would have to be handled carefully.

"You're not real Marines!"

"Yes we are, sir," Gunny Sands said calmly. "United States Marine Corps. Full controlling legal authority. Major, you need to put the weapon down or we're going to fire on you with prejudice."

"Answer my question, Gunnery Sergeant!" the major said. "Who the hell authorized personalization of vehicles?"

"LantFleet, sir," Gunnery Sergeant Sands said. "And you shall place the weapon on the deck or you're not going to survive."

"You can't give *me* orders, Gunnery Sergeant! The commandant would never approve personalization of vehicles! You're not Marines!"

The guy had family or something. Hopefully family.

There was a young male watching the tableau from the home he'd emerged from.

"Until you are psych cleared you are functionally a civilian, sir," Gunny Sands said. "We've had this issue before in clearance, sir. Now you are *going* to stand down or my troops are going to have to shoot you in front of your child, sir. I don't want that to happen, sir."

The major started as Trixie pivoted and backed. The main gun swung around with a squeal until it was inches from the major's head.

"PUT . . . THE WEAPON . . . DOWN." Faith said over the speaker system.

The major put the weapon down.

"Now, sir, if you'd like to go retrieve your son we'll be happy to transport you to the evac ships for eval . . ."

"Looking for Master Gunnery Sergeant Evan Walters," Faith said after sticking her head in the compartment.

Lejeune was a big area. Even with a company of Marines in five times the number of tracks a company would use, it was taking time to clear the whole thing. They were done with the base and working on the nearby towns. That was where they'd stopped at the gunny's for a cold beer and picked up his friend.

"Be right with you, ma'am," Evan said, rolling out of his rack.

"Just uniform or whatever, Master Gunnery Sergeant," Faith said.

Faith led him down to one of the "civilian" bars in the liner and took a table.

"I understand the whole thing about back pay," Evans said, grinning. "But you may be buying, ma'am."

"Glad to," Faith said as a server came over. "Hey. What do you have that has no carbonation and no alcohol that is not coffee or tea?"

"Water?" the woman said. "Fruit juices. I'm not sure what we've got available."

"Water, then," Faith said. "Give the master gunnery sergeant whatever he'd like."

"Coffee?" Evans said. "I've been out for a while."

"Anything to eat? We've got some frijoles?"

"Sushi?" Faith asked.

"And that, yeah," the waitress said. "Most people are pretty over that."

"Sushi if it's *fresh*," Faith said. "I mean *really* fresh. I've been eating it practically quivering for a while. Tataki if it's possible."

"I'm good with sushi," Evans said.

"I'll check," the woman said.

"So," Faith said. "While we wait on sushi that's probably stinking... I've been with the gunny since we pulled him off the *Iwo*."

"Yes, ma'am," Evans said.

"And the one time that someone brought up... female company, he pointed out that he was married. Waiting for the float to be over and get home for his cold-beer. And the first spot that we went to when we hit the civilian side of the bay was the gunny's house. Which was... Well..."

"Yeah," Evans said, nodding.

"I'm sorry for your loss as well, Master Gunnery Sergeant," Faith said quickly. "I don't mean to..."

"Not an issue, ma'am," Evans said. "Gladys was

my third wife and the first one that was worth a damn. But she died as peaceful as you can from that damned disease."

"Having had it, I know it's not the best way to go," Faith said. "But it's better than turning."

"Yes, ma'am," Evans said. "It really wasn't all that bad. Quick, anyway."

"Days of agony," Faith said. "But I was sort of bitten."

"That's double tough," Evans said.

"Think that's bad," Faith said, holding up her scarred left hand. "Alligator."

"Shark," the gunny said, pulling up his pants leg. "Little one in surf off Phuket."

"Since we've established our CVs," Faith said. "The gunny just made that one comment. It was his crazy. Everybody's got at least one. But . . . he must have really loved her. I don't think he's ever talked about her except that one time. That's how people who can't really handle it . . . deal. They don't talk about . . . who they lost. I'm just wondering . . . What was she like?"

"You really want to know, ma'am?" Evans said as the waitress came back over. She had a beautifully prepared plate of thinly sliced tuna and their drinks.

"Try it," the lady said. "The chopping guy says it's fresh yellowfin. He was also real excited you were in the restaurant but he speaks some weird language. I couldn't get what he was gabbling about. You famous or something?"

"Or something," Faith said, taking a bite. "Tell him thank you. That's great. Really incredible."

"You got chit or scrip?" the lady asked. "That's ten chit, eighth piece, or two-fifty scrip."

"Card," Faith said, handing over her charge card.

"Scrip it is," the lady said.

"Eighth piece?" Evans said.

"We get paid some in gold or silver sometimes," Faith said, shrugging. "We got some from banks, people turn junk in and it's minted at Blount."

"Pirate days," Evans said, shaking his head then grinning. "That could be fun."

"True," Faith said. "Some of this stuff is. Not much. So . . . I don't even know her name. The gunny's wife."

"Charlotte," Evans said, taking a sip of coffee to give himself time. "And the truth is, ma'am . . . You know what a dependapotamus is?"

"No?" Faith said, frowning. "Dependent of the river?"

"What?" Evans said.

"Potamus is 'of the river,'" Faith said. "Hippopotamus is 'horse of the river.' Figured it was mixed with dependent."

"A dependapotamus, ma'am, is a dependent that supplies *nothing* to the relationship, ma'am," Evans said, shaking his head. "Sands was one of the finest young Marines I've ever had. I mean right from the day he reported as a boot, you could see the makings of a gunny. Motivated, dedicated, competent. Just fucking squared away. Dad was a Marine. Granddad was a Marine. Sort of guy who really should have gone to OCS. Sort of gunny, when he made it . . . You ever hear that in Vietnam they took gunnies and just promoted them straight to brigadier general?"

"It's come up," Faith said. "Been discussed in this situation. We've tended to get two kinds. The kind you could do that if we had unlimited bodies, which we don't, or the type that can't get their heads around the fact that this is a zombie apocalypse we *have* to win, not a guerilla war in some foreign country that really doesn't matter a hill of beans. Generally, if the first thing they look at is the shine of the troop's boots or whether they have their hands in their pockets...we put them out to pasture. But you're saying Sands was one of those. Which I agree about. But his wife...wasn't."

"She was his millstone, ma'am," Evans said. "Fat. Ugly. Well, not ugly. Just one of those women who might have been cute at eighteen but they went downhill fast. Slovenly. Hoarder. Sands' room was always neat as a fucking pin. God-damned house was a fucking wreck. Always. Covered in unemptied ash trays, piles of junk. She had two little dogs that crapped everywhere. Jesus would they bite. *And* they hated Tommy. Just a fucking wreck. He'd just say that when he made a commitment it was till death do they part. In that way, this damned plague is the best thing that's ever happened to him."

"Jesus," Faith said, shaking her head. "Why would... Seriously? The gunny? Why marry somebody like that in the first place?"

"Sands is all about honor, right, ma'am?" Evans said. "But you know, this was *years* ago. When he was a boot, practically. She 'got pregnant,'" Evans said, making quotes in the air. "I told him it probably wasn't his and he should wait or just pay the child support. But he upped and married the scheming little bitch. Then she 'had a miscarriage' after they were married. I'm not even sure she was really pregnant. Or she might have had an abortion. She sure as hell never got pregnant afterwards. Sands wanted to. She said she was off the pill. But . . ." He shrugged again.

"Hell, and he might not have fooled around but she had a parade of hog fuckers in and out of the house every time he was on float, pardon my language, ma'am. If she wasn't on the Pill she'd have had some other guy's kid."

"That is fucked up," Faith said.

"That it is, ma'am," the master gunnery sergeant said. "I made much the same mistake myself when I was a youngster. Just didn't feel I had to torture myself the rest of my life for it. You saw the beer, ma'am?"

"He said that he was waiting for the float to be over," Faith said. "Wanted his cold-beer. One word. I told him the first place we were going was his house so he could have his cold-beer. He did point out that what with the power out and all it probably wouldn't be cold."

"She was a serious drinker, ma'am," Evans said. "They were always short on money what with her either buying cheap stupid shit or spending it on booze. I kept hoping cirrhosis would kill her. Thought about just feeding her some margaritas with antifreeze in it.

"I had Sands on his first float. Squared away. Perfect fucking Marine, ma'am. Hard worker, fast learner. Never fell for the tricks people play on the new guys. I got him promoted to first class as fast as I could. He was too good to have mosquito wings.

"Got back from the float, looking forward to his new mamasan. She never even turned up at the homecoming. He had to catch a ride to the apartment they had. She'd gained thirty pounds and there was no beer in the house. He just went off about the beer. I mean, he was losing his military bearing at the unit; I'm sure he was going off about it at home. There was something about that that got through her thick head. So every time he came home from float, there'd be one beer left. Just one. Maybe it was one of her sick games. But he always had his cold-beer when he got home. Only thing she ever got right as a dependent in all the years I've known him."

"Fuck," Faith said.

"He's free of that she-devil, ma'am," Evans said. "I miss my Gladys, but he's free of that she-devil. I just hope like hell he don't make the same mistake."

"I'll make sure he doesn't," Faith said.

"You just for the first time made me realize you really *are* fourteen, ma'am," Evans said, shaking his head.

CHAPTER 22

"Well, that's a pisser," Faith muttered as the doors of the supply warehouse were cracked open. The first person through the door was a two-star general.

She'd learned to just let the gunny handle the senior guys. They couldn't see past the Barbie and the bars. Unless, like Evan, they'd had a hand-crank radio. Which they never seemed to have in the "official redoubts."

"General," Sands said, saluting. "Gunnery Sergeant Tommy J. Sands, First Marine Battalion."

"Good to see you, Gunny," the general said, returning the salute. "Major General Lowell Ramos, deputy post commander. I'm going to hope that there's a damned good reason Marine vehicles are painted up like ghetto cruisers."

"That, sir, is my platoon leader," Sands said, pointing up to Faith. She wasn't watching the interplay, just keeping an eye out for leakers. "Who holds two Navy crosses for actions against infected, sir, from just the *first six months* of her tour, sir. Lieutenant Smith is fourteen and earned both while *thirteen*, sir. Officers who cannot grasp that a fourteen-year-old girl is the baddest-ass zombie-killer in the post-Plague world, and that that is the *only* criteria right now for how good of an officer you are, have repeatedly broken their careers on Shewolf, sir. There is no actual need for camouflage, sir, and some arguments against it. So it's a test, sir. Can you adapt, react and overcome to this new world or are you 'pre-Plague' and just need a nice quiet desk job, General?"

"Had issues in the past?" the general said.

"Yes, General," Sands said. "Current standing orders are that rescuees are to be treated with due military courtesy but, as with prisoners of war, until they have passed evaluations and are cleared for duty, they have no actual authority, sir. So we don't have to break any more careers of officers who don't get that you're looking at the Chesty Puller of the post-Plague world, General. And because people who cannot are really not much good to us, sir. Those that cannot . . . There are plenty of desk jobs, generally at lower rank, waiting on them, sir."

The general thought about that for a long moment.

"Chesty Puller," the general said.

"Not an exaggeration, sir," Sands said. "Fourteen. Two Navy Crosses. Really deserves more."

"This is going to be a very long brief, isn't it?" the general said.

"You're getting there, sir," Sands said, breathing out. "Considering that LantFleet is a directly promoted civilian Navy captain whose previous military service was as an Aussie para, CINCPAC is a commodore who was an Army lieutenant general and took a voluntary demotion and service transfer, the CJCS is an Air Force brigadier, the NCCC is one hundred twenty-*sixth* on the list and we're finding between zero and five percent survivors world-wide . . . Yes, sir."

The general took a deep breath and breathed out. "*Long* brief. Major! Get everyone loaded! Time's a wastin'."

"Come!" Faith said at a tap on her door. She'd just gotten out of the shower and was drying her hair.

"Lieutenant?" the major who had been in the warehouse said, opening the door.

"Sir?" Faith said, startled. She was in shorts and a T-shirt, which wasn't nude or anything but she wasn't expecting a major.

"The general and I have been cleared for duty," the major said. "He was wondering if you could spare him some time. If you're uncomfortable with that, I'll tell him you'd already turned in."

"No, sir," Faith said. "But my hair's obviously a wreck and I'll need to get dressed. Ten minutes?"

"That will do fine, Lieutenant," the major said. "We weren't introduced. Major James Skelton."

"Pleasure to make your acquaintance, Major," Faith said. "And each second is another I'm keeping the general waiting, sir. What compartment?"

"Seventy-two, thirty-three, Empress deck, Lieutenant," the major said. "I'll tell the general about ten minutes."

"No time for make-up," Faith said, rubbing her hair. "Damnit, I hate being in the Marines!"

"Have a seat, Lieutenant," General Ramos said.

The stateroom was one of the better ones on the liner. Since it was a "mega-liner," that was very nice indeed. An "ocean view" suite was the general luxury of a suite in a five star hotel, if smaller.

Faith carefully sat at the edge of the indicated chair at attention.

"Would you care for a drink, ma'am?" the major asked solicitously.

"Water, sir?" Faith said, starting to stand up.

"I'll get it, Lieutenant," the major said.

"Just water?" the general said.

"I don't drink alcohol, sir," Faith said. "It has almost no effect on me and I don't like the taste of most kinds. If it's an issue, sir, vodka. It doesn't taste horrible and it won't bother me till I've had a bottle or so."

The general started to say something, then just shook his head.

"If you could get the lieutenant some water, please, Major. I'll take coffee in that case."

"Yes, sir," the major said.

"Is my not drinking an issue, sir?" Faith asked. "Vodka is fine, sir."

"Not at all," General Ramos said. "Just another . . . I was informed that there is an acronym post-Plague—ZAM."

"ZAM or zammie, yes, sir," Faith said. "Zombie apocalypse moment."

"Just a zammie," General Ramos said. "I've been reviewing the written histories. I was quite surprised by their professional quality given the circumstances. Then I recalled your father's background pre-Plague. I have also had the various 'introduction' videos running. Given your experiences, I had expected you to be a *heavy* drinker."

"Yes, sir," Faith said. "Most people do, sir. I think drunk people are stupid and I don't like looking stupid, sir."

"You've cleared ships like this before," General Ramos said.

"Yes, sir," Faith said.

"How?" Ramos said. "I've only been through a very small portion. This is an enormous amount of deck space."

"One compartment at a time, sir," Faith said. "At this point, all personnel in staterooms like this are assumed to be dead. No food or water. Therefore we concentrate on crew areas, which the crews often stocked, as well as storage points primarily below the main water tanks. The *Voyage* took two weeks, sir. We can rough-clear a liner in a couple of days at this point, sir. That is, one that was in service. This one was rough-cleared in a few hours, sir. Took about a week to get it back in operation, although I understand there are still some issues with the plumbing. Sir."

"I also reviewed the incident with Colonel Downing," General Ramos said. "I'm not getting involved. The incident should not have been unexpected, all things considered, both your own combat record and the situation. The original DI violated established procedures, and the colonel was given a chance to redeem himself, which he failed. It's not specifically stated anywhere, but that would seem to be the rationale for the 'no authority until cleared.'"

"That and other issues, sir," Faith said.

"Which are?" General Ramos asked.

"The direct reason given is that these sieges people have been in are similar to being prisoners of war, sir," Faith said. "Everyone coming out of a compartment is dealing with various stressors, sir. They may think they are ready to just get going, and when we were critical on personnel we *needed* them to get up to speed as fast as possible. But some people have a harder time adjusting than others, sir. Specifically, all of the personnel recovered from Parris Island were . . . not in the best shape, sir. The DIs had had to continue to be DIs night and day for ten months and instead of reorganizing as a combat unit and training for infected combat, they'd essentially kept the trainees in boot mode. They were all *highly* inflexible, even for Marines, sir. The boots required extensive retraining on initiative and combat actions. The DIs had to be retrained for leadership of combat forces and many of them simply could not cut the mustard, not at their pre-Plague rank. So the new approach is to take a wait and see attitude and in the meantime, to keep from having similar incidents or worse, do some evaluation. Sir."

"Have you been evaluated?" General Ramos asked.

"I took the evaluation after my leave, sir," Faith said. "I was found to be fit for duty."

"Clearly you are, Lieutenant," the general said. "What are your goals, Lieutenant?"

"A zombie-free world, sir," Faith replied.

"That is a big order," Ramos said.

"I am young, sir," Faith said. "I have time, sir."

"In terms of your career as a Marine officer, Lieutenant," Ramos said.

"My career, sir, is to create a zombie-free world, sir," Faith said. "Currently, sir, my Marine career enhances a zombie-free world, sir. If that were to change, I would find a career which did so, sir."

"I don't see us stopping the fight against the infected any time soon," Ramos said. "But if we were to do so you are saying that you would find some other job that involved killing zombies?"

"Yes, sir," Faith said.

"What if the mission was to help people, instead?" Ramos asked.

"The biggest help we can give people right now, sir, is killing zombies, sir," Faith said.

"Agreed," Ramos said. "And as noted that is probably not going to change any time soon. I've only spoken to your father briefly. And he was . . . reticent on clearance strategy. Are you aware of his plans in that regard on the strategic level?"

"No, sir," Faith said.

"Never discussed them around you?" Ramos asked.

"Captain Smith is . . . cautious about discussing plans, sir," Faith said. "That has always been the case, sir. His reference to that is usually the American general Stonewall Jackson who was notorious for keeping his plans close to his vest, sir. He doesn't like to make promises he can't keep and he has a staging process for plans, sir. There is an acronym I forget, sir." Faith thought about it for a moment. "Desires, Intentions, Goals, Concepts, Plans, Actions, sir. Believe that is the series, sir. Each of those up to 'actions' may have several forms of equivalent value until they're evaluated. Some are discarded leading to the next stage, sir. I'm not sure where the captain is in terms of strategic clearance in that series, sir. My father desires a zombie-free world, sir. So far his actions have been to build forces with very little strategic or even operational clearance. Probably because he's somewhere in the middle of the series, sir."

"Are you familiar with mechanicals, Lieutenant?" Ramos asked.

"I saw the ones in the Canaries, sir," Faith said. "I haven't seen any of the new ones in action, sir. I've read the reports, sir."

"What do you think of them?"

"I think they're slow and somewhat inefficient, sir," Faith said. "I discussed that with my father on leave, sir. They do well for the first week, sir. But it takes a fairly stupid zombie to walk into one, sir. After the first week, their clearance rate drops, sir. I did more clearance in one night with an Abrams and a platoon in amtracks than all the mechanicals in Miami. On the other hand, they just keep going, sir. A tank is a high maintenance item, sir. And there is a limited supply of M1028 in this fallen world, sir. There are arguments both ways, sir."

"And they only work on coastal cities," General Ramos said.

"Or riverine, sir," Faith said. "And mechanicals don't drop a city to low orange. The best they do is high orange. Dropped from red but not even to yellow in most cases. I could clear New York or D.C. with my platoon in three or four days, sir. At least Manhattan, sir. Up to the point we run out of M1028 at which point . . . I can't crush them all, sir."

"No," Ramos said. "And you don't know if mechanicals are your father's only plan?"

"No, sir," Faith said. "At least, I don't think they are. Again, Da keeps things pretty close to the vest. But he's said mechanicals are only part of the plan, sir."

"I'd considered asking you to be my aide," General Ramos said. "Then I realized that would be a bad idea. Good because you are, unquestionably, the best known and one of the most knowledgeable fighters of the post-Plague environment. Having your experience close would be an asset. Bad because it would be far outside your skill-sets and you would probably hate it. Especially since it would be junior aide, mostly handling the social side. You've been a second lieutenant for more than six months, haven't you?"

"Yes, sir," Faith said. "The general idea, sorry, is that I'll probably stay a two LT until I'm at least sixteen if not older. Which I'm fine with, sir. I'm really not about rank, sir. Just want to clear zombies, sir."

"Are you continuing your education?" Ramos asked.

"Yes, sir."

"How's that going?"

"I'm up to eleventh grade class-work, sir," Faith said. "Mostly self-taught through computer classes with some occasional assistance from other officers, sir. I'm not sure I could go back to a classroom, sir. Meetings are bad enough, sir."

"It will be a while before we stand Annapolis or the Point back up," General Ramos said. "But you need to get your head around going back to school at some point. You'll need the professional education as your career advances."

"Yes, sir," Faith said.

"Disagree?" the general asked.

"My career is killing zombies, sir," Faith said. "Not sure what decimating Chaucer has to do with that, sir."

"I believe the word you were looking for there, Lieutenant, is deconstructing," Ramos said after a moment of furrowed brow.

"As you say, sir," Faith said. "It will be a while before it becomes an issue, sir."

"Agreed," Ramos said. "Very well, Lieutenant. Thank

you for your time. It was a good chat. Look forward to working with you in the future."

"Thank you, sir," Faith said, setting down her nearly untouched water. "By your leave, sir?"

"She *meant* decimation, didn't she?" Ramos said.

"I suspect she did, sir," Major Skelton said.

"Turn in, Jimmy," the general said, picking up another briefing book. "I'm going to keep doing my own homework. If a fourteen-year-old Lieutenant can trip me up, I clearly need to get my brain in gear."

"Aye, aye, sir."

"Ugh," Faith said, taking off her blouse and hanging it up. "That was worse than spinning out on infected."

She looked at the stack of books by her bed, then sat down at the computer and brought up her latest class. She had a full day of clearance tomorrow but she also had a ton of homework. She popped the top on a Razzleberry tea and started the video.

"No rest for the wicked," she muttered, taking a sip. "Ah. Sweet nectar of a lost world. What *shall* I do when you are no more . . . ? And I meant *delineating*, General. The Lyf So Short, the Craft So long to Lerne . . ."

"Got a civilian sailboat approaching from the west," Petty Officer Third Class Marc Dunross said, looking through the binos. "Fifty-five foot ketch."

They'd been getting a trickle of refugees at Gitmo. People who had radios and were able to break out by boat had been steadily streaming in. This looked like another group.

On the off chance that some group had "bad"

intentions, there were two "forts" guarding the entrance again. They had Mk19 40mms which didn't have much range compared to previous generations of "coastal artillery" batteries but could take on most of what they would expect in terms of post-Plague piracy. Which had so far failed to materialize.

What people *didn't* see was the fast attack boat sitting deep and silent. Anybody with bad intentions the Mk19s couldn't handle were going to be in for a very *brief* shock.

Mayport had a similar set-up.

The standing watch on the East Harbor Watch Tower had been fairly bored up to this point in the watch and would probably go back to being bored. The boat didn't seem heavily armed.

"Roger," Petty Officer Second Class Andrew Stagg said. "I'll call harbor control."

"Welcome to Guantanamo Bay!" Master-at-Arms Mate Second Class Warren Hall said as the Zodiac came alongside the ketch. "Permission to come aboard?"

"Granted," the captain said. He was a tall and very handsome man with a bright blond beard, long unshorn hair, blue eyes and unsurprisingly a dark tan. He was wearing a faded Hawaiian shirt and worn cargo shorts. The shirt had stains on it that might have been from fish blood. Might.

There were a bunch of refugees on the deck; the boat was loaded just to the point of over-loading. Most of them were women and children with the exception of the captain and two other men. Several had side-arms and one of the men was carrying an M4 as if he knew how to use it.

Hall pulled himself aboard and smiled at the group.

"Where are you out of?" he asked the captain.

"Tampa," the man replied.

"Good to see more new faces," Hall said. "I am Master-at-Arms Mate Hall. I need to give a brief familiarization class before you proceed.

"When you arrive you'll be given the choice of land- or sea-based refugee housing. Sea-based is on a cruise liner and is more secure than land-based. There are still a few infected on the land side. Sea-based, no weapons, explosives or ammunition are permitted carried onboard. You'll have to turn them in to a master-at-arms for storage in an arms room. You'll be given an opportunity to clean them either at the time you turn them in or afterwards if you prefer. When you leave the boat you can pick them up.

"On land, open carry is permitted and encouraged. There are, as mentioned, still a trickle of infected on the land. Any use of a weapon other than on infected is charged in the normal sort of way with the exception that it's . . . quick. If you kill someone because you got into a drunken brawl and shot him or her, you're given a very short trial, a very limited appeal, then shot as well. Period. Rape with intent if proven before a jury of your peers is *also* a capital crime for both military and civilians. We've had some people come out of compartments that got used to not hearing the word 'No.' We have fewer now. Or you'll end up with a short trial and a bullet in your brainpan. For lesser crimes like theft, the sentence is hard labor, which is mostly body clearance. You're back in civilization. Be civil, be safe.

"Any persons who are current active duty military

or reserve are automatically reactivated as are most former military who are in the age range for reactivation. Veterans outside the age range who wish to volunteer can do so. Anyone wanting to *volunteer* for military service, you'll get the opportunity. And I probably shouldn't mention this but probably stuck either up on the watch tower that spotted you or doing something like this. There are civilian jobs as well. Plenty of work to go around.

"When you get into the harbor, dock at the liner," Hall said to the captain. "Your people will be given the choice of land or sea. Then get vaccinated, not an option if you're staying in cleared zones, get some food in them, get quarters and a shower. No ration, currently, on water. Shower as long as you'd like."

"That sounds fabulous," one of the women said. She was holding a new baby in her arms. She wasn't the only one.

"We've got some medical care freeing up," the petty officer said. "Now that the baby wave is passing. Not much, only one MD and you'll probably never see him. But corpsmen and some others with training. Babies get vaccinated as well if they're old enough. Are there any questions?"

"When do we report in?" the captain asked.

"As soon as you fill in your social security number you're activated," the petty officer said. "What were you?"

"Admiral Josh Hiscock," the captain said. "I'm the SOCOM Commander."

"Admiral," Steve said, saluting as the admiral landed from the Zodiac. He'd "checked in" at the liner, gotten showered, shorn and changed and headed over to the piers. "Welcome to Guantanamo Bay, sir."

"Commodore Wolf," Admiral Josh Hiscock said, returning the salute and sticking out his hand. Someone had found him a set of NavCam and he'd brought his own stars. Like Steve, he had an H&K USP on his hip, which he'd also brought along. "I've been keeping up with your exploits by radio. To say the least, I'm impressed but not surprised. I'd worked with Aussie paras before and you represent them well."

"Thank you, sir," Steve said. "Very glad to have you aboard."

"Nobody seems to know what to do with an admiral," Hiscock said. "I agree with Night Walker that booting you out is not in the best interests of the nation."

"We're getting a bigger and bigger force, sir," Steve said, waving to the waiting car. "This world needs all the help it can get. We're extending ops all over the world at this point and having an experienced flag officer who *gets* this is a zombie apocalypse is a boon. Very glad to have you aboard, sir."

CHAPTER 23

Despite the parking lot in Baie Saint-Paul being plowed, there was a white-out when the Sea Dragon came in to land. White-outs sucked. The world and all your spatial references just disappeared. They were one of the major causes of crashes by helos on landing.

Commander Sanderson was expecting it and kept his eye on the belly radar return, coming in slow, listening to the drift calls from the scanners and the airspeed and altitude calls from EZ. They all took a deep breath when the wheels touched down with just the smallest bit of forward movement. Soft landing.

"I'm glad you were on that and not myself, sir," Lieutenant Chrysler said. "I've flown in snow before, but never with a rotor this big." Bigger rotors meant more rotor wash, which meant more snow or dust or whatever being flung into the air.

"That was why I took it, Lieutenant," Sanderson said. "Do the post-flight. I'm going to go meet this Air Force sergeant. Jesus, the guy's got to clang when he walks."

"Yes, sir," Chrysler said.

"Sir! Sergeant Williamson, Air Force Security Force, sir," Williamson said, saluting Sanderson as he walked through the cargo portion of the bird.

The Sea Dragon wasn't overloaded but that was just because of how much it could carry. The back was packed with material. Most of it was medicine and medical equipment. The Fall had stripped most hospitals and pharmacies, not to mention killing practically every doctor on Earth. Medical support was the number one need of every community in the world.

Two coolers, however, were critical.

"First of all, Sergeant," Sanderson said, returning the salute, then sticking out his hand. "If you'll do me the honor, let me shake your hand. Fifteen hundred miles through *this*?" the commander said, waving at the snow-covered post-apocalyptic terrain.

"No issues, sir," Williamson said. "Survivors along the way were very friendly. Happy to see some signs of recovery, a uniform at least, and more than willing to give support. Had to help out a few times with clearance, sir. No issues, sir."

"Double tough, Sergeant," Sanderson said, shaking his hand. "I will never again refer to it as the Chair Force."

"Thank you, sir," Williamson said.

"The vaccine cannot be allowed to freeze," Sanderson said. "It has to be kept cool but not frozen. That's clear?"

"Yes, sir," Williamson said. "We'll separate the containers between two of the MRAPs, sir. The Cougars are handling the road pretty well, once the SnowCats plow them down a bit. And they're climate controlled, sir."

"Ooyah," the commander said. "Good luck on your return voyage, Sergeant. I'll be looking for word of your safe arrival."

"We'll get it done, sir," Williamson said.

"That, right there, is one very brave sergeant," Sanderson said as the Sea Dragon lifted off.

"Yes, sir, he is," Chrysler replied. His tone was faintly wistful.

"You disagree?" Sanderson said.

"No, not at all," the former actor replied. "I'm actually thinking if I wasn't already doing important stuff and if I wasn't so God-damned old, I'd want to join him. Say what you want about the current horror. It is, absolutely, horror. But a world that was once humdrum now . . . isn't. Adventure awaits at every turning for the survivor. It is impossible to *avoid*. I liked doing the movies I did but I liked, even more, the thought of *being* that character. Of going on those adventures. I loved doing the on-scene since it took me to places that were at least wild and beyond. It's why I was so addicted to the role.

"That sergeant and his team, crossing fifteen hundred miles of howling wilderness. Possibly bandits. Probably infected. Lions and tigers and bears, oh, my. Bringing medical supplies, radios and hope to people along the way? That right there is adventure. I hate what has happened. I would turn back the clock if I could. But this is a world made for the adventurous. I wish I was forty years younger."

"If we can get rid of the damned infected," Sanderson said.

"There is that . . ."

"Welcome to Gitmo, General," Steve said, saluting.

General Ramos saluted as soon as he reached the bottom of the stairs, then shook Steve's hand. The band broke into the Marine Corps Hymn as a cannon started firing the salute for a two-star flag officer. There was a selection of military personnel lined up in ranks on the tarmac in their best kit, including a company of Marines in combat gear.

"Commodore Wolf," Ramos said. "It's an honor to meet you."

"The honor is all mine, General," Steve said. "Would you care to troop the line?"

"It would be an honor," Ramos said.

"That was quite the pomp and circumstance," Ramos said afterwards as they were sitting in Steve's office.

"I aim to please, General," Steve said. "And we rarely get the chance. Being specific, we've *never* before gotten the chance. General Montana turned it down flat the one time I suggested it and Admiral Hiscock arrived so fast we were taken off guard."

"I'd heard even before the Plague Night Walker was a bit of a character," Ramos said. "I don't usually go for full honors myself. But I could see you'd gone to a lot of trouble. The Marines are part of Task Force Charlie?"

"Roger, General," Steve said, "Just back from clearance operations in St. Martin. We really didn't like leaving those cruise ships behind on the last sweep. They found some survivors. It's possible some people ran out of stores in the meantime. I just try to ignore that sort of thing."

"Understood," Ramos said. "I had some interesting conversations with your daughters on the way down. Possibly illuminating, possibly not. Let me first say, as I'm sure everyone does: Wow! Holy crap on a cracker. Good job, there, Captain."

"Thank you, sir," Steve said. "It wasn't all me, General. Stacey not only bore them, she was right there raising them. It was a team effort."

"I hope to meet her at some point and will add my compliments," Ramos said.

"If you're prepared for it, we're scheduled for dinner en famille, General," Steve said. "Up to you."

"Again, I'd be honored," Ramos said. "This . . . bootstrap has been not only incredible in its drive but competently done. Which was not meant to be an insult. Competence was what was needed."

"Much of the competence, as always, relies on others," Steve said. "Commander Isham, although we did not start out well, was a blessing. Amazingly competent guy. Most of the people we recovered were competent. The conditions tended to sort for those. Incompetence in the compartments was a death sentence as I'm sure you're well aware, General. Heinlein once said 'Ignorance is its own death penalty.' That wasn't generally true, in fact it was rarely true, in the pre-Plague world. Competence couldn't save you from the disease but only competence could keep you alive in the sieges afterwards. Even Colonel Downing is too competent to keep at menial tasks indefinitely. There is simply too much to do."

"Agreed," Ramos said. "I'll have a chat with him at some point."

"His response has been very Marine, sir, I'll give him that," Steve said. "He agrees that his actions were not the best and based upon both the stresses of relief and ignorance of the post-Fall conditions. I don't actually have him as a stevedore. He's one of the clerks in the shipping office and, naturally, superlative at it. Faith agrees her actions were not the best. She's actually kind of mortified even if she doesn't show it.

"The truth is, General, that the fault on the incident lies on my shoulders. Both for not implementing the orders regarding determination of competence post-rescue earlier and insisting that the lieutenant and her men take a break earlier. We should have taken the stand-down at the point the Force returned from England rather than later. We live and learn, sir."

"Some people do," Ramos said. "You're clearly one of them, Captain."

"I try, sir," Steve said.

"The one bit that was illuminating in my discussions with your daughters was that you indicate a strategic plan for eliminating the infected threat," Ramos said. "But you are also reticent on specifics. Both of them discussed your planning philosophy. I wrote it down," Ramos said, pulling out a sheet of paper. "Desires, Intentions, Goals, Concepts, Plans, Actions. Care to lay that out for me? I didn't ask either one to explain it."

"A person has a desire, General," Steve said. "I'll avoid alternate metaphors and just talk about this world, sir. My desire, most people's, is a zombie-free world, sir. That is a fixed point. One item. From there it gets complicated. Intentions are the next step and the alternatives start to expand. Possibilities become fractal. At a certain point, I had an intention to use Bermuda as a staging base. I followed that fractal and discarded it, mentally, before proceeding. Another intention was to use the Canary Islands or the Azores. Again, discarded. Eventually I settled on the intention of using Gitmo.

"What were the goals that derive from that intention? Sufficient force to clear it was a clear goal. At a certain point I might have chosen to clear PI, early. It was isolated and no more difficult to clear than Gitmo. That was a mental goal at one point which I discarded, again. Fractals branching out, sir. Finally they collapse onto a few clear concepts. Gunboats for clearance. Sweeping methods. At that point you have to start testing them to see if they are functional. Even if it is, again, a thought exercise. Those that have some functionality, you push down to plans. At which point I bring people in on it, sir, and start pushing the work-load down. Does that make it clearer, General?"

"Yes," Ramos said. "Where are you on that fractal of clearing the continental areas of the United States?"

"The mechanicals do not work as well as I had hoped, sir," Steve said. "So that plan, while not a bust, has been dropped in terms of importance. We'll continue to use them since they at least *reduce* infected presence. Some people in the Miami area are self-extracting. The mechanicals have a value especially since they are easy to produce and just keep working. My other main plan, sir, involves what I call bots."

"Robots?" Ramos said. "I'm virtually certain you're not talking about making T-1000s."

"No, sir," Steve said, smiling faintly. "Although if I had the capacity and was sure they wouldn't turn on us I'd do it. No, sir, the bots are otherwise. I would prefer, though, to let that ride for now. I have a briefing on them set up for you, sir. We have a covert planning and development group over at Camp Delta. It seemed an appropriate spot and it's possible to keep it away from the main base and base personnel. That something secret is going on over there is known. *What,* I think we've managed to *keep* secret."

"May I ask why?" Ramos said.

"Because if it's a nonstarter I don't want people getting their hopes up, sir," Steve said. "And because if it *works* it's going to make me the biggest mass murderer in history, sir."

"General, Lieutenant Commander Tami Mitchell," Steve said the next morning.

Camp Delta, the terrorist detention facility at Guantanamo Bay, was set up in general like a minimum security prison. The design was based on "Club Fed" prisons in the U.S. with an additional "high security" wing for particularly dangerous detainees. There were leaders and followers in the terrorist field as in any other. The followers were in open barracks with access to external yards where they could play soccer and basketball. The leaders were in individual cells designed to prevent "tap code" or other communication and only saw guards.

All in all, though, it wasn't by any stretch a horrible place. Set right on the Caribbean, the view was great and the climate was mild. It was the sort of spot you would otherwise put a Sandals resort. Every time the subject of closing it came up, the main complaint of the detainees was they didn't want to go to either federal Super-max, which was set up with even tighter security than the "High Security" wing, or third party prisons such as Tunisia or Romania. Which was worse was a toss-up.

And it was remote from the main base, securable and had both a now-cleared hospital as well as a helipad. Throw in some equipment and you had a nice base for clandestine research.

"Lieutenant Commander," the general said, shaking her hand. The first thing he noticed about the lieutenant commander was her eyes. He was pretty sure she had *not* passed the psych profile.

"Lieutenant Commander Mitchell is the head of Project Subedey, General," Steve said. "The bot program. The commander had the unfortunate experience of seeing one of her children killed by infected, sir."

"I deeply regret that, Commander," the general said.

"Not as much as I do, General," Mitchell said. "But we've got a solution."

"A final solution as such," Steve said. "By the way, General, all of the personnel assigned to Project Subedey have similar experiences to the commander. That is deliberate. I wanted people who had zero compunctions working on this project, sir.

"The way that these briefings usually go is we have you sit through a PowerPoint presentation which you cut short and ask a couple of questions then leave. If you will do me the favor of amending that to a short helicopter flight, I think we can skip most of the dog and pony. However, you'll need to get into a silver suit."

"Very well," Ramos said. "After you, Captain, Commander."

It wasn't only the general in silver suits. The helo crew, the people handling the helo and Steve were all in NBC gear.

The helo took off from Delta and stayed low to the water on exit, heading west.

"We're technically violating every bit of Cuba's territorial rights," Steve said. "Not to mention, well . . .

treaties, laws, regulations, international agreements, the UN charter and Executive Orders en masse. However, better to test things on Cuban than on U.S. soil."

"I doubt they're going to go to war over... chemical weapons?" Ramos said. "Especially since there is no Cuba. I can see the efficacy but you'd have to spray every inch of the U.S. with them. And that would cause some issues. I don't have a problem with use of chemical weapons. Contaminating half the U.S. I have an issue with, Captain."

"We won't, sir," Steve said. "About one percent. Possibly ten percent of urban areas. If I may ask the General to just wait. The flight is short, sir. And it works better as a visual, sir."

"I'll wait," Ramos said.

They went feet-dry over the sprawling port city of Santiago De Cuba. It was a much better port than Guantanamo in terms of geography, a deepwater port cut inland that was highly protected. Also surrounded by a huge city which sprawled all over the hills surrounding the port. There were some mechanicals working in the port. The water wasn't packed with bodies but they were noticeable even in the dim moonlight from the blacked-out helo. There were so many the sharks had clearly gotten full.

Besides the moonlight there were four sets of lights showing. They appeared to be rotating spotlights. The helo was headed for one of them.

The helo proceeded inland to a park, then began circling at about five hundred feet.

In the park there was a... device. It was lit up bright as day with flashing red lights and spot-lights that looked like car headlights pointed upwards. And there were bullhorn speakers on it. Even from the high-circling helo the general could hear some sort of announcement in a female voice but he couldn't make out the words.

The lights permitted him to see the general design. Spread legs to hold it upright. Spikes to keep infected off of it. A cup attachment on the top that he suspected had to do with sling-lift. All the gear just below that. Down from that . . . it had some sort of heavy circular sleeve, the purpose of which wasn't clear, and a down-curved circular shield, also quite large. The sleeve looked as if it was designed to drop, which would bring the shield down to just about cover the landing legs. He couldn't get a good look below the shield. But whatever was below was the smallest part of the system.

And there were infected. Dozens, *hundreds* of dead littered the ground around the device and even more were feeding. There were probably ten thousand infected below, with most of the dead being within fifty meters of the device. Some of them seemed . . . sluggish. As he watched, one stopped feeding and just lay down. A few moments later, another started feeding on him. The pile was getting large.

"Jesus Christ," Ramos said quietly. "Radiation?"

"Gamma radiation to be precise, sir," Steve said. "Two mostly spent fuel rods from the Jacksonville nuclear power plant with a metal cover to prevent beta emissions. Pilot, back to Delta. I think we've seen enough."

"My first thought was gas, sir," Steve said as they proceeded back to Gitmo. "I'd come to the conclusion the best choice was Amidol, which is similar to VX but a bit less stable so it breaks down faster. Issues. Yes, it breaks down. It does *not* break down evenly or quickly unless it is exposed to sea water. It requires the NaCl for the reaction. If it gets into ground water, it breaks down very slowly indeed. We started by trying other chemicals with less permanency. But, well, war gases are war gases for a reason. The efficiency just was not high enough. Not even things like phosgene, which we tried, as well as chlorine and even a carbon monoxide generator. But only the war gases really worked well and ground soil and water tests indicated there would be large contamination zones after their use.

"Counterpoint: Every city in the world's ground water is *already* so contaminated just by having *been* an industrialized city, I'm not sure it matters. New Orleans, post Katrina and all the way up to just pre-Plague, was still a toxic spill zone that nobody would be *allowed* to live in were it not for politics. It was a city-wide Superfund site worse than Love Canal. What should have been done with it was level all the contaminated areas and fill in with dirt. Past issues. They're all back under water, anyway, and back to being a toxic stew. The same toxic conditions exist for most of the cities. Hell, most of the major rivers in the U.S. are not potable at this point. The only thing that's going to fix it is time. Time heals all wounds, even chemical. Rivers should be useable in five years or so. Point being that contaminating all the cities would not have been an insoluble issue.

"Killer issue: Production on the scale we'd have to produce it. Models said clearing *all* the urban areas of the U.S. would require fifteen thousand one hundred and forty-two sorties. Or seven *million* five hundred and seventy-one gallons of Amidol. Which is a hell of a lot of poison gas, General."

"I would have discarded the thought at that point," Ramos said. "When you talk about 'millions of gallons' of complex chemicals in *this* environment. Infeasible."

"I came to the same conclusion, sir," Steve said, grinning. "What's that thing about the proof of another man's intelligence, sir? I had come to the reluctant realization that we were going to have to use pied piper and artillery. Which meant at the least starting up or finding an artillery plant. Nitrates . . . Et cetera.

"Then we found the *Nebraska* turned over pierside at King's Bay. And after discussion with various officers who knew more than I about nuclear reactors, we decided we *needed* to right it and pull the reactor. Which set off a *very* serious discussion by *very* serious nuclear engineers of just how deadly dangerous that was going to be and how insanely safe we were going to have to be to keep from killing the salvage crews."

"Deadly dangerous being a good thing in this instance," Ramos said, nodding.

"The mechanicals are nothing more than a deliberate industrial accident, sir," Steve said. "So I decided 'why not a deliberate *radiological* accident?'"

"Contamination?" Ramos asked.

"Very minimal," Steve said. "The device is filtered for gamma. Gamma rays don't really leave much residual radiation behind, sir. We did a test of a spot one had been sitting on for two weeks and in another two weeks it was barely above background. They just zip through the infected and somewhat slowly kill them.

Biggest problem is secondary contamination from the metals in the bot. Since you can't feel, smell or touch gamma rays . . . the infected flock and feed. And die. And die. They're not even heavily irradiated. But over time they get enough to kill them.

"We'll have to dispose of the bots eventually. *They* are seriously contaminated. But not the ground. And although gammas keep going, they also spread in every direction. They're basically a nonissue beyond a few dozen meters. Biggest problem is their limited range and the fact that the closer infected act to absorb the radiation. That one is going to have to be moved soon. What we're looking at, now that we have some empirical data, is how often they'll have to be moved to maintain utility. Again, that may turn into a killer logistical issue. There are no easy solutions to hundreds of millions of infected. So far."

"You're going to need a lot of nuclear material," Ramos said.

"There are sixty-five nuclear power plants in the U.S., General," Steve said. "Each has spent fuel rods in cooling ponds available for use as well as their internal fuel rods. That is quite a bit of material. We also have several thousand nuclear weapons in inventory, sir. They, too, can be used. Once you break them down to materials, sir, they're not useable as nukes of course."

"I was the guard commander for a site, Captain," Ramos said. "I know how hard it is to get a sustained explosive reaction. This may seem 'old school' but the materials could be used for terrorism. Dirty bombs . . ."

"Until they are done with their work, they are extremely well guarded by infected, sir," Steve said.

"A tough nut for anyone but a military unit to crack. Some people may eventually have helos as well. We'll patrol the drop points with Gunhawks night and day. That should discourage theft. And approaching from the ground would be . . . difficult. Gamma radiation goes through just about everything. You noticed the curved shield, sir? The reason there is a shield is so you can't actually *see* the core from above. If you could, we'd eventually lose crews.

"When the helo drops a specially designed connector into the cup, that releases the shield, which drops and cuts off emissions. The bot is picked up and carried to another spot and begins again. Refueling the small generator on it is an issue, as is any other 'maintenance' on the system. It is *very* hot. We rotate the crews working on them and they use lead-lined gear. We can also use plutonium from warheads, although it takes two warheads to make a good emitter, or a couple of fuel rods from a civilian reactor. There are several dozen just in the cooling ponds at the nuclear plant in Jax. There are other sources. We can make at least three hundred with nuclear material currently available or that we can avail ourselves of. One reason we're going to have to clear the *Stennis* at some point. We need the rods."

"How many estimated infected in the U.S.?" Ramos asked.

"About seventy million at this point, General," Steve said. "Based on models. Number is dropping slowly. There was a large initial die-off just after the Fall for a variety of reasons including cannibalism, then another during the winter. Unfortunately, things appear to generally be stable at this point. Current rough models are that we'll drop to something like thirty million in ten years. In ten years, any survivors in sheltered redoubts are going to be out of materials. If the U.S. isn't cleared in three years or so we'll lose an estimated eighty percent of the remaining survivors. So we're going to have to do this as fast and as brutal as possible. Ask me for anything but time."

"Biggest mass murderer in history," Ramos said. "I see why you told Lieutenant Smith there were more efficient ways to clear than a tank."

"Notional plan is as follows, sir," Steve said. "Move the ground force via railroad. Roads are blocked, railroads we can clear. Move into area that has been rough-cleared by Subedey. Set up a secure forward airfield. Have the helos fly in and prep. Helos pick up the devices, then move into surrounding area. Once the area is yellow cleared by the Subedey devices, move into it, away from the particular points, and do it all over again. And that's all we've got at present, sir. The rest is details which, well, we've got the PowerPoint if you'd really like to sit through it."

"Possibly at a later date," General Ramos said. "You have discussed this with the Joint Chiefs?"

"Yes, sir," Steve said. "Every flag officer is briefed, General. I ran this same brief for Admiral Hiscock just the other day. I, by the way, see this as an Army program, not Navy. Navy may use some for clearance on coastal cities but we're mostly looking at it as Army. The Joint Chiefs see the potential efficacy, sir, and the issues. The current group is onboard."

"I'll need to see the full details and talk to some of the nuclear officers," Ramos said. "But notionally so am I."

"The cities are the problem, General," Steve said. "Cities and suburbs. They are where the mass of survivors remain. Getting them cleared out is going to be key to freeing the world. We can't simply nuke them. It would take out half the world's survivors."

"All understood," General Ramos said, shaking his head. "It's a big task."

"It's a small world, General," Steve said. "But I wouldn't want to paint it. Unfortunately, it appears we must."

"What were your immediate plans for your forces?" Ramos said.

"Every task requires trained personnel, sir," Steve said. "There are more of those in the military than in general civilian areas. Thus: Continue clearance of coastal bases is the near-term plan. Norfolk is, alas, a very big ticket. Lots of population density, lots of infected. We've been looking at it and rubbing our chins. We're cutting out ships but clearing even the base, which has multiple perimeter breaches, is going to be a chore. We may start Subedey there. I've been talking with my staff about concentrating our forces to do so. *After* we'd cleared Lejeune and the surrounding bases. Once we have sufficient force, clear Savannah to get to Hunter and Stewart at which point we'll stand the Army back up. There's a notional plan for a deep strike to Bragg as well. Lots of high quality forces there and we'd anticipate similar survival levels to Lejeune."

"I'm going to make one recommendation," General Ramos said. "It is a recommendation, only. It is still up in the air whether I will continue at my current rank or take a position at a lower one. Given the numbers we have, that's understandable. Especially with the example of General Montana, whom I'd met prior to the Plague and, like most warriors, admire. I'm not going to say 'I'm in charge!' like Al Haig just because I have stars. Recommendation only."

"Yes, sir?" Steve said.

"We're coming up on one year since the announcement of the Plague," General Ramos said. "I would suggest that we need something to show how far we've come back."

"As you say, sir?" Steve said.

"Norfolk is important," Ramos said. "We need the personnel, we need the facilities. If for no other reason than to bring them to Jax. And the survivors and dependents are going to be our people. That is important as well. But I would recommend a mostly symbolic mission."

"Yes, sir?"

"Time to clear D.C., Captain," Ramos said. "My recommendation is that by the one-year anniversary of the announcement of the H7D3 virus, Americans own our capital again."

"General," Steve said. "I have no objections to that plan."

"And one additional recommendation," General Ramos said. "Use tanks, not bots."

"Will do, sir. Care to command the ground force, General?"

"That would truly be an honor, Captain."

CHAPTER 24

"You know," Faith said as the LCU entered the cavernous well-deck of the USS *Bataan*. "Maybe having a great big freaking hole in the middle of a ship *isn't* such a bad idea."

The *Bataan* had been "cut out" from Norfolk where it had been alongside when the plague broke out, then towed down to Mayport along with the out-of-commission *Iwo Jima*. By cannibalizing the *Iwo Jima* and quite a few other work-arounds, crews had gotten it back into commission in record time. Which was useful since they were going to need it for Operation George.

"Yuh *think*," Sophia said, leaning her arms on the railing and watching Trixie being brought aboard. She was still in her flight suit, having just brought in "her" Seahawk. She'd qualified as an aircraft commander. Her copilot had been a Marine F-18 pilot who was now a Navy lieutenant, two ranks above her. She was still in charge when they were in the air. Which was cool. Weird, but cool. "Most stuff the Navy does makes sense. Eventually."

"White caps?" Faith said.

"You can use them to hold water," Sophia said.

"Bullshit," Faith said. "I know that's the supposed reason but it's bullshit. Bell bottoms. Thirteen-button fly. It's just a traditional and stupid uniform unlike our *glorious* ones. Manning the rail. On a man-o-war it sort of made sense. People could hang onto stuff and there was a fucking railing on the deck. On a carrier, it's insane. You're right by a five-story drop to the water. There's not even a rail to *man*. It's just so admirals and captains can jack off."

"And the Marines are any better?" Sophia said, ticking points off on her fingers. "You start off marching on the wrong foot, you can't get your rank acronyms into a simple three-letter scheme like every *other* service in the world, and what the hell is the thing with 'Good night, Chesty'?"

"Those all make perfect sense," Faith said loyally. "Well, I'll give you the acronym thing, but we're sticking with 'Good night, Chesty.'"

"Lieutenant Faith Smith to Briefing Room Four," the tannoy blared. *"Lieutenant Faith Smith to Briefing Room Four."*

"I'm not scheduled for a meeting," Faith said, looking at her watch.

"Looks like you are, now," Sophia said, waving. "Have fun."

"Ensign Smith to the ready room! Ensign Smith to the ready room!"

"Hah, hah!" Faith said, grinning as she opened the hatch. "Have fun in *your* meeting, Sis . . ."

"Barrels on miniguns do wear out, sir," Lieutenant Wilkes said. "And once they wear out, replacement is currently problematic."

"We've got a lot more fifty caliber barrels than miniguns . . ."

"Body clearance..."

The problem was while Washington, D.C. only had six hundred thousand residents, more or less, prior to the Plague, and most of the affluent had probably fled, there were more than six *million* residents within a ten mile radius from the Washington monument. That meant at current rates of infected survival, something like two million zombies. And zombies were people. They'd travel quite a ways for a nice meal. Any signs of life in the downtown areas and the surrounding hordes would close in. There was no point in clearing D.C. if they couldn't turn on the lights of the Washington Monument for fear of being swarmed.

The other problem was that they still had barely a regiment. Besides equipment, Da had sent about a battalion strength of Marines to the West Coast. General Montana needed them just to make a dent in the Southern California zombie brigades. The zombies had, unfortunately, survived better than people. Southern California had a great climate with the exception of a decided lack of rainfall. Where the East Coast people could figure out how to make something resembling cisterns and survive on rainfall, many of the redoubt compartments that would otherwise have survived on the West Coast succumbed to lack of water.

Where they'd gotten ten percent survivors at PI, they had found less than three percent at Pendleton and Coronado despite the best efforts of the survivors. Water had just run out.

Then there was the problem of the roads. They were choked with cars. Even more so than Jax. Tighter road network and people had waited later to flee, assuming D.C. couldn't *possibly* fall. So, many of the roads were impassable to vehicles. *All* of the many bridges were choked. Which also meant that blocking them was going to be an issue. Infected could get through the cars but you couldn't just set down containers to close them. Then there was the fact that D.C. wasn't anything resembling an island. It had rivers on two sides and Rock Creek but Rock Creek was open to infiltration and to the north it was *entirely* open. There was no realistic way to close the city with the forces they had.

Last but not least, they were running out of M1028. There had been a stock at Lejeune and more on the *Iwo* but not, in Faith's opinion, nearly enough. Of course, in her opinion there could *never* be enough canister.

She and Sophia had ended up in the same meeting in the end, which was going around in circles.

"Ensign Smith," Colonel Ramos said. He'd taken a voluntary demotion to colonel and taken over all "field" forces, which included the Navy forces forward. Hamilton had stepped aside with total grace. "Everyone has voiced various opinions except you and your sister. Would you care to chime in?"

"I'd start with gunboats," Sophia said. "The same way we did in the Canaries and Caribbean."

"Gunboats are not going to clear the city, Lieutenant," Major Sanskeld said. "We've been over that."

Sanskeld was one of the PI officers who had managed to avoid reduction. He was good enough, but PI officers, in general, were not high on Faith's "like them" list and were low on the "trust them" list. He also was a huge "what-if Dave," in that every single suggestion had to be countered with a "what-if" or a "that won't work." Not, not, not.

"I said *start* with them, sir," Sophia said. "D.C. is a river city. Why not use our proven riverine and oceanic abilities?"

"Go on," Colonel Ramos said.

"That's all I've got, sir," Sophia admitted. "I agree with Commander Wilkes that clearing from the air is problematic, sir. Just so damned *many* of them. We could look at water-cooled on the helos. But you really don't need fifty to kill zombies, sir. We've never looked at water-cooled two-forties or even Barbie guns. Both have possibility. I'm not sure you can convert a SAW to belt-fed, but if you could, and you cooled it . . . the infected eventually bleed out."

"Leaving piles of rotting bodies all over the city," Sanskeld pointed out. "Which without the infected to keep them in check means rats explode!"

"She is making salient suggestions, Major," Colonel Ramos said. "Objections and issues are for later. So . . . water-cooled machine guns from helos?"

"I'm not very happy with it, sir, but it's the best I've got," Sophia said. "And it would take both some serious mechanical work and some testing, sir."

"Understood," Ramos said, making a note. "Even if we don't use it here, it's something worth looking at for the future. Thank you, Ensign. Your suggestion on gunboats is definitely worth looking into. We also need to stop throwing away our brass. At some point we're going to have to make more ammo and we can do reloading. Remelt the brass at the very least. Any idea how many it would get in terms of population?"

"Depends on how long you did it, sir," Sophia said. "We only did one attack on each point in previous missions, sir. I would suppose you could do multiples.

Eventually you would draw infected from quite a distance. How far I'm not sure. I would roughly estimate five miles if you just kept doing it, sir. How far can you see one of those vertical spot-lights, sir? Have a division with one on a barge as we did in Jax. Fire up at dawn, stand down until the next dawn and do it again, sir. Eventually you'll reduce the numbers quite a bit, sir. And if fifty is in short supply, we can switch to something else if we water cool them, sir. Two-forties will do the job, sir."

"All good points," Ramos said. "Now what are the objections?"

"The same thing will bring infected into the city from the distance," Sanskeld said. "There is going to be a continuous stream. And the piles of rotting bodies are, again, a major health hazard."

"Disposal, period, is going to be an issue," Ramos said, making another note. "But the concept has merit. Ensign, what would you think of being temporarily grounded?"

"Wouldn't prefer it, sir," Sophia said. "And Lieutenant Commander Chen has much more experience at this point on small boat ops, sir. If you're thinking of sending someone up there to get started, Commander Chen is the man."

"Thank you so much, Sophia," Lieutenant Commander Chen said. "And I'd second the notion of using something other than fifty. But that is what is currently loaded. So if you wish us to get started and see how it works, we can do so, sir. I'm more than used to converting ideas on the fly. We're flexible that way," he said, shooting a glance at Sanskeld. Chen had already raised the point about gunboats.

"It's worth a shot," Ramos said. "Any other suggestions we haven't already covered? Lieutenant Smith, I note that you've been engrossed by your laptop. I take it you're not watching movies."

"I *was* looking at the satellite images, sir," Faith said. "Currently I'm reading Patton's biography."

"No inclusions to the meeting, Lieutenant?" Ramos asked.

"Words, sir," Faith said. "Not liking talking. Especially around autonegators, sir. And more goal-concept than plans, sir."

"General order," Ramos said. "Let the lieutenant talk and don't insert what-if or other objections until I so direct. Lieutenant, just . . . talk."

"Sophia beat me to gunboats, sir," Faith said, looking up. "Maybe we're stuck in our ways but they work. And if you do it day after day, maybe move around a little, you're going to get the numbers down. But what the major said is right. There's the bodies, which are going to be a big problem. And there's going to be more moving in. Not just attracted in, sir. The infected have territories, sir. They fight over them some. When you take them out, there's going to be a big movement of territories shifting. Not sure how to use it to our advantage but until you hit the edge of the suburbs in clearance, there's, yeah, going to be infected infiltrating in for freaking ever.

"So you got to go out and round those up. Then kill 'em. Then dispose of the bodies, sir. Best way to dispose of the bodies is probably burn pits, sir. So you need them in burn pits and you want them as close as possible just for the logistics, sir.

"So . . . The piles from the gunboats you can't get

in burn pits. So you just burn them . . . there. Words. Institute?"

"*In situ,*" Sophia said, rolling her eyes.

"*In situ,*" Faith said. "I don't know how smart it is or anything, but I'm thinking using one of the tankers or a support ship and mounting big flamethrowers on them. Maybe not *on* them. Maybe a pipe to a ship or a barge that's the flamethrower ship. Fire up a particular point for a day or two. Bodies start rotting. Come in with the flamethrower rig and just keep burning them till they're bones or ash or whatever. Probably should bring in some of the fire-fighting boats to keep the buildings around them from burning or whatever. Use pure petroleum, sir. We got a shit ton of it at Statia and we're not refining it. But it's a glut compared to diesel or kerosene, which we need. So if that's an idea we go with, get the petroleum. Hell, it will burn, which is all you need. Sir.

"So then you go ashore and start digging up the Mall . . ."

"The *Mall*?" Sanskeld said.

"Major?" Ramos said dangerously.

"Shit grows back, Major," Faith said. "Parris Island was going back to nature when you were there, Major. Shit grows back. Big fucking . . . osteoporosis or something in France, which is all the dead from some big battle in World War Two. Do that in fifty years or whatever. Make a memorial. We can replant or whatever later. Yeah, *the Mall*. It's got trees, too. Which we're gonna need. Send in a combat engineering team during the day and dig trenches, pits or whatever in the Mall. All the grassy areas. Maybe except around the Washington Monument. I get that's sort of . . .

Not around the Washington Monument. But down past the Smithsonian, over on this Ellipse thing... Put a bunch of wood in the bottom. Bunch of wood. Cut trees all over wherever we've taken, take down busted-up houses, whatever. Bunch of wood. Cover it in petroleum to get it burning nice.

"Then send ashore heavy armored platoons like we already do, sir. That's going to be a *big* logistics thing. Fuel, repairs, recovery, support... Going to have to look at how many amtracks and such we can stand up and support, sir. And get there. I'm talking about more than you can fit on a LHD. Send them in night and day. Night more than day. Maybe an M88 in the lead. HERCULES can run over cars just like Abrams and they can stay buttoned up. Once the cars are crunched, amtracks can roll over the crunched cars most of the time. Follow with an Abrams. They can pull amtracks out that get stuck and the HERCULES can pull out the Abrams. Infected might be able to swarm HERCULES. That's what forty mike mike is made for. If a Herc gets stuck or breaks down, send a Herc from a nearby team. Combined arms teams with a wrecker 'cause we're gonna get stuck and getting out of a scrum when you've got a stuck armored vehicle sucks, sir.

"But don't shoot up the infected. We've only got so much ammo. I mean, we got a lot, but only so much, sir, no planned resupply and a big world to clear. We'll need a secure point, big one, in artillery range of the Mall. Preferably somewhere we can roll on and off with ammo. When you lead in a pied piper, fire it up with artillery. Then bring in the bulldozers, at some point, bulldoze them into the pits and you're done. Fire up the pits probably in the evening. Fill with more wood in the morning. Do it all over again that night. Keep doing that till the whole area's clear. Minimum use of bullets, lots of arty, but we've got that sitting around. And artillery kills better than bullets, from what I've heard.

"Rolling offshore every day will be an issue. We may have to set up some sort of secure area to roll to. Maybe where the artillery is. But it should have the back-door of being able to roll offshore in case shit hits the fan. So, close to the water.

"We're going to need five times the amtracks you'd normally use for a MEU, one HERCULES and one Abrams for each three to five amtracks and a shitload of speakers. We don't have to use the psyops ones all the time. Any big ass speaker will do. Drive around doing that until all the infected are toast, sir. Take some time but we can really clear all the way out to . . ."

She looked at the map.

"There's this ring road, right? 495? We can probably clear everything inside that ring road in, say, four weeks? Not yellow, but low orange. Yellow inside the D.C. city limits. Maybe put up some definite barriers inside there and get it down to greenish in a certain area. By then we'd have moved out from the Mall to other areas to use as mass graves, sir. And probably have the arty sitting in the Mall to support it.

"That's not so much a plan, sir, as concept, you understand," Faith said. "I don't know how many arty troops we got or what it takes to fix their gear up to standard. Don't know if that's all doable, sir. Probably the thing about the amtracks and Abrams isn't. I don't think we have five times as much or can get that many up and going in that time even if we did. But the more we use, the faster it goes, sir. That's all I got, sir."

"So, to dial it down a bit," Ramos said. "One team of an M88, three to five tracks and an Abrams rolls through D.C. When it has a fair following it heads to an area of the Mall that has been pre-selected. As it passes through that area, it is fired up by one-five-five using variable time fuse. The infected are killed by the VT fire and the unit continues on. End of the day, bulldozers push the infected bodies into pits pre-laid with wood, start the fires and let them burn. Do it again the next day."

"That's the general idea, sir," Faith said. "Probably roll out hot and fast, then slow down on the way back in. We may be able to build up maps that can see where the roads are clear and where they're not. That's where the helos are going to come in handy. Also . . . if a team gets totally stuck, they can probably be pulled out by helos direct from their tracks. More Soph's thing than mine but Gunhawks for cover and Dragons for extract. We could probably STABO out most of the team. Or something. Not my asteroid, sir.

"Then when we come back in, refuel, rearm if we need it, then roll back out. Do that over and over again. When we've gotten to the point we're not getting many takers in the middle, move out to other areas and set up the same sort of central kill and disposal point.

"Big tactical problem is that you get more infected following you at night. Do day runs, then night. Turn the thing about the fires around. Fire them up in the morning and let them cook during the day. Then the tracks roll out again at dusk. In the morning, the tracks make sure the area is cleared for the bulldozer crews, bulldoze them in all at once. That way we can be sure there's not a friendly-fire incident. Is it going to take a lot of logistics? Yes, sir. Way lot of logistics and support. I mean, if we do it big. We can do it smaller and it will just take more time, sir. I'm not sure what we can really support, sir. Way above my paygrade, sir."

"Major Sanskeld?" Ramos said.

"Do a thorough air reconnaissance, first, sir," Sanskeld said. "And build the map to which the lieutenant referred. Possibly some SAR but mostly build the map. Video, where possible, of every road. Even if it is hand-held as long as we can figure out what we're looking at. Build up a map of which roads are passable and impassable and use that to determine routes that avoid, unless necessary, running over the cars. My objection to that, sir, is less the mess than that you'd have fuel on the streets which combined with weapons and sparks from the passing tracks would cause fires. Which would kill survivors and you can't actually drive your tracks through it."

"Noted," Ramos said.

"But those are details, sir," Sanskeld said. "In general . . . I begin to see the logic. Very complex operation that will require a good deal of intelligence and initiative on the part of the team leaders, sir. That is another issue."

"And they'll need to be able to figure out where they are and where they're going," Sophia said. "Which leaves Faith out."

"Bite me," Faith said. "Car GPS saves the day, there."

"That is a point," Ramos said. "We can build the map to note blocked routes. And use standard GPS where possible. It's easier to reprogram that than in BFT."

Faith nudged the captain next to her.

"BFT?" she whispered.

"Blue Force Tracker," the captain replied.

"Secure point for artillery and fall back?" Ramos said.

"Pentagon?" Lieutenant Colonel Hamilton said. He had taken over as the MEU S-3. "Fenced and gated. We may need to do some clearance on the Arlington side, first. The infected can swarm the fences if they are in enough density and a camp that size will attract them from miles around. But the artillery would be in easy range of the Mall. Close to the water. No direct access but, well, that's what bulldozers and C4 is for. Possibly Reagan National. More area. Also fenced and gated. Better over-water access. Issue. We have stood up no artillery *at all*. All artillery MOS personnel were transferred to infantry duties."

"That's a matter for the G-1 to unfuck if we decide to do this," Colonel Ramos said. "I take it Captain Smith will have no objections to the Marines having organic artillery at least. Lieutenant Commander Chen."

"Sir?" Chen said.

"Gather up all the gunboat squadrons and head up to D.C.," Ramos said. "Start the music. We'll bring up the MEU later. Start on the Pentagon side. Try to find a good spot away from what we're going to use, which means the Pentagon or possibly Reagan. But start the music. Keep going until we get there or until you're not getting much on the Arlington side of the Potomac. Then switch to D.C. We'll see about alternate weapons to the fifties on the fly as you said. Clear?"

"Aye, aye, sir," Chen said.

"Colonel Hamilton, I want a more detailed look at this overall plan," Ramos said. "It sounds like to hold either the Pentagon or Reagan we'll need to do some ground-level clearance on the Arlington side, first. Look at where to set the kill zone. Arlington National Cemetery is off the list."

"Absolutely, sir," Hamilton said. "But, bad news, sir."

"Which is?" Ramos asked.

"Best alternate impact area and burn pit zone is probably the Army-Navy Club golf course, sir," Hamilton said.

"Ouch," Ramos said to a series of grimaces around the table. "That was a damned good course, too. Was. Past tense."

"Aye, aye, sir," Hamilton said, grinning. "Army's never going to let us live it down, sir. I mean not in a hundred years, sir."

"They will if we can get enough free to stand them back up," Ramos said. "I want the Phase One plan complete by seventeen hundred tomorrow so we can look at what we need for Phase Two and Three planning. Looks like a concept, though. Lieutenant Smith."

"Sir?" Faith said, looking up from her computer.

"Your idea," Ramos said. "You are going to have the honor of first landing in the AO. Rack them up, Lieutenant."

"Aye, aye, sir."

"Jesus," Sophia breathed as the Seahawk circled over Arlington. "I thought *London* was bad . . ."

The Greater D.C. Metropolitan area had a larger number of wooden based buildings than London and that had been a major issue. Also, during the summer it dried out a good bit and was very arboreal. What had swept across Arlington was as much a forest fire as house fires. The result was that about half of Arlington and D.C. had burned. And while undoubtedly many infected were killed by the fires, anyone trapped in a home or other building by the infected had definitely perished.

It was spotty, though. In this case, spots of unscorched ground were often entirely surrounded by devastation. And there were survivors. She could see them on rooftops, signaling for pick-up. In some of the balcony high-rise buildings the survivors were using ropes on the exterior to move around. In others they'd apparently cleared the interiors or the infected had died off.

They passed over a killzone of one of Chen's gunboats and she shook her head. The pile was . . . huge. Massive. Sick. Piles of twisted and probably rotting bodies, most of them in pieces from .50 caliber fire. By her experienced count, over a thousand, probably over two. She was glad she couldn't smell it from up here.

And the infected were still swarming on it. The gunboat division, which had backed away from the pile for the day to get some sleep away from the smell, would be back in the morning to make more carrion. Probably half their rounds at this point were just chewing up corpses. If she'd been in charge, she'd have them move.

"That is . . . sick," Lieutenant Simms said. The former F-18 pilot was still a newbie at helos even compared to Sophia. Despite that, both had already rotated to Mayport as IPs.

"We built up some kills in the Canaries," Sophia said. "Thought those were something. Was I ever wrong.

"Okay," she said, looking at the civilian GPS strapped to the flight panel. "What's next?"

"25th Street South," Simms said.

"Port. 25th Street South at my order," Sophia said, bringing the bird around to the target street. "Begin film . . ."

"Starting, aye," Olga said. "And the answer is: 700 block: blocked and charred and blocked again."

"Seven Hundred: Bravo comma Charlie, aye," Simms said, making a note on his iPad.

"Mark it as mostly bypassable," Sophia said.

"Marked," Simms said. "You sure?"

"The road's blocked. The houses are burned flat and mostly slab. The amtracks can move through the rubble."

"Hell of a thing," Simms said. "I lived in Aurora when I was stationed here."

"Sorry for your loss, sir," Sophia said automatically. "26th Street, south . . ."

CHAPTER 25

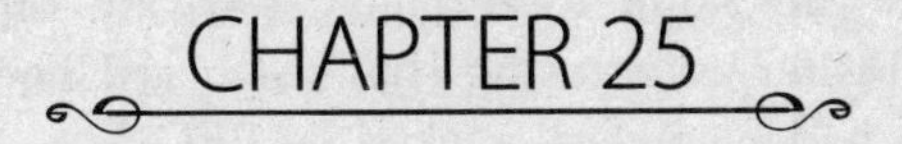

"Let the bodies hit the floor," Faith sang, drawing her USP. "Let the bodies hit the floor. Let the bodies, let the bodies . . ."

Infected had inhabited Reagan National. It was accessible due to busted gates and all the broken glass on the front and it kept them out of the weather. Despite all the gunboat clearance in the area, the place was still fairly populated. Not bad; the platoon wasn't going to get into a scrum with this density. But quite a few.

Trixie was parked outside baggage claim. Technically, Faith should be *either* an infantry *or* armor platoon leader. But while her specialty was infantry, the very few suggestions that Trixie be taken away had been met with cold, blank stares from not only Wolf Marines but pretty much all the senior officers. So when the infantry unassed, she popped out of the tank and slid down the glacis to go have fun in the sun.

Or the baggage claim as the case may be.

About half the platoon was newbies from PI fleshed out by Wolf Marines and trained jarheads from Lejeune. The boots and Lejeune Marines heard the tales from the "Wolves" as the scattered Wolf Squadron Marines were called. But this was their first experience of fighting with "The Skipper." Seeing it was a different deal.

"Does the Skipper ever miss?" Private First Class Bryant Fisher asked as he changed mags. The former PI boot had been fast-tracked to PFC as one of the few who could think beyond direct orders. He wasn't freaked out by the fight. He'd spent about half the time since being released from the horrors of extended boot camp clearing liners. Clearing liners was a picnic compared to a ten month boot camp at PI.

"Oh, *yeah*," Curran said as Faith switched to her first pistol. Twelve rounds and twelve infected were on the floor bleeding out. She holstered the pistol and drew another. "Everybody misses a shot *once* in a while. I've seen her miss . . . twice, I think? And her sister's better at over a hundred meters. Just stay on target . . ."

"Well, that was boring," Faith said, reloading her pistols. "Just another bug hunt."

"Game over, ma'am," Curran said. "Game over!"

"I say we nuke the site from orbit," Faith said, finished reloading. "It's the only way to be sure." She had an iPod bud in one ear and her comms in the other. She keyed the comm and held up a hand to Curran.

"Alpha Company, Shewolf. Lobby's clear but this is going to be a bug. . . . Stand by . . ." She drew one of her pistols and fired off to the side, nailing the infected climbing out onto the baggage carousel. "This is going to be a bug hunt. We're going to have to sweep the whole place. Roger . . . Roger, copy that."

"Bug hunt time," Faith said. "We've got Terminal A. Second's got B and so on and so forth. Bravo is getting the gates closed and securing the perimeter. First job, clear up in here. Then find a security station with a really detailed map. Jan, take the port side, I'll take starboard. Make sure your loads are up. Drink. Then let's go get some . . ."

"Wheeee!" Faith said, sliding down the baggage carousel. She had her USP in a two-handed grip and was nailing infected as she slid. She was missing but that was to be expected. The angles were just insane.

She hit the slideway at the bottom on her back, padded by a recent kill, with infected coming from either direction. She dropped the empty USP, drew her chest pistols in each hand and started firing, looking back and forth and firing carefully.

"They need to make this an amusement park ride," Faith yelled.

The platoon was farther up in the complex snake-maze of the baggage movement area. They were trying to cover their lieutenant but the intervening carousels made it nearly impossible. The up and down carousels twisted through the warehouselike baggage movement area like so many metal strands of spaghetti. There were essentially no clear sight-lines much less clear fire zones.

"Fisher," Januscheitis said. "Get down there and cover the LT."

"Aye, aye, Staff Sergeant," Fisher said, hopping on the slide. "Look out below, ma'am!"

"Take port," Faith said, getting up on one knee as Fisher slid in beside her. She dropped both empty pistols, switched to M4 and started firing to the right.

"Aye, aye, ma'am," Fisher said, getting up on a knee as well. He tried to ignore that he was in standard combat gear and kneeling in infected blood.

The slideway was nearly two stories up and, with the platoon moving down from above, the only reasonable way to access the two-some was along the slideway. Which was rapidly filling up with bodies.

"Scrummin' time," Faith said, letting the M4 pull back on its sling and drawing her kukri. She slid the knife across the first infected's throat and hip-flipped him to the side to fall into the distance. But there was another infected behind that one. When it charged, she just tripped it and hip-checked it off the slideway. "Don't fall."

"Aye, aye, ma'am," the PFC said. He was out as well and let the M4 withdraw then took a horse stance. "Fortunately, Staff Sergeant Bumwaldt was a Marine hand-to-hand instructor. It was about the only thing I learned in the warehouse besides that staff sergeants are total pricks, ma'am."

He blocked the rush of the first infected and knife-handed it on the side of the neck, stunning it. Then he just pushed it off the slideway. He did the same thing with the next but reversed the direction. It was enough of a fall that they weren't going to survive. Which he kept in mind was equally the case with himself.

Faith was, meantime, doing the same thing but with a knife not a hand. It was much bloodier. However, she could see infected crawling up from every direction. It wasn't the thousands it looked like but it was too many for two to take on and they were *way* out in front. Fun as it was, this was getting out of hand.

"Jan, we could use more bodies down here," Faith yelled. "Live Marine ones!"

"On the way, ma'am!"

"Note for the after action report, Staff Sergeant," Faith said, sharpening her kukri. "Clearance of baggage areas in airports should be done from the bottom, up, *not* the top down. And all personnel should wear full clearance gear. Should be considered confined space clearance."

"Aye, aye, ma'am," Januscheitis said. He pulled out his green notebook, wiped some blood off his hands, and made a note.

"Alpha, Shewolf. Unit needs to RTB for a wash down. We've got sticky mags. And, well, everything else . . ."

"The terminals appear to be mostly clear, sir," Captain Frank Dobbins said. The commander of Alpha Company, First Infantry Battalion, First Marine Regiment, A/1/1, was the former commander of a similar unit at Lejeune and Faith's company commander. "Chartreuse at least. Probably betas left but there always are. Clearing the bodies out will be . . . problematic."

"Unless we can get the luggage system working again," Faith said. "Then we just ship them to Houston to get lost . . ."

"You look like you could use a shower, Lieutenant," Lieutenant Colonel Grant Dawson, the 1/1 commander, said.

"Had one, sir," Faith said. "In gear. Could use another. Several. This stuff does *not* come off easy. It's like you can *never* get it out of your hair. Definite item for the AAR: Do not clear baggage areas without full clearance gear."

"Noted," Colonel Dawson said. "I'm going to contact higher and declare the area clear for landing. We'll lay low and hope the infected don't swarm the fences till the rest of the gear gets here..."

"Remember trying to get the magazine on that Coast Guard cutter open?" Faith said, watching the unloading process.

The *Bataan* and three LCUs had supported the initial landing. Now the MPF ship USNS *2nd Lt. John P. Bobo,* recently returned from the Pacific, was anchored just off the airport unloading over a "floating dock." Track after track was rolling ashore, most of them towing artillery pieces or trailers loaded with artillery ammo.

The first unload had been seven tons with rolls of wire to "upgrade" the defenses of the airport. Marines were hard at work reinforcing the perimeter fence as well as building Combat Operations Bases scattered around the airport. Each would support a Marine company and one platoon of artillery. It had been decided to do it that way so the different COBs could provide supporting fire if one COB came under attack by massed infected.

The infected were out there, that was for sure. Despite all the fire from the gunboats, which was ongoing, and the fact that operations ceased at dark to avoid attracting them, they were gathering by the airport fences. The first part of the plan was leading them away so they didn't have more bodies built up in the area.

You could smell the decay from the ones in the terminal despite being nearly eight hundred meters away and more or less upwind. That was one of the things drawing the infected: the smell of carrion. You'd think they'd go for some of the easier to access piles the gunboats had built. But if they were smart they wouldn't be zombies, would they?

"The hard part is remembering that was less than a year ago," Sophia said. Her bird was parked on the tarmac getting refueled. One of the first cargoes to go ashore was a forward air support team. That kept the crowding down on the *Bataan,* which was overloaded with helos. "But at the rate we're going through ammo, we're going to need to open every magazine on the planet."

"That's about to change," Faith said, watching the artillery landing. "Let's hope these things are as good as they're cracked up to be."

"Let me remind everyone that you need to have your hatches *closed* as soon as we near the golf course . . ."

Just getting there had been a nightmare. "Fast out, slow back" was not an option. Every road was blocked and often by "stuff" the helos had missed. Tracks could not cross whole trees blown down by storms. Or for that matter power poles downed by being hit by a truck. The truck might be off the road but the power pole wasn't.

They'd spent half their time driving through yards. Often with infected hammering the sides of the tracks. Fortunately, there was essentially no one who was not a veteran at this point. For green troops that was a bit nerve-wracking.

Tracks had gotten stuck and had to be towed off of hidden obstacles. While the infected were swarming.

That had required a lot of rounds and a call to a Gunhawk to fix. Fortunately, they were doing this first run by day. Doing it at night would have meant scrumming. And with the infected density, that would have meant an LRI situation.

But they were finally approaching the golf course with Hell's own pack of infected on their tail. There were . . . thousands. The last Gunhawk pass had been for video, not fire support. That had been uploaded to the Hole, where it was massaged by a computer and come back with better than fifty thousand infected, trotting along behind trying to get to the tasty treats.

Faith could believe it. She was observing them through her commander's vision blocks.

"I need a read back from each track that they are closed up, tight," Faith said. "Track One . . ."

When all the tracks had confirmed that they were closed up for the night, Faith switched to the fire control frequency.

"Fire Control, Fire Control, Alpha One, over," Faith said.

"Fire Control."

"Going to try to lead them down to the ninth tee," Faith said. "Down by Glebe Road, break. Will call for fire when in the basket. Over."

"Roger. Have that zeroed and are ready for fire for effect at your call, over."

"Stand by," Faith said, checking the GPS. It was hooked up to an external, unarmored, antenna so they were probably going to lose it as soon as the rounds came in. "Roger . . . How long on the time of flight, over?"

"Fifteen seconds, over."

"Roger. . . ." Faith looked at the group, thought about where they were and shrugged. "Fire control, approximately fifty thousand targets on Target Point Nine, break. Fire for effect, over."

"Fire for effect, out," the firing battery called. *"Shot, over."*

"Roger," Faith said.

"Your response is 'shot, out' saying you heard that."

"Shot, out," Faith said.

"Splash, over."

"Oh, yeah, that's a splash," Faith said as the variable timed artillery exploded over the heads of the infected. It wasn't centered on the mass but it tore a huge chunk out of one wing. There was no clear *reason*, just pops of smoke overhead then . . . infected just fell. "Nice. Keep it coming, over."

"That is what fire for effect means. You have five more stonks on the way, over."

"I need somebody who actually knows how this works," Faith muttered. The fire was tearing up the infected but most of them weren't actually in the basket. About half the group of infected were making it past. Some of them were stopping to feed, the rest were just following the damned music. "Fire control, Alpha One, over."

"Alpha One, Fire Control."

"Most of them didn't get hit, break," Faith said. "I'm going to go right to Target Point Two, right on top of the point, and just park and let them swarm. Then scratch my back. We'll see how that works, over."

"Roger," Fire Control answered a moment later. *"Your call."*

"Maxim Twenty: If you're not willing to shell your

own position, you're not willing to win," Faith said. "Should be a lark. Switch to target point two . . ."

"Fire Control, Alpha One."

"Fire Control," Lance Corporal Paula Winters said. She looked over at the battery FDC chief. "Is it just me or did she sound nervous?"

"Nervous," Staff Sergeant Lefre Delmont said. "She's about to have fifteen rounds of one-five-five drop on her head."

"Yeah, are you ready to fire on Target Point two, over?"

"Roger," Winters replied.

"Now might be a good time, break. They're sort of all over us. Like banging on my top hatch all over us. Over."

"You have to call it," Winters said, rolling her eyes.

"Fire Control, Alpha One. Fire for Effect, five times, stonks, whatever, target point two. Over."

"Fire for effect, out," Winters said, sending the command to the guns. There was a distant series of booms. "Shot, over."

"Shot, out."

"Splash," Delmont said a few seconds later.

"Splash, over."

"Yeah . . . Wow. Sounds like rain on a tin roof . . . Could you pass to support that the tracks are gonna need a wash down? Oh, and, tell your guys they rock. That got the rest of 'em. Over."

"Any idea on total kills, over?" Winters asked.

"Twenty thousand or so in the two sets or whatever. Still quite a few left. We'll roll and see if any follow. There's feeders on the first set at Target Point Nine. I don't know if you want to fire that up. Or . . . break.

We'll roll back there and park and you can fire us up again. How's that work?"

"Up to you, over," Winters said, shaking her head.

"We'll figure it out. Always do. Oh, I think you blew up my speakers..."

"The main problem, besides the roads, was the artillery," Faith said. "It worked great where it worked but the area of impact was too small. Fifty thousand people take up room. I don't know for artillery but they're either going to have to shift it around as they fire or more guns or something. That's pretty much all I got. Oh, and if we have to back scratch every time, we're going to need to armor up the speakers or something. *Now* that's all I've got."

"Fire support?" Colonel Dawson said.

"Right now we have one battery in support of our battalion, sir," the fire support officer said. "We can have them do adjustment in fire. But it would seem we need more tubes in support."

"All the batteries aren't firing all the time," Colonel Dawson said, making a note. "I'd suggest that we have all the batteries fire every time there's a call rather than the support battery. But that will have to be a decision of higher. And we probably should send in an ANGLICO team to see how the fire is working and make adjustments. Do we have one available?"

"We have a member, sir," the fire support officer said. "One for the MEU. ANGLICO took a bit of a hit in the plague, sir. But we should be able to send him along to see what's what."

"I'll pass that up the chain, too," Dawson said.

"Oooh," Faith said as the brigade time-on-target hit. They'd gathered up another nice group of infected following them and the fire had hit direct on the mass. And it hit a much larger footprint, covering the entire group. "Splash, out. Good effect. *Big* mass of bodies. When you're finished, we'll finish off the survivors. Out." She switched to the platoon frequency.

"Turn around and follow me. Use turret guns to clean up. Out."

"You gotta hope these guys are okay with this," Faith said over the intercom as Trixie rumbled through Arlington National Cemetery.

The normally well-kept grounds were overgrown with weeds and a fire had scorched many of the trees. Robert E. Lee's house had burned to the ground.

Despite all that, they weren't finding many infected in the area. Should have been prime stomping grounds for them.

"They understand, ma'am," Decker replied. "Can't you hear them, ma'am?"

"That is your gift, Staff Sergeant," Faith said.

"These are not unquiet dead, ma'am," Decker said. "This is usually a place of great peace. To lie here means that you have cast aside the burden of duty for the feather of honorable death. But they know the turmoil of our nation and have wished to rise to its defense could they again. We quiet them, ma'am, by the rumble and squeal of our treads and the thunder of our artillery, for they know the nation is protected, still. It was only before our arrival that they were unquiet. I doubt that any infected *could* nest in these hallowed grounds."

"Decker," Faith said, her eyes misty. "Like the

rest of us, I don't know if you're crazy as a bedbug or gone through crazy to some other side of insane sanity. But I'm glad you're you."

"Thank you, ma'am," Decker said. "The nice thing about ghosts is you always have someone to talk to..."

"I'd like to pass to the aviation people the request for an overfly and survey of the course before we go to free-fire tonight," Faith said, looking at her notes. "I'd like to know which holes are sort of clear. The combination of blood and dirt is making things treacherous. We got an amtrack stuck on the ninth hole last night and that was no fun at all. And we need to figure out a way to tell platoons from Two One that when there's a check fire on a hole it means that another unit is trying to extract an amtrack or something and to keep driving around in circles till the kill zone is clear. Not, let me repeat, NOT bring fifty thousand howling infected down onto the course while we are deployed hooking up towing cables, however funny this will seem in retrospect, and I quote. If there is a bar fight at the O club sometime this week, I hope you'll understand why a certain platoon leader from Two One is in the hospital..."

"Time to go full rig," Faith said, looking up at the Pentagon. There were infected. They'd survived. How many on the interior wasn't as clear. "This ought to be a lark. And tell the wash point guys to be on standby; we're gonna need it."

"How's it going, Lieutenant?" Colonel Ramos said.

Faith was at her "command post" deep in the bowels of the Pentagon. The mini-base had been set up with ammo, food and water resupply in a secured section of rooms in the Army portion of the massive building. Troops could rotate back from combat and get some rest before continuing clearance.

"Slow, sir," Faith said. "This place makes a liner seem straightforward, and it's hard to prevent infiltration. We're getting constant leakers. Then there's the damned security doors. Some of 'em you can barely scratch, sir."

"I'm surprised by the infected density," Colonel Ramos said. "I can't believe so many survived."

"If anyone had mentioned this thing had basements I'd have expected it, sir," Faith said. "Basements flood. Water equals infected. And they'll find a way in even if we can't. Did it get so high that they're moving through the ventilation, sir?"

"We got that," Ramos said.

"Going to take a while, sir," Faith said. "Just another bug hunt."

"Nuke it from orbit," Ramos said. "It's the only way to be sure."

"Don't joke, sir," Faith said. "I know where there's a bunch of special weapons just sitting around collecting dust. And we're finding dick all for survivors."

"Bravo, One One is closing in on the Tank," Ramos said. "It's the only spot that might have them. We've checked every other supply point in the building. If it's empty, I'm calling this. We'll just seal the doors. Maybe pump it full of chlorine gas."

"Works for me, sir," Faith said. "There's better uses for our time."

"Where the fuck are they all coming from?" Faith asked tiredly. She was looking forward to getting back to the ships and getting a shower. Clearing the Pentagon, to the extent it was clear, had been a fucking bitch. And now infected were *still* turning up in Crystal City.

There was a constant *pop-pop-pop* of fire from the back of the seven-ton. Despite Arlington County being repeatedly swept, infected just *kept* fucking appearing.

"Alpha One One, First Platoon," Faith said. "Permission to deploy for a short sweep, over."

"This area has high infected, First," Captain Dobbins replied. *"That's a negative."*

"Roger," Faith said, watching an infected crawl out of a store-front window. "Then request we come back and do a forced reconnaissance. I've got a crawly feeling, over."

"Discuss at the firebase, over."

"Let me get this straight," Colonel Dawson said. "You want to do a ground level dismount sweep of . . . Where? Crystal City? Which is still orange at least."

"Yes, sir," Faith said. She'd gotten a shower, food that wasn't MREs and some more or less solid sleep in a comfortable bunk on the *Festival Dawn*. "On return to base after the Pentagon sweep I noted not only solid orange level infected presence but infected exiting numerous buildings along the return route, sir."

"I saw the same thing," Colonel Dawson said. "We can't get them all, Faith."

"Understood, sir," Faith said. "My issue is that it is something with which I am unfamiliar, sir. When I hit something that's new, I want to know how far it goes, sir. Because, sir, sometimes when I've just gone 'Oh, big deal' in the past, it has risen up to bite me in the ass, sir. I've got the creepy-crawlies, sir. I'd like to figure out why there are so many infected just popping the fuck up, sir. Jax is pretty much yellow to greenish at this point, sir. Why isn't Arlington?"

"Do you have something besides 'I'd like to go back to Arlington and get in a scrum'?" Dawson asked.

"I'm not planning on scrumming, sir," Faith said. "Not if I can help it. Return to Arlington with the company in amtracks, sir. My platoon will do a reconnaissance trying to figure out where infected are coming from. If we can get some determination quickly, great. No more than a few hours recon. I'd like the company on standby to pull us out. I . . . I don't know what is there, sir. Could be a few infected up in buildings and basements and they'll eventually go away. Could be something new, in which case . . . I'd like the company on standby to pull us out. I do not want to do another LRI. But something is very very wrong, sir. And it's got me concerned for planned future operations, sir. I know the joke about lieutenants and 'in my experience,' sir . . ."

"No one questions your experience, Shewolf," Dawson said. "Not for more than the first conversation. If you're this concerned . . . We'll put it on the mission schedule."

"Thank you, sir," Faith said.

"And you'll go rigged for close combat," Dawson said.

"Oh, God, yeah," Faith said. "I just hope we can self-extract. Sir."

"Wait," Faith said as Hooch was about to bang on the bulkhead with a crowbar.

They'd entered by an underground parking garage exit. They'd swept down towards the bottom and found the bottom level filled with water. There were the usual bits and remains of every kind of dreck, mostly identifiable human bones. But no infected. There were some doors with signs into other areas, but they hadn't checked those, yet.

"This is a recon," Faith said. "I know the whole thing about letting them come to you. We're not doing clearance. So for once, we sneak."

"Roger, ma'am," Hooch said, putting away the crowbar.

"Check the hatches," Faith said. "Infected can only use a simple hatch. Find one that's open."

The corridors were a maze but they weren't lost. They'd been carefully marking their trail. So far, they had yet to encounter a live infected. Lots of sign. Even some nests. But no live infected.

Then Fisher, on point, quietly opened a door and made a "stop" sign. He then just as quietly closed the door and made a cutting sign with his hand, shaking his head.

Apparently his lights had been enough. Faith could hear the growling starting up. Lots of growling. It was coming from every direction and felt like it was shaking the ground.

"Fall back!" Faith shouted through her gas mask as the door burst open and more infected than she'd ever wanted to see again at close quarters poured into the tight corridor. There was "target rich environment" and "okay, this is Tango Uniform." The situation had just gone Tango Uniform.

"Go hot! And see if we can find a hatch to block!"

"Exit is blocked!" Hooch called. "We couldn't melee through that, ma'am!"

"Can you hold them?" Faith yelled. Hooch was around a corner from her but she could hear the continuous fire from his team.

"For now, aye," Hooch called.

"Jan, go through the left hatch," Faith yelled.

"Aye, aye, ma'am," Januscheitis said. "Do this hatch, Curran!"

"Aye, aye," the lance corporal said, hooking the lock with his Halligan tool. "Fisher, hammer!"

The PFC hit the head of the Halligan tool with his own on the hammer edge and the lock popped off. A moment later they were through, including the two teams in contact. It had gotten to scrum at one point but they'd finally broken contact.

"I'm totally turned around," Curran said. "But it's clear down here!"

"Get it prepped to block," Faith yelled, firing her Saiga through the crack in the hatch. She was glad she'd brought the nonstandard weapon with her. She hadn't seen infected density like this since LRI. On the other hand, they were in much tighter quarters and so far they hadn't been forced to scrum once.

"First, Alpha. Status, over."

"We're having to take an alternate exit route," Faith radioed. "Main route is blocked. Do not commit at this time. This is bad on toast down here. This would swallow a company. It would probably swallow a battalion. I've got an inkling of an alternate route we can use if this building is to form. We may require helo extract from the roof. So far no casualties and we're not yet yellow on ammo, over."

"Roger. I'm contacting higher for helo support and possible ground support. Can you comment on the threat, over?"

"This appears to be some sort of underground mall or something, break," Faith said, handing her assault pack and empty mags to Fisher. "Load those," she snapped. "There are *extensive* underground areas. Infected density is high red. Floor plans are stupid complex. Break. Going to try to find the elevators. Should have built in ladders. Break. Shall try to find ground level exit method. Absent that will climb to roof and extract through roof hatch. Over."

"Understood. Will maintain overwatch. Got some coming out but not in a wave. Over."

"Radio's starting to not work as well," Faith radioed. "Deep underground. Will try to keep in commo. We're getting out; just a matter of when. Out." The hatch was effectively blocked but the infected could be heard howling and clawing beyond it.

"Oorah," she said to the gathered Marines. "I had a class what seems like thirty years ago on how these buildings work. If I read one of the maps correctly, and I'm better in buildings than streets, there should be a service elevator up ahead and to the right. We'll access that. Problem will be if the elevator is up rather than down. If it's down, we'll hit the ladder and just climb. If we have to go out on the roof, we'll go out on the roof. Welcome to shit-has-hit-the-turbine One-Oh-One. It happens to be my specialty..."

"Gimme," Faith said, taking the Halligan tool. "Like this..."

She slid it into the gap between the elevator hatches,

slid down, cracked the lock and levered the hatches open an inch.

"Now, pull," she said, handing the tool back to Fisher. In case there were infected on the other side she covered the opening with her Saiga.

The elevator had two long-dead corpses in it. She hardly noticed details like that anymore. Especially since they weren't kids.

"Hatch," she said, pointing up. "Fisher, Bowen, boost."

She drew her .45 and let them boost her up to the roof hatch of the elevator. Topside was clear. She could hear infected above but it appeared all the elevator hatches were closed.

The ladder was on the left side of the door bulkhead. Opposite of the Bank of the Americas building she'd wandered around so long ago but big diff. And, thank God, this building was only about ten stories not thirty-seven. If they couldn't get one of the doors above open or if none of them were clear they'd just go up to the roof and call for a Gunhawk for cover.

There was a flurry of shots from below and Faith keyed the platoon radio.

"Status?"

"They're slipping in from somewhere, ma'am," Januscheitis said. *"Just a trickle. We've got it."*

"Jan, can you figure out how to relatch the elevator?" Faith said. "Or do I need to come down there?"

"Got it, ma'am," Januscheitis said.

"We're going to need everybody to hook up," Faith said. "I don't want anybody falling to their death. Then, well, we just climb for freedom."

"Aye, aye, ma'am."

"I've got lead, you've got trail," Faith said. "Squad leaders, let's get this organized."

"Fuck a freaking duck," Faith said when they'd gotten to the roof hatch. Every time they'd come to a door that might be good there'd been infected on the other side. She was pretty sure they were following them up. Which meant they might be on the roof. And she was shot. Upper body strength was not her asteroid. Her arms were noodles. She knew she wasn't the person to do the top clear. And it *was* going to need clearance. She could *hear* the infected. "Hooch. Pass me. Your clear. Stand by."

She hooked one arm into the metal ladder, hooked her safety line, shuffled to the side a bit and fumbled for her radio.

She'd lost contact with higher earlier. But they were high, now. Maybe she could get through.

"Alpha, First Platoon," Faith radioed.

"First platoon, Alpha. Good to hear from you again."

"We're going to have to access the roof. Request cover fire, over."

"Gunhawk is up and already firing. Infected on the roof in large numbers."

"Fuck a freaking duck," Faith muttered. Then she heard the sound of the rotors and a rattle of the rounds striking the roof somewhere to their right. "Roger. Will exit and pop smoke. Do not fire on smoke. Over. Hooch, have a smoke grenade *in your hand*."

"Aye, aye, ma'am," Hooch said, pulling one out of a cargo pocket.

"Do not fire on smoke, aye."

"Check fire for exit, over," Faith said.

"Stand by," Alpha called. *"Check fire confirmed."*

"Go, Hooch," Faith said.

The sergeant opened the hatch, tossed the smoke grenade and hurried through. She could smell the smoke as he popped it. And hear the tidal wave of infected closing on him.

"Go!" she shouted, tapping the troops past her. "Go! Go! Go! Move it, Marines! And stay in the smoke! Alpha, we need support fire from Gunhawk. Cover the stair exit. Drop the infected level!"

"Roger. Check fire lifted . . ."

"Clearly your gut was with you again, Lieutenant," Colonel Dawson said as Faith slumped out of the Seahawk.

With support fire from the Gunhawk and their own fire they'd finally gotten the stair hatch to the roof closed. After that it was just a matter of getting on the helos. Quite a few of the Marines had gotten in the scrum and were as usual covered in infected blood. Just another day in the post-Plague Marine Corps.

"Hotwash, how bad is it down there?" Dawson asked.

"Hundreds?" Faith said, shrugging. "Thousands? I don't know, sir. Not as bad as LRI but it was serious, sir. And that was under *one* building, sir. I had a little time to think about it, sir. Big cities like this are honeycombed with tunnels under them, sir. Homeless live in them in big cities since they're under cover. Figure infected do, too, sir. And if we tried to clear that, sir? I think it would swallow our whole force and we'd never get it to so much as yellow. Out in the open, easy. Down there? Forget about it.

"Sir, I don't think we're getting the big cities back

in our lifetime. Not fully. And people are going to have a hell of a time self-extracting. In Jax the water level was up and there were gators, sir. Up north . . . Some of 'em will be flooded and that will help but . . . I just . . . That's all I've got, sir. Too tired to even think, sir."

"Get cleaned up and get some rest, Lieutenant," Dawson said. "Even if they break out in numbers, I'm sure the firebases can hold them."

"They've got one-five-five, sir," Faith said. "And they brought canister. I checked."

CHAPTER 26

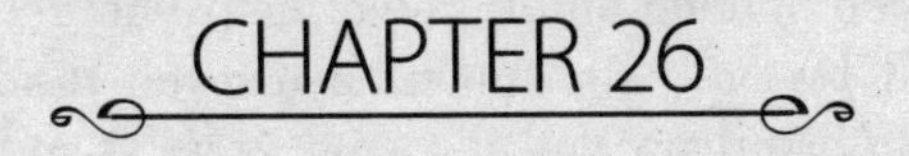

"Mine eyes have seen the glory of the coming of the Lord," Faith sang as Trixie humped up the shoreline. *"He has trampled down the vineyards where the grapes of wrath are stored . . ."*

Being the lead force for the entry to Washington was another playlist that had taken some care. But given *where* they were going ashore, there was no other reasonable choice.

With the bridges blocked by cars and in most cases incapable of taking the weight of an M1, they'd had to cross amphib. The amtracks were pulling up out of the water, dripping and looking as if they wanted to shake themselves to get dry, while Trixie landed from the LCU. But that left them at the level of the river. The main planned impact area was above them. And having taken various looks at the situation, there was really only one viable way up. The question being not *if* the tanks and tracks would do damage but how much.

"Sorry about this, sir," Faith said, saluting the memorial. "I'm sure you'll understand. Let's mount it. Take this slow, Condrey."

"Aye, aye, ma'am," Condrey said, engaging the tank and slowly mounting the steps to the Lincoln Memorial.

"We have builded him an altar in the evening dews and damps," Faith sang as the seventy-three ton tank started to grind the marble stairs to dust. *"We can read his righteous sentence by the dim and flaring lamps."* She fired bursts from the cupola gun into the infected coming down the stairs in a tide. Many of the bullets passed through or over and hit the monument to the last president to lead a war on American soil. He'd understand. *"His day is marching on . . ."*

"Ma'am, you okay?" Decker said from below.

"Great, Staff Sergeant," Faith said; she was snorting from trying not to giggle. "Take a look at the sign on that building, Staff Sergeant."

"Ah," Decker said, swiveling the turret to get a look at the sign. "I see the irony, ma'am." He didn't seem amused but then she'd never heard him amused. He was worse than Germans.

"You are just too oorah, Decker," Faith said, continuing to machine-gun the infected pouring out of the United States Institute for Peace.

"General," Ramos said, saluting, as U.S. Army General Tommie Hammond, Commander Materials Command, climbed out of the amtrack.

"Ram," Hammond said, returning the salute and sticking out his hand. "Good to see you. What the hell are you doing wearing chicken wings again?"

"Because all we have is a regiment, General," Ramos said, shaking his hand. "And the Army is essentially stood down until we get enough people, sir. Also, LantFleet is a captain who's a direct commission. NCCC is Undersecretary Galloway. Night Walker is back and has CINCPAC as a commodore. The brief is long, sir."

"Sounds like it," Hammond said, shaking his head. "Do you have people available?"

"Got a team on standby for just this occasion, General," Ramos said, waving to a major. "If you'll follow Major Withers, sir?"

"Is that a potential issue in the chain of command, sir?" Major Skelton asked as the general drove away in an MRAP.

"Oddly enough, no," Ramos said. "The general's permanent rank is the same as mine. But you can retire at rank and it's permanent. So General Montana outranks anyone but another retired lieutenant general or general. And if they're retired, the NCCC can decide whether to bring them back at rank or not. Most of this is worked out in the TS codicils of the Succession Act that get into lower level successions in the event of, well, a total fucking collapse. The only issue that might arise is if there's one of the upper level actual 'acting President' successors or someone much higher than Undersecretary Galloway in the NCCC ranks."

"Then God help us if the Secretary of Health and Human Services made it, sir," Major Skelton said.

"If she has, we'll obey her orders, Major," Ramos said. "While making pointed suggestions what those orders might be. What is the status on Two One?"

"Decker, I have a puzzler for you," Faith said as Condrey sideswiped a black Expedition out of the way of the following tracks.

"Yes, ma'am?" Decker said. They weren't engaging infected but they did have a nice trail of them.

"Why is the State Department more armored up than the Pentagon?" Faith asked. "We could barely get Trixie though those defenses. Although they're low enough the infected aren't having any problems."

"I'm not sure, ma'am," Decker said.

"'Cause people don't like them as much, ma'am," PFC Twitchell said.

"That makes sense," Faith said.

"Crap!" Faith said as the adjustment round hit right in the middle of the WWII memorial. "No, no, no, NO! Gawwwd DAMNIT! *LEFT* YOU DUMB SONS-OF-BITCHES!"

"They can't hear you, ma'am," Decker reminded her. The adjustment was being done by their one surviving ANGLICO NCO, who was up in a Gunhawk.

"I know, Staff Sergeant," Faith said. "But it's a crime and a waste."

"And, again, ma'am," Decker said. "Those who are honored will understand."

"Still a crime and a waste, Staff Sergeant . . . Okay, looks like they're on target . . . Alpha, First. We free to call the rain, over?"

"One more adjustment, First, over," Alpha replied.

"Roger," Faith replied. "We'll just cruise up and down the square . . . Sergeant Major, marching up and down the square . . ."

"I'm getting calls that if you hit the Memorial again, they're going to open fire on us," Sophia said over the intercom.

"Please pass to them that adjusting rounds in here is like threading a needle in a thunderstorm, ma'am. Would they prefer I hit the Vietnam Memorial, the World War Two Memorial, the Reflecting Pond or the *Korean* War Memorial? Possibly the Washington Monument? As it is, the German American Friendship Garden is about to be toast . . ."

"There are eighty-seven secure bunkers in the D.C. area alone," Colonel Ramos said. "That does not count the extensive underground works of the Smithsonian, assuming they are not totally flooded. Then there are the dispersal sites. Some of those we don't know the status. Some we do. Mount Weather reported itself as H7D3 compromised then went off the air. Given that most of the Congress and the SCOTUS was evacuated there by that time . . ." The colonel shrugged.

"Wasn't the President reported at Mount Weather, sir?" Faith said.

"The President was evacuating *to* Mount Weather when communications were compromised, Lieutenant," Ramos said. "However, since his Marine pilots had not been vaccinated and the detail *was*, it was elected to take him by ground vehicle. That was the last anyone heard of him. It is possible he is in one of the bunkers or could have made it out of the D.C. area and be somewhere else or could be dead. We don't know. Raven Mountain, which had pretty much the entire remaining Congress as well as half the Supreme Court, just went off-line. Nobody knows why. H7 presumably, but they could have just lost all their commo nodes. And the SecState was reliably reported there. The SecDef was in the Tank. He's been positively identified as KIA.

"However, all the major successors—Speaker, President of the Senate and Cabinet Secretaries—as well as the Secret Service details for the President and the Vice President, were vaccinated. Other details the data is sketchy. Bottom line: There may be high officials of the government remaining in these bunkers. Now that conditions are down to yellow, on the surface at least, we will begin active inspection of each of the facilities. Back to confined space combat."

"Oorah, sir," Colonel Dawson said. "As my junior lieutenant would put it, it's scrummin' time."

"Speaking of which," Colonel Ramos said. "There are two major objectives which I'm sure *all* the lieutenants are hoping to breach: The White House and Eighth and Eye."

"Eighth and Eye?" Faith whispered to Captain Dobbins.

"Marine Barracks," Dobbins whispered back.

"We'll draw objectives out of a hat," Ramos said. "Most of them are company or platoon objectives. Given Lieutenant Smith's adventure in Crystal Land, there will be an additional company or platoon as backstop as well as a response unit. Once we've determined the objectives, we will look at how we're going to work that out..."

"First Platoon, Alpha Actual."

"First," Faith said, firing one-handed at an infected charging out of a cross corridor.

The basements of the buildings in D.C. *all* seemed to be interconnected. You just couldn't "clear" the damned things. And they were as rife with infected as Crystal City.

The basement of the Department of Commerce was no more or less awful than the Department of Agriculture or EPA. So far, Faith had yet to get a "good" target. Other lucky bastards had gotten to clear the Capitol and the White House and Eighth and Eye. Although it was taking most of 2/1 to clear the Smithsonian. And so far she had yet to find a "secure facility" that had held out. She'd heard they'd found some in the Department of Education of all places.

Just another bug hunt.

"Abort operation. Return to base using minimum force necessary to successfully extract your personnel. Is that order understood?"

"Abort, aye," Faith said, shooting another infected in the face. "Could you define minimum force, over?" It was still moving so she shot it a couple more times just to be sure. Didn't want an ankle biter. They tended to trip people up.

"No further and I quote wanton slaughter of afflicted individuals close quote. Pull out using minimum force. Just get back to base. We're stood down. Alpha, out."

"What the fuck?" Faith said, switching frequencies. "Platoon. Mission abort. Pull back to the tracks. No worries, no sweat, we just got an abort from higher. Don't know why. We're Romeo Tango Bravo. Rearguard, you're now point. Let's plow the road . . ." She didn't even bother passing on the "minimum force" thing. *What the fuck?*

"What the fuck, sir?" Faith said when she got to the forward command post. "We were practically to the fucking bunker!"

"We're breaking down and pulling back to Reagan,"

Captain Dobbins said, his face tight. "The Secretary of Education is number thirteen in the line of Presidential Succession. Her first order on getting in touch with Command was to stop the clearance. So we're stopping clearance unless that is clarified. That is an order, Lieutenant. We're determining fall-back lanes at this time. As soon as we have them figured out, we're pulling back to Reagan. Is that understood?"

"Aye, aye, sir," Faith said.

"What the fuck?" Faith said, setting down her tray.

The combined mess in the *Festival Dawn* was massive but she could always seem to find Sophia.

"Sit," Sophia said quietly, shaking her head. "Just... You haven't seen the new directive?"

"No," Faith said, sitting down. "What new directive?"

Anna silently slid a folded sheet of paper to her.

"While the zeel of the United States Military in suporting there nation in this time of difficulty is apreciated, their reminded that the persons aflicted by H7D3 are human beeings and should be treated as such...."

The photocopied Executive Order went on like that for a full page. Someone had beat her to red-lining it. *"Genoside will not be tollerated by this administration..." "Invesigations possibly leading to crimnal charges..." "detaled serch for crtical indiviiduals."*

There wasn't one single line which lacked a misspelled word and most had some egregious grammatical error.

It was signed "Elizabeth Sovrain, Secretary of Education, Acting President."

"The positive to that missive is that the issue of

American schools is clarified," Anna said in her most impeccable British accent. "The person in charge is a bloody loon."

"So no more clearance?" Faith said. "And did we lose the ability to run spell-check entirely?"

"No," Sophia said. "We're back to tag and bag like before the Fall. Where we're going to find the Tasers and sed-a-gives is fortunately not my concern."

"What about vaccine?" Faith asked. "We going to be slitting the throats?"

"No," Sophia said. "We're going to be administering care."

"Cutting their throats *is* administering care," Faith said. "Or are we supposed to keep them strapped to a bed for the rest of their lives?"

"*I don't know*, okay?" Sophia snapped. "Did you catch the part about 'child soldiers'?"

"No," Faith said. "I think my brain shut down before that point. I'm no grammar Nazi, just ask Captain Dobbins, but *my* eyes started watering. Who can't spell 'genocide' for God's sake?"

"'There shall be no more use of child soldiers, and all such persons shall be discharged immediately,'" Anna quoted. "I was informed persons who were admitted without regular training standards—'here's a gun, go shoot zombies'—are being allowed to voluntarily discharge. And one line hinted at criminal charges for 'crimes against humanity.'"

"I heard Da's on his way up by P8," Sophia said. "He might be facing charges."

"She'd have a mutiny," Faith said mulishly.

"What happened to Semper Fidelis?" Sophia asked.

"Always Faithful to the *nation*, Sophia," Faith said.

"And this is *not* faithfully discharging our duty to the *nation*! There are survivors! What about *them*? They can't get out without us clearing?"

"She considers the *infected* to be survivors, Faith," Sophia said. "Her daughter apparently broke containment right after the Fall. So she wants us to *find* her, okay? Well, she wants the 'military' to find her. *We're* out on our ass. And Da is probably breaking rocks."

"There has to be *something* we can do," Faith said.

"We haven't found anyone higher on the list," Sophia said. "And since we're not actively clearing, we're not going to. If something doesn't break, we're looking at that... She could be Acting President For Life."

Faith looked at her nearly untouched plate and picked it up.

"Where there's a will, there's a way. I'll see you gals later."

"One state cannot introduce and ratify a Constitutional Amendment!"

Jerry Carter was the chief counsel for the State of Texas Recovery and Reestablishment Committee. Based in Hamlin, the committee was in the process of finding and counting enough citizens to be eligible for reestablishment of statehood.

So far they'd gotten a hard count, with documentation of citizenship and residency, of forty-five thousand people. Sixty-five was the magic number. Twenty thousand more and they'd be the only state with one congressman and two senators.

And, technically, the ability to amend the Constitution. Including the Twenty-Fifth Amendment, which was the current sticking point.

"Show me where it says how many states have to be in the Union," Acting Governor Brad Thurman said. The former head of the Texas Rangers was nearly eighty and still hard as nails. Ask any of the infected that had had the bad luck to run across him.

"It doesn't. When we meet the test for a state, we can have a by-election for Congress, an election for governor—think I'll be running unopposed there—the governor chooses two of his 'cronies,' that'd be Charlie from Amarillo and Bubba from B'ville, then we can introduce an amendment. At which point, only verified states get to vote for ratification. We can introduce and ratify as many as we want. And the quorum of the Senate and Congress will be one congressman and two senators from Texas. Sarah's a shoe-in for the congressman's spot. And Sarah, Charlie and Bubba are already onboard."

"This is insane," Carter said.

"No," Thurman said quietly. "What's insane is what's going on in Arlington. And we're going to *fix* that. Either that or hoist the Lone Star and that's a can of worms we'll only crack if we're forced to . . ."

"The Secretary is no more nor less insane than any other person previously judged competent to assume an office of authority," Colonel Hamilton said. "Her insistence that we suspend all 'wanton slaughter' of the infected together with performing aggressive search operations for her daughter are forms of obsession that rise to the level of neurosis, not psychosis. The fact that it is a very bad order does not make her insane. 'Competence' in regards to the articles and Amendment is a matter of psychological competence not technical competence. There is no medical reason to *not* swear her in as Acting President."

"At which point she supersedes Undersecretary Galloway and her . . . okay not 'insane' but clearly impossible-to-effect orders go into effect," General Brice pointed out. "There is no way the forces we have can 'secure and maintain afflicted.' We're outnumbered a hundred to one. And you can't sweep the tunnels for her daughter, who is either dead or infected, without 'wanton slaughter.' Ergo, she is not *technically* competent to be the acting President under the current conditions."

"The military does not decide technical competence, General," Steve said. "If it did, half the Presidents we've had elected would have been overthrown by a coup. Which is why civilian control of the military is holy writ. What we are currently doing is considering mutiny. I am *not* onboard. The world does not need America led by a junta. In a year and a half there is a regularly scheduled presidential election. That's if Texas does not act first. I doubt she will get reelected, and we continue from there. Well, *someone* does. She's already said she's charging me with crimes against humanity and insists that the military cannot use 'child soldiers.' She seems to feel Stacey and my parental rights should be suspended for deliberately 'traumatizing' our children. So Sophia and Faith are both going to have their commissions revoked as soon as she is sworn in.

"I'm resigning. I was a 'hostilities only' officer and if we're not continuing the war there's no reason for me to be involved. If I need to take the fall to keep our country from being torn apart by a civil war, I'll do that. My life, my fortune and my sacred honor. I'm shooting for house arrest and leaving everyone else out of it. If she attempts to try the entire upper command or my daughters... Then we'll probably have a mutiny no matter what."

"I intend to resign as well," Montana said. "I've got a nice little house in Coronado all picked out. Might go down and see about clearing a little town in Mexico since it will be outside her jurisdiction."

"I'm thinking Med," Steve said.

"We can't *all* resign," Colonel Ramos said.

"No, but I am, Colonel," Steve said. "I must. That way, you can put all the blame on *me*. I'd even go for house arrest since it's going to be lifted as soon as she's out of office. But I will *not* support a mutiny, coup or junta. I guess you can say I'm putting my faith in Texas."

"I'm putting my faith in Faith," Colonel Ramos said.

"Colonel?" General Brice asked.

"Sorry," Ramos said mildly. "Forget I said that. I mean, seriously, forget you *ever* heard me say that. Having *not* said it, I need to go make sure all *sorts* of people are involved in *very* important meetings..."

Faith didn't have much use for computers. Didn't mean she didn't know how to use them. After a class from Sophia, she'd been putting in more and more time. And she also didn't do intel. But she'd learned to hum the tune.

She started by finding out who was superior to the Secretary of Education in the hierarchy. Turned out it was just about everyone in the Cabinet. But to turn this around without a mutiny, she needed someone with some *sense*. Then there were the known facts. SecDef was dead. He'd been found in the National Military Command Center, aka "The Tank," which had been lost to "turned" individuals. He was only identifiable by his dog-tags. Turned out in emergencies, the entire Cabinet had high-tech dog-tags. Bottom line: Off the list.

President, who was last reported moving by ground convoy with his family, had never reported in at Mount Weather, which had *also* been lost. Raven Mountain was a question. It had gone off-line but no reason was known. It hadn't reported being infected. But Raven Mountain was way the hell deep in West Virginia. No way to look there.

VP: Convoy reported H7 compromised, contact lost. Probably KIA. Speaker of the House was in the same vein as the SecEd. *Might* have more sense but she'd only get one shot at this. Off the list. Also probably at Mount Weather but not for sure. President of the Senate. She recognized the name from some rants by Da pre-Plague. "Senile idiot" was what she remembered. Oops . . . Raven Mountain. Off the list. SecState. Mount Weather. SecTreasury . . . Intel reported him as having been killed in a helo crash on the way to Raven. The reason that the President had been moved by ground. Attorney General . . . Possible. Nope, Boulder. Off the list . . . Interior, Agriculture and Commerce she'd all checked. They were either outside D.C. or location unknown. Off the list . . . Off the list . . . Off the list . . .

"Fuck," she muttered. Every "higher" point in D.C. had been checked and there were either no survivors or the Secretary or whatever was gone.

Locations unknown or low probability of info were: POTUS; SecState who had not been in State's "secure facility" and only "reliably" reported at or near Mount Weather; AG, "reliably" reported in Boulder and had not been in the local bunker... VPOTUS, maybe. Compromised convoy sounded like T-O-A-S-T. That was it. The only remaining viable "possible" was the President. And he and his family were last seen leaving the White House headed for Mount Weather in a convoy.

But...

They had enough resources these days that there was an intel group. And they'd been questioning survivors about what they'd seen prior to the Fall. Also, all the teams had reported "notable vehicles or other indications of senior officers" during the sweeps. Faith's platoon had found some LAVs abandoned...

She dug into the intel using a search for "President" and "POTUS."

Survivor: *I'm sure it was the President. The convoy had some tanks with it and that big armored limo he uses...*

Survivor: *I'm pretty sure it was the President's convoy. It looked like one, you know? You see it in D.C. all the time. But it had some tanks with it which just made sense. That was when I tried to run, you know? If the Prez was leaving, so was I...*

Survivor: *...it was the President's car, you know? That one they call "The Beast." And, like, four tanks...*

There was already a map. There'd been a team tracking the locations. But nobody had seen the Beast. One other indicator that the VPOTUS was toast was that they'd found her armored limo abandoned in downtown D.C. No way to tell which of the corpses around it might have been her or her family. Which was a shame since she'd be *spar* as President in a ZA.

But . . . tanks. *She'd* called every armored vehicle she saw in Blount Island a "tank" until she was gently corrected by Gunny Sands and Staff Sergeant Decker. To a civilian, or a lieutenant who'd been a civilian before the Plague, anything with a gun and armor was a tank.

She started looking for reported positions of armored vehicles, then putting them into the map of the suspected locations of the President. Some of those locations were way off the map in odd areas. Some were reported as "low probability" based on the convoy being headed west. But all those roads were blocked as hell. At a certain point the Secret Service detail would realize there was no way out of D.C. To the west there were rivers and bridges. And every single bridge was blocked as shit.

So they'd turn around. Why not the White House? Who knows. Blocked roads? Where *would* they head?

She'd head for Eighth and Eye or the Navy Yard. Pentagon was out of the question; bridges. Did they have commo, still? Probably. Where? Would? They? Head?

It's an emergency. You have to save your primary. Getting out is impossible. Helos are compromised. She'd *been* in the Fall. She *knew* what the chaos was like. Where do you go?

It was like that night in NYC. You go to ground. You find the best facility you can that is closest. Period.

It's an *emergency*.

Three Marine light assault vehicles had been spotted outside the Federal *Emergency* Management Agency building. They'd been on a recovery list. Why LAVs at FEMA, nobody had asked. Because they *weren't* tanks. Intel said they were looking for M1s or the

Beast as a sign of the President. Faith would have dumped the Beast and gotten in the LAVs.

And FEMA was bound to have one hell of a "disaster center." Which the Secret Service would know.

POTUS was a bit of a fucktard but not as bad as the Acting POTUS. Any port in a storm.

Time to find Sophia.

"You're insane," Sophia said.

"Yuh *think*?" Faith said. "I can swing my side, can you swing yours?"

"We'll be in a cell next to Da," Sophia said.

"The family that does time together, stays together," Faith said. "Come on. What are they going to do to us? We're *juveniles*! *And* we've been traumatized by all the shit we've been through! Boo-hoo, it's been so *terrible*! We'll plead temporary insanity. Worse comes to worse, we'll share a cell. It'll be like being back on the *Mile Seven*."

"You're supposed to be arguing in favor of the plan, Faith," Sophia said.

"Even *if* this works, no matter what we'll be in a heap of trouble," Faith said seriously. "The Prez was no great shakes. But it's not about *us*, Sophia. It's about our nation. If it works, the nation will be better off. With the SecEd in charge... The U.S. is screwed. Texas will probably secede. Do you want my Marines having to fight *Texans* instead of zombies?"

"I can get the gear," Sophia said, sighing. "Once more unto the breach, dear sister?"

"Once more," Faith said, grinning. "Or close up the wall with our American dead."

Timing was everything.

Amtracks were still moving around. You fixed one, you gave it a test drive. They might never again be used for any reasonable purpose but they had to be used or they'd go bad. They'd learned that.

Faith knew which Marines were the PI guys. You could tell. They looked like Decker when he was just off the boat. They still weren't real good at questioning orders, especially from an officer, especially from Shewolf.

She found some PI Marines to load an amtrack with seabags. That's all they were, seabags. Just heavy seabags. And PI Marines followed orders.

Then she drove the amtrack to the ammo point that *also* had PI Marines working at it and ordered them to load the track with .50 and 40mm, 5.56, .45 and 12 gauge. Then signed for it with a flourish. Every I dotted, every T crossed.

All the brass were busy preparing "transformational plans for low-impact assistance of afflicted persons." Like, *all* of them were busy. Even the gunnies and master gunnies were in meetings. There was no one senior to her to say "you can't do this." While she was loading ammo one staff sergeant had walked over with an expression of curiosity on his face, stopped, turned around, put his hands behind his back and sauntered away whistling.

But timing was still everything.

"Just in case" they kept a loaded Gunhawk on the hot pad. Good news. Bad news, the crew was sitting in a ready room with the helo in view. They had to be . . . disposed of. With extreme prejudice. Sophia wasn't looking forward to what she was about to do. She was deeply ashamed. But it had to be done. For the good of the nation, they had to be removed from the equation.

"You're going to love this," Sophia said, sticking her head in the hatch of the ready room. "You are hereby ordered, as of this moment, to attend a mandatory class on 'Consideration of the feelings of the Afflicted' in number six conference room. Now. Well, at thirteen hundred. Conducted by one of the 'Acting President's' staff."

"You have GOT to be shitting me!" Lieutenant Commander Wilkes swore.

"And Da has officially been charged with crimes against humanity," Sophia said.

"That we'd heard, Soph," Wilkes said. "I just... There's no way it will stick."

"I'm under the impression that there's going to be a compromise," Soph said. "Da always said all he wanted was a stout ship and a star to sail her by. House arrest at worst. Anyway, orders. Conference six. Sorry. Now, sir."

"Roger," Wilkes said, standing up. "I would rather die a thousand deaths."

"But now you really must go," Sophia said.

"What about you?" Wilkes asked.

"As a grounded and soon to be discharged for the good of the Navy officer, I'm exempt," Soph said. "I'll just sit here looking at a bird I'll never fly again."

"Going somewhere, ma'am?" Staff Sergeant Decker said.

He'd been waiting at the lowered ramp of the

amtrack when Faith walked back from signing for the ammo. He was carrying two very heavy-looking seabags.

"Just taking it for a test drive, Staff Sergeant," Faith said.

"I am not that stupid, ma'am," Decker said, throwing the bags into the amtrack. "Nor inflexible anymore. And you can either wait around and have this op—whatever it is—blown, or you can enter the vehicle, ma'am."

"Decker, they will bust you to dooley," Faith said, getting in the amtrack. "*And* throw you in jail."

"I am very high-level PTSD, ma'am," Decker said, raising the ramp. "I have been verified as having a psychotic attachment to my officers, ma'am. The proof being I kept that fucktard Lieutenant Klette alive as an 'afflicted.' The worst they will do is stick me in a padded room, ma'am. And they're probably going to do that anyway, what with the new regime. I'll drive. You man the guns, ma'am."

"Oorah," Faith said.

"By the way, ma'am," Decker said, as he started the amtrack. "What *is* the op?"

It took about five minutes to walk to the "conference room," which was five tents hooked together. Which was about when Lieutenant Commander Wilkes would know he'd been conned. Sophia waited one minute to walk down the corridor, pick up her flight bag then walk to the bird and get in. There would be no pre-flight. Then she looked at her watch again. Bang on twelve fifty-seven. She looked over to her right and saw an amtrack headed for the water. She hit the start button. The bird was kept warmed. She wouldn't have to wait for it to get to temp. Everything was in the green. Full power.

Operation Actions of the Tiger was a *Go*.

She keyed the radio and selected the Regiment Combat Ops frequency.

"Once more unto the breach, dear friends, once more,
"Or close the wall up with our American dead!
"In peace there's nothing so becomes a woman
"As modest stillness and humility;
"But when the blast of war blows in our ears,
"Then imitate the action of the tiger!"

"Very nice," Olga said over the intercom. "Very touching."

"You think you're going anywhere without *us*, you are sadly mistaken, Ensign," Anna commed.

Sophia just shook her head. No time to argue.

"Gunhawk Nine, light on the pad."

She switched frequencies, pulled up on the collective and was gone.

Getting to the FEMA building had been a nightmare.

They'd stopped by the Washington Monument to change. She couldn't board the amtrack in full clearance rig without the mission being obvious. There were still a buttload of infected in D.C. In keeping with orders, they had not engaged them. But they didn't want to be sitting outside the building changing.

So all her gear, and the staff sergeant's, had been in the seabags.

Then it was just a matter of shaking their trail of infected and finding their way through the blocked streets to FEMA. The likelihood that the President of the United States was there was low. But it was the only shot they had of getting this ungrammatical idiot out of power.

The FEMA building was a massive right trapezoid with dark brown windows bounded by C Street and Virginia Avenue. The ground floor had been lined with shops and the main entrance was a walkway between the FEMA building and the flanking Holiday Inn on the 500 block of C Street; the Virginia Avenue side was blocked by a retaining wall.

There were, sure enough, three LAVs parked higgledy-piggledy on the street. But no Beast. Some armored SUVs were *nearby* but no limousines per se.

They'd come this far. They weren't going back.

There were infected filtering out of the building, blocking the walkway entrance.

"Gunhawk, Ground," Faith said. "Can you clear the poor innocent bystanders?"

"Will do," Sophia said, bringing the Gunhawk in to hover over the amtrack. "Whenever you're ready."

"Let's roll, Al," Faith said.

"Aye, aye, ma'am," Decker said, opening up the passenger hatch. There was an infected right outside and he blew him away with three rounds of 5.56. "This is gonna be a hot one, ma'am."

"Just the way I like it, Staff Sergeant," Faith said, getting her knees under a full-sized ruck full of ammo and hoisting it up. It was going to be nearly impossible to scrum until they'd blown some of it off, but she figured they were going to need it. Heavy as a motherfucker though. "Gunhawk," she grunted. "Start the music."

The Gunhawk opened up with all four miniguns, shredding the infected blocking the walkway as Olga and Anna covered the sides. The door miniguns could aim almost straight down and they walked the rounds out from the amtrack, littering C Street with zombies.

"Maxim Four:" Faith said, dropping out of the track. "Close air support covereth a multitude of sins."

Second Lieutenant Faith Marie Smith and Staff Sergeant Alfred J. Decker, USMC, marched forward into a scalding deluge of brass. . . .

CHAPTER 27

ABOUT TWELVE MONTHS EARLIER:

"I told you we should have used the LAVs in the first place, Special Agent!" Vice President Rebecca Staba said as they boarded the vehicle. Her limousine was high and dry on a pile of infected bodies. "Marine!"

"Ma'am!" the Marine PFC sitting next to her in the light assault vehicle barked.

"Are there any spare weapons?"

"Ma'am . . ." Special Agent Jerry Phillips started to protest.

"Spare me, Special Agent," Staba snapped. "Zombie apocalypse. These Marines are unvaccinated, unfortunately. Some of them, sorry, *will* turn. And I am NOT going to be unarmed in a *zombie apocalypse*!"

Staba had been one of those compromises that you have to make in politics. The former lieutenant governor of Oklahoma, she had not been near the top of the rankings in the primaries. She was not beloved of the Republican Party leadership—she got not only zero support but constant criticism from them—and she was frankly hated by the media and her much more "nuanced" and "bi-partisan" running mate.

What she *did* have was a massive following among the "Guns and God" conservative base. And since the former governor of NY who had won the primaries was looked upon as not much more than another Republican-In-Name-Only, he needed the shoring.

A former high school math teacher who had gotten into politics to try to get some sense into education, Vice President Staba was a mother of four children with a husband who was a successful businessman in his own right. She had supplemented their income in the early days of the marriage as an NRA firearms instructor. She invariably had more people show up at her rallies than her running mate's. Which did not enamor him more with her. The fact that she was an "over-endowed" smoking-hot blonde who was *never* seen in public other than fully made-up and well-dressed was constantly criticized by the news media. The snarking, mostly by female commentators, about her make-up, hair and wardrobe was half her coverage during the primaries. Fuck 'em. She looked good and liked it that way.

Her intense devotion to her Christian faith, the Second Amendment and her "large" family was pretty much the rest of her coverage. Never in a good light.

The staff sergeant across from her unclipped his M4 and thrust it out. "Locked, loaded, on safe, ma'am!"

"Not your own, Staff Sergeant," Staba said. "You're going to need it."

"Here, ma'am," Phillips said, defeated. He opened up a ZIP bag and pulled out an MP5. "Also locked and loaded."

"And *not* on safe I see," Staba said, safing it. "Now, who's got one for Dave?"

"I'm fine, honey," Dave Staba said. "I'm sure some will turn up."

Among other actions that had seriously pissed off her

detail, the Vice President had ensured her family was aboard the LAV *before* she boarded. Most people had come to the conclusion that in a reverse of an earlier First Family, Dave Staba was the brains of the outfit. He'd been her political manager for most of her career and was the "back room" dealer. He was *not* the brawn. Capable, mind you, but not the "in your face" type.

"Are we gonna be okay, Mom?" Sherry said. The youngest didn't sound traumatized so much as curious.

"We're going to be okay, sweetie," Rebecca said, leaning forward. "We've got Devil Dogs to keep us that way . . ."

"Can *I* get a weapon?" Thomas, the fifteen-year-old asked, raising a hand.

"Not unless we really need to," Rebecca said. "And if we really need to, yes."

"Ma'am . . ." Phillips said, shaking his head.

"Tommy has more firearms training than most members of Federal Law Enforcement, Special Agent," Staba said. "He is not the level of the detail but he is proficient. If we have to dismount, and if there are weapons available, he and Dave and Christy will *all* be armed. Sherry is not ready, yet. That is not for discussion."

"Roger, ma'am," Phillips said, wincing as the LAV bumped over something large. "Continue for the FEMA building."

"Can we make it to C Street?" Staba asked.

"Ma'am, unlike your limo, we will make it to C Street if we have to drive over *cars*," the staff sergeant said.

"Oorah," Staba said.

The FEMA bunker was, unsurprisingly, well designed. Besides a very large fuel supply, generators to maintain power and pumps, and all the usual food and medical supplies, it had "recovering power" exercise systems. The stationary bike, Stairmaster and rowing machine were connected to mini-generators similar to those in a Prius, which fueled the massive banks of batteries. The lights were low-wattage LEDs. More or less continuous use of the exercise equipment could even keep up with the sump-pumps—especially important given that the bunker was barely below water line for D.C. The toilets were hooked up to water-recovery systems designed originally for the cancelled NASA Mars mission. They used hand power to run them.

It was also occupied, by about twenty FEMA managers *and* their families. In a bunker designed for twenty, total. With the addition of the Marines and her detail and family, things were tight. And only her detail and family were vaccinated. Or so they thought. They later learned the FEMA managers had "procured" vaccine for their families. Where and what type, they were reticent about. She wasn't going to bitch. *She'd* have turned every infected in the world into vaccine.

The first order was that everyone unvaccinated was to secure themselves. One of the Marines had already turned on the trip. That was unfortunate, but on the bright side it gave Dave a weapon. The efficacy of the vaccine was proven when Thomas was bitten subduing one of the Marines. He got very sick but recovered.

Food was an issue. The bunker was stocked for five years. With even the shortest possible rations, they had at best a year and a half. The Marines had volunteered to evacuate the bunker. And Staba stomped her foot on that. They'd all make it or they wouldn't.

Then there was another issue, sort of: it wasn't

bad food. One problem of long duration missions like "being stuck in a bunker in a zombie apocalypse" was called "food ennui." People just got sick and tired of the same damned crap. They would stop eating and eventually succumb to malnutrition.

FEMA's response was to acquire long-duration foodstuffs from, well, all *over*. Many nations besides the U.S. made long-duration food supplies. And FEMA had a "test and share" program with other nations. There were German rations, British rations—surprisingly good—Indian, French, Chinese, Italian, stuff from Singapore which was . . . all sorts of different nationalities. The Chilean rations included a small bottle of not-bad wine. MREs were right at the *bottom* of the list.

The problem was not eating *too* much. Not enough rations. But they also had to have the energy to run the exercise machines.

Greatest weight loss program in *history*. If she ever got out of the damned place she was planning on starting a weight loss program based on it. Her butt was in the best shape it had been in years.

Of course . . . that was *if* they ever got out.

The Marines had had to fight their way in and lost people to bites. Being Marines, as soon as one was bitten, he took the rearguard and stayed. Semper Fi, Marines. Semper damned Fi. They'd also used up most of their ammo. She'd used up all but five rounds for the MP5. The detail was out. *Nobody* had had the concept of fighting their way *into* a bunker in the plans. And, honestly, there wasn't *any* way to carry enough ammo to fight through all the infected. There were a zillion of the bastards.

The bunker was hooked into the building's security

feeds. They could see what was happening. Naked zombies just . . . took over. And they were *everywhere*. In the streets. In the lobbies. In the hallways. In the corridors outside the bunker. The Marines estimated that after a month the LAVs probably wouldn't start right up. And even if they had enough rounds to get to them . . . where to go? Most of the cameras had failed with the power. The only two remaining, internally powered by the bunker, were outside the main door and the secondary door. They were using the intervening space to hold the bodies of those who turned. After a while they turned off the light at the outer door. There was nothing to see but infected and it was just wasting power. From time to time they turned it on and waited. Eventually, the corridor would fill with infected. They timed it and started to get a feel for how bad it was. At first the corridor filled in less than five minutes. After six months, it was up to ten. And so on. That was all the intel they had. Still far too many to attempt a breakout even if they knew where to break out to.

The bunker was *supposed* to have continuous communications. No joy. All the comms were down. Damaged, inoperable or nobody on the other end, nobody knew. They couldn't even get anything from the radios on the roof. As far as they could tell, they were the only remaining humans on the planet. Well, sentient, uninfected, humans. There were plenty of the other kind.

"Is someone humming?" Rebecca asked calmly, looking up from her iPad. Fortunately, she had thousands of books stored on the device. And she finally had all the time to read that she could possibly want.

Humming was *verboten*. Lots of things were *verboten*. She blessed the fact that they had chosen the FEMA bunker. Everyone, the Marines, the detail, her own family and the FEMA people understood the importance of allowing people their personal space in both body and other forms. They couldn't continuously take showers but people maintained hygiene. They might talk but they used "inside" voice. They didn't hum. Singing was only for the few, including Rebecca and Sherry, with really good voices and only as part of a group thing that was planned. You didn't do things that might annoy others. It was too tight. Everyone not only "hot-bunked" but "hot-sat." There weren't enough horizontal spaces, even on the floor, for everyone. And *everyone* understood that.

"It's more of a rumble, ma'am," Staff Sergeant Jason Cordova said musingly. The staff sergeant, NCOIC of the detail supporting the Secret Service in extracting the Vice President, was one of the survivors. Which had been a good thing. He had a font of good jokes which had taken a while to come out. Things had just been too damned grim for too many months.

It was one year and three days from the date the President had announced the Plague. They had been in the bunker just over ten months with no clue what was going on except the slow and unsteady decrease in infected drawn to a light like moths.

Whatever it was, it shortly went away.

"Do an exterior infected count," Rebecca said, looking back to her book.

Special Agent Phillips flipped on the exterior light and waited. And waited... And waited...

Rebecca was trying not to be too curious. Everyone was acting as if they were doing something else.

"We have full corridor, ma'am," Phillips reported. "Thirty minutes."

"That's a big change from just last month," Rebecca said.

"Not enough of a change to break out, ma'am," Phillips said, turning off the light.

There was another rumble, closer, the next day. This time Phillips got out a stethoscope and applied it to the bunker wall.

"Tracked vehicles," he said, pulling the phones out of his ears. "Staff Sergeant?"

"Tracked vehicles," Cordova confirmed. "Fading. Wait . . ."

Everyone in the room heard the thump. It was faint, but you could feel it through your bones.

"Main gun on an Abrams would be my guess," Cordova said, grinning. "Maybe a Paladin. But I'd guess main gun on an Abrams, ma'am."

"Someone is clearing the city," she said, smiling. "'Bout time. Special Agent Phillips. I want a daily check on infected numbers."

"Yes, ma'am."

There were rumbles, some distant, some closer, for several days. Although the time for the corridor to fill dropped to nearly forty minutes, other than the first big drop it didn't drop much. And that was *still* too many to make a breakout.

Then the rumbles stopped. And there were still infected.

"It's possible that they have essentially cleared the streets but the tunnels remain inhabited," Phillips said. "Or that they are clearing buildings or bunkers. It may be some time before they get here."

"At a certain point, we're going to be out of food," VP Staba said. "We will go to heavier rations for the Marines, detail with the exception of Special Agent Bryant—sorry, Maryann, but melee truly is a man's game—and . . . Misters Kraznewski and Flaherty. Those persons will begin working out and training on hand-to-hand. We will secure every bit of coverage for them we can and if push comes to shove . . . we'll *melee* our way out. These things don't use weapons. We'll be tool users even if it's a crowbar. Everyone will arm themselves and fight as well as they can. We'll get up on the roof and signal for help. Modified ration schedule now; two weeks and we break out. It is that or starve to death."

"Understood, ma'am," Phillips said.

"Oorah, ma'am," Staff Sergeant Cordova said, grinning.

It had been a week and a half with no sign of rescue. Daily they checked the infected density. If anything, it had gone up but that might just be because they were turning the light on every day. Which would make getting out trickier. The zombies were going to be waiting for them.

They'd decided on a plan of heavy firepower at the beginning. Blast through the ones nearest the bunker, then work their way to the stairs. Marines would lead the way with the detail and two of the biggest FEMA guys either interspersed or at the rear. The bunker contained some full-coverage "silver suits" that the fighters would wear to protect from bites. Rebecca had pointedly refused them even for her family. They went to the people most in harm's way.

Quietly, they had discussed the likelihood of surviving the breakout and it didn't look good. The infected showed no signs of leaving the underground areas and there were tunnels from FEMA to other basements. They would come flooding in at the first attempt to break out. And the people in the bunker didn't have any really good melee weapons except one clearance tool.

But it was the only reasonable option. That or cannibalism, which had been discussed. In retrospect, they should have eaten the people who turned. They had microwaves.

They'd all decided trying to break out, even if the chances were low, was the better alternative. There were fewer infected. It might work. Might.

"Freeze," Sherry said.

There had been a lot of cross-training in the bunker. The Marines had shared their experience and training. The FEMA guys and gals were managers but had all spent time in the field and had their own training and experience. Even the detail had opened up about personal protection. So everyone knew what "freeze" meant. And did.

"I hear something," Sherry said. "Stethoscope?"

Phillips applied it to the wall and frowned.

"You try," he said, offering it to the girl.

"Something," she whispered. "Tracked vehicle I think. But . . . it stopped. It didn't fade. Just stopped. Now all I can hear is something . . . odd and you guys. Wait . . . that's . . . You?" she said, offering it to Jerry again.

Jerry listened carefully, then shook his head.

"I don't know what that is," he said. "Maybe . . . I

think it might be lots of infected moving... could be massed running... Wait... There's thumps..."

"More grenades, Staff Sergeant!" Faith shouted, pulling the pin on two M87s and tossing them through the crack on the hatch one after the other.

"Aye, aye, ma'am!" Decker said, pulling more out of her rucksack.

They'd managed to fight their way to the building security station and get the hatch jammed against the infected. There was a shit-pot of them, though. Not like London but they only had two people.

The security station had been a nice secure point. The hatch was sturdy and they had it nicely blocked. Gave them time to water up, get a map, find the location of the bunker and reammo. Now all they had to do was get *out* of the room.

She leaned back as fragments pinged into the room. Not many, though. They were being caught by the bodies of infected blocking the hatch.

"We *will* eventually kill enough we can get out," Faith said.

"Oorah, ma'am," Decker said, handing her two more grenades, one at a time. "Caution. Pins are pulled, ma'am."

"Thanks for that helpful safety tip, Staff Sergeant..."

"Lots of grenades," Staff Sergeant Cordova said. "Has to be. More... More... Jesus. *Somebody* believes in peace through superior firepower... It's stopped."

"I think we should be prepared to break out," Staba said. "Fighters, rig up."

"Aye, aye, ma'am," Cordova said. "Let's get it on!"

"You ever see the movie *Predator*, Staff Sergeant?" Faith shouted over the fire.

They were getting hit from both directions. Wave after wave of infected. They barely had time to reload. And the basement of FEMA was flooded. Really rancid water, too.

The only thing that was allowing them to move forward was her Saiga. And she was running out of pre-loaded magazines. She'd also carefully avoided dropping her pistols. She wasn't going to go fumbling for them in the water.

"Yes, ma'am!" Decker said, drawing his 1911 and firing carefully.

"That scene where Jesse Ventura fires up the trees with the minigun," Faith said, drawing her chest pistol. "Zumwald told me that was live. They didn't use 'squibs,' whatever those are; they just fired the minigun. I should have seen one of those Navy nukes about getting a shotgun minigun!"

"That would have been useful about now, ma'am," Decker said.

"*After* we find the President," Faith said, holstering the gun. "Assuming we don't get court-martialed. Need to reload."

"Roger, ma'am," Decker said, stepping backwards carefully so they were beside each other.

Faith dipped into his pack and started pulling out magazines, sliding them into pouches and weapons. The bottom of the pack was filled with ammo but the top was filled with pre-loads. On the other hand... She ran out of Saiga pre-loads before she got all her magazines filled.

A couple of infected had trotted up while she'd been loading. She took them off-hand and kept on going. Decker was dipping into her backpack at the same time, switching empty M4 mags for full.

"We gotta move before they cluster again," Faith said. "Right up ahead if I'm reading the map correctly."

"Aye, aye, ma'am," Decker said, firing at an incoming infected.

"Let's roll . . ."

"The man trap where the bodies are is going to be an almost zero oxygen environment by now," FEMA Deputy Director John Rossman said. "If we aerate it, we'll temporarily overload our own filters. We can do that but it cuts down on our air time. I know we're breaking out but . . . air is air. You'll need to use the air pak to move forward. If we open up both doors, we'll get air from both directions and it will clear. But not until then."

Staff Sergeant Cordova was moving forward to try to hear if there was any sign of movement in their direction and getting a safety brief from the director.

"Roger, sir," Cordova said, his voice muffled by the air pack and silver suit.

"Good luck, Staff Sergeant," Rebecca said as a phone rang.

"Or not," Phillips said, picking up the red phone and keying on the external light and camera.

There were two people in what looked like fire-fighter bunker suits and just *covered* in weapons at the external phone. The one with the phone to his ear was firing a pistol off-camera one-handed.

"HELLO! HELLO! TELL ME SOMEBODY'S IN THERE!"

"This is Special Agent Jerome Phillips," Phillips said. "Who is this?"

"Lieutenant Faith Marie Smith, United States Marine Corps!"

She momentarily dropped the phone, whipped out a kukri and chopped the neck of a zombie that was clawing at her companion.

"Open the damned hatch! We need to reammo! Stand by!"

The woman dropped the phone again, holstered faster than he'd ever seen a detail member manage, pulled out two grenades, one in either hand, pulled the pins, flipped off the spoons, waited a moment then flipped them up and out. Both of the figures scrunched into the water, up against the wall, holding their arms inward.

"Holy fuck no!" Cordova said. "Sorry for the language, ma'am."

"I was thinking much the same thing, Staff Sergeant," Staba said.

Both figures stood back up after a moment and the grenade thrower picked up the phone.

"You've got ten seconds and we're leaving," the woman said, holding the phone with her head and reloading one of her pistols. It was apparent she'd taken some fragments in her arm. *"We cannot hold this position."*

"Unlock the exterior door," Staba said.

"Ma'am," Phillips replied.

"Not a request!" Staba said.

"Unlocking the door," Phillips said.

"Vent the mantrap," Staba added.

"Already done," Kraznewski said. He was the official systems engineer for the bunker.

"Thanks *so* much."

The woman on the pickup . . . might be young. Might. It was hard to tell even with the gas mask off. Scarred of face, lined and weary, she had flat, dead, eyes. If the smell in the mantrap bothered her, it wasn't apparent. It had seeped into the bunker when they vented the environment and it was gagging. It had to be worse in there.

"I need to see ID," Phillips said.

"You want my ID?" the woman said. "Staff Sergeant, turn around." She reached into the man's backpack and pulled out a box of military grade 5.56. "That's my ID. You want to reammo or not?"

"I still need to see ID," Phillips said.

"Staff Sergeant, did *you* bring your ID?" the woman asked. "I left mine in my other pants."

"Yes, ma'am."

"Show the jerk your ID."

"This will take a moment, sir," the man said, starting to loosen his gear.

"Can you give a brief on the exterior conditions?" Phillips asked.

"Fucked up and then some," the woman said, pulling more ammo out of the sergeant's ruck and beginning to reload. "Long damned story. Short version is we were clearing D.C., found the Secretary of Education and she called a halt to all clearance operations. We have to be 'kinder and gentler to the afflicted' or some shit. This is a totally illegal and unauthorized operation but the worst they can do is arrest me and my sister, who's providing top-cover. Besides, my da is *already* under arrest. If the Prez isn't in there, we're fucked. Hell, we're probably fucked anyway. Not a big fan. If he's listening... still not a big fan. Don't give a fuck. Whatever."

Rebecca leaned forward and pressed the talk button.

"The President isn't," Staba said. "The Vice President is."

"REALLY?" the, definitely young, woman said with a squeal. "I'm, like, your BIGGEST fan!"

"Open the door, Jerry," Staba said. "I think we'll be okay."

"Holy shit, it really *is* you!" Faith said then threw a salute. "Madame Vice President! Lieutenant Faith Marie Smith with a party of one! Permit me to introduce Staff Sergeant Alfred J. Decker, U-S-M-C, who has previously been declared totally bughouse due to PTSD and therefore is *not* responsible for his actions in this matter, ma'am!"

"I take it the President is missing or dead?" Staba said, returning the salute.

"MIA, ma'am," Faith said. "You're the highest ranking official we've found, ma'am."

"Then neither of you have a *thing* to worry about," the Vice President said, grinning. "But whoever obeyed the order to stop clearance operations may have a thing or two to answer for."

"Semper Fidelis, ma'am," Faith said. "There were reasons. My da agreed to house arrest to keep her from charging everyone in the world with crimes against humanity, ma'am. Ma'am..." Faith frowned for a moment.

"Rather than pull your party out, I should probably fight my way back to commo. There's a Gunhawk driven by my sister up top. She can commo to Colonel

Ramos that you're here. That will give him the cover to break out. It's pretty nasty out there, zombies, rats and nasty, stinking water, and we'll have to fight our way to the surface. The staff sergeant and I can make it back topside. I've done weirder shit."

"Oh, *hell* no," Staba said. "I barely got a chance to shoot zombies on the way in. But no throwing grenades like popcorn, Lieutenant. Got it?"

"Aye, aye, ma'am."

There was, unsurprisingly, a helipad on the roof of the FEMA building. Sophia had set down on it gently. Just because it was a helipad didn't mean it was rated for a Gunhawk. But the building didn't collapse. And the hatch was, for a change, locked.

So she'd been sitting there for four hours, occasionally restarting the engine to keep it warm, hoping against hope for word from Faith. She intended to wait until someone flew in and told her to leave at gunpoint. So far, so good.

"G . . . k . . . G . . . hawk . . . Wolf . . ."

"This is Gunhawk Nine," Sophia said. "Broken."

"Gunhawk . . . Got the . . . V . . ."

"Faith, you're broken and unreadable," Sophia said, starting the engines. "Olga, Anna . . . I've got Faith."

"Thank God," Olga said, test-firing her weapon.

"Gunhawk, Shewolf, over."

"Hear you, Faith, over," Sophia said.

"Heading to roof with Vice President," Faith said. There was a background of fire but that was normal for Faith. *"You are going to fly her and her family out. Six packs. You got the lift, right?"*

"*Vice* President?" Sophia said. "And yes I do, over."

"Make that President," Faith replied. *"Already sworn in. Call ops. Order of the President, not, say again,* not *acting. Need extract for twenty-three, say again, two-three, packs. That is* after *you pick the President and her family up. Over."*

"Roger," Sophia said, grinning and changing frequencies. "Combat Ops, Combat Ops, Navy One. Say again . . . Navy *One* . . . Over."

EPILOGUE

"But, Madame President," Steve protested. "I had this great little island in the Mediterranean all picked out! Ponza. Beautiful place. Charming ruins. Blue grottoes. Saltwater pools the sharks can't get to . . ."

The White House was surprisingly clear—it had been evacuated and the gates locked during the Fall—but D.C. in general was horrible. So the President had repaired to the *Festival Dawn*. And for the foreseeable future, the capital was going to be Jacksonville. D.C. was still too rife with infected. Guards would be left at critical points, notably the White House, the Capitol and Arlington, but once their resumed clearance ops were done, they were pulling out.

"Too bad, Steve," Rebecca said. "Duty calls. You're probably right that Project Subedey is too large and complex for your skill sets. Certainly for your interest. So we'll be handing it off to others. And we're going to change some titles around. I've been reading all the histories as well as the documentaries and who has turned up. So these are my first executive orders.

"General Montana is coming back east. He will reactivate his lieutenant generalcy and become CINCONUS as well as Commander-in-Chief Joint Forces, none of this 'chief of staff' bullshit. We'll be working closely with him. General Hammond will be CINCARMY, which will be a major general position. Since most of the mission for the Army will involve genocide rather than battle, I'm sure that the former commander of Army Materials Command can run it. If he can't, I'll find someone who can. Admiral Soames will take over as CINCPAC, Commodore. Admiral Hiscock will become CINCLANT and CINCNAVY, rear admiral. General Ramos will be Marine Commandant, brigadier.

"General Brice will take over managing the Subedey construction and management programs. And, yes, we will be proceeding with Subedey. Brilliant, by the way. Air Force will be stood down for the foreseeable future. Key West agreement is out the window. Navy will handle all cargo aircraft. All Naval Aviation continues to be Navy, for the time being at least. Army can have fixed wing if they have a justifiable use for them but transport aircraft are Navy.

"I'm going to partially forgive Colonel Downing, move him to Navy as a captain, give him a small but reasonably sized task force, about the size of what you had in the Canaries, and send him to the Indian Ocean. We have bases there that need clearing. He'll be the IO Squadron commander. We have a lot of gear and people between Diego Garcia and all the bases in the Gulf. We need to see if we can get any of that back. Diego will be the permanent base for that."

"If I may, ma'am," Steve said. "Thank you. I know that Faith has felt bad about how that worked out, and Colonel Downing is not that bad an officer. It was just an unfortunate incident."

"Which is why I'm doing it," Staba said. "IO is not by any stretch a great posting but it's an important one. If for no other reason, we need the pre-po site on Diego. Those are permanent positions. Even if other flag rank officers turn up, we're not going to keep slotting them in higher. I'll be appointing appropriate Secretaries who will be acting until we get advice and consent. I'm also going to unofficially go back to the old terms. Screw this 'Department of Defense' stuff. We're back to the Departments of War, Navy and Army. I'll include the commandant as one of my advisors."

"Yes, ma'am," Steve said. "But I don't see where I fit in there."

"I considered reactivating Wolf Squadron as our goodwill ambassadors to the rest of the world," Staba said. "Anyone with a radio apparently knows who you are. But right now we're primarily going to be concentrating on the U.S. I'll send forces and supplies to our allies, absolutely. But clearing the U.S. has priority. However, I was in a hole for a year and probably will never be caught up on details of who is what and what is important. And you did resign, right? So you're a civilian, now. Who do you think I want for my Secretary of War, Steve?"

"Ick, yuck!" Steve said. "I was getting tired of sitting at a desk in *Gitmo*! *And* I thought the force size was getting beyond my reach! Now you want me to be in charge of *the whole damned thing*? What about Secretary Galloway?"

"Secretary of the Army," Staba said. "And you'll be working directly with General Montana. You can feel free to lean on him. It's not the vast force we once were. You'll do fine. I don't have a person in mind for Secretary of the Navy. That is one place where I'll need your advice."

"Yes, ma'am," Steve said. "Anthony Connor, ma'am."

"Who?" Staba said.

"One of the gentlemen we picked up in St. Barts, ma'am," Steve said. "Like Zumwald and Isham, he was a bit of an arse at first. Former CEO of a large defense contractor after a twenty-year career as a surface warfare officer. He had retired to St. Barts. He's been running most of the civilian side of the ship refurbishment programs. And doing so *extremely* well. The only reason the *Bataan* got up and going as fast as it did was his work. He's the right guy for the job, in my opinion, ma'am."

"I'll need to meet with him," Staba said.

"He's at Mayport, ma'am," Steve said. "I'm sure you'll get along. He's not the arse that most defense contractors tended to be. Sharp as a whip and very dedicated to the nation, ma'am."

"Sounds good," the President said. "Again, need to meet him, first. Then there's the really important appointment of Vice President."

"I don't have the requirements, ma'am," Steve said. "And I hope you're not thinking of your husband, Madame President. That would be . . . an awful precedent."

"Not Dave," Staba said, grinning. "I agree it's a bad precedent, and he wouldn't want the job. And you don't have the qualifications. But *Stacey* does. I don't intend to die but if I do, your wife takes over. We cannot, again, get advice and consent. But I will have each of the upper echelon swear to follow her lead until a regular election. Even if Secretary Sovrain or any other potential 'acting President' we may find throws a hissy fit."

"Aye, aye, ma'am," Steve said.

"You wanted a stout ship and a star to sail her by, Mister Secretary," the President said. "That's going to have to wait."

"Yes, ma'am," Steve said.

"And it will allow you some family time," the President said. "Since you took all the aviators away from the Marines, I'll have to be flown by the Navy. Guess who one of my pilots is going to be?"

"She really is not . . . tremendously experienced, ma'am," Steve said.

"She's experienced enough to have pulled me off a roof when everyone else was dutifully following orders," Staba said. "She'll do. As a copilot at least. And I need a platoon leader for my Marine Guards. I think Faith needs a little dialing in on certain aspects of being an officer, and that will give her a chance. The Marine dress blues are quite pretty, even the officer ones. They're even flattering on women."

"Aye, aye, ma'am," Steve said, wincing. "Her deportment and tact are not . . . Faith *has* no tact, ma'am."

"That is what I'm *looking for*, Steve," Rebecca said. "This is a world of pain. I'm not even going to vaguely sugar-coat that. This is blood, toil, tears and sweat time. Tomorrow we relight the flame of the Unknown Soldier. We will be burying next to the others a body identified as a Marine from the Pentagon to represent all the servicemen and women we lost to the Plague and the battles with infected. She's only recognizable as a probable Marine by her tattoos. And she *was* an infected. We may need to kill them off to save our nation, but they were our people, too."

"Absolutely agree, ma'am," Steve said.

"There will be an armed guard, Marine for now, marching twenty-one beats at post. The first such being Staff Sergeant Decker who will be the NCOIC for the guards. We will rotate in Marine platoons from combat duties to guard the Flame until we can stand up the Old Guard again.

"But Decker will *only* be able to march, unhindered by zombies, due to *more* guards, not in pretty dress blues but full battle rattle, surrounding him and piling up the infected attracted to The Flame. That *has* to end. It will take people like yourself and your children to do that. I don't intend to be stuck in Mayport the whole time. I *shall* go and visit the other states, no matter *how much* force that takes. The only way to visit my constituents in Texas will be to roll hot onto an infected held beachhead. And I *will* be going forward with the Marines whether it is by helo or amphibian. If it is by helo, Seawolf will be a pilot and if it is by amphib Shewolf will be in charge of the Marines. I don't need the perfectly polished Annapolis grad for that. I need Faith and Sophia. Like Grant, they *fight*. And so do you and Stacey. Which is why I need you, this nation that you chose over the nation of your birth needs you, still. All of you."

"Yes, ma'am," Steve said.

"We are going to retake our nation," the President said, looking out the window of the cabin. "We are going to save whoever is left. We are going to bring *everyone* we can *find* . . . home."

The fires were burning again on the Mall. They would burn for years. Incendiary piles of the infected, a light in the darkness, beacons of smoke and flame showing the way back home.

THE END

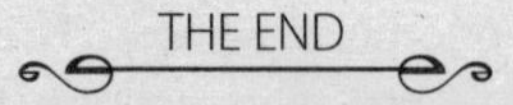

The following is an excerpt from:

GENTLEMAN JOLE AND THE RED QUEEN

LOIS McMASTER BUJOLD

Chapter One

It was a good day on the military transfer station orbiting the planet Sergyar. The Vicereine was coming home.

As he entered the station's Command-and-Control room, Admiral Jole's eye swept the main tactics display, humming and colorful above its holo-table. The map of his territory—albeit presently set to the distorted scale of human interests within Sergyar's system, and not the astrographic reality, which would leave everything invisible and put humans firmly in their place as a faint smear on the surface of a speck. A G-star burning tame and pleasant at this distance; its necklace of half-a-dozen planets and their circling moons; the colony world itself turning below the station. Of more critical strategic interest, the four wormhole jump points that were its gateways to the greater galactic nexus, and their attendant military and civilian stations—two highly active with a stream of commercial traffic and scheduled tightbeam relays, leading to the jump routes back to the rest of the Barrayaran Empire and on to its nearest neighbor on this side, currently peaceful Escobar; one accessing a long and uneconomical backdoor route to the Nexus; the last leading, as far as forty years of exploration had found, nowhere.

Jole wondered at what point in the past

double-handful of years he'd started carrying the whole map and everything moving through it in his head at once. He'd used to consider his mentor's ability to do so as something bordering on the supernatural, although the late Aral Vorkosigan had done it routinely for an entire three-system empire, and not just its smallest third. Time, it seemed, had gifted Jole easily with what earnest study had found hard. Good. Because time bloody *owed* him, for all that it had taken away.

It was quiet this morning in the C-and-C room, most of the techs bored at their stations, the ventilation laden with the usual scents of electronics, recycled air, and overcooked coffee. He moved to the one station that was brightly lit, letting his hand press the shoulder of the traffic controller, *stay on task*. The man nodded and returned his attention to the pair of ships coming in.

The Vicereine's jump-pinnace was nearly identical to that of a fleet admiral, small and swift, bristling more with communications equipment than weapons. Its escort, a fast courier, could keep up, but was scarcely better armed; they traveled together more for safety in case of technical emergencies than any other sort. None this trip, thankfully. Jole watched with what he knew was perfectly pointless anxiety as they maneuvered into their docking clamps. No pilot would want to make a clumsy docking under *those* calm gray eyes.

His newest aide popped up at his elbow. "The honor guard reports ready, sir."

"Thank you, Lieutenant Vorinnis. We'll go over now."

He motioned her into his wake as he exited C-and-C and made for the Vicereine's docking bay. Kaya Vorinnis was far from the first of the techs, medtechs, and troops from the greatly expanded Imperial Service Women's Auxiliary to be assigned to Sergyar command, nor the first to be assigned directly to his office. But the Vicereine would approve, which was a charming thought, though Cordelia would doubtless also make some less-charming remark about how her natal Beta Colony and a like list of advanced planets had boasted fully-gender-integrated space services since forever. Personally, Jole was relieved that he only had to supervise the women during working hours, and that their off-duty arrangements here on-station and on the downside base were the direct responsibility of a rather maternal and very efficient ISWA colonel.

"I've never seen Vicereine Vorkosigan in person," Vorinnis confided to him. "Only in vids." Jole was reminded not to let his long stride quicken unduly, though the lieutenant's breathlessness might be as much due to incipient heroine-worship, not misplaced in Jole's view.

"Oh? I thought you were a relative of Count Vorinnis. Had you not spent much time in Vorbarr Sultana?"

"Not that closely related, sir. I've only met the count twice. And most of my time in the capital was spent running around Ops. I was put on Admin track pretty directly." Her light sigh was easy to interpret, having the identical content to those of her male predecessors: *Not ship duty, dammit.*

"Well, take heart. I was put through a seven-year rotation in the capital as a military secretary and aide, but I still caught three tours on trade fleet escort duty afterward." The most active and far-flung space-based duty an Imperial officer could aspire to during peacetime, culminating in his one and only ship captaincy, traded in due course for this Sergyar patch.

"Yes, but that was aide to *Regent Vorkosigan* himself!"

"He was down to Prime Minister Vorkosigan, by then." Jole permitted himself a brief lip twitch. "I'm not *that* old." And just kept his mouth from adding, ". . . young lady!" It wasn't merely Vorinnis's height, or lack of it, that made her look twelve in his eyes, or her gender; her recent male counterparts were no better. "Although, by whatever irony, my one stint in an active theater of war *was* as his secretary, when I followed him to the Hegen Hub. Not that we knew it was going to end up a shooting war when that trip started."

"Were you ever under fire?"

"Well, yes. There is no rear echelon on a flagship. Since the Emperor was also aboard by that point, it was fortunate that our shields never failed." Two decades ago, now. And what a top-secret cockup that entire episode had been, which, glued throughout to Ex-Regent Prime Minister Admiral Count Vorkosigan's shoulder, Jole had witnessed at the closest possible range from first to last. His Hegen Hub war stories had always had to be among his most thoroughly edited.

"I guess you've known Vicereine Vorkosigan just as long, then?"

"Nearly exactly, yes. It's been . . ." He had to calculate it in his head, and the sum took him aback. "Twenty-three years, almost."

"I'm almost twenty-three," Vorinnis offered, in a tone of earnest helpfulness.

"Ah," Jole managed. He was rescued from any further fall into this surreal time warp by their arrival at Docking Bay Nine.

The dozen men of the honor guard braced, and Jole returned salutes punctiliously while running his eye over their turnout. Everything shipshape and shiny, good. He duly complimented the sergeant in charge and turned to take up a parade rest in strategic view of the personnel flex tube, just locking on under the competent and very attentive supervision of the bay tech. Exiting a null-gee flex tube into the grav field of a station or ship was seldom a graceful or dignified process, but the first three persons out were reasonably practiced: a ship's officer, one of the Vicereine's ImpSec guards, and Armsman Rykov, the only one of the new Count Vorkosigan's personal retainers seconded to his mother, in her other hat as Dowager Countess. The first man attended to mechanics, the second made a visual and electronic scan of the docking bay for unscheduled human hazards, and the third turned to assist his liege lady. Vorinnis tried to stand on tiptoe and to attention simultaneously, which didn't quite work, but she dropped from Jole's awareness as the last figure cleared the tube in a smooth swing and flowed to her feet with the aid of her armsman's proffered hands.

Everyone snapped to attention as the color sergeant piped her aboard. Admiral Jole saluted, and said formally, "Vicereine Vorkosigan. Welcome back. I trust your journey was uneventful."

"Thank you, Admiral, and so it was," she returned, equally formally. "It's good to be back."

He made a quick initial assay of her. She looked a trifle jump-lagged, but nothing like the frightening dead-gray bleakness that had haunted her features when she'd returned alone almost three years ago from her husband's state funeral. Not that Jole himself had been in much better form, at the time. The colonists of Sergyar had been entirely uncertain if they were going to get their Vicereine back at all, that trip, or if some stranger-lord would be appointed in her place. But she was wearing colors again now, if subdued ones, Komarran-style trousers and jacket, and her unmistakable smile had warmed to something better than room temperature. She was still keeping her tousled red-gray hair cut short; the fine bones of her face held out, like a rampart that had never fallen.

Her left hand, down at her side, gripped what appeared to be a small cryofreezer case. Lieutenant Vorinnis, like any good admiral's assistant, advanced upon it. "May I take your luggage, Your Excellency?"

Cordelia cried, sharply and unexpectedly, "No!" twitching the case away. At Jole's eyebrow-lift, she seemed to catch herself up, and continued more smoothly, "No, thank you, Lieutenant. I'll carry this one. And my armsman will see to the rest." She cast a quick head-tilt toward the girl, and a plea of a look Jole's way.

He took the hint. "Vicereine, may I introduce my new aide, Lieutenant Kaya Vorinnis. Just assigned—she arrived a few weeks after you left." Cordelia had departed six weeks ago to present the Sergyaran Viceroy's Annual Report to Emperor Gregor in person, and incidentally catch a little of Winterfair Season with her family back on Barrayar. Jole hoped that had been refreshing rather than exhausting, although having met the Vorkosigan offspring, he suspected it had been both.

"How do you do, Lieutenant? I hope you will find Sergyar an interesting rotation. Ah—any relation to the young count?"

"Not close, ma'am," Vorinnis replied, an answer Jole suspected she was tired of offering, but she did it without grimacing here.

The Vicereine turned and delivered a few well-practiced words of thanks to the honor guard. Their sergeant returned the traditional, "Ma'am, yes, ma'am!" proudly on their behalf, and marched them out again. Cordelia watched them go, then turned with a sigh to take Jole's arm proffered in escort.

She shook her head. "Really, Oliver, do you have to do this every time I transit? All I'm going to do is walk from the docking bay to the shuttle hatch. Those poor boys could have slept in."

"We never did less for the Viceroy. It's an honor for them as well as for you, you know."

"Aral was your war hero. Several times over."

The corners of Jole's mouth twitched up. "And you're not?" He added in curiosity, "What's in the box? Not a severed head—again—I trust?" It seemed too small for that, fortunately.

Cordelia's gray eyes glinted. "Now, now, Oliver. Bring home one dismembered body part, *once*, mind you, *once*, and people get twitchy about checking your luggage ever after." Her smile grew wry. "But that we can *joke* about that now . . . ah, well."

—end excerpt—

from *Gentleman Jole and the Red Queen*
available in hardcover,
February 2016, from Baen Books